"*And Again* was contin[_]
just when I thought I kr[_]
they surprised [_]
—Susan Straight, author of [_]

"*And Again* delivers a stunning journey
challenging the nature of identity, weaving
four stories into a cohesive narrative."
—*Paste* magazine

"Chiarella is . . . a pioneer as a writer, spinning a
plot that's as groundbreaking as the medical procedure
Linda, David, Connie, and Hannah undergo."
—*Chicago Review of Books*

"Chiarella's entrancing prose and fully fleshed characters
should garner widespread, enthusiastic praise."
—*Booklist*

"Chiarella's engaging writing creates so many haunting
moments that readers will find themselves moving quickly
through the story, as well as awaiting her next work."
—*Kirkus Reviews*

"Utterly absorbing. I never wanted it to end."
—Rebecca Johns, author of *The Countess* and *Icebergs*

"Strength and resilience abound in this deeply felt debut."
—Shelf Awareness

"Moving and beautifully crafted." —LAILA LALAMI

Dear Target Reader,

It is such a joy to be able to write this letter and an honor to have *And Again* selected as a Target Club Pick. As a (perpetual) grad student, I've spent a lot of time in Target over the years, be it for notebooks or interview outfits or late-night provisions before a deadline. And, of course, for novels. It is always difficult for me to leave each time I visit without browsing in the book section. I've found it's a perfect mix of literary favorites and new, essential books for me to discover. I rarely walk away without adding a book to my cart. For me, that's what reading is—an exploration, whether coming back to a classic with new eyes or finding the next book that makes me look at the rest of the world from a fresh perspective.

That's also what writing *And Again* was for me: an exploration. It started with a simple question about identity, became a way to grapple with ideas about illness and mortality, and eventually developed philosophical and spiritual meaning. But, in the end, it was not the ideas that continued to bring me back to the page: it was the characters. *And Again* began as Hannah's story, a character so flawed and conflicted and uncomfortable in her own skin that she quickly became the most dear to my heart. But as I wrote I found that I could not stop thinking about David and Linda and Connie, about their lives and their struggles, their happiness and their humor. They were characters who demanded to be written, and I knew I could not stop writing this book until I had captured their lives on the page.

None of them are perfect people—far from it, in fact. Sometimes (perhaps a lot of the time) they act in ways that are not admirable. Sometimes their thoughts betray terrible and selfish impulses. That was both the easiest and most difficult aspect of writing such a varied group: trying to make them human, despite the fact that humanity is always conflicted and very often messy. Sometimes we love the people in our lives—and sometimes we don't. Sometimes we don't like ourselves. Each of these characters is at times just like me, and each of these characters is completely unlike me at other times. And what I hope more than anything is that you find the same thing, dear reader. That there is something in Hannah, David, Linda, and Connie that feels true, even if they seem flawed beyond measure (because really, they all are). I hope these characters are ones you'll carry with you, as I have for the past few years, and as I have carried the characters of my favorite books with me long after I've finished them.

Yours,
*Jessica Chiarella*

"What a stunning first novel! *And Again* was continually haunting me, and just when I thought I knew these characters, who are so vivid and singular in their desires and frailties, and yet so universal in their humanity, they surprised me once more until the pages were finished and I was left pondering our lives, our future, and how love still works. Jessica Chiarella has so much talent."

—Susan Straight, author of *Between Heaven and Here*

"*And Again* is a moving and beautifully crafted novel about the frailty of identity, the illusion of control, and the enduring power of love. A fantastic debut."

—Laila Lalami, author of *The Moor's Account*, Pulitzer Prize finalist and longlisted for the Man Booker Prize

"Contemplative . . . Chiarella's entrancing prose and fully fleshed characters should garner widespread, enthusiastic praise."

—*Booklist*

"Chiarella's engaging writing creates so many haunting moments that readers will find themselves moving quickly through the story, as well as awaiting her next work. This is a novel about what it means to be human, with all the flaws and vulnerabilities that implies, and whether we can ever truly begin again."

—*Kirkus Reviews*

"It was the unique premise of *And Again* that pulled me in, but it was Jessica Chiarella's luminous writing that kept me reading page after page. The characters were gorgeously observed, the world fully believable and utterly absorbing. I never wanted it to end."

—Rebecca Johns, author of *The Countess* and *Icebergs*

"[Jessica Chiarella] does an amazing job moving from character to character and delving into their inner thoughts. The idea of creating human clones is already a controversial subject, but this book offers an eye-opening view to the mental and psychological strain that it can cause. The vulnerability and self-consciousness of the characters make them easy to relate to and endearing."

—*RT Reviews*

"Chiarella provides a finely nuanced look at four people whose return to the living feels miraculous but provides no magical answers or happy endings in the long run. The body transfer serves easily as allegory for any major life change; we are called upon in life to remake ourselves at some point. Strength and resilience abound in this deeply felt debut."

—Shelf Awareness

"Chiarella's characters are well drawn, and their anguishes ring true. Do the people who love us in sickness and health really love us, or do they act out of a sense of duty? The SUBS have gotten a reprieve; what will they do with their second chance? Chiarella expresses their deep desires and yearnings with poetic compassion."

—*USA Today* (3.5 out of 4 stars)

"*And Again* delivers a stunning journey challenging the nature of identity, weaving four stories into a cohesive narrative. You'll meet Hannah, an artistic prodigy; David, a congressman; Connie, an actress; and Linda, a wife and mother who lived completely paralyzed for eight years. As Chiarella gradually reveals the characters' pasts in tandem with their present courses, she illuminates the reality that their bodies—and our own—determine identity far more than [is] expected."

—*Paste Magazine*

"Chiarella is a pioneer as a writer, spinning a plot that's as groundbreaking as the medical procedure Linda, David, Connie, and Hannah undergo."

—*Chicago Review of Books*

"Chiarella's debut novel is an intriguing tale of the everyday efforts of medical advancement. Though the premise is [science fiction], the story is realistic and largely character-focused. Chapters are set from the perspective of the four individuals and woven together to tell a story that deals with commonplace issues in everyday life. Similar to Karen Thompson Walker's *The Age of Miracles*, this is a great choice for fans of that novel."

—*Library Journal*

"*And Again* is a fascinating and disturbing glimpse of a medical technology that some believe the future may hold for our society."

—*San Diego Book Review*

"*And Again* is a heartbreaking exploration of what it means to be human as well as the moral dangers of scientific advancement."

—*(The) Absolute*

# And Again

A Novel

Jessica Chiarella

TOUCHSTONE
New York   London   Toronto   Sydney   New Delhi

TOUCHSTONE
An Imprint of Simon & Schuster, Inc.
1230 Avenue of the Americas
New York, NY 10020

First Touchstone trade paperback edition August 2016

TOUCHSTONE and colophon are registered trademarks of Simon & Schuster, Inc.

For information about special discounts for bulk purchases,
please contact Simon & Schuster Special Sales at 1-866-506-1949
or business@simonandschuster.com.

The Simon & Schuster Speakers Bureau can bring authors to your live event.
For more information or to book an event, contact the Simon & Schuster Speakers Bureau
at 1-866-248-3049 or visit our website at www.simonspeakers.com.

Interior design by Erich Hobbing

Manufactured in the United States of America

1   3   5   7   9   10   8   6   4   2

The Library of Congress has cataloged the hardcover as follows:
Chiarella, Jessica.
And again : a novel / Jessica Chiarella.
pages cm
Summary: "A debut novel about four previously terminally ill people who must grapple with the
reality of reentering their lives after being granted genetically perfect copies of their former bodies,
and the unimaginable consequences and entanglements that follow."— Provided by publisher.
1. Terminally ill—Fiction. 2. Human cloning—Fiction. I. Title.
PS3603.H536A53 2015
813'.6—dc23
2015010621

ISBN 978-1-5011-5710-3

*To my parents,*
*Joanne and Frank Chiarella,*
*and my brother,*
*Christopher Chiarella*

"He could see plainly that she was not herself. That is, he could not see that she was becoming herself and daily casting aside that fictitious self which we assume like a garment with which to appear before the world."

—Kate Chopin, *The Awakening*

# August

# Hannah

Maybe it's like being born. I don't know. It's impossible to compare it to something I cannot remember. When I finally come back to myself, it takes me a moment to realize I haven't died. I choke my way back to consciousness, my eyes full of milky brightness, my heart a seismic pulse of energy inside me. I reach out, fumbling for something to anchor me here. I am lost, panicked, and adrift with the idea of death, when the room begins to take shape around me. Details sharpen, forms appear. It's a small room with a window. Everything is colorless, washed-out, and overtaken by light. Unfamiliar. Then I register the smell, the metallic bite of antiseptic in the stale air, and I know I'm still alive. It's a hospital smell. And even though I'm disoriented and sleep-addled and half-blind, I know for certain that Heaven would never smell like this.

I take a breath, try to slow my heart and pay attention. People will want to know what it's like, how it feels, being born for a second time. They will want it to be tunnels of light and choruses of angels, messages from the other side. They will want God to have something to do with it. But it feels more like waking from a night of heavy drinking than anything profound. I feel wrung out and groggy. Dehydrated. I blink against the brightness of my room, breathing deep the acrid hospital smell, and realize that I'll probably have to lie to them.

Sam is sitting by the window. He looks older in these shades of white and gray, gaunt and worn and sapped of blood. As if all of his lingering boyishness has been finally wrung out of him, and suddenly his dark hair and sharp nose, the unshaven shadow around the calm fullness of his mouth, all of these things serve to make him look hardened. Even from here I know it's his eyes that have changed the most, lingering somewhere far off, the pain in them. I think of my first drawing class in high school, how the teacher taught us always to begin a portrait with the eyes, how you can map a whole face once you get the eyes right. The sight of him brings with it a relief that is so potent I could cry. He's here.

I try to say something, but the words are hot little barbs that stick in my windpipe. Sam glances up at the small sound I make, as if he is shocked to see me there. He moves toward me and reaches for the side table, retrieving a cup, and offers me a spoonful of ice chips.

"You're okay. It's the respirator. They took it out a half-hour ago."

I accept the ice, and it's shockingly vivid, the taste of it like cold chlorine, blunting the soreness as I swallow. He glances down, taking my hand and squeezing it, almost to the point of pain. He looks afraid. I wish I could tell him that I'm all right, but I can't speak, and I'm not even sure if it's true anyway. Has the transfer worked? Is it supposed to feel like this?

Sam pushes a button next to my bed, calling a nurse. I shake my head, wishing I could tell him not to. I need a bit more time, to wade into this like the waters of an icy pool, slowly, so as not to shock the system. But then I notice my hand, the right one, the one he's holding so insistently, and for the first time my eyes register a color. Red. My hand is bleeding, the IV catheter hanging loose, a piece of medical tape curling where it was pulled free from my skin. Great work, Hannah. I haven't been awake five minutes and already I've managed to draw blood.

And my nail polish is gone. Penny came by yesterday afternoon and painted my fingernails a slippery wine color when the nurses weren't watching. Harlot, she'd said, showing me the label on the top of the bottle, giving me that crooked smile of hers. I'd told her there was no point. After all, what did a discarded body need with red fingernails? But she'd insisted, and I was too weak to even consider arguing. Now my nails are bare. It hits me, the certainty that I've shrugged off my former self and taken root within something else. I think of a snake shedding its skin, leaving the dry, crusted remains to the whims of the sun and desert sky.

A nurse hustles in, stopping briefly to shine a tiny light into my eyes that feels like it's piercing my brain, and then attends to my damaged hand.

"She pulled it out when she was waking up," Sam explains, as if we've accidentally broken something very valuable in someone else's house. "She seems disoriented."

The nurse nods. "It takes a few minutes for their eyes to adjust to the light," she replies, packing the back of my hand with gauze and fastening it in place with medical tape. "Some of the others have said they couldn't see anything at first."

"But she can see now, right?" Sam asks.

"Of course," the nurse replies, peeling her gloves off and tossing them in a waste bin. "She can hear, too."

"I know that," Sam says, reddening. It's habit for him now, managing me and my care and my disease with little input from me. I've been a passenger in my own illness ever since the beginning, with Sam squarely at the helm.

"The doctors should be by in a few minutes," the nurse says, scribbling something in my chart and heading for the door. "When they're done I'll be back to put in a new IV."

Sam sits next to my bed, his fingers around my wrist, sparing my damaged hand. It is quiet again, quiet but for the beep of the machines next to my bed, and all of a sudden it's too much. I want Sam to say something, to look me in the eyes, but he does neither.

"You're here," I whisper through the rasp in my throat. Sam glances up.

"Of course. Of course I'm here."

"I was afraid you'd be . . ." *Gone*, I think. "Sick. The flu."

Sam shakes his head. "I only stayed away because the doctors told me to, you know that. But nothing would have kept me away from you today."

He looks so sincere when he says it, and it's just what I want to hear. Sam believes in the truth the way my grandmother believed in the Holy Spirit, as an intangible force of righteous power, worthy of lifelong devotion, and I feel sick for doubting him at all. I want to kiss him, to dig my fingers into his hair, to use what little strength I have to erase this fault line that has split us from each other since I was diagnosed. But instead I reach forward and touch the crease between his eyebrows with the pad of my thumb, wishing I could smooth it out, as if I were working with wet clay. That crease, which appeared almost simultaneously with my cancer, has grown deep during the past few months. It is so unfair, that Sam should have to carry a mark of my illness on his forehead while I can start over fresh. It feels like walking away from a terrible car wreck without a scratch.

I begin to register the torn puncture of the IV, the low, aching pulse of it, and that's when I know that if this second birth was meant to be profound, if it was meant to be something rare and overwhelming, then I'm certain I've done it all wrong. Because it's only that small, insignificant pain in the back of my hand that makes me realize all of my other pain is gone.

It's impossible that I haven't realized it until now. I'd wished for this specific mercy every moment I was in pain, and I'd been in pain for months. Worse, too, was imagining what caused that pain, the dense, parasitic tumors cropping up along my spine. Sam and I both became well acquainted with each other's powerlessness in those months; mine in the face of my own body's betrayals, and Sam's in the face of the medical establishment that had become the sole governor of our lives. His inability to negotiate for an increase in my morphine or his futility in protecting me from the barrage of small, necessary agonies that accompanied each of my days in the hospital made the pain that much more difficult. His powerlessness undercut my own. Now I've forgotten, it seems, those months of hot wire tightening inside me, those months of chemical burning through my bones, metal puncturing my skin. How easily a body forgets, I think. But no, not this body. This body has never known such pain at all.

"You look like you've gotten about twelve years of sleep," Sam says. "How do you feel?"

"I can breathe." I exhale the words, drawing them out. I feel like I'm describing a lover, something illicit.

"I know," he says. "Your pulse ox is above 95. That's the first time in ages."

I smile, glancing over at the readout on the monitor beside my bed. It would have been a mystery to us a year ago, that machine, but now we are experts in the weights and measures of my illness. Sam has a particular knack for memorizing numbers and the dosages of my medications and the names of all of the nurses. He's the one who takes the notes, asks the doctors questions. He says it's the journalist in him, but I know better. He's particularly skilled at this, at being the caretaker, because he had a lot of practice with his father.

"It's amazing how afraid I've been of that little number," Sam says. "I keep waiting for it to drop. It seemed like I'd come in every morning and it'd be lower than the day before. That fucking number used to ruin my whole day."

I nod. I wonder if I'm allowed to kiss him. I decide it's better not to try, not right away.

Sam leaves to check his messages when the doctors descend. Dr. Mitchell gives a quick knock on the door as he enters, less a request for permission and more of an announcement of his presence. There's no stopping anyone in a hospital; you're on their turf, a supplicant. The doctor is an older man with bright silver hair and an oblong birthmark on his right cheek. Dr. Shah follows him, and the contrast of her youthful exuberance could not be starker against his measured, practiced calm. She practically skips into the room, teetering in her high heels, looking more like an extra in a Bollywood movie than the scientific savant that she is. The third man is less familiar to me. He's tall, middle-aged, and has a certain bureaucratic exactness to him. I wonder if he's from the government, one of the doctors who will be reporting on all of the SUBlife patients during the next year before the program goes up for FDA approval. The three of them close in around me.

"How are we feeling today Hannah?" Dr. Mitchell asks, taking a penlight out of his pocket and shining it in my eyes. I smile because he always speaks about me in the plural and because, of all my doctors, I like him best.

"The pain is gone," I reply, a bit afraid to say it out loud, lest I tempt it back with my words. A nurse elbows her way between Dr. Shah and the other doctor, unceremoniously grabbing my arm for a blood test. She plunges a needle into the distended vein in the crook of my arm. It's almost a welcome sight; my old veins had been so shot in the last few weeks that the nurses in the ICU had to draw blood from the tops of my feet. Dr. Mitchell checks the glands in my neck as the nurse removes the full vial of blood and tapes a lump of cotton to my injured arm, then disappears without a word. The brusqueness and efficiency of the hospital staff has become commonplace for me, and I long ago surrendered any resistance to their needles and catheters and tubes and relentless prodding. It's been a long time since I felt that my body was in any way my own. But this is the first time that I wonder if this body is mine at all, if I even have the option to refuse any of the medical demands they will make upon it.

I answer Dr. Shah's questions and read the flash cards she puts before me as Dr. Mitchell listens to my heart and lungs, tests my reflexes. I recite the words they asked me to remember before the transfer. Glass. Curtain. Snapshot. When she holds up a card with a blue box in the middle and asks me what color it is, the smart-ass in me wonders what would happen if I tell her that it's yellow. I feel like a seal with a ball balanced on my nose, clapping my flippers for their amusement. But I give the correct answer instead. My guess is FDA guy doesn't have much of a sense of humor.

"What did you do for your seventh birthday party?" Dr. Shah asks. The question surprises me a bit, because I haven't thought about any of my childhood birthdays in years. She must have gotten her information from my sister.

"Horseback riding," I reply, recalling the coarse feeling of the horse's mane beneath my hands. The memory brings with it a flood of relief. It must all still be there, I think. All of my memories must have transferred over, even the ones it wouldn't occur to me to remember on my own.

Dr. Mitchell presses on my stomach. FDA guy looks bored. I wonder how many times he's been through this before. I wonder how many of us there are in the Northwestern pilot program. Or maybe he has to fly around, go to all five of the hospitals that were approved for SUBlife trials. How many times can someone watch a human clone wake up for the first time before it becomes boring?

Dr. Mitchell pulls out a pen and scribbles in my chart. "Everything is looking great, Hannah," he says. "You should expect some differences at first. Your muscles are still underdeveloped, so we're not going to get you up and walking just yet. And we're going to work our way up to solid food to make sure your digestive system is in good order. But none of that is out of the ordinary for this stage post-transfer."

"Has anything gone wrong with any of the others?" I ask. Dr. Mitchell glances at Dr. Shah. She's the one who answers.

"We only have data for our SUBlife patients here at Northwestern. But so far, everyone has responded very well to the transfer."

"How many have there been?"

"You're the fourth. You'll meet the others next week when you start attending your support group meetings."

"And you're sure—" I swallow hard against the lingering dryness in my throat, trying to get the question out. "You're sure the cancer isn't going to come back?"

There's a slight pause in the room. FDA guy looks at me like I'm an idiot, probably wondering why his taxpayer dollars are funding a study to save someone like me, someone who can't even grasp the most basic of concepts. But if I don't ask the question, here, out loud, I know the lack of an answer will plague me forever.

Dr. Mitchell is kinder than his counterpart. He takes my hand, leaning forward a bit. Maybe he knows how badly I need to hear it again now, even though I've heard it a hundred times before. "We were able to isolate the defective genes, Hannah," he says, smiling a bit, a kindly old man calming his grandchild after a nightmare. "We removed them completely when we began developing your SUB. No, the cancer is not going to come back." He squeezes my hand.

Now I start to cry, which clears the room pretty effectively. Sam steps back inside as the doctors leave, and he brings me a handful of tissues, but doesn't sit back down. I wonder if his instinct is also to flee at the sight of my tears. Maybe he's finally reached his limit, too.

"Penny left three messages. I told her I'd call as soon as you woke up, do you mind?" He holds up his phone.

"No, I'm sure they're going crazy," I say, drying my eyes as he steps back out into the hallway.

I wad up the damp tissues and toss them in the direction of the wastebasket. They fall short, of course. I take a deep breath, revel in it, and decide to take stock. I haven't been alone yet, in this new body, and it feels a bit like waiting to become acquainted with the body of a stranger, a new lover. It's something that must be done in private.

The skin of my arms is very pale, dusted with a fine down of dark hair, unbleached by the sun into its usual golden invisibility. Trails of cerulean veins stand prominent beneath the skin of my wrists. I can't tell if the patterns are still the same as they were before. I don't remember, and it scares me how little I memorized of the body I'd lived in for twenty-seven years. All of my freckles are gone, giving my skin a strange, placid sort of appearance. As if it's not quite real, as if I've pulled on a pair of perfect, silken gloves that reach all the way up to my shoulders. There are dark, damp thatches of hair in my armpits, and I begin to feel itchy as soon as I discover them.

My hands look small, their joints thin and supple, and I move them experimentally, testing to make sure my synapses fire with the same precision as before the transfer. They are foreign objects now, like the pale, delicate petals of a lily. These hands have endured none of the years I spent scribbling on sketchpads or being sliced up carving linoleum in a printmaking class or trying and failing to learn the piano. I wonder if I can hold a pencil. Or a paintbrush.

I flex my feet, stretching my legs under the bedspread, then fumble a hand under my hospital gown, taking care not to detach any of the EKG leads fixed to my skin. I laugh a little to myself when I find the soft dent of scar tissue in the middle of my stomach, testing it with my fingertip, wondering at the thrill of familiarity in provokes within my chest.

"What?" Sam says as he reenters, noting my reverie.

"For a second I was afraid I wouldn't have a . . ." I motion to the middle of my stomach. "I mean, does a clone need an umbilical cord?"

"I guess there were one or two things we didn't think to ask, huh?" he says, leaning close as I tuck the hospital blanket around my waist and draw up my gown, revealing the pallid skin of my stomach, with the little knot of my navel in the center. "Looks the same to me," he says. I smile.

"What did Penny say?"

"She called me a very nasty name for not updating her sooner," he replies. The thought of Penny's famously quick temper hits me in a tender spot somewhere in my chest. I turn my head as Sam settles back into his chair, so he won't see that I'm on the edge of tears again. I feel as if I have no skin, as if every emotion that wells up inside me will immediately spill out. I can hold nothing back, not in this new body; I can't control it like the body I remember.

"I told her that they can come by as soon as visiting hours start. And, of course, she ignored me and said they're coming over now. I didn't see any real point in trying to argue with her."

"Smart man," I say, though I'm grateful that my oldest friend is dragging her boyfriend into their car and heading toward me, probably at blinding speeds. I need Penny's eyes, and her honesty, to tell me if I'm the same as I was before. Sam has been so wrapped up in the mechanics of my disease, and the day-in, day-out of my life at the hospital, that I'm not sure he'd be able to tell. Maybe I'm afraid that he doesn't remember what I was like before I was sick, even though it's only been a handful of months since I was diagnosed. Or maybe, despite his righteous honesty, the journalistic ethics that have seeped into every bit of his life, I'm still afraid he'd lie to me.

Penny breezes in like a wash of winter air, crisp and bracing, the tiny dark ropes of her braids animating around her as if caught in a wind that belongs to her alone. She strides over and clasps my face in her hands, the silver of her rings cool against my skin. She studies me, her heavy eyebrows furrowed above the dark scrutiny of her eyes. I hold still, feeling very much like I'm showing her one of my paintings, watching her eyes scan with passionless appraisal. I'm about to interrupt her concentration and demand a response, when she breaks into that lovely smile of hers.

"There you are," she says and kisses both of my cheeks, releasing me.

"Am I?" I ask, still internally bracing myself. I don't doubt Penny's judgment; I'm just unaccustomed to walking away unscathed by it.

"You look pretty decent, actually," she replies. I grin, because to Penny, decent is just this side of tremendous. She turns to Sam, who is sitting by the window reading something on his laptop. He's been on a leave of absence from the *Chicago Tribune,* where he covers national politics, though it hasn't stopped him from working during every spare moment. I wonder what it's costing him, these weeks away from his job, and wish I could signal to Penny to lay off him, at least for today. But I'm already out of luck. "You, however, look dreadful," she says.

"Thanks, Pen," Sam replies, barely glancing up from his work. Penny's friendly dislike of Sam is nothing new, and he's as familiar as I am with the smooth clarity of her whims and the depth of her candor.

"Connor'll be up in a minute. He stopped downstairs to get coffee," she says, flopping down into the seat next to my bed. Every time she moves there's a dull clatter of bangles and beads. I'm sure I look bare and unformed next to Penny's intricate, well-curated beauty. "So how do you feel?"

"Good. And really strange. A bit naked." I roll up the thin cotton sleeves of my hospital gown and show her the pristine skin underneath. My arms are spindle-thin, broken only by the joints of my elbows like dense knots in sapling branches. They are as unmarked as porcelain.

"A waste of good artwork," she replies, and sends another pointed glance in Sam's direction. "Better for the country club though, I guess. Finally smoothing out all of those pesky rough edges, aren't we?" Sam isn't listening, or he's choosing to ignore her. Either way, changing the subject is best.

"I keep feeling like I should have my glasses on." My battered frames sit on the table next to me. I grabbed them out of habit a few minutes ago, sliding them on and recoiling at the warped blur that clouded my vision.

"What happened here?" she says, motioning to my bandaged hand.

"Pulled out my IV," I reply. "Accidentally."

"See," she says, making a soft tsk-ing sound in mock reproach, "this is why we can't have nice things."

"Do you have a mirror?"

Penny goes fishing in her bag, an old gray corduroy satchel that seems to hold a good portion of her worldly possessions at any given time. I've seen paintbrushes, lace underwear, antacids, spools of thread, condoms, even bottles of perfume produced from that bag at a moment's notice. And yet somehow, magically, Penny is always the first one to dig out her ID when we go to bars together. She hands me a tortoise-shell compact with a circular mirror inside.

"You haven't seen yourself yet?"

"They won't let me out of bed," I reply, peering at my right eye, which is huge and bright and the color of coffee under a shapeless, overgrown eyebrow. I move the mirror down, trying to glimpse more, to get a sense of my face as a whole. But it's too small, that scrap of reflection. I can only see one feature at a time.

The freckles on my nose and cheeks are gone. My skin is poreless, scrubbed of its ruddiness and even the barest hints of sun damage, like a doll's face. The small dent of an old piercing is gone from the right side of my nose. The mirror reveals hollow cheeks, a chin that is more pointed than it was before. I am all bone structure, a skull that has been dipped in wax. My upper lip sports dark fluff, a shadowy contrast against the muted pallor of my face. I'm a bit mortified by this discovery. I think of Sam and the waxing strips I hide behind a bottle of lotion in our medicine cabinet. Such petty dishonesties that have always existed between us, where our bodies are concerned. How piteous it is that they linger still, even through the worst of circumstances. I snap the mirror closed, handing it back to Penny. It's too close, too fragmented an image to satisfy me.

"So here's a question," Penny says, dropping the mirror into her purse and sitting back. "I know they supposedly have the genetic side of this all figured out. But what happens if you take up smoking? All bets are off?"

I shrug. "I guess. They can't do much about environmental risk factors."

"Actually, you can't take up smoking," Sam says, glancing up from his reading. He's been listening after all. "It was in the paperwork you signed before the transfer. You're not allowed to do anything unnecessarily dangerous to your SUB."

"What the fuck does that mean?" Penny asks, before I have the chance.

"Smoking, skydiving, driving drunk, things like that," Sam replies. "That's an expensive bit of medical research you've got there."

"And what are they going to do, take her body back?" Penny's crisp diction holds the slightest hint of her father's thick Parisian accent.

Connor interrupts Sam's answer by appearing in the doorway, flush-faced and jubilant in his thick glasses, a tray of coffees in his hand. The three of us cheer as he distributes the spoils, kissing me on the forehead as he passes, his patchy attempt at facial hair prickling against my skin.

"You look gorgeous, Han," he says, handing me a steaming cup. "Are you allowed a little jolt?"

"Who cares?" I reply, popping open the cup's lid and blowing a ripple of steam across its contents. I inhale the scent of dark-roasted beans. That smell used to immediately conjure the frosted mornings Penny and I spent in the coffee shop across from our first apartment, eating sticky Danishes and sharing the discarded sections of other people's newspapers, flirting with the baristas. But the memory doesn't come easily now. Something is missing, some connection that I can't place. I take a sip of the coffee, and it's so shocking, so appallingly bitter, that I spit the hot mouthful back into the cup.

"Jesus, where did you get this shit, Connor?" I ask, meeting three pairs of startled eyes.

"The coffee stand downstairs. Did you want cream and sugar?" Connor asks.

"No, of course I didn't . . ." There was an ancient coffee maker in the School of the Art Institute's Fine Art building. It produced sludge so thick you could almost stand a paintbrush on end in a cup of it, and I was infamous for drinking it with religious devotion. Now I glance at Sam. "Yours is okay?"

He nods, the crease between his eyebrows deepening.

"I can get you something else," Connor offers, but it doesn't do much to diffuse the sudden wary tension in the room.

"That's all right," I say, unable to brave anything else from the coffee cart at the moment. But I do need something, something to get the burnt, tarry taste out of my mouth. "Maybe just some water."

Sam goes to get it for me, and no one says anything while he's gone.

# David

Within an hour of waking up, all I want is a shave and a cigarette. Through all of it—Beth's tears and the stop-and-frisk from my doctors and the Skype conversation with my son—my beard itches. Politicians don't grow beards, at least not unless they want to look like hippies, or worse, Communists. I haven't gone more than three days without a shave in my entire adult life. But here I am with a half inch of thick brown hair rooted to my face. I look a hell of a lot like a teenager when I wheel myself into the bathroom to take a piss. Under the green flicker of fluorescent lighting, I see an overgrown kid, like those pock-marked hipsters who always show up to protest at town hall meetings, scrawny boys in tight jeans with perfect teeth and long eyelashes who bitch about the evils of free trade or the plight of the polar bears. The kind of kid who has to grow a beard so he won't be mistaken for an ugly, broad-shouldered girl. I only hope my real face is waiting for me underneath the facial hair.

My slightness is the biggest surprise. I'd almost forgotten what I looked like before college, how small and inconsequential I once was. And here he is again, that wisp of a boy, with his thin frame and bony arms. My skin is chalk white and shows none of the lines that sprouted from my eyes or parenthesized my mouth during the past few years. I never minded the wrinkles, even when Beth did her best to talk me into getting them injected with Botox for the sake of the cameras. They made me look older, more distinguished, like I'd worked for what I'd earned in my life. For a congressman, that kind of perceived credibility was worth its weight in gold. I run a finger over the skin on the outside corner of my eye. It's smooth and tight, flawlessly supple. *Fuck.* The last thing I need is to look like I took this leave of absence to get some work done at a fancy spa somewhere.

It's ironic that returning to this particular body has actually saved me. It's a body that looks spindly and wan compared to the one I had yesterday. I'd spent years cultivating and maintaining the muscle mass I had, enough that *GQ* ran a cover story on me for their fitness issue. "The Best Abs in Congress," it read, and the guys in my caucus ribbed me constantly for it. But privately, I was damn proud. It was part of my dogma; hard work and personal determination had literally shaped me into the person I was. And now all of that effort has been wiped away.

I want a cigarette. It's a Pavlovian impulse, like an itch you don't know you have until scratching it feels delicious. Smoking in bathrooms has become a habit for me. During session breaks, in the middle of black tie events, before press conferences. Blowing smoke out windows or into exhaust fans. Hell, I once smoked a cigarette in a bathroom on Air Force One. After all, the vice president can only bum so many smokes during a flight before you realize that the smoke detectors in there are mostly for show.

The sudden gnawing of the craving pisses me off. The doctors all but guaranteed that I'd be rid of my chemical dependencies in this new body. They were as gleeful as doctors get about an untested theory, a mix of earnestness and lustful salivation over the idea of it. A body that has never tasted nicotine, never had a sip of Scotch. And yet, the memory of that long-suffered impulse has me patting the pockets of the scrubs I cajoled from a cute nurse, looking for cigarettes I don't have. I bang my way out of the bathroom, startling Beth where she sits, watery-eyed and still breathless with exultation at the miracle of it all.

"Where's Jackson?"

"Camped out in the hallway, I think," she says, spinning her wedding ring around her finger. She started wearing it again when

I got sick, and she plays with it now like she did when we were first married, as if it is something new and not quite comfortable. "It's the only place he can get cell service."

I wheel my way to the door, which takes considerable effort, and bang the side of my fist on it in three jarring beats. I'm halfway back to the bed when Jackson steps into the room behind me. He's grinning, his mouth full of teeth that are one size too large for his face, and combined with his orange hair he looks a bit like the kid from *MAD* magazine.

"You rang?"

I use the last of my upper-body strength to haul myself into bed and slide back between the covers. I try to hide the fact that I'm winded when I speak. "What am I missing out there?"

"There's going to be a floor fight on the farm bill. Apparently the Democrats have some issues with the rider the minority leader attached. The Dow is down, but it'll rebound as soon as we vote on the budget. And the AP is reporting that Keith blew a point-one-five last night during a traffic stop and then tried to show his ID to get out of it."

"What was it, some crusader cop?"

"A rookie. Second week on the job, if you can believe it. Had Keith in handcuffs before his partner even realized what had happened."

"Bad luck for Keith," I say. The worst that usually happens is a cop with an oversize conscience makes you leave your car and drives you home in his squad. But most just send you on your way when they see the seal on your badge.

"Looks like there's a new bad boy on the Hill," Jackson says. He's in a good mood; he's grinning like he's done something really disastrous this time and no one can pin it on him.

"Hey, he's pinch-hitting. I won't be out for long. Speaking of which, where are we on the polling?"

Jackson pulls a manila folder from under his arm and hands it to me. "You're not going to believe it."

I glance over the data, a breakdown of percentages and their corresponding questions. My eyes catch on a number. "Rehab? You're kidding."

"We pitched everything from autoimmune diseases to exhaustion to sex addiction. Turns out, Wisconsinites think a man who has to get dried out is more trustworthy than one who is sick or tired."

"Or balling prostitutes," I add, and then catch a look from Beth. "Sorry babe. Jackson is a bad influence on me."

Beth leans over to squeeze my hand. Her blonde hair pools in front of her shoulders and the silk of her blouse whispers as she moves. She's wearing red lipstick. She always wears lipstick, even on international flights and while playing tennis and during midnight trips to the pharmacy for baby aspirin. I seem to remember her lips were a particularly bright shade of pink when she was in labor with David Jr.

"How about I get you something from the cafeteria, hmm?" she says. "Leave you two to talk?"

"Great, babe. Anything with chocolate, right?"

"Right, because you need junk food in your condition," Jackson quips.

"Eat me."

"Don't kill each other while I'm gone, please," Beth says, giving me a brief kiss on the lips, not enough to smudge her lipstick. I realize a moment too late that it's a first kiss, of sorts. But then she's already heading for the door, her heels clicking on the tile of the floor in a perfectly measured rhythm, and I don't even have a chance to savor it. It's already gone.

Jackson sits down in her chair once we're alone, leaning back with a stack of files balanced on his knee. He waits for me to speak, to ask the question. I try to wait him out, to see how long I can stretch the silence, but after a few moments my resolve crumbles.

"So what's the real damage here?"

Jackson chews the inside of his lip, the way he has ever since we were kids, the way he did the time we dented his father's truck playing baseball and tried to think up a good excuse to keep from getting throttled.

"We're going to take a hit, no matter what. But if we can make the rehab story work, it might buy us enough time for things get back to normal before SUBlife goes up for FDA approval. The public has a short memory, and a year is a long time. If we do it right, they won't connect the dots when the word 'cloning' starts to get thrown around."

"And if they do?" I ask, though I'm not sure I want to know the answer. Jackson shrugs.

"You'll have a lot of time to perfect your hook shot, I guess. Or hey, I could run for your seat and you could be *my* chief of staff. That could be fun."

"Right." I scratch at the prickle of thick hair on my neck. My fingernails are trimmed short, and for the first time I realize that someone had to have trimmed them for me. Someone was in charge of maintaining this body as it was being grown, before my memories were transferred in. The idea makes me feel a little sick.

"And the support group?"

"Apparently nonnegotiable. But there will be iron-clad confidentiality agreements all around. The others can talk all they want about their own experiences, but the minute your name comes into it, we'll be taking fifty cents of every dollar they make for the rest of their lives."

"Good. Hopefully they make enough for that to be a motivating factor. Get me the background information on them, will you?" I say, picking up my cup of water from the side table and toasting him with it, wishing it were three fingers of Scotch.

But the more Jackson and I talk, the more this seems possible. I could wake up next year and be back to the man I remember. Better even, the man I promised Beth I would be when she came back and began wearing her wedding ring again. I could quit drinking altogether, quit smoking, spend more time in my district, even live at home with Beth and David Jr. for most of the year. Yes, this will be a beginning. I polish off the water in a large gulp and then crush the cup in my fist, tossing it at Jackson, who deflects it with his forearm.

"You must be feeling better."

"I feel like a million dollars, brother. But tell me, who do I have to blow to get a shave around here?"

# Linda

It amazes me, sometimes, how small a world can be. Not the world as a whole, from horizon to horizon, but the world as it exists for a single person. Sometimes it feels like a person's world can shrink to a size that would fit within the shell of a walnut. I think of prison cells and agoraphobic poets and people who are born and live and die inside the limits of the same small town. It must seem impossible to them that highways actually lead anywhere. A person could believe that airplanes are the size of flies, if she only ever sees them from afar, trailing their way across the sky. If she can even see the sky.

I envied all of those people. People who drove from one side of their little town to the other. Prisoners pacing in their cells. Poets who watched birds through their windows and wrote about them from behind large wooden desks. I hated all of them for the size of their worlds. Because mine was much, much smaller. What I wouldn't have given for four walls and a window.

Since the transfer, wiggling my toes has become my favorite pastime. It's the simplest of pleasures for me; I could spend hours this way, peering down and watching the sheet twitch and flutter over the twin mounds of my feet. It's always what you see in movies after a car accident, when some poor bloodied actress is being strapped into a neck brace, her face wet and vacant in the red light of the road flares surrounding the wreck. The paramedics ask her to move her toes, and she can't. And that's when you know it's all over for her.

That's not how it was for me, of course. After my accident I didn't regain consciousness for eighteen days. And, by the time I did wake up, there was no question of the damage my poor body had sustained. I would never wiggle my toes, or move my fingers, or even lick my lips, not ever again. I could blink. That was it. One for no. Two for yes. An entire language distilled down to two words.

So having movement now, even the smallest of muscle twitches, feels like such an immense gift I dare not ask too much of it. Sometimes I lie still, afraid of the crushing disappointment, a blackness so deep I'm sure I would never recover, if I were to try to move and fail. I do not dare to imagine walking, or writing, or going to the bathroom on my own. I barely dare to speak. It's been my experience that life has a way of ripping the rug out from under you just as you're finding your footing. And I have no fortitude to withstand disappointment, not anymore.

In truth, I never thought any of this would actually work. It sounded absurd to the point of comedy when the doctor first described it to me, sitting on the edge of my bed, detailing the Substitute body they would clone from my DNA and the hormone treatments that would accelerate its growth, from infancy to adulthood in a matter of months. The way they would open my skull and remove a few precious bits of my brain, like seeds, that would take root inside the SUB. It took me a very long time to realize that the nurses hadn't accidentally hooked my IV up to some fantastic narcotic, something they give to hospice patients to make them numb with euphoric, hallucinatory happiness before the end.

The doctor wanted my consent to do it, even though Tom still had power of attorney over my medical decisions. The risk of death was too great, I guess, for them to cut into my brain without my permission. I gave it readily, blinking twice even before the question was complete. It seemed like the best choice possible. I would either be cured, or I'd be dead. Both options were preferable to remaining as I was.

They had to put me under general anesthesia for the transfer. It was ironic, really, because they could have sawed my legs off and I wouldn't have felt a thing. But cutting into my skull, that was a different story. That was one of the only places I still had any feeling.

Tom was there, in the operating room, hovering over me and eclipsing my view of the packed gallery above me. I watched him, from flat on my back, the slice of his eyes that showed between the gauzy scrub cap he was wearing and the mask over his face. Maybe he held my hand, I don't know. It would have been for his own benefit, if he did. All I could do was lie there and watch his eyes and wait for the drugs to stretch everything like taffy and then blot all of it out. Wait for death if it was coming. Tom looked so afraid in those last moments. He couldn't know how I welcomed anything that would come next, even if it was death, even if it wasn't. All I could do was blink until my eyelids became thick with weight, and even then, again and again, yes, yes. Yes.

# Connie

Nobody comes to visit me in the hospital that first week. And that's fine because nobody was really around for the past five years when I was sick, either. They were around at first, before it got really evident that I wasn't kidding. People seemed to care when I told them. I feel like the percentage of people who cried upon hearing of my condition was pretty impressive, especially considering the only friends I had were paid to be on set every day. But the minute it started to show, within weeks of that first KS lesion on the side of my neck, bleeding purple through all the makeup I slathered onto it, the orbit of friends and industry players around me seemed to loosen and widen. The minute people could see the disease, they began to care a whole lot less. People stopped looking at me. Which was strange, because people had been looking at me my whole life, people I didn't even know. But the sicker I got, the more people saw the disease instead of me. It got to the point where my own mother couldn't look me in the eye.

Looking in the mirror now feels like revenge. I've always had good bone structure, the kind of thing talent agents can spot in a pre-pubescent schoolgirl at a mall, the straight nose and high cheekbones and pointed chin that grows up with you no matter how much weight you lose or how deep the lines around your eyes become. Now my skin is no longer sallow and lined, my eyes aren't ringed in deep, sucking sockets of shadow. My hair isn't gray and sparse; my lips aren't cracked or pocked with sores. I look like I did at twenty-five. Better, even. I'd been smoking for ten years by my twenty-fifth birthday, and my skin never looked this pristine, like polished stone, even when I was at my best. My hair is thick, back to its shining honeysuckle blonde. My lips are soft and full of blood. I smile at my reflection, winking an eye ringed with long lashes. Give me a pair of tweezers and a good blow-out and I'm Grace fucking Kelly.

Let them try and show their faces now. Those hangers-on. The agents and managers and makeup artists who fled so quickly when they realized their paychecks would fade along with my looks. Let them try and flock back now that I've been reborn, fully-formed, like Athena springing from Zeus's skull. Excitement brims within me. I trace my fingertips down the perfect column of my nose, over my chin, an eyebrow, circling my eye. Checking to make sure it's all real, it's not some illusion brought on by whatever they're putting in my IV. But it's me, or at least the version of me who used to leave talent agents and directors and teenage boys slack-jawed and gaping. I'd watched this woman shrink and wrinkle like a raisin during the last five years, giving way to age and disease and despair. This woman, I think, looking at my reflection, this woman is afflicted by none of those things.

It's a nearly breathtaking thought. I've spent so much of my life trying to blot out the version of myself who came before, first the long-limbed girl in cutoffs from the trailer park in Illinois, then the teenage catalog model selling trashy clothes and bubblegum, then finally the up-and-coming soap star who contracted the A3/02 strain of HIV the week her first independent film premiered at Sundance. Now I've got all that time back. I have no past. I was born from nothing, conceived in a tube, and grown in a lab. And showbiz has the memory of a goldfish. All I'd have to do is pick a good stage name and no one would remember the blonde girl who won a Daytime Emmy a decade before. No one would want to remember, not when I look like this now.

I'm up and walking without assistance by my second week in the hospital, though at times it still feels like my joints could flop out of place at any moment. The first thing I do is tiptoe my way down the hall when the nurse's station is clear and Google the number for Val, my building's maintenance guy, on one of their computers. It takes much longer than I expected. My typing is slow and dreadfully clumsy. If I close my eyes, I can imagine the placement of every letter on the keyboard, but my fingers refuse to fly over the keys like they once did. I must tell each finger where to move. When I finally find the number, I'm almost certain one of the nurses is going to catch me, but still I pick up the phone and dial.

"Yeh?" his voice comes over the line.

"Yes, this is Connie from apartment 537? I was wondering if you could do me a favor."

"You put in a maintenance request?" Val's accent is thick and Eastern-European, all of his consonants feel earthy and guttural over the phone.

"No, see, I just want you to knock on apartment 538, Dr. Grath's apartment? Could you let him know that I'm away on vacation, and not to worry?"

"Vacation?" Val says it as if he doesn't understand the word.

"Yes. Tell him Connie, from apartment 537, called and told him not to worry. Okay?" The nurses won't be gone for long. I glance down the hallway to the door with the light flashing above it. I sort of hope someone isn't dying in there. Seems like a bad way to score a free phone call. Though, I wouldn't have to resort to such methods if they let me use my cell. The rules in this place are starting to get on my nerves.

"Sure, sure," Val says, though I'm only about forty percent sure he'll actually do it. Considering how long it took him to fix the leak in my bathroom ceiling, I might be home before he actually gives the message to the old man.

I've been thinking about Dr. Grath a lot during the past few days, and I am feeling pretty bad that I didn't tell him that I'd be gone for a few weeks. I imagine him tapping on my door with the top of his cane and getting no answer from within. I wonder if he's frightened, thinking that maybe I'm lying dead in my apartment like the doomed heroine in one of his Hitchcock films. But no, Dr. Grath is sharp enough to realize that if I were dead in my little studio, he'd probably be able to smell my corpse from across the hall. Still, I wonder if he's lonely.

I've been traipsing down to his apartment a few times a week for years now, because I burn through my medical marijuana much quicker than he does, and he's always willing to share. He says it doesn't do a lick for his glaucoma anymore, everything has been a dark blur for him for years now, but his ophthalmologist just keeps prescribing it for him. Probably out of pity. It was always our joke, mine and Dr. Grath's. Because we both know that anyone who pities Dr. Grath is just wasting his time.

It was a mistake, not to mention my impending hospital stay to the old man. I simply said good night to him one evening and left for the hospital the following morning. If I died when they cut into my brain during the transfer—which had been a risk, according to Dr. Mitchell—I would've preferred Dr. Grath to think I just disappeared. I talked a lot throughout the years about hopping on a plane to Bermuda or Iceland or Brazil and never coming back. If I had died on the operating table, I would want him to imagine me on a beach somewhere instead of holed up in my moldering, poorly heated studio.

Even now, I don't know how I'll explain what's happened to me. I think of his eyes, those cloudy blue eyes that look like milk billowing into a cup of tea. If I lied, told him I was visiting family or on a bender, or that Bermuda wasn't really all it's cracked up to be, he wouldn't be able to tell that I was lying. He wouldn't know that I've been cured, while he must still live out the rest of his life looking at the world and seeing nothing. It doesn't seem fair.

I go back to my room, steadying myself on the doorjamb before stumbling through, and flop back onto the rumpled sheets of my hospital bed. And I barely have time to register my mistake, to see the unfamiliar book on the side table and the sagging balloons in the corner and hear the flush of a nearby toilet, before a small Asian woman emerges from the adjoining bathroom. She stops where she is, and we stare at each other for a moment.

"Sorry," I say, sliding off the bed and onto my already-exhausted legs. "I guess I got the wrong room." She looks peculiar, strangely ageless. Her hair is dark, her eyes wide-set and topped with sparse eyebrows. Perfect teeth peek out from between her full lips. Her skin is dewy and placid, totally without texture, baby skin. There is a maturity in her features; seen from afar I might peg her somewhere around thirty. But up close, she has all the signs and markers of youth, of girlhood, and I see in her so much of myself that the recognition is immediate. "You're another one, aren't you? In the pilot program?" I lower my voice a bit. "SUBlife?"

"Who—" the woman says, still gaping at me as if I am some foreign creature, something unnatural, an intruder.

"I'm Connie. From the room next door. I think. I never figured that they'd put us all on the same floor. But then again, why not, right?" The woman says nothing. Maybe something has gone wrong with her transfer, maybe they weren't able to get all the data mapped correctly into her brain. She looks at me like she's got a screw or two loose.

"It's weird, right?" I say, trying to help her along, buying time to pause and get my balance before starting to walk to the door. She nods a little in reply, and then makes her way to the bed in two unsteady strides. She sits down gingerly.

"Are you Mary Jane Livingston?" she says, finally. Her eyes are a pretty color, gray ringed with brown. Her question makes me laugh.

"I am," I say, delighted that she recognizes me. *Stratford Pines* was the first real acting gig I landed when I moved to Hollywood, a bad soap opera but a good jumping-off point for a film career that never materialized. Still, it's gratifying to be connected to my former self. "At least, I was. In another life."

"I don't like the woman they replaced you with. She's not as pretty."

"Susanna White. She plays Mary Jane all wrong, much too emotional. I mean, I know you're a soap star and all, but Christ, have a little artistic integrity, won't you?"

The woman smiles awkwardly, as if it is an uncomfortable expression for her.

"What's your name?"

"Linda." She looks like she's about to say more, so I wait a moment. But the smile fades from her face and her lips press together.

"So you've been watching for a while then, huh? It's been, God, about five years since I was on the show."

"I used to watch it every day." She has a strange conversational style; she stops talking just when it seems like she's picking up steam. Maybe I make her uncomfortable. I should really leave. I've barged in on this nice, unremarkable woman as she's recovering from a traumatic medical procedure. But the idea of going back to my empty room makes me tired in a way that is not wholly physical.

"Who was your favorite character?" I ask, trying to keep the conversation going by sheer persistence. Again, her teeth appear in a shiny stripe between her lips, as if she's trying to remember how to smile.

"Jake." Her eyes drop when she says it.

"He's very pretty, isn't he?" I'd gone home with Bradley Jennings, who plays the character of Jake Westerfield on *Stratford Pines*, more than once for a little post-production. I consider telling Linda this, and then decide against it. She looks like she might shock pretty easily. "I haven't really kept up on the story since I left the show. It's funny, you work with the same people every day for years, and you think that you'll all keep in touch when it's over. You'd be surprised how quickly something stops being a part of your life." I think of Dr. Grath again, how easy it was to check into the hospital, to disappear for weeks, without even wondering about him.

"I have a TV," Linda says. She motions toward the television mounted on the wall. "I could tell you what's happened."

"In the last five years?"

Linda nods emphatically. Who was this woman before the transfer? There's something painfully disjointed about her, the way she looks and the way she talks. After all, not many Rhodes scholars are watching *Stratford Pines* every day for the past half decade. But she has an earnestness that I find endearing, particularly so, given the weight of my loneliness.

"Maybe," I reply, because I'm still wary of committing pieces of my future to anyone else. I have been, ever since I got sick. It's why Dr. Grath never invites me over, I always simply stroll down the hallway and knock on his door, unannounced. I hated plans, and appointments, things that need to be scrawled on a calendar. It felt like handing over bits of time, time that no longer belonged to me, without knowing how much I had left.

# Hannah

My sister visits the week after the transfer. She's called a couple of times during the past few days, and I've been putting her off. Lucy is particularly high maintenance when she's trying to get pregnant, and I've been telling Sam that I don't have the energy to contend with her yet. In truth, I'm a little afraid of what she'll think of me now. I run my fingers through my hair and it's heavy, unwashed, thick with grease. I wonder how I'll look to her.

She starts crying as soon as she enters the room, with one hand over her mouth. I glance wide-eyed at Sam, a silent plea for help. He's always been good with Lucy. Better than I am, at least. She blubbers in the collar of his shirt as he envelops her small frame, rubbing circles along her back. It used to be that way with Sam and me, back when I was first diagnosed. I remember crying on our bathroom floor, the force of his arms gripping me, the damp press of his face into the back of my neck. Now, it seems like whenever I cry, he finds an excuse to leave the room.

When Lucy releases Sam she descends on me, her face wet against my cheek, her curly hair soft and fresh-smelling as it falls into my line of vision. She has the same fair features as I do, though her hair is a shade lighter brown, her eyes a bit smaller. She looks tired and very lovely.

"God, you look fabulous," she says, groans really, sniffling and releasing me, wiping her face with her palms. "Think I could get a new body after I have another kid?"

"What if you want to have more?" I ask.

"I swear, three is enough. Too much, probably. The next one

33

won't get breastfed at all, I'll need a cocktail so badly," she says. "But what about you? How are you feeling, honey?"

"Good, I'm good. Sam is taking excellent care of me."

"Of course he is." Lucy's smile is always genuine when she turns it on Sam. "I knew he would."

I try to ignore the private bit of affinity that passes between them. I think of being twelve years old and watching from the living room on Friday nights as Sam waited for Lucy at the bottom of the stairs. Of looking at their prom photo, sitting in its frame on my mother's desk. Of waking up cold and gasping in my hospital bed, and finding Sam gone. It was Lucy who told me Sam had the flu, that the doctors wouldn't let him in the ICU. Lucy blinks a lot when she lies.

Thinking of that morning sours my stomach. It is the source of all of my doubt; it makes me wonder what sort of secrets remain between the two of them, the ones that linger from their time together, all those years ago, and the ones that are as fresh as a new wound.

"Mom has been calling," Lucy says.

"Here, too," I reply. "Sam talked to her. Something about the water purification systems getting caught up in customs?"

Lucy lets out a little huff. "It's the Sudan, honey. You know they would be here if they could. So many people are depending on them out there."

"I know," I say, nodding. Trying to remember the last time I spoke to my parents, in between one of their Africa trips for Clean Water First, the nonprofit they founded when I was a teenager. We were angry when we spoke, I'm sure. We always seem to be angry at one another, because they're off putting their wealth to good use saving lives, and I'm in Chicago painting pictures. They are good people, the way Sam is a good person, the way I have never been. I try not to wonder if their anger, their disappointment, is part of the reason they didn't come back when I got sick.

"I mean, they didn't come back when either of the boys were

born," Lucy says. "It would take an act of Congress to get them out of there in the middle of a project."

"I know," I say again. Lucy straightens.

"Did you get the flowers Roger's firm sent?" she asks, glancing around the room, its flat surfaces crowded with a kaleidoscope of bouquets and balloons and miniature stuffed animals.

"Yeah, the ones by the window. Be sure to thank him for me, they're lovely," I reply, as Lucy gets up and walks to the overflowing bouquet.

"You would think his secretary would know better than to order anything with baby's breath. It's like sending carnations. Jesus," she says, turning the vase a bit. I can almost see the flowers wilting under her scrutiny. I feel the same way when she glances back at me. "Your face looks so different. You know those reality shows where people lose all that weight and they show before and after shots? It's sort of like that."

Sam winks at me over the screen of his laptop. It's impossible to have a conversation with Lucy that doesn't somehow wind its way toward the topic of her lingering baby weight. I try to keep from grinning. "Hey, thanks."

"Have you set a date for the wedding yet?"

My desire to smile evaporates. "Lucy, it's only been a couple of days."

"But that was the deal, right? That if the transfer went well . . ." she says. Sam's face is impassive. His eyes track over the screen in front of him.

"I can't even walk down the hall on my own, Luce. I think planning a wedding is a little beyond my reach right now."

Lucy perches on the edge of my bed. "I'm not saying you need to start planning. Just set a date. Something to look forward to. Anyway, you know I'll take care of whatever you don't feel up to dealing with." She takes a curl of my hair between her fingers, pulling it lightly until it straightens. "You'll make such a beautiful bride," she says. I take her hand and kiss the back of it. She clears her throat, blinking fast, and turns to Sam.

"You enjoy that new body of hers while you can, because once you two start having babies, it's nothing but stretch marks and flab everywhere, I swear."

"I'll keep that in mind," Sam says, nodding sagely, as if he's taking her seriously.

"You remember what I looked like in high school," she says. "Believe me, no amount of Pilates will get my ass back to where it was back then."

"Well you can always hope you have the gene for metastatic lung cancer too," I say, because I can't stop myself. Lucy looks like she might begin to cry again, and I press my fingers against my lips, just in case there are any more choice words threatening escape.

"That's really not funny," Lucy says.

"I'm sorry," I say, catching Lucy's hand as she tries to extricate it from mine. "Cabin fever, you know? It makes me a total ass."

"Right," Lucy says, looking at our intertwined hands. Hers is puffy and worn, her fingernails short and utilitarian despite their bright pink polish. A mother's hand. Mine might as well be a child's for how delicate it appears. She notices the contrast, I'm sure. It's a terrible feeling, Lucy's unhappiness. I'm always the one to apologize, the one who requires forgiveness. The one who brought her curly fries and ice cream and rubbed her back for hours when Sam broke her heart in high school, as if it were my crime to atone for instead of his. As if I knew, somehow, that his crime would become mine, in her eyes, years later.

"How are the boys, Luce?" Sam asks, and Lucy's face lifts and reforms into something more serene. Even her eyes smile, when she looks at Sam.

"A handful," she replies. "They think my new sectional couch is the best jungle gym they've ever seen. And Roger just encourages them, of course. I'm all by myself, trying to keep the barbarians at bay." Sam has a marvelous talent for handling my sister. Somehow, what would take hours or even days of pandering and groveling on my part, he manages in a matter of moments. Lucy pulls her hand from mine and moves toward him, as he promises that we'll be by for dinner soon, that he'll bring the boys some of his old baseball cards to trade. I watch the two of them, reminded so well of the days when I lived on the periphery of their vision, when being five years younger made me all but invisible to them. And I wonder, again, about the morning I woke to find Sam gone, and the sort of secrets they're keeping from me now.

# Connie

I'm able to beg a pair of tweezers off of one of the nurses before my first support group meeting. My eyes water as I pluck my eyebrows into something close to arches, the pain of it more acute than I remember. Everything is fresh and vivid in this body, nothing dampened by time or wear or damage. I shudder to think of what my first bikini wax will be like. There's really nothing to be done about my hair, which is lank and flat and unwashed, but I find an elastic band in my purse and pull it back into a knot at the crown of my head. And there she is, the woman with no history. Helen of Troy. The face that launched a thousand ships.

It's not hubris, or at least not just hubris, that informs my opinion of myself. While I was growing up, my mother was a connoisseur of beauty. A failed actress/model/dancer herself, she raised me to be a passionless appraiser of aesthetics, and I was always an eager pupil. Together we would paw through fashion magazines and critique the women on the shiny silk of the pages, or watch a continuous loop of barely clothed dancers in music videos. She would hold a mirror in front of my face and demand that I contort my expression into a whole slew of emotions, correcting each flaw she witnessed, smiling her prim little smile when she was pleased. Now my reflection is just as flawless as it was then, at twelve, before the world had a chance to work at it.

It was what made my disease doubly cruel, that the death of beauty in me would precede my actual death. I did everything I could at first, to salvage and prolong what little of it was left, scraping fungus from underneath my fingernails and having my withered face injected with fillers until it bruised black and dyeing my hair to keep its bright blonde hue until it was all too much. Until I was just a silly, saggy, ugly woman with a bad at-home dye job. After that I stopped going out so much, began spending my evenings with a blind man. I got rid of all my mirrors.

A nurse appears in the doorway to bring me to the meeting. It's the sort of thing I always avoided when I was sick, crowded little rooms full of skeletal AIDS patients trading stories about toxoplasmosis and Pneumocystis pneumonia. I never understood people who derived comfort out of shared experiences, particularly bad ones. I preferred to be alone, to ride out the spells of grief and depression and hopelessness under my own steam, instead of unloading them to a room full of strangers. The last thing I wanted was to be around other people who were sick too; it felt too much like looking in a funhouse mirror and seeing a hundred reflections of myself, all my problems multiplied and manifested again and again. Though it's probably much easier to go to a support group where no one is actually dying—quite the opposite, in fact.

Linda is already there, sitting in the small conference room with a younger woman when I arrive. We're all dressed the same, in cotton hospital robes over our gowns and cheap cloth slippers. They glance up when I enter, and I can feel that familiar current of electricity in the air as I move through it. It's like a held breath, something palpable in its absence. I want to grin. It's been years since I've lit up a room just by entering it. I give Linda a little wave, and her jubilation shows in the quick breath she takes, her shoulders pinned to the back of her chair.

I take a seat across from them. There's already an awkwardness in the room, as they avoid my eyes, and each other's. I wonder how long they've already been sitting there without talking. The one is so small she looks like little more than a girl, but pretty. She has huge dark eyes and a tiny nose and thick, curly hair, what people in the business would call ethnic-chic. She could easily be French or Irish or Jewish or maybe even Hispanic, in the right lighting.

Natalie Wood, singing on a fire escape. By comparison Linda, with her wandering eyes, looks a bit unhinged. I can't tell if she's tamping down some manic, wall-climbing energy or if she's terrified of sitting in this room, but she looks like she might make for the door at any moment. There are two other empty chairs in the circle. When I glance back to the girl, she meets my eyes for a moment before looking away. I take it as an invitation.

"I have a pair of tweezers if you want to borrow them," I say, motioning to the space over her nose, where her eyebrows nearly meet. She looks at me like she's not sure if I've insulted her, but then lets out a little laugh. Rising to the occasion. A girl with a backbone. Before she can answer a man enters, one who is clearly not a SUB from the creases in his face, all his edges soft and withered. Good bone structure, though, and it leaves him with a somewhat dashing edge. That's the thing about good bones, they hold up even after everything else has lost its steam.

"We're not all here yet, I see," he says, taking a seat between Linda and me. He checks his watch, obviously annoyed to make his entrance before an incomplete group. The fifth member arrives a few minutes later. At first I think he's another young doctor; he's wearing blue scrubs and he's clean-shaven, with a certain air of importance around him. But when he comes to sit in the remaining chair I realize, with more than a little surprise, that he's a SUB as well.

"My apologies," he says, with a feigned sort of antebellum bashfulness. "I didn't mean to hold everyone up."

His face is too perfect, like a corn-fed high school quarterback, though he carries himself with the calm assurance of a much older man. He has dark hair and perfect cheekbones, and a mouth stuffed with bright white teeth. You can tell, just by looking at him, that he is blessed in just about every way a person can be. And already, I don't trust him.

# Hannah

He says his name is David. We all go around the circle and intro-
duce ourselves. There's Linda, who sits next to me, close enough so
I can feel the ripples of anxiety washing off of her like the rhythmic
gust of an oscillating fan. And then there's Connie, the bombshell,
sitting with her arms crossed as if she's posing for a camera. And Dr.
Bernard, the psychiatrist in charge. But David is the one who holds
my attention, because even though he looks ten years younger than
he is, even out of context, out of his usual expensive suits, isolated
from his gaggle of aids and lackeys, away from the TV cameras and
microphones, I know who he is. He's David Jenkins, and he's a U.S.
Congressman.

I can't count how many times I've seen this man on TV, when
Sam turns on MSNBC after work and we flop down on the couch,
letting long minutes slip away before we're hungry enough to cook
dinner. People have said that, one day, this man could be president.
And Sam swore up and down that he'd leave the country forever if
that happened.

He's handsome, up close, and I have no control over this body
yet. I cannot curtail its impulses, instruct it not to want the wrong
people. So attraction hits me like a sledgehammer, pulsing in my
stomach with the insistence of starvation. David must notice that
I'm staring at him because he looks me right in the eye, a testing
glance, a challenge too well controlled to become a threat. I look
away on reflex alone and realize that Dr. Bernard is already in the
middle of his introduction.

"This is the forum," Dr. Bernard says. "Not only for your questions, your experiences in recovery, but for your fears and your frustrations as well. This is uncharted territory for all of us, medical personnel included, and no one has any illusions that this is going to be an easy process for any of you."

David is still looking at me. He cocks an eyebrow as my eyes meet his, and again, I'm forced to look away. I can feel my perfect skin grow ruddy with the mix of embarrassment and attraction and anger that this man's presence has created within me, out of nothing. Whatever game it is that we're playing, I'm certain that I'm losing.

"I have a question," Connie the bombshell says, half-raising her hand, though she doesn't wait for his acknowledgment before she keeps talking. "What exactly is the point of this whole exercise? I mean, as far as I can tell, everything worked the way it was supposed to. I don't get why we have to come here and talk about it every week for the next year. It seems like a waste of time, if you ask me."

"You signed an agreement to participate in this support group when you were admitted into the program," Dr. Bernard replies, and Connie gives a little laugh.

"What are they going to do, sue me? They can take me for all I've got doc, believe me, it won't exactly be worth their time." Dr. Bernard's mouth seems to constrict a bit, though he doesn't look angry, not exactly.

"It does seem sort of strange," I say, thinking of the single cancer support group I attended after my diagnosis, a group for terminal patients that met once a week in the school room of a local church. I remember how traitorous I felt, knowing that the slick SUBlife brochure was sitting on my dresser at home as I listened to the others describe the agony of chemo, the indignities of colostomy bags, or the triumph of climbing a flight of stairs. "I mean, isn't this sort of thing usually reserved for people who aren't going to get a miracle cure?"

"I think we all need to recognize what a wholly significant event you've all been through here," Dr. Bernard replies. "Just because you're not going to die doesn't mean that your journey won't require support."

"Isn't it funny how the only people you hear describing life as a 'journey' are bad poets and shrinks?" Connie says. I'm beginning to like Connie. She has a quality I've always envied in Penny, the ability to speak without being careful, without worrying what others will think of her. I wonder if it is the privilege of beautiful women, or if it's a freedom that comes from not being the daughter of wealthy philanthropists or the girlfriend of a crusader journalist. I wonder who I've become, after so many years of being polite and appropriate and unassuming, so as not to reflect badly on the people in my life. I wonder who I'm allowed to be now.

"Listen, doctor, all joking aside," David says, fixing Dr. Bernard with what appears to be his best 'come to Jesus' expression, a mixture of earnestness and condescension that makes me bristle. Dr. Bernard, to his credit, holds David's gaze with a look of calm, professional interest. "I think what we're all saying is that we just want to get on with our normal lives now that the medical legwork is done. We're all tremendously grateful to be part of this program, but coming here every week is just going to serve as a constant reminder of what we've been through."

"I appreciate your opinion, David," Dr. Bernard replies. "But this group serves a dual purpose within the pilot program. Not only are you coming here to provide support for the other group members, but these weekly meetings give us the opportunity to monitor your recovery and quickly address any issues that might arise over the next few months." He pauses. "I also think it's important that all of the members in this group have the opportunity to speak for themselves. So, I would ask you in the future to feel free to express your own opinions, but to please refrain from generalizing about the group as a whole." I think I hear Connie snicker at this, but her face is placid, with only the barest hint of amusement.

"Linda," Dr. Bernard says, everything in his posture and demeanor gentling, as if he's speaking to a small, lost child. "There must have been questions you wanted to ask before the transfer, and couldn't. Do you want to share any of those now?"

Linda seems to shrink into her seat, her gaze darting from person to person as we all turn expectant eyes in her direction. I wonder who she was, in her former life. It's Connie who finally gets her to speak, nudging her in the arm, which has the same effect on Linda as if she had administered an electric shock. At first I think Connie is being cruel, but Linda looks at Connie as if she's her own personal Jesus. Connie smiles, and then so does Linda, a slightly dimmer version of Connie's radiance. "You must have questions," Connie says. "I know I do."

Linda nods, suddenly eager to please. "I do. I have questions."

We all wait for her to continue, and when she doesn't, Connie prods her again. "What's the biggest one you've got? Let's see if the doc here can answer it."

Linda sits for a moment, chewing on her bottom lip, considering. Then she turns to Dr. Bernard.

"I want to know if my family still loves me," she says.

# David

"Congress votes on the FDA's budget right?"

A woman's voice stops me on my way to the coffee cart. There was no coffee at the support group meeting, which seems like an error of the highest order to me. If it were AA, there would have been a coup d'état if people didn't have Styrofoam cups to cradle when they needed something to do with their hands. How did anyone expect us to talk without something to stir, something to sip, something to blow on? How do they expect us to sit like good patients and cooperate? It's how you get a bunch of volunteers organized and knocking on doors and making phone calls. You give them free coffee, as much as they want. Even the worst gas station rotgut imaginable will do. You could run an entire army off of coffee.

The voice catches me off guard. I didn't realize anyone had followed me off the elevator, and when I turn it's Hannah, the brunette, the one who looks like she's young enough to be jailbait. It's difficult not to be disappointed that it isn't the blonde following me into the lobby. I have to remind myself that I'm not like that anymore.

"What?"

"Congress," she says. "They're the ones who fund the FDA."

"If you say so."

"And in a year the FDA is going to decide whether or not to approve SUBlife."

"If that's what the doctors said," I reply, half-turning away from her to resume my progress toward the hiss and bubble of the steel carafes.

"So what are you doing in the pilot program?" she asks, not following. She doesn't move. She knows her question will make me turn back toward her, the clever little thing. And it does.

"I'm not sure what you mean," I say, trying to maintain a note of calm disinterest in my voice, but it's not quite genuine enough. She's got me on my heels, and she knows it.

"Well, you're the Chairman of the House Budget Committee, if I'm not mistaken. That seems like a hell of a conflict of interest to me."

"Well, apparently the good people at SUBlife disagree with you," I reply. The girl carries herself as if she isn't very pretty. Perhaps she wasn't, before the transfer. Add a few pounds, maybe uneven those teeth a bit, dim the luminousness of her skin, and she could be plenty plain. But it's there now; she looks like the androgynous women staring out of Beth's fashion magazines. Women with mismatched features, huge lips and jutting cheekbones, large, thick eyebrows, and gaps between their front teeth. Women you'd think were almost ugly, if they weren't so fascinating. "What are you, a reporter?" I ask, letting a bite into my tone.

"No, just a concerned citizen, I guess."

"Concerned about what?"

"How on earth you were chosen for SUBlife. It was supposed to be a lottery system, right? From what I heard there were a few hundred qualifying patients in the Chicago area. So I'm wondering how a congressman was lucky enough to get on the short list." She's flushed a bit; blood is seeping into her skin the way a drop of wine blooms outward on a white tablecloth. She's angry.

"I qualified. Brain tumor," I say, tapping my temple to demonstrate. "Size of a golf ball. But listen, sweetie, before you start slinging around accusations, I'd suggest you consult the confidentiality agreement you signed when you got that new body of yours." I draw closer to her, lowering my voice, until I'm nearly whispering in her ear. "Because if I ever hear anything like what you just said coming from the mouth of a reporter, or if I read it in a newspaper, or on a blog, or even in the fucking *Red Eye*, you'll be paying my rent for the rest of your life. Understand?"

I step back. Her jaw is tense, and there's an angry sheen in her eyes. I wonder if she's cried yet, in this new body of hers. The thought bothers me a little, that I might be the first person to make her cry. But what bothers me even more is that something, maybe our proximity, or the tension of our little exchange, or the way this girl looks in her sad little hospital robe, something makes me feel an immediate spark of adrenaline in my blood. The first flicked switch in that cascade of neurotransmitters and churning internal chemistry that accompanies attraction.

It's amazing how physically aware I am, as if every vein and hair follicle and muscle fiber is suddenly dense with nerve endings that had never existed in my former body. As if my subconscious knows that this body is something foreign and new, something that must be monitored and measured and experienced fully. Whatever the case, my physical response to this woman makes it difficult to remember my former resolve, the desire to be faithful to my wife. I do my best to ignore the feeling, to chalk it up to the way winning an argument has always turned me on a little, no matter who it's with. After all, I'm a better man now.

She nods, a terse movement.

"Good. Now how about I buy you a cup of coffee?"

"You're getting coffee?"

"You heard the doctor; we're going to be spending quite a bit of time together this year. I don't want us to start off on the wrong foot, do you?" It's the way I talk to my opponents during debates, with a bit too much folksy charm, just enough so they know that it's an act, and underneath is something much more dangerous.

But she smiles, all traces of her momentary weakness gone. She's found her footing again. "You go ahead. I'll take a pass on this one."

"Suit yourself." I head toward the coffee cart, eager to put distance between us.

"And Congressman," she says, not loud, but enough to stop me in my tracks for the second time today. Maybe it's this girl who is more formidable than she appears. She is still smiling when I turn. "You call me sweetie again, and I'll make you miss that tumor."

# Linda

I haven't told Tom yet, that Connie wandered into my room last week. Until I saw her again in the support group today, I'd almost convinced myself that I imagined it. Stranger things have happened to me, I guess. Tom looks exhausted in the blue flicker of the television. It's late, and he's been here most of the day, though I'm not sure why he bothers. It's not like we've said much to each other. You'd think, after eight years of not being able to say a word, I'd want to tell him things, spill every thought that's been pent up inside me, like the pop and gush of opening a bottle of champagne. But that's what happens when your world gets small. You can't remember what you used to say to people, because you're so out of practice. You realize you don't have much to say anymore. One for no. Two for yes.

I used to wonder about the lengths I'd go to in order to stay alive. If I would be the type of woman to survive a shipwreck, or being stranded out in the wilderness somewhere alone. You read about things like that sometimes, or watch reality TV specials on the Discovery Channel, about stranded scuba divers who grip on to buoys for days at a time, or mountain climbers who crawl their way back to base camp with two broken legs. I always wondered if that would be me, if I had the kind of mettle that could withstand the most harrowing of circumstances. If I could tie a tourniquet on one of my own limbs, if I could saw off my own arm to escape a desert canyon. But, as it turned out, my canyon was my own body. And I was powerless to fight my way out of it.

It took me a long time to accept all of those hard truths that accompany a traumatic brain injury, especially one as severe as

mine. There was the respirator and the feeding tubes and the catheters. The paralysis, that crushing feeling of being trapped in a body
that would no longer listen when I told it to move. Those were terrible lessons to learn.

But for the first four years, at least I was at home. With Tom,
and our babies, and a home-care nurse named Cora. Tom converted
the office at the front of the house into a bedroom for me, and it
got sun in the afternoons and a western breeze. I could look out the
window and watch storms roll in over the roofs of the houses on our
block. And Cora was not such bad company. I worried at first, when
she leaned over me and I caught sight of the tightness of her scalp
between the braids in her hair and the long sharpness of her fingernails and the rose tattoo peeking out from under the neckline of her
scrubs. I wondered what she thought of me, the Chinese woman
with the white husband, the expensive house, a life so charmed and
so cursed at once. But when we were alone she talked, sometimes for
hours on end, telling me about her twin sons who had just left for
the army and the mother who could no longer remember her name.
She told me stories that would have made me laugh, or would have
made me cry, if I still had the ability.

My eyes would fill sometimes, and tears would leak down my
cheeks, and I would lie there and feel the droplets disappear into the
fuzz of numbness below my nose. There was no rhyme or reason to
when that would happen. Something about faulty tear ducts. My
brain and body were almost fully separate by then. Cora knew that,
and she would just dab my cheeks with a tissue and keep talking.
Tom never understood, no matter how many times Cora explained
that it was a reflex more than anything. He would shake his head
and cover his mouth with his hands, and his own eyes would fill.
And Cora would ease him out of the room and wink at me when she
returned. We were good friends, I think, Cora and me.

"What are the others like?" Tom asks, talking over the sound of
the TV on the wall. And, for a moment, I don't realize that he's actually waiting for an answer. It's shocking, really, how out of practice

I am at this. I try hard to figure out what sort of answer he wants. Their names? Their occupations, or their diseases? If they're nice or arrogant or disinterested? An appropriate answer seems too heavy to conjure, too broad for me to process. I panic a little. The air in the room feels thin, and I wonder if I'm allowed to open the window. But no, I have to say something to Tom, because he asked a question and he's waiting for an answer. I try and get out a few words without showing him that I'm short of breath.

"One man, two women. One of them is very pretty. An actress." I don't elaborate. It feels good to have a secret from Tom, something that is just mine. I remember Cora's winks, the secrets we kept from him.

Cora was the one who turned me on to *Stratford Pines* in the first place. I used to silently scoff at the other mothers at the playground when they talked about their soap operas, the endless cycle of inane story lines and the stock characters who change partners more quickly than in a square dance. I was already a bit of an outsider with them, that group of blonde North Shore mothers, a clique that came together with the same pettiness and backhanded cruelty as a high school cheerleading squad. It felt good to be the smart one, the mother with a five-year plan, a half-finished master's in English Literature from Northwestern and dreams of a doctorate. I'd palm one of the books I carried in the basket of Katie's stroller and feel the quiet heat of my own superiority.

But when your world shrinks with the speed and ferocity that mine did, when you can no longer escape into books, you begin to understand the allure of slipping into someone else's life for a while. And if it's a made-up life of intrigue, of kidnappings and long lost children and lovers separated by the manipulations of others, all the better. During the eight years of my stasis, of my conscious coma, of being locked inside my own body, those characters became as dear to me as any of the friends I'd had before my accident. They became residents of a secret world, one that existed within the useless, hollow body in which I was trapped. And, as shameful as it is to admit, those characters became the one source of comfort that I carried from my family's house to the cold isolation of the nursing home. Not my husband. Not my children. When I was scared or sad or lonely, I thought of *Stratford Pines*.

"Did you tell them you were a runner?" Tom asks. It seems a stupid question. I was many things before I was paralyzed. None of them seem particularly important anymore. When you are one thing, only one thing, for eight years, everything that came before it begins to feel less substantial. Sure, I was a runner. I was also a toddler, once, and no one cares to hear about that either.

"No," I reply, because it's an answer I'm used to. One blink.

"Well, why not?"

It's agonizing, sometimes, having Tom around so much. Tom and his questions, always waiting for me to answer with a look of expectation that makes me feel like a moth tacked on a wall, his gaze intrusive as a pushpin. I liked it better when he came once a week, a new bouquet of fresh flowers tucked into his armpit, his meager, persistent attempt to liven up the dinginess of the nursing home. I liked it when he did all the talking and never expected an answer.

Before the accident, I always imagined myself to be an ordinary sort of person. A kind person, someone with a large heart and certain perseverance. Maybe not enough to cling to a buoy or saw off one of my arms. But a good wife, a good mother. And then the settlement money from the accident ran out. Suddenly Cora's services were too expensive. Suddenly, Tom began to talk about finding me a place where I could be cared for around the clock.

Within my first month at the nursing home, my world shrank so small that it siphoned every bit of kindness or perseverance right out of me. The cage of my body took on a terrible, crushing weight. Like being buried alive. I didn't have four walls and a window. I had one wall, and a bit of ceiling, and a TV that was mounted there. Gone were the clouds and sunshine. Gone were Cora's stories, and the sounds of my children running down the upstairs hallway, and the smells of garlic bread and tomato sauce wafting up from our kitchen.

The four years I spent at Shady Glen Nursing Home felt like fifty. I read once that all anyone ever truly wants out of life is more time, that the search for immortality is the basis for all human achievement. And I knew I was the exception to that rule. Time was my enemy. Time was a slow drip of agony in my IV. I prayed for infections, for fluid in my lungs, for bubbles of air in syringes. But, as neglectful as the nursing home staff was when it came to just about everything worthwhile in a life, they were uncannily good at keeping me alive. If I could have told Tom one thing during his weekly visits, just one, it would not have been that I loved him, or our children. It would not have been that I missed my life, even the scraps of it that I had in those first years after the accident. If I got a single message in a bottle, floating up from the ocean of my isolation, I would have told him to cut off my oxygen and leave me there. My world had grown so small that the only thing left to do was to leave it.

So, there it was. I was the type of person who would let go, swallow mouthfuls of seawater and sink below the surface. I would stop moving and let myself freeze to death on the side of a mountain. I would find the highest cliff on my desert island and throw myself off. And because I could do none of those things, because I was utterly powerless to change the terrible current of my pulse or rid myself of the machine that kept me breathing, I lost myself in the lives of the characters on TV. I lived for those afternoon hours, more than I ever lived for Tom's visits, or even my own children. I drank those stories up, letting it anesthetize me like an opiate flooding into my bloodstream. I could ride for hours on that high, sometimes. I could close my eyes and write myself into their stories, touch their lovers, relish the sweet pain of their tragedies. And I understood it, finally, for what it was. It was a secret world. It was my window.

And then. And then. Two blinks.

"What did you talk about?" Tom asks, maybe because I still haven't answered him. It's hard to focus for too long, especially with the TV on in the background.

"I mostly just listened."

"Well, what did the rest of the group talk about then?" Tom has a mousy quality to him now. His hair has gone thin and gray in the past few years, which makes him look like he's in his late forties instead of thirty-five. He looks decades older, instead of three months younger than me. He looks so tired, and I wish he would go. It's the feeling I've had on so many occasions, when he'd come to visit me with the kids, when the day was bright and sunny and I knew they were missing out on it because of me. I wish he would go, instead of sitting here trying to talk to me. It seems like a waste of an evening.

"I'm not supposed to tell," I finally say, hoping that will be enough to send him out, on his way. I wonder what he would be doing on a normal Thursday, if he weren't here.

"The kids want to see you," he says then. I nod, because I don't know how to answer. "Jack thinks you're like Han Solo. That's the only way I could think of explaining it to them. Where Han gets frozen and then thawed out? It's the best kid-friendly analogy I could come up with."

"Snow White," I say, not looking at him. "Sleeping Beauty."

"Oh, right," he says, and he sounds so abashed that I force myself to look at him and smile, which takes some effort. It takes my eyes away from the TV. I've been working on smiling in the mirror when I stumble across the room to use the bathroom. It's as if I've forgotten that I can smile and laugh and frown, and I'm so out of practice that I have to make the decision to smile before I do it. Nothing feels natural anymore. Nothing, that is, except lying in my hospital bed, staring at the TV that's mounted on the wall, and wiggling my toes. Everything else feels too massive, and too terrifying. One for no. Two for yes. Things were so much simpler before.

# Hannah

David walks into the meeting five minutes late. Connie, Linda, and I glance up when he bangs his way through the door, his stride measured and unhurried. He pauses at Dr. Bernard's still-empty chair.

"Good. I'm not holding things up today," he says, to no one in particular. Connie rolls her eyes.

"Looks like you're only the second most important person in the room this week," I say, giving him my best faux campaign-ad smile.

"Thanks for warning me about the coffee," David replies, his voice gruff in my ear as he passes my chair. He takes the seat next to me. "That first sip ended up down the front of my shirt."

I stifle a laugh with my hand, and my stomach hurts at the effort. I wonder if I've laughed before this moment, since the transfer. I can't remember. But the image of David spewing coffee all over himself is too good to keep a straight face. He scowls at me.

"I really appreciated that. I thought we were supposed to be in this together."

"And I really appreciated you voting to cut funding for the NEA," I reply.

"Ah," he says, sitting back in his chair and crossing his arms. Triumphant. "I see you Googled me."

"Don't flatter yourself. I know a few people who lost their grants after that vote. Really talented people, ones who are better than having to work at Starbucks to pay their rent."

"Maybe they should have gone into something more useful to society."

I feel young and whitewashed under his gaze, stripped of the signs and markers of my roughness, the hard edges I'd chosen and cultivated so specifically. I think of Sam, the way he looked at me when we met again in college, with my dyed hair and my nose ring and my tattoos. He looked at me like I'd been melted down from the girl he knew and forged of something harder and more brilliant. Some shining metal. Now I feel like clay, barely formed.

"Like garbage collection. Or politics," I quip.

Dr. Bernard enters before David can say anything else. The good doctor is a full eight minutes late, all apologies, waving his hand in the air as if batting away all of the obligations that have trailed him into the conference room. Connie winks at me.

"So to begin this week, I think we should explain a little about what brought each of you into the program," Dr. Bernard says, clicking his pen and preparing to write on the legal pad that's balanced on his knee. "David," he says, turning toward the other man, "would you like to start us off?"

David seems less than pleased at Dr. Bernard's little show of authority. "I can give it to you in five words or less. Metastatic brain cancer."

"And a little about yourself, please," Dr. Bernard replies, coaxing him like a professor in a room full of bashful freshmen.

"Well, I work for Uncle Sam. I have a wife, Beth, and a son who will be eleven in October."

"And how are they coping with what you're going through?" Dr. Bernard asks. David pauses, wiping the back of his hand across his mouth, and then shakes his head.

"They're fine. Beth is, well, she's used to handling chaos. She's excellent at it. And she knew I wasn't going to die. She knew, one way or another, that I wouldn't let something like that take me down."

"And your son?"

David is silent for longer this time. "He's fine. He's a strong little kid. Takes after his old man that way. Right now he's in Wisconsin with his grandparents. Beth, she thinks it's better to keep him away from the hospital, you know?"

"And what do you think?" Dr. Bernard asks.

"I think a kid has to grow up sometime. I was never protected from anything as a child, and I don't think my son should be either," he says, all hard authoritarian bluster, but then something shifts in him. I can almost see the set of his shoulders soften. "Anyway, I'm his father. He shouldn't need to be protected from me."

I want to tell him that he's wrong, that we are capable of such great damage, that it's only by the grace of God or modern medicine that we haven't ruined the lives of the people who love us. But he looks so angry, and so vulnerable in his anger, that I'm sure he already knows. It's a startling feeling, to look at David Jenkins and see something familiar.

"That enough?" he asks. "Did I sing enough to earn my supper this week?"

"I appreciate your willingness to share with us," Dr. Bernard replies, and I'm still too distracted by David to realize that I'm on deck. "How about you, Hannah?" Dr. Bernard says. I straighten in my chair, fumbling with all of the things that I no longer know about myself.

"I'm a graduate student at the Art Institute. A painter. I live with my boyfriend, Sam." I falter, thinking of Lucy's visit. "Well, I guess he's my fiancé, now. Since I didn't die."

"Congratulations," Dr. Bernard says. "What was it that brought you here?"

"Lung cancer," I reply, trying to keep my face impassive, even as the words still feel so dense with agony that their shape is strange in my mouth. "Not the kind you get from smoking cigarettes. The kind you get from a really bad roll of the genetic dice."

"What was that like? To be diagnosed and be chosen for the program so suddenly?"

"One minute I was dying, and then I wasn't," I reply, as if it is a trifle. In truth, I've been thinking a lot about the beginning, as if pinpointing the genesis of my illness will hold the key to how everything went so wrong so quickly. It was spring, and it was windy. I was heading home from a class at the Art Institute as dust and dead leaves skidded along Michigan Avenue in a series of wild gusts. Hurrying, I think. Late for dinner with Sam. My large canvas portfolio was catching the wind and propelling me at odd angles as I struggled down Harrison, heading for our apartment. I ran across the street during a gap in the rush-hour traffic, the pressing itch accumulating in my chest, gaining in heaviness as I fished my keys out of my pocket. I coughed hard, breathless, doubling over. Trying to force the feeling out of my lungs. Trying to clear them of whatever had taken root there. It was the first time I wondered if it was not a lingering cold that was keeping me up at night, soaking me with sweat. It was the first time my body became a source of fear.

"I'm fine." I smile at him, the fake smile, my first new trick in this new body. Thinking of riding the L home after the diagnosis, the SUBlife brochure in my hands, trying to read the pages through the glassy swell of my tears. And later, crouched on my bathroom floor, making the profound mistake of hyperventilating while having lung cancer, when Sam came home and found me. "I'm dealing with it fine," I repeat, so Dr. Bernard will move on to someone else.

Dr. Bernard nods. "All right. And you?" He motions to Connie.

The bombshell fixes him with a slightly weary look. "What's there to say, doc? I was an actress with a hell of a promising career when I shot up with the wrong people. Spent the last five years living off my Social Security checks in a rat hole of an apartment in Uptown."

"You contracted an aggressive strain of HIV," Dr. Bernard says.

"Lucky, right? Though," she motions to the rest of us, "I guess I'm in good company when it comes to the luck department, aren't I? We're all either very lucky or very unlucky, hell if I know which."

"And how does it feel, now that you have a second chance at the career you thought you lost?"

Connie sits back in her chair, her legs stretched out in front of her, crossed at the ankle, her feet almost reaching Dr. Bernard's.

"Peachy," she replies.

Dr. Bernard adjusts his tie, pulling it away from the skin of his neck. "Linda. Could you tell us a little about your situation before the transfer?"

Linda is still wide-eyed and twitchy, but some of last week's terror seems to have left her. She swallows.

"I was in a car accident. Eight years ago."

"And what happened as a result of that accident?" Dr. Bernard prods.

"I couldn't move. I could blink, but that was all." She blinks now, as if to demonstrate.

"I read about a guy who had that same thing," David says, nodding, his face a phony attempt at gravity. "He wrote a book by blinking the letters of the alphabet. Or something like that."

"I guess I didn't make good use of my time then," Linda replies, looking at her feet. I can't tell if she's trying to be funny.

"Linda, last week you asked us a question that we couldn't answer, about your family, about whether they still love you. What made you ask that?" Dr. Bernard leans forward in his seat, his hands steepled in front of his mouth, his eyes intent on her.

"I don't know," Linda replies, simply, her voice devoid of emotion. "I guess I wouldn't love someone who left me like that."

Her words hit me in the stomach. Not because her situation is awful, though it is, terribly. But because in that moment I think of Sam. Like a reflex. I think of waking alone in that hospital room, of Lucy's explanations. As if part of me knows a secret that the rest of me is trying, desperately, to unlearn.

# David

I follow Hannah up to the roof after the support group disbands. It's curiosity more than anything. She sat there like a stone for the last twenty minutes of the session, unmoving, her eyes fixed in middle space. It was something in Linda's story, I think, that sunk her so far into her head that she only resurfaced when Dr. Bernard repeated her name, twice, before we finished.

Hannah has fascinated me ever since our little tête-à-tête near the coffee cart. Some part of me must have feared that I'd been lost in the transfer, too changed to return to my old life, until this girl turned all of her wrath in my direction. It's amazing, how familiar it is to be hated, almost like coming home.

I follow her up five flights of stairs, pausing at each landing to regain the strength in my lungs and my legs, listening as she does the same a flight or two above me. She must hear me panting below her, but she doesn't wait, and I wonder if the mood she's in has divorced her from any hint of the world outside her own mind. She reaches a door marked "Authorized Personnel Only" and walks through with such unflinching confidence I wonder if she's ever gotten in trouble for breaking a rule in her life.

Following her out onto the roof feels like summiting a mountain, all fresh air and endorphin-filled exhaustion. I'm sweaty and drained, and when I find her collapsed against a brick wall with her legs stretched in front of her, I drop like dead weight next to her. Street noise—the honking of horns, the squeaky breaks of city buses, and the rumble and jostle of traffic—wafts up around us, like music being played in a faraway room. It's sunny, but gusts of late-summer wind drive heavy, fast-moving clouds above us. Their shadows crawl their way across the concrete of the roof.

"I did Google you, actually," she says, as if continuing a conversation we've already been having.

"I knew it," I reply, feeling a small swell of triumph beneath my sternum.

"You were one of seventeen congressmen congratulated by a group called American Evangelicals for Life. For your opposition to, among other things, abortion and stem cell research."

"I've been congratulated by a lot of people for my opposition to those things," I reply.

"I wonder what American Evangelicals for Life would think of you taking part in a medical study involving human cloning." She kicks off her sandals, flexing her feet. They are the color of frozen milk, so white they are almost blue. "Think they'd be cool with it?"

"Stem cell research takes a life in the name of medicine. I've done no such thing."

"So you believe in God?" she asks. I venture a glance at her. She's looking at me with such earnestness that I wonder if she's fucking with me.

"Of course I believe in God. Don't you?"

She shrugs. "I did when I was a kid. I guess I sort of grew out of it."

I bristle a little at this, the way I do when faced with any sort of atheism, the people who believe they are superior and enlightened for believing in nothing. As if closing your eyes to the light is somehow the braver decision. "Believing in God isn't like believing in Santa."

"How does someone like you take part in this study? If there is a God, I think SUBlife is tantamount to laughing in his face. How do you believe in God and also choose to defy everything you've been taught to believe?"

"I'll tell you and anyone else the same thing. That God put a gun to my head and asked me what I was willing to do to save myself, to save this life that he gave me. And I answered that I would do anything. Because life is that precious to me."

"I guess I can understand that," she says, nodding. "But I'd bet you that congressman's salary of yours that the AEL won't."

"Maybe not," I reply. "Maybe I'll get lucky, and they'll never find out."

"And what if they do? Have you thought about what you'd do if you can't go back to who you were before?" she asks. Her arm is brushing against mine. I wait a moment to see if she'll move it, and when she doesn't I press a bit more toward her.

"I haven't thought about it much. There's a lot about me that my constituents haven't ever found out." I want to shock this girl, because I think maybe she's the type who is impressed by things that shock her. "You know, I used to steal cars as a kid."

"You're kidding."

"Nope," I reply, "there was this dealership in our town with a real shitty security system. We'd break in at night and get the keys, joyride around. I think to this day Mr. Beecham is wondering why the cars on his lot were always low on gas." My body is suddenly drunk on the recklessness of being seventeen, punching through the darkness of rural routes without streetlights, hollering into air that was empty for miles. The thrill is so sharp, even in memory, that gooseflesh erupts on my skin. "And you? What will you do if you can't go back?"

She doesn't say anything for a moment. Then she shifts, and I feel her arm pull away from mine. Her mouth tastes like heat when she kisses me, like the muggy, asphalt-baked air of summertime. It's an appalling taste, and wholly intoxicating, like so many things I've experienced, a muddling confusion of attraction and revulsion. Coupled with my lingering memories, it's overpowering. But she pulls away before I can give myself over to it. I move a hand to my mouth, wiping away the sheen of wetness there.

"I don't know," she says. "I don't know what I'd do. Reckless things, probably."

"I can't afford to be reckless anymore," I reply, trying to temper everything that is rioting inside me. There are a lot of thrills to be had down that rabbit hole. I've been so marooned in this new body, so diminished and altered, that to be recognized by this girl feels like a small bit of salvation. But I cannot be that boy again. I cannot be this man. "I'm married."

She nods, eyes downcast. But she doesn't apologize. "You know, you look married."

"What does that mean?" I ask, endlessly curious about how others perceive me, especially now. Especially her.

She shrugs, settling back against the wall. "Comfortable, I guess. Like you're interested in the world, but not too interested, because you've not supposed to be looking for anything anymore."

I'm not sure what to say to this. I'm not sure, not exactly, what it is I've found in Beth. A woman of great beauty, certainly. A political wife of the highest order. A competent, if not always exuberant mother to my son. I try and remember what it was I wanted on those nights, flying through the darkness, just careless enough to be free. I don't remember wanting any of those things. And the thought scares me a little, scares me in a way driving ninety on a marginally paved road in a stolen car never did.

Hannah motions to my hand. "No ring?"

"Too big." My fingers are tapered, almost feminine, when I'm used to seeing hands that belonged to a laborer, rough and calloused. Knuckles that had been cut and bruised in fistfights. Palms that never grew clammy, no matter how nervous I was. The broken thumb that gave a baseball the perfect bit of spin when I threw it. Hands that had shaken those of presidents and union leaders and billionaires, and demonstrated that I was just as formidable as any one of them. These hands are not mine. They are not the sum of my experiences. These hands belong to someone much weaker. "What about you?" I ask. "Aren't you supposed to be engaged?"

"Sort of," she says, playing with the hem of her scrub shirt. "We agreed that we'd get married after the transfer. If everything went the way it was supposed to."

"So why are you up here being reckless with me?"

"Because you followed me up here at the wrong moment. Because nothing feels the way it's supposed to," she says, turning toward me, fixing me with those huge eyes of hers. "Can't you tell? Nothing tastes the way I remember, everything is so bright it hurts, everything feels so . . ." She stops, and I understand it now, why the doctors brought the four of us together. It's because I understand what she means, exactly what she means, and no one else in the world will. "How can I be the same person," she asks, "when nothing feels the same?"

"Maybe we're not the same people. Maybe we're better than we were," I reply, though I know it's not the answer she wants.

"I guess we'll see," she says and rises, steadying herself on the brick wall, stepping over my outstretched legs to get to the door. I have to tamp down the sudden impulse to follow her, again, to make her stop, to keep her here. I think of Beth, flawless Beth, who never really tastes like anything I can discern, who is so familiar to me that the smell of her hair is as inconsequential as my own. Hannah opens the door and then pauses, turning back to face me.

"We're not really off to a great start, are we?"

# Linda

The world outside of my hospital window feels so huge I expect the air to be too thin to breathe. One morning last week a flock of birds blew around the sky like a swarm of bees. I watched for an hour as they gusted around, breaking and reforming like sea foam riding a wave. I sat there wondering at how full the world was, how huge, to include flocks of birds that do nothing but spend an afternoon riding the air. It reminded me of looking out my window at home, with Cora dozing in the chair next to me.

Connie visits one afternoon, a few days after our support group meeting. It's just as jarring this time as it was the first time, to see Mary Jane Livingston step out of *Stratford Pines* and into my hospital room. It's as if a wall between my two worlds has been breached, and one is leaking into the other. I want to ask her everything, ask what her secrets are, she who has seen so much more of life than I have. But it's difficult to say anything, because what is the right thing to ask a person like her? I'm afraid of saying something silly, of scaring her away like a skittish bird landing on my windowsill. So I stay quiet because this is the best way to deal with people, from what I can tell.

"I hope you don't mind me showing up again," Connie says, taking a few steps in. She's wearing scrubs too now, and I wonder what the trick to that is. I asked Tom to get me some earlier in the week, and he told me that only doctors and nurses wore them. I didn't want to tell him that it wasn't true, that I knew for a fact he was wrong. But now I feel dowdy and a bit infantile in my hospital gown and bathrobe. She crosses the room and takes a seat in the chair next to my bed, Tom's chair. But he's not coming by until after work. And Connie is here now, looking as if she's been gilded by sunlight against the gray sterility of the room.

"*Stratford Pines* starts in five minutes," Connie continues. "I didn't want to miss it. I'm so behind already. Do you mind?"

I shake my head. This is not the time to say anything, because what do you say if Paul McCartney stops by with a copy of *Sgt. Pepper's* and wants to play it for you? Nothing, that's right. You'd shut up and listen.

We watch the show together, like Cora and I used to do, with me lying in bed and her sitting on the chair next to me, her feet propped up on the edge of the mattress. It feels like sitting in a pool of sunlight, being next to her. She asks questions as we watch, about why Star and John are together, and why Kyle is suddenly named Tony, and why Krystal is living with her most hated rival, Sarah. And I tell her, as best I can, about evil twins and stolen babies and old enemies falling in love with each other. Things that I have lived, and get to live again now, in the telling.

Connie's reactions to each of my revelations thrill me like gusts of soft heat pouring through my limbs, as if the show were something I myself created. As if it is my life that I'm recounting. How I have lived, I think. How many lives I have lived, from my hospital bed, and how wondrous it has been.

"What was it like?" I ask. "Being on the show, was it amazing?"

"It was a lot of long hours," Connie says, and then she must see the slight fall in my expression, because she quickly adds, "But I made some great friends there. Good people. It was kind of like a halfway house for actors, you know?"

I nod, though I have no idea what she means. On screen, Chrissy throws a drink in Damien's face. I grin, because boy does he deserve it, but Connie doesn't seem to notice.

"There was always someone new coming on, new characters, or new actors taking over old parts," she continues. "And there was always someone leaving, because they wanted to get into prime time or they got a part in a movie or something. We used to take bets on the new blood, who would make it, who wouldn't. You could tell the people who were meant to be lifers. I think they were the happiest ones of any of us." She looks far away, and it's lovely just to watch her, the perfect downward curve of her nose in profile, the little shells of her ears. She looks like she's been carved from ivory. Even her nail beds are slender and delicate in her long fingers. It seems almost unfair, that someone should possess so much beauty.

"Why did you leave?" I ask.

"To make it big," Connie says, the thin arches of her eyebrows bobbing as she says it, a playfulness in her tone. "All the money was on me. And when I got the lead in a movie, everyone was prepared to pony up. It was just a little indie flick, but it premiered at Sundance that year. And let me tell you, that was a trip and a half." She glances back at the screen. "For a while after I got sick, I wondered if I would have been happier as a lifer on the *Pines*. I certainly wouldn't have ended up with a super-strain of HIV at twenty-eight."

"If you could go back . . ." It's the beginning of a question I can't finish. It's a game I've played with myself too many times. I know all of my own answers. Don't get on the highway; don't change lanes to get out from behind the truck. In fact, don't even get into the car. Lose your keys. Don't pick up the call when your cell phone rings. But I know the trap in that particular game. If you wish for too long, if you go back far enough, you could wish your whole life away, every choice you made to get you to this point.

But Connie looks like she's considering the question. I wonder if she's ever thought about it before, or if she's one of those people who can exist only in the present, in the reality of things, and not the endless possibilities and alternate worlds that seem to exist for me.

"No, I don't think I could have stayed," she says, finally. "I never got past the idea that I was meant for more than that. And once you think something like that, you can never un-think it, can you?"

"I guess not," I reply. But as I watch Stefan and Jamie slow dance across the screen in a pool of fake moonlight, I realize I will watch their whole love story spark and bloom and die, and even if it takes years for that to happen, I will see it. And it will be beautiful and terrible and poignant and bitter, and so much more of everything than it ever is in real life. How could anyone want more than the possibility of that?

# Hannah

It is certainly strange, to live the first few weeks in my new body. Perhaps the strangest part is how inconsequential the change feels sometimes. Not dying, no longer being in pain, these differences are so startling and so complete that it's easy to forget that I was ever sick to begin with. There is no scarring, no residual damage, no daily reminder of the months I spent being mutilated by tubes and wires and needles. I have a full, thick head of hair. And I'm no longer as frail as I was in the beginning; slender stretches of muscle begin to form under the skin of my arms and legs. I look like I'm closer to running a marathon than dying of anything.

There are other things, too. Little things. My hearing is pin sharp, instead of muted by my years of rock concerts and riding on Jake Mariano's motorcycle as a teenager and the clattering din of taking the Red Line. The little aches and pains I used to carry with me—waking up with a stiff neck, cracking the ankle I sprained playing soccer as a kid, the enduring tightness in my hips and the backs of my thighs from painting for hours on end—are gone. They are removed so thoroughly that I can't remember exactly what they felt like. Any and all excess fat has been spirited from under my skin, leaving a thin, supple sort of body it its wake. The dimpling in my thighs and the small crevices of stretch marks in my sides, the handful of scars I'd amassed in my twenty-seven years, all have been replaced by tight, flat skin. It's a body so perfect it is difficult to inhabit sometimes, because it's difficult to imagine it's really mine.

I focus on these things, the miraculous little details, the perks, to keep from thinking about why I kissed David Jenkins on the rooftop. I tell myself it was idiotic to let him follow me, particularly when I was feeling lost and wistful and unusually vulnerable. I think of the kiss, imagining myself as separate from my body, as if it had moved of its own accord because it needed so badly to be touched. It certainly doesn't help that Sam is keeping his distance, as if I'm some foreign thing, a wax figure come to life, or the Stepford version of my old self. I try to ignore it, to focus on other things, my physical therapy, learning how to write again, practicing typing out text messages to Penny on my phone.

I told Penny about the kiss when she came to visit me on Friday afternoon, bracing myself for the hardness of her expression even as I let the words spill out between us. She chewed on the inside of her cheek, the way she does when she's working on a painting that she can't get quite right.

"Who is this guy?" she asked.

"Just a guy from my group. No one, really." I pause, trying to think of something that will mitigate the awfulness of it. "He's kind of a dirtbag, actually." Nothing changes in her face in response to this, and I can't tell if I've made things better or worse by saying it. Finally she releases her mouth back to its rightful shape and turns the soft pink of her palms to the sky.

"I don't know, Han. I'm not going to be the one to tell you how you should or shouldn't process all of this."

It made me feel worse, I think, that she didn't scold me, or reassure me. It made me feel even more adrift.

By the next Thursday I know any chance I've had of driving David Jenkins from my mind has been futile. Because there he is, ten minutes late, taking the seat across from me in our support group.

"Does anyone feel like they got the wrong body?" he asks, cradling a cup of hot cocoa between his hands. It seemed childish and silly to me, when we showed up to last week's meeting, to find packets of Swiss Miss and a carafe of boiling water on the conference room table. But now we all drink it, tearing open the paper packets with our teeth and stirring lumpy chocolate powder into the piping hot water. It's a good excuse to ignore one another for those first few awkward minutes, until someone gets up the nerve to speak.

"I mean, maybe not the wrong one, obviously, but, maybe the knockoff version?" David continues. Linda nods a little, but says nothing. Connie seems to be paying more attention to a chip in her nail polish than to what David is saying. Dr. Bernard scribbles on his notepad before looking up.

"You think that this body is somehow inferior to the one that you had before?" Dr. Bernard asks.

"What I mean, doc, is that I can't prove this is my body," David says. We've all adopted Connie's habit of calling Dr. Bernard "doc" because it seems to annoy him quite a bit. It feels kind of good, to have someone to gang up on. Six weeks, I think. Six weeks was all it took to go from strangers to a merry little band of rebellious clones. "Everything I could point to," David continues, "everything that I could identify as mine is gone. That's a lot of history to lose."

I brush my hand over my forehead and it's perfectly smooth, though I persist in trying to find the little indent that used to be there. It was a scar from when I went head-first into a rocking chair as a toddler. I was too little to remember it, but my mother always seemed to enjoy recounting that particularly harrowing bit of childhood lore. Now the last bit of evidence is gone. The memory belongs only to my mother. If she forgets it, it will be like that unfortunate afternoon never even happened at all. So I know what David means about losing history.

"You know, even our fingerprints are different now," I say, examining the pads of my fingers, as if I can tell that the patterns etched into my skin are altered. It occurs to me, again, how little I knew of the body I left. "They're not genetic, fingerprints. They're developed in utero, environmental, so there's no way they could be the same."

"I guess if you ever wanted to rob a bank, the time is now," Connie quips.

"I can't stop thinking of what they've done with our other bodies," Linda says. "What does it mean to donate it to science? Is it just sitting in a refrigerated drawer somewhere? Or, did they cut it to pieces like those fetal pigs we had to dissect in high school? Did they burn it? I know I shouldn't be thinking about it, but it still feels like me. It's still enough of me that I care what happens to it."

We all look at her, flabbergasted, because this is the most any of us has ever heard Linda say. She's twisting a piece of Kleenex between her fingers as she speaks. I wonder why Linda cares what they did with it, after eight years of being trapped within that defective vegetable of a body. I would expect her to be happy to be rid of it. But now that she's said something, I feel it too, a sense of disconnection from my old self, like an amputee that still feels itching in a phantom limb. Though that body is pocked with tumors and damaged beyond repair, it's still so kindred to me that leaving it to the whims of my doctors feels like abandonment. I try not to think of it, watching Linda twist her tissue. I'm sure a person could go crazy, thinking about it for too long.

Dr. Bernard is, as always, scribbling away in his notepad. Connie raises an eyebrow at me and I shrug. The questions are pointless. It's been clear from the beginning that this man doesn't have any answers for us. It's how the pioneers must have felt, the explorers, riding their horses through tall, wind-swept grasses. That feeling of danger, lingering around the edges, making everything bright and clear and evident. How significant they were, by simply crossing that bit of earth. And I realize, perhaps for the first time, how alone we are, the four of us.

# November

# Hannah

Our apartment feels cold when I step inside, an empty cold, as if no one has been moving around enough to stir heat into the air. We share a two-bedroom condo in Printer's Row that my parents bought for me when I finished college, where Penny and I used to live until she moved in with Connor. My boot heels click on the wood floors as Sam opens the living room curtains, letting the afternoon light in. The space feels foreign now, despite the five years I've lived here, as if someone has replaced all of my belongings with props that look the same but are actually false, subtly inauthentic.

Everything is where I left it. There are the plush gray sofas, the bright glass of the coffee table, the floor-to-ceiling bookshelves Sam's parents had installed for us as a Christmas gift last year. There is the woven rug, the gleaming wood of the dining table we custom ordered from an artisan I met in school, the granite countertops and stainless-steel appliances we bought to update the kitchen after Sam moved in. It looks like something out of a catalog, the trendy kind that employs just enough detail—a stack of books, a wok on the stove, something scribbled on a notepad hanging from the fridge—to make it look as if people really live there.

The first time I brought Sam to this apartment, I was afraid it would be the end of us. We were drunk, stumbling the handful of icy blocks home after seeing a Swell Season concert at the Auditorium Theater, and I pulled him inside without thinking what it meant, to show him where I lived. I'd been to his studio a handful of times and always thought its sleek bareness had more to do with disinterest on his part than any aesthetic preference. But the farther he ventured into my apartment, with its walls painted a deep ocean-spray of turquoise, crowded with unframed canvases and well-worn posters, the more aware I became of how garish it seemed. I watched him take it in, the purple futon and huge wicker armchair, with its overstuffed blue cushions. Penny's funky blown-glass pillar lamp standing in the corner. The card table against the wall of the dining area, covered with a tablecloth I'd fashioned from a patchwork of silk scarves, with about a dozen low-burned tapers in an assortment of candlesticks on its surface. The kitchen, worn and outdated and adorned with my battered copper pots and Penny's red ceramic Buddha cookie jar and lines of empty liquor bottles. A mural-size black and white print of an ocean-scape, wheat-pasted to one of the walls. He appraised all of it in a glance, smiled a little, whispered, "You have interesting taste," in my ear and then, "Where is your bedroom?"

"Penny's the one with the interesting taste," I told him later, lying in bed, watching the streetlight fracture through the sun catcher hanging from my window. Desperate not to seem childish, in my apartment filled with cheap, gaudy trappings. Desperate, already, to be a chameleon, to be the sort of girl who could fit seamlessly into his life. Because already I was in love with him.

"I like it," he said, and it was the first time I realized I could tell when he was lying. He was no good at it. It was one of the things I loved most about him, that he was so honest he couldn't even lie well.

When Sam moved in, I participated in each decision that undid that former home and created this one in its place. I helped Sam strip the floors, repaint the walls, spent endless weekends at Home Depot picking out track lighting and fabric swatches and high-tech dishwashers. I did not mind it then, being the one to change. Sam's inherent goodness, his love of justice, his idealism, made me believe that loving him could make me all of those things, too. I realized that if one of us had to change so we could be together, it should be me.

None of it feels like it belongs to me now. I feel like an intruder here, standing in the middle of the living room with my coat on, afraid to dispel any of the room's silent perfection with my presence. It's as if the apartment has shifted a few degrees from where it was, skewing my sense of direction.

"Want me to make you something?" Sam asks, turning on the baseboard heaters to dispel the cold. He is constantly in motion because, after all, it would be silly for us both to stand, useless, in the middle of the room. It seems we don't know how to live around each other anymore, after my months in the hospital. We lost the knack for it that quickly. "I haven't really had the chance to get to the store these past couple of weeks, but I could make you some oatmeal."

"Sure." Oatmeal is one of the few foods I've been able to stand lately. Flavors are so strong they've become intolerable, and I've been subsisting on French fries and hospital Jell-O, applesauce and Honey Nut Cheerios. Peanut butter and jelly on white bread. Packets of cocoa. Children's food. I haven't been able to stomach meat either, since the transfer. From the moment the nurse put a tray of grayish Salisbury steak in front of me, I knew I wouldn't be able to get it down. It had some new association with death for me, one I never considered before the transfer, and I still haven't worked it all out yet. There is simply too much to figure out so soon.

The apartment looks recently cleaned, as if Sam removed all evidence of his weeks of living alone here while I was in the hospital. I can imagine what it must have looked like before, with discarded dirty socks on the living room floor and dark flecks of shaved whiskers in the bathroom sink. I know his bad habits, the lazy little traits that we both keep in check for each other. I don't know what it would be like to live alone for months in this place. I've never lived alone, and that fact feels more significant now than it ever has.

I sit on the kitchen counter and watch as Sam cooks. It's one of my favorite pastimes, watching Sam in the kitchen. He moves with a deliberate expertise balanced with a casual, practiced ease. He eyeballs the amount of milk he pours into the pot, chopping dried cherries as he waits for it to boil, then adds the oatmeal and stirs in a few shakes of cinnamon. It smells delicious. I sip weak tea that's full of sugar and begin to feel warm again. Perhaps all we need is to keep busy, to not let the silence drag on for too long.

"I miss my tattoos," I say, rubbing my wrist against the leg of my pants, as if I can unearth the design still hidden underneath my blank skin.

"Yeah, me too," he says, holding up our nutmeg grinder. I shake my head, and he returns it to the cabinet.

"Liar," I say. "What was it that you said when we first started dating? That I should consider what I'll look like when I'm seventy?"

"I liked your tattoos," Sam said, handing me a steaming bowl of oatmeal and a cup of brown sugar. I heap in a few heavy-handed spoonfuls.

He picks up my wrist and presses the blank skin of it to his mouth. There's potential in this moment, the first time we've touched outside the hospital, in an apartment with a locked door and no chance of anyone banging in to draw my blood or clear my tray of food or test my memory. All of my nerve endings seem to rush to the surface of my skin, crackling with the electric potential to feel. An image of David comes forward, unbidden, the way he squinted against the sun before I kissed him on the roof. And then Sam is stepping back, looking as if he's shaking off an ill-conceived impulse. He clears his throat and scratches at the nape of his neck, where his hair is just a bit too long.

"Do you think you'll have them redone?" he asks, picking up the pot and rinsing it out in the sink. Keeping busy so he won't have to look directly at me.

"What?"

"Your tattoos."

"No," I say, my voice too sharp, trying to turn my attention back to my breakfast, trying to ignore my own ill-conceived impulse, to throw my bowl and its steaming contents in his direction. All he has for me is kindness and pity, and I want neither. The brown sugar melts into my oatmeal, and I eat a few hot mouthfuls to distract myself before I continue.

"It wouldn't be authentic, if I just got them all over again. I wouldn't be getting them for the same reasons. They wouldn't mean what they used to."

"Right," Sam says, as if he understands. He acts as if he understands all of it, the bits of me that I've never quite been able to smooth out, the pieces that I never quite managed to fit into this life of ours. But the truth is, he never has.

Sam and I met for the second time during my fourth year at the School of the Art Institute. It was at a gallery in River North, during a posh up-and-coming event where my friend Trevor was showing one of his paintings. I had always liked Trevor's work. He had a modern Egon Schiele thing going on, and I'd sat for him a couple of times when he wasn't happy with his other models. Trevor said he always preferred to paint other artists anyway; he had a theory that painting another artist watching him created a double-mirror effect, opening a corridor of space that hadn't existed in his work before. Of course, he would have had to pay one of the gamine young women who posted fliers on the SAIC bulletin board, whereas for a while I was willing to take my clothes off for him for free.

There must have been something to his theory, though, because it was one of his paintings of me that had created enough of a stir to get him into the show. I dragged Penny with me that night, unwilling to venture into a gathering of North Shore art collectors by myself. We tottered in on stiletto heels, looking like a pair of lost hippies in thrift-store cocktail dresses. The painting, of course, was on its own wall, seven feet tall and vibrant with color, me in purple knee socks and nothing else, lying on rumpled sheets and walking my feet up Trevor's bedroom wall. My eyes peered right at the observer. Looking at it made me a bit dizzy, seeing myself the way he'd seen me in his head, all swirls of color and those huge, demanding eyes. It made me wonder if all my mirrors had been lying to me my whole life, though I couldn't exactly decipher the nature of the lie. I couldn't tell if I was more beautiful or less, the way he'd painted me.

Penny, of course, was unimpressed. "In the future, please make sure the men who see you naked know how to use a paintbrush," she said.

"All of them?"

"All of them. You want a drink?"

I glanced back up at myself. "I think I need one."

As Penny floated off, I tried to put space between my portrait and me. I wandered toward a collection of photographs on the opposite wall, unimpressive shots of abandoned bicycle frames locked to various racks around the city. Trevor was across the room, holding court among a small clot of older women wearing perfectly tailored silk dresses and intricate jewelry, and when I caught his eye he winked at me. As I tipped my imaginary hat to him, I felt someone sidle up next to me.

"It's you in that painting over there, isn't it?"

"Not exactly," I replied, glancing over and swallowing my next breath when I realized that the man next to me was Sam. His boyish features were the same as ever, the light shadow of stubble on his chin the only evidence of his age.

"You have the same tattoo," he said, motioning to the lacy lines of ivy swirling their way from my left shoulder blade down to my elbow. Those same lines crawled their way over my bare shoulder on the canvas.

"You're very observant," I said, searching his face for any signs of recognition. I'd dyed my hair a faint lavender color in college and invested huge amounts of money getting it chemically straightened from its usual tight ringlets. He'd also never seen me in makeup, particularly not the kind of heavy eyeliner I was sporting that night. It was exciting, like wearing a mask, to stand in front of Sam as a stranger. It made me feel powerful.

"So it is you," he said.

"Not really. It's only what Trevor sees."

"Seems like Trevor sees an awful lot."

I laughed, peering at him from under my bangs. There were differences, when I looked at him long enough. His brown hair was shorter than it had been in high school. His jaw was a bit wider, his mouth broader. All of his lankiness seemed to have hardened, become more defined. Maybe he wasn't the best-looking guy in the place, but he was mine, a little, by virtue of having been my sister's once. That familiarity alone drew me to him.

Penny reappeared then with a couple of vodka tonics. "Who's your friend?" she asked, handing me the cold, sweating glass. I took a sip, relishing the sweet tang of it, preparing to enjoy my new game.

"Penny, this is Sam Foster," I said, watching the rush of confusion overtake his expression. To his credit, he recovered quickly.

"I'm sorry, have we met before?" he asked. I could almost see him pawing through his mental Rolodex, hoping to find my face.

"Ages ago. If I remember correctly, you gave me a bootleg of the Smashing Pumpkins farewell show at the Metro for my twelfth birthday. Which was nice, considering my sister got me a gift card to The Gap."

"Holy shit," he said, taking a step back, as if seeing more of me would draw everything into focus. "You're Lucy Reed's little sister. Hannah. Jesus, I can't even remember the last time I saw you."

This struck me as odd, because I could remember exactly when I last saw him. It was at his father's funeral, only days before he ended his relationship with Lucy. But I smiled anyway, brushing off the memory. "Probably back before I got my braces off," I replied as Penny watched with curious amusement. It was a break in my pattern. I didn't usually go for the jacket-and-tie types.

"How is Lucy?" Sam asked.

"Married," Penny replied, before I could. "To a banker, no less. They're picking out their white picket fence next week."

Sam's face showed no discernable signs of disappointment, only faint, polite interest. It was reassuring, to imagine how little Sam cared about Lucy and her banker husband in my presence.

"Well, tell her I say hello."

"So what do you think of the show, Sam?" Penny asked.

"Can you keep a secret?" Sam asked. Penny motioned to him to indicate that he should proceed. "I don't know much about art."

"So what are you doing here on a Saturday night?"

"I'm writing up the show for the *Trib*."

"You're a reporter?" I asked, and he nodded.

"And they're sending you here, even though you don't know anything about art," Penny said, and didn't wait for an answer, waving her hands in front of her, as if she could fend off any additional conversation. "Christ, I don't even want to know. You two have fun, I'm going to go rescue Trevor and pretend there's still a thing called culture in this country."

"Don't let her bother you," I said to Sam once Penny was out of earshot.

"She's got a point. I'm new at the paper, paying my dues in Arts and Leisure for the moment, trying to work my way up."

It's the sort of thing that would one day bother me, the idea that my life's pursuit was his purgatory, his stepping stone into more practical and important matters. That he would arrive at the gallery, fully prepared to write about the work, and yet harbor no desire to learn anything about it that wouldn't fit into a page of text. But those concerns would come later. That night I would have overlooked anything to keep him talking.

"What do you want to write about?" I asked.

"Politics," he replied. "Political corruption, really. How money and patronage influence the system."

"So you're a crusader then. Trying to make the greedy and corrupt pay for their misdeeds?"

"Maybe just trying to shine a little light into a system that's the worst at serving the people who need it most," he replied.

"An idealist."

He shrugged, completely self-possessed. "Maybe."

"Well, you're certainly a better person than I am," I said, feeling myself drawing closer to him by degrees, even if my body wasn't moving. "I would want to make them pay."

"Hannah Reed," he said, as if testing out how my name felt in his mouth. "You're not at all what I remember."

"You're a lot like what I remember," I replied. "Well, except your hair is shorter." I brushed my fingertips over the close-cropped hair at his temple, watching him twitch a bit at the contact. "It was always so curly."

"And you were such a shy little kid," he said, glancing back at my painting, at the burnt umber and gold Trevor used for my eyes, the peachy swirls of skin, the dark russet of my nipples.

"It's easier than you think. Sitting for a painting," I said. "Once you've painted a portrait yourself, you realize it's just about what's in the artist's head. It's not really about the subject at all. It could have been anyone up there."

"But doesn't it feel a little weird? With that on the wall in front of a crowd of people?"

"Maybe," I said. "But no one really sees me when they look at it. Here." I took his arm and pulled him in front of it. "What did you think when you first saw it?"

"I'm not sure if I want to tell you," Sam replied, and his expression made me laugh.

"I'm not thirteen anymore. I can legally drink and everything. Please, humor me."

"I guess I thought she looks lonely," Sam said. "I wondered what kind of idiot would leave a girl like that alone in his bed."

I had to look away from him for a moment then, until the sear of heat across my cheeks subsided. "See, it's not me. I'm not lonely."

"No?"

"Well, you're here, aren't you?" I said, and I wanted to be thirteen again, so the younger version of me would know that Sam Foster would one day look at me the way he used to look at Lucy. To reassure her that her loneliness wouldn't last forever.

Sam saw all of my tattoos that night. The dark lines of poetry on my ribs, the oleander blooms sliding down my thigh. The roman numerals on the insides of my wrists. The marks I had amassed in the years since I realized that it was easier to love my body as a collection of stories than as something sacred and holy, the body my mother had given me. It was easier to make myself into something I recognized, something I could love.

He asked about them, of course, about what their stories were. Men always asked. But he was easy to distract in the inky darkness of his bedroom. It took him three years, finally, to get all the answers. And then in the fourth year I was wiped clean, and there was no point to the questions anymore.

# David

I've never liked Chicago much. It's a city just big enough for its residents to have an overinflated sense of their own importance, while still harboring a deep inferiority complex because they don't live in New York or L.A. That, and the Democrats have such a stranglehold on the political system that there hasn't been a clean election here in the past hundred years. It's the perfect example of liberal hypocrisy; the bleeding hearts and the unions and the welfare-dependent masses have had their way for so long that they've created a bankrupt clot of buildings surrounded by war zones on two sides, and one side by water. It's a microcosm of corruption and institutional failures. Everything from its school system to its police force to its public transit system is either irreparably broken or chronically useless. And everyone who lives here thinks the deep-dish pizza makes up for it.

My home is a house in upstate Wisconsin, in my district, where the people also might have a chip on their collective shoulder, but they work damn hard to make up for it. Unfortunately, somewhere in the stack of paperwork I signed before the transfer there was an edict requiring me to remain within an hour of Northwestern Memorial for the next few months, so for the time being Beth and I have rented a condo on Lake Shore Drive.

I'm sprung from the hospital on a Friday afternoon, and that's where we go. Beth drives, because I technically don't have a driver's license yet. It's something you don't really think about when you get a new body, that you've never passed a driver's test and not even the photo on your license is accurate anymore. I don't know if I'm even capable of driving a car. After all, I just learned to walk again.

Beth waves to the parking attendant as she pulls our gray Audi into our parking space. She's been living here alone for the past few months while I've been in the hospital. This is her turf. It's an off-putting sensation, like I'm an intruder in my own house. But considering how much time I'd spend in D.C. every year, Beth is well accustomed to living alone by now. It was one of the reasons she stopped wearing her wedding ring. One of the reasons there were divorce papers waiting on my desk only a week before my diagnosis.

Beth leads me into the building and unlocks our door with a silver key, just one of many on her key ring. I can't remember where my keys are. It turns out getting released from the hospital isn't much like getting out of prison in the movies; they don't hand you a plastic bag full of the clothing and possessions you had on when you went in. No, I only signed some paperwork in my shaky scrawl and was wheeled out to the curb like a helpless invalid. Hospital policy, of course.

The apartment we rented is modern and fully furnished, all chrome and glass and well-lacquered wood. It makes me homesick for the high vaulted ceilings of our remodeled farmhouse in Wisconsin, or even the antique faux-European accents of my apartment in D.C. This is yuppie artifice, as inauthentic and gaudy as a stretch limo. But Beth doesn't seem to mind. She cares less about the soul of a place than I do; all she cares about is the price.

The apartment is so far-flung from the house I grew up in, it's almost comical. Simply the fact that it's two stories already makes it a step up. My family lived in a squat little ranch house on sixteen acres of farmland just outside of Athens, Wisconsin. My early life was flat and gray, speckled with mud, sweat stained. Everything was like that, the house, the land, my family. Everything smelled like hay and manure and empty air. The idea of living in an apartment like this was laughable; of being a congressman, unthinkable.

I was never the smartest guy in my high school. Or, if I was, I worked too hard on the farm to ever spend much time studying, so my grades never reflected it. But I knew how to talk to people. I learned it early, after my mother died and my father took off, leaving my grandmother to take care of me and the farm by herself. I was suddenly the one to haggle with our equipment suppliers and barter with our grain distributors and fight with the mortgage lenders. I learned fast, how to get what I wanted. It was a survival skill back then, as important as knowing how to build a fire or find water in a desert. I loved my grandmother, probably more than anyone else in the world, but had it been up to her alone, we would have lost the farm in that first year. It was my responsibility to step in, to keep everything running as it had. And no matter what I did, it wasn't ever enough.

In the end, we had to get help from the federal government to keep from losing everything. That was the worst part of those years, the food stamps, the subsidies, the government relief for small farmers. I hated those checks, hated my free lunches at school. Those were indignities my grandmother and I should not have had to bear, not in America. It should have been enough that we worked, and worked hard.

Of course, the Wisconsin where I live with Beth and David Jr. is very different from the Wisconsin where I grew up. Beth was New York City through-and-through when we met, when I was a freshman congressman and she was a budding reporter for one of those trendy Internet news sites. I had to all but crowbar Beth out of the Big Apple when we married, and she's never been quite at peace with Wisconsin, even though we live in a veritable estate, even though she plays tennis at our country club every weekend, even though David Jr. is attending the best private school in the whole damn state.

"How's David Jr.?" I ask.

"Well, he got into an argument with one of the other boys at school the other day," Beth says, as she pulls a bottle of Perrier out of the fridge with perfectly manicured hands. "I guess he saw some cartoon of you on the Internet or something."

"An argument or a fight?"

"His teacher called it an argument. She says he's been volatile lately, and it was only a matter of time. But don't worry, I'll handle it."

"No," I say, leaning on the counter to give my legs a break. "Tell him I'll Skype him this weekend and we'll talk about it. I don't want him getting pushed around."

"Sweetie, I've got it," she says, her perfect rows of teeth showing under red lips. "It's kid stuff. Don't bother with it."

Time was, I would've been more than happy to let Beth deal with our son's problems. After all, how could they compare with what I had to deal with at his age? I had work on the farm and a part-time job and a grandmother who would forget to eat if I let her stare out the window for too long. It's been a concern of mine for a while that my son has it too easy, the child of a congressman with his private school and our big house and the best of everything. How on earth will he be prepared for the world with that kind of an upbringing? It's been easy to blame Beth for coddling him, for giving him the sort of posh lifestyle she grew up in. But now I think it's my own failing, not being around enough to insure he's got his feet on the ground. It's just one of the things I intend to address now, with my second chance.

"No," I say to Beth. "No, I'll handle it. I'll make it a priority."

"All right," she says, her mouth quirking up at the corners, as if she is afraid to smile too wide just yet, when my reform is still so new. I'm beginning to feel like everything is a test, to show her proof that I am truly changed, that she made the right decision in tearing up the divorce papers and taking care of me when I got sick. She rounds the counter to me, smoothing out the shirt I'm wearing, her hands brushing down my chest. "I'm happy you're home, you know," she says, sniffing a bit, batting at the corner of her eye with her fingertips.

This is such an uncharacteristic turn from my wife, such a strange show of emotion for a woman who is so deft and elegant and remote, that I'm caught off guard. Even more so when she takes my face in her hands and kisses me, full-on, in a way I remember from when we were first together. It takes me a moment to get the hang of it, this suddenly fervent kissing thing, because I would have been out of practice kissing Beth even if I wasn't in an entirely new body. Just when I'm really finding my footing, she pops the button on my jeans with her fingers, and my fortress of concentration collapses in on itself as if it were made of toothpicks. She slips her hand into my boxers and it feels soft and cool and my hips lurch forward of their own accord.

The disaster begins slowly, as disasters usually do. I begin to think of Hannah. Hannah, on the roof, pressing her mouth to mine. And I have to stop it, to stop all of it, because I can't allow myself to think of some girl while my wife has her hand down my pants. I try and think of Beth, perfect Beth, with her bubblegum pink mouth and perfect breasts and blonde hair. But it is like a switch has been flipped inside of me, everything shutting down from the inside out. I grab her wrist.

"What's wrong?" she asks into my throat.

"I can't right now, baby," I say, extracting her hand.

"Can't? Oh . . ." She drops a step back. "Is it something about . . . your SUB?" She says it like it's some sort of fungus. Not the thing that's saved my life.

"I have work to do, Beth," I snap. "I can't just drop everything in the middle of the day."

"Oh. Of course," she says, running a finger below her bottom lip, fixing the line of lipstick there. Perfect, my wife. "I just thought . . . Never mind."

I let out a breath, wishing I had something to offer her. "Everything is still so new," I say, because it's all I can muster. She nods, though I can tell her impassive veneer is back in place, impenetrable. It doesn't matter what I say now. "I'm gonna call the office. Are you making dinner or are we ordering in?"

"I was going to make us a couple of steaks for your first night of freedom," she says. The idea of red meat conjures images of my other body, lying in a refrigerated drawer somewhere. I start to feel sick.

"Not steak," I say. "Something else. Pasta, maybe?"

She nods, looking at me like she's sprung me from a psych ward instead of the hospital. I feel that way, a little. Shifty, like something disastrous is about to happen. I have to prove to Beth, somehow, that I've turned a corner. I have to forget what happened on that rooftop.

"All right. Whatever you want," she replies, as if nothing in the world has ever mattered less to her. I want to linger, want to try to explain how everything feels now, how everything in my mind seems to be wired wrong. But Beth doesn't want explanations. She wants her husband back, and there's nothing I can do to convince her that things will go back to normal. That things will be better than normal. I go in the bedroom to call Jackson. He picks up on the first ring and begins talking without any introduction.

"I want you to do a phone interview with the *New York Times*," he says. "Prove to your constituents that you've still got your wits about you. They're skewering you over the whole rehab story."

"Fine, what else?" I walk the perimeter of the room as I talk, opening drawers and flipping lamps on and off. My hotel room procedure, checking everything out. But this isn't a hotel, this is home for the better part of the next year. I slide open the closet. It's mostly full of casual clothes. A dozen polos and my favorite Yale sweatshirts. Jeans and track pants and basketball shorts. There are a couple of suits hanging toward the back, and I pull out one of the jackets, holding the hanger up to my shoulders and looking at myself in the mirror.

"Burt Leeland wants to get on a call sometime next week," Jackson says, as I study my reflection. The jacket dwarfs me. I toss it onto the bed as I head through the master suite to the hallway. The gym is two doors down, with its mirrored wall and its black and white exercise machines. I run my palm over the rows of hand weights sitting on their rack against one wall.

"Think it's possible he's calling in that favor already?" I ask, lifting a twenty-pound barbell off the rack and pumping my bicep experimentally against the resistance. It feels like it weighs about triple what it should. I set it down with a clang of metal on metal.

"I think it's doubtful that he's calling to wish you a speedy recovery," Jackson replies, and I know he's right. Burt is the CEO of S&J Holdings, a conglomerate that deals in everything from airplane parts to media outlets to pharmaceuticals. And he was the first call after my diagnosis because he's the only man I know with enough pull to break a double blind in an FDA trial. Or rig a lottery, in my case.

"Tell him I can speak to him at his earliest convenience," I say, sitting down on one of the leg machines and pumping out a few reps on a sickeningly light weight. My muscles sear inside me as I count in my head. The weight crashes back into place on my last rep, and I sag a little in the hard cushion of the seat. I have such a long way to go. "I guess I was never going to be able to avoid paying the piper, huh?"

"Doubtful, sir," Jackson replies.

"Well, let's see what we can do about mitigating the fallout from this. I don't care what he wants, I'm not selling the whole fucking farm, all right?" I reply, wiping the slight sheen of sweat from my forehead onto my sleeve. Beth won't be happy if I show up for dinner smelling like a construction worker. I decide to forego any more leg presses for the evening.

"Of course, sir," Jackson replies, though his voice has no conviction in it. Everyone is placating me these days. Everyone, of course, except for Hannah, who challenges me at every turn. I can almost hear the scheming that must be going on in Jackson's head. I'm sure he's already planning ten ways to reign me in on this. He doesn't have the conviction to go up against S&J, risking exposure and their sizeable contributions to my campaign in one fell swoop. If Burt Leeland asked me for nuclear launch codes, Jackson would find a way of delivering them. But he doesn't know what I know, what I've always known. He doesn't know struggle, or the feeling of true power. He doesn't know what it's like to be me.

"Let's get this over with," I say, not waiting for an answer, clicking the phone off and going to change my shirt before dinner.

Later I find Beth in the study that Jackson set up as a temporary
office, leaning over the desk, reading something by the light of the
small lamp beside her, the intensity of her focus almost startling.
I watch her for a few moments from the doorway, unnoticed, as
she closes a folder and puts it back into one of the drawers. I duck
back into the hallway as she flicks off the light, pretending I haven't
caught her going through my things. She starts as she sees me, shutting the office door behind her. Then she smiles, her perfect veneer
pulled back into place.

"You coming to bed?" she asks.

"In a bit. I have a few ends to tie up first."

"Of course." She presses a hand against my chest, her wedding
ring glimmering there like an accusation. She kisses me on the cheek
this time, an admonishment of my earlier mistake, and then heads
for the stairs.

I go back to my study after Beth has gone to bed, opening the
drawer from which she'd pulled the folder. There are four files in
the drawer. One for me, one for Hannah, one for Connie, one for
Linda. Our SUBlife profiles, the background information collected
on us before the transfer, the ones Jackson had to call in a few favors
to get. Something in me prickles with displeasure, that my wife
would be snooping into this part of my life. I put the files away,
trying to ignore the quiet instinct inside of me that says something
awful has happened, though I'm not quite sure what it is.

# Connie

I knock softly on Dr. Grath's door, four short raps, the way I always do, so he knows it's me.

"It's open," he calls from inside, and I enter. His apartment is dim. The amber glow of evening sunlight cuts through the shut blinds on his window; it's the only other light in the little room besides the flicker of the TV. He sits in his armchair with a mug of tea next to him on the side table and a joint balanced in his thick-knuckled hand. He's surrounded by bookshelves stuffed with books he can't read anymore. His plants are dying, their leaves curling on yellow stems. I tried to overwater them a bit before I left, but apparently it wasn't enough. I wonder if he remembers they're even there. "Your vacation is over just in time. *I Confess* is on." He motions toward the TV. I smile because Dr. Grath knows Montgomery Clift has always been a favorite of mine.

"Perfect," I reply and then stop short when Dr. Grath stands up so quickly he drops the joint. It trails hot sparks down the front of his dark green cardigan and lands on the carpet, still glowing. I'm about to rush to stomp it out when Dr. Grath's voice stops me.

"Who are you?" he says, his face trained on me, as if he could conjure some saved-up stores of sight, if only he concentrates hard enough. He's a small man when he stands, probably about my height, with a thin nose and wisps of white hair on his head. He paints a sweet, feeble picture, standing there in his rumpled clothes. Like a baby chick before it opens its eyes, all damp, downy feathers and shriveled legs. Only his mind remains sharp, in a body that has failed him a hundred times over by now.

"It's me," I say, laughing a little, as if this is a game I don't quite understand. "I haven't been gone for that long, have I?"

"Your voice," Dr. Grath says, his own voice wavering with fear. Then he recovers himself a bit, because his next words are stronger, more resolved. "I don't believe you."

"Dr. Grath, it's me," I say, taking another step toward him. He shrinks back a bit. "Jesus, what do I have to say to prove it to you?"

He seems to consider the question for a minute. "Did you happen to get new vocal chords on your vacation? Because the Connie I knew smoked a pack a day since she was a teenager, and you could hear every single one of those cigarettes when she talked."

I'm unprepared for this. I hadn't considered that he'd be able to tell I've changed. I hadn't even decided if I should tell him anything at all. I want one place in the world to be just how I remembered it. I want there to be one place where it doesn't matter if I had been changed or not. "And what if I did?" I say.

"Impossible, my dear," Dr. Grath replies. I shrug, though he can't see me, not with the apartment this dark. He can barely see me in full sunlight, as it is. Just variations of shadow, he said to me once. Just figures moving around in a dark room.

"Your wife's name was Maureen. Like my mother's." I leave it at that. The one thing we have in common. Dr. Grath frowns, and I can tell I've won him over, because he drops back into his chair. "You sound like a different person." His tone is gruff, as if I've done it intentionally to inconvenience him.

"It's a long story." I step forward and pat him on the arm, reaching down to pick the joint up from the carpet at his feet. It's too late; there's a charred little hole where the fibers of the rug have been singed away. He'll never know, though, so I don't mention it. I hand the unfinished joint back to him. "Be more careful, old man. You don't want to be the one to burn the building down."

Dr. Grath chuckles, turning back to the TV. "Yes, because if someone is going to burn down the Chelsea Hotel, it had better be its resident Edie Sedgwick." He pats my hand, accepting the joint and bringing it to his lips. The light flickers off his cloudy eyes; nothing is absorbed. "Was it a good vacation?"

"Not bad," I say, settling into my usual spot on his tiny couch, watching Montgomery Clift cross the screen dressed in black priest's robes. "I'm glad I'm back in time for this. Monty dressed as a priest is even better than watching him in *Red River*. There's something much more alluring in the forbidden, don't you think?"

"You are lucky you live when you do, my dear," he says, and I can almost feel the lapsed Catholic in him stepping up to his lectern. "It wasn't so many decades ago that a woman like you would be branded a Jezebel."

"Oh please," I reply. "It wasn't so many decades ago when women like me were burned at the stake."

He laughs then, but his eyes hover in middle space, so I can't tell if he's trying to look at me or the television.

"Tell me what's different," he says.

"Everything," I reply. "Everything is different."

"Is it a man?"

I'm the one to laugh now, and it's a clear sound. It's the first time I notice what he means, that the husky scrape is gone from my throat. I sound younger, less world-weary. I hadn't even noticed before. "You give your gender a lot of credit, as if all it took was a few months with a new beau to fix me right up, huh?"

"I've seen whole worlds turn upside down in less time than that," Dr. Grath replies.

"Yes, but not lately."

"Careful now. You can't tease me anymore if it turns out you're cured and I'm not."

I don't say anything for a long time. He waits, remaining silent, letting me figure out what to say next. *Old bastard,* I think.

"How did you know?" I ask, finally, blinking hard to keep the sting in my eyes at bay.

"Val's caller ID. He said the call came from Northwestern Memorial. And here I thought you weren't coming back at all, after he gave me that message. I thought that was your good-bye. I had a good cry over it, actually. But then you show up smelling like fresh milk, with that voice of yours. It's like you've been scrubbed clean."

"What did I smell like before?" I ask, a little taken aback.

"Vinegar. And damp hair. Like you were dying."

"I *was* dying."

"And now?" he asks. I look at the TV. Montgomery Clift and Anne Baxter are having a tense, passion-filled exchange. It occurs to me that he looks a bit like David.

"I guess I'm not anymore."

"And how does that happen, exactly? I mean, I've heard of remissions, but never cures. Not with your strain. Believe me, I've asked around."

"Trying to fix me, doctor?" I ask, flirting a little, because it's the only way I know how to repay men who are kind to me. But he's having none of it, as usual.

"I'm not keen on the idea of outliving anyone I know," he says.

I let a long stream of air out through my nose, as if I've just taken a long drag on his joint. "Well your plants are going to die."

"Maybe not," he replies, "now that you're back."

Dr. Grath falls asleep in his armchair, and I leave him there. He spends most nights there now, with the TV flickering over his well-lined face, his vacant eyes moving beneath his eyelids. I wonder what he sees when he dreams, if he ever wakes up forgetting that he's blind until he opens his eyes. That was how it was for me for a long time. I'd wake up and for one dizzying moment I'd forget that I was sick, as if I were suspended mid-fall. Then the world would rush up to meet me.

I wash out his teacup in the sink. Killing time, mostly, before I have to go back to my apartment. I turn down the volume on the TV, though not all the way, not to the point where he won't realize it's still on when he wakes up in the morning. And then I venture back across the hall, with its thin felt carpeting and musty smell, into the apartment I didn't bother locking while I was gone.

I don't like it anymore. Not that I ever particularly loved it, but I feel now an active repulsion when I flick on the lights and shut the door behind me. It's nothing like the apartments I had in L.A., even the little place I'd shared with another model when I first moved into the city. That place had been cramped and hot, with foggy windows and a communal pool that was always overrun with algae and dead leaves. We'd slept on mattresses on the floor, she and I, with a curtain hung on a wire between us to divide the room. But it had a view of the Hollywood sign and it had been unfailingly sunny, like everything in California. And after growing up in a trailer, it might as well have been Buckingham Palace.

This apartment only ever served as a place for me to convalesce. I moved out of L.A. as soon as my disease started to show, as soon as the people around me began to back away. People could tolerate a lot in that city, but a beautiful woman's descent into the grotesque was not acceptable, at least not in the industry. And people were still a bit afraid of my particular strain, which had developed a resistance to nearly all of the standard medical treatments. So I retreated back to Chicago, abandoning the sea air and the mountains and the sunshine for a tiny studio apartment in Uptown that seemed like a good place to die. And this was the apartment I'd chosen, because it was cheap enough to be covered by my Social Security checks and nothing about it reminded me of California.

It has a smell, like dying flowers, like something sweet rotting. I never really noticed it before. Now, with all of my senses sharp and new, it assails me in the doorway and has me trying to force open my windows, a futile endeavor, as they've been painted shut since before I lived here. I'd never cared much what my apartment looked like. But now everything around me, from my threadbare couch to the yellowing tile in my kitchen to my leaky, moldering bathtub, seems to be suffused with disease. It never occurred to me before how dim my apartment is. My bed is unmade and my sheets smell sour. I strip it down to the mattress and haul the bedding to the first floor laundry room, throwing it into the washer with a few capfuls of bleach, enough to make my nostrils sting from the fumes, but at least it's better than the other smell.

Upstairs, I root around under my sink until I find a soft cardboard box full of trash bags. I'd left a half-full can of garbage in my kitchen before I checked into the hospital, and now it's teeming with fruit flies and reeks so badly it makes my eyes water as I bag it up and rush to the trash chute in the hallway. Another survey of the space under my sink produces a bottle of kitchen spray and a can of Ajax, and even though it's three in the morning I begin to tear into my apartment with the fury of a meth addict in an after-school special. This place is unsuitable I think, again and again, unsuitable for the person I am now. I should be back in L.A., where I could open the window and smell hot wind and desert flowers. I should live in a place decorated with silk curtains and ornate mirrors, with a wrought-iron bed frame and huge photographs hanging on the walls. It was what I told myself again and again as a child, sleeping in the stagnant air of my mother's trailer, listening to motorcycle engines and angry voices drifting in through my window. I told myself I belonged somewhere beautiful, that God had made a mistake when I was born there. That was back when I believed in God.

I sleep on my couch when I'm finally exhausted, too drained to retrieve my sheets from the laundry room. I hope they'll still be there in the morning, though I doubt it. At least the place smells better now, the odor of rot beaten away by the sharp, acrid scent of ammonia and the treacly lavender of my kitchen cleaner. Everything is still dingy, though, battered away by years of activity. I think of all the hours I've spent here, all the endless days shuffling around, wearing down the cushions of my couch, eating out of delivery containers and not seeing the sun for weeks at a time. How easy it was to remove myself, almost completely, from the world around me. I chose to be absent, when even Dr. Grath had been finding his way around the city without his eyes. What a coward I was, I think. How weak.

I don't sleep well. It's a terribly uncomfortable couch. Things don't really look better in the morning, there's just a haze of natural light added to accentuate the ugly details of the place. I wonder if I should move, leave everything and start over somewhere else. It's a fleeting thought. The only person in the world who knows me lives right across the hall. And, no matter how much I've changed, I'm not prepared to give that up yet.

# David

David Jr. looks like a young bird in the light of his computer, making his skin a pale blue and his black eye looks even bigger. His soft, fair hair is mussed, and he can't keep his hands out of it. It makes him seem nervous, the way he plays with his hair, digging his fingers through it, twisting tufts until they stick out from his head like thorns. I wonder if he is nervous, talking to this man who resembles his father in only shadowy, utilitarian ways.

He has always been small for his age, my son. He was born nearly six weeks premature, and even after he outgrew the delicate, alien visage of those first weeks he never quite caught up to the other kids his age. I think of how he must look to the other boys in his class, like he's made of china, like he could break if you handled him just a bit too roughly.

The image of his split lip is glaring magenta on the computer screen. It makes me furious to see this sort of damage to my son's face, first at the little fucker who hit him and then, irrationally, at my son for being such an easy target. For being too much like me, at his age, with a father too disinterested to teach me how to avoid getting my ass kicked. It's a shameful feeling, being angry with my son because he got hurt, because I haven't been around enough to teach him all of the things I was forced to learn for myself.

"Mom said it was you who started it," I say, trying to coax some sort of satisfactory explanation from him. He nods, fingers curling into the hair above his right ear.

"They were laughing at me."

"Who is 'they'?" I ask.

"Jimmy and Bradley Simmons. A few others," he replies. I know those little shits. They look like they could be in high school, though they have the intellect of second graders. Their father owns a company that manufactures tractors, one of those unlikeliest of success stories, in which someone with very few valuable faculties makes millions by accident alone. The sort of success story that makes me wild, burns in me like chemical waste, goring holes in my stomach when I think of the way my grandmother toiled for so little. Or my mother, who could read books in Russian, who knew the names of the constellations, whose sadness seemed born of knowing what she could have been if she hadn't been saddled with a farm and a son and a worthless husband. My mother, who didn't live to fifty, who didn't live to see me start high school.

"Jimmy and Bradley Simmons are bigger than you. Why would you try to go after them yourself?" I ask, feeling the sting of my own hypocrisy. I would be riotously proud of my son if he'd had the brawn to go after them and come out on top. David Jr. shrugs. "Come on, you can do better than that. Tell me, why would you start a fight with boys who are twice your size? It's not a smart move, buddy. You shouldn't be starting fights you can't finish."

"They had a cartoon from the Internet. You were wearing a sheet like a dress, and they were laughing at you," he says. I know the cartoon he means. The *New York Times* ran it the week after my rehab story broke. It shows me as an overgrown frat boy, showing up to a vote in a toga with a bottle of whiskey taped to each hand.

"Look, buddy, there are going to be plenty of people who will say mean things about me. That's what it is to be a leader. People need someone to ridicule, and it's always the person who steps up. Understand?" I ask. He nods, though his expression borders on vacant, like I've awakened him from a deep sleep. "Tell me that you understand."

"I understand," he says, the split in his lip bobbing as he speaks. Maybe I'll have one of my buddies in the IRS run an audit on Simmons Tractor and Freight. Maybe I'll reroute the new highway in my district so it runs right through the Simmons' family home.

"When I get home, I'm going to teach you how to fight, okay? I'm going to teach you how to throw a punch and mean it."

"I did mean it," he replies. *A baby bird*, I think. Or maybe a baby mouse. It makes me a little angry, that he doesn't have the sense to know he's too damn small to be picking fights.

"You don't have to fight my battles for me, understand? I can do that myself. I don't need a little kid to stand up for me," I say, and watch him deflate in front of me. *Shit.* This is not what it means to be a better father. "I just don't want you getting hurt on my account, buddy. It's not worth you getting hurt, all right?" He nods, but he doesn't look at me. "All right. Are you surviving grandma's cooking?"

"She made me eat goat cheese."

"Did you like it?" I ask.

"No, it was gross," he says.

"Well, listen, Mom is going to be back with you in a few weeks, and then it'll be just a few more months until I'm home too. And hey, I'll take you to a Brewers game, how about that? We can get those seats behind the dugout again, would you like that?" I ask, painfully aware that I'm pandering to my son, giving him whatever he wants so he won't be so damn sad anymore. I'm just as bad as Beth, I think. Every time I try to toughen him up a little, I end up coddling him.

"Yeah, sure, Dad," he says.

"You keep your chin up okay?"

He nods, and we sign off. I sit back in my chair, my fingers at my temples, trying to resolve the mix of pity and guilt and shameful disdain that always curls through me when I speak to my son. The unqualified optimism I felt that first day in the hospital room feels like a shrunken, petrified memory now. A better man, I think. Yeah, I'm fucking father of the year.

# Linda

*It's the same house.* That's all I can think when I follow Tom inside. He didn't sell it after all, which I know had been a consideration when money started getting tight after my accident. I'm grateful that it's still here, this house on Hinman Street in Evanston, because it is so achingly familiar even though it's been eight years since I've run my hand over the smooth wood of its banisters or felt the floors echo under my feet.

Jack and Katie stand at the foot of the stairs when we enter, Katie with her hands behind her back while Jack stands on the bottom step, twisting himself back and forth from the end of the banister. They both look a little frightened of me. In truth, I'm a little frightened of them.

"Mom's home," Tom says, with an almost sing-song exuberance to his voice, then moves to pay the babysitter, a wisp of a girl who doesn't look much older than Katie, and usher her out. She looks like she might prefer to hang around and watch the family drama that's about to unfold, but she finally ducks out the front door when Tom thanks her for the third time. The door shuts behind her with the firm insistence of the lid of a pressure-cooker. There is nothing left to do now but to meet my children.

Jack moves first, with a grin that is all pink gums and empty spaces, launching himself at me and gripping me around the waist with such force that I nearly topple. "Mommy!" he says into my side, and I'm sure if I were a real mother I would know exactly how to match this display of emotional hunger. If I were not a woman living inside herself, if I had not been separated from my children so viciously and for so long, I would know what to do. But my hands do not seem to work. I cannot quite figure out how to hold this small creature who has attached himself to me, so all I manage is to pat the black silk of his hair. Tom lets the moment go on for longer than I would prefer, before he rubs the boy's back, taking him by the arm and releasing his grip on me.

"Okay, Jack," he says. "Okay." Jack is still grinning as Tom gathers him up with an arm around his shoulders, kissing him on the top of the head. I think maybe I haven't done so badly after all, but then Katie bursts into tears, clapping both hands over her face, and runs up the stairs. I can hear a door slam at the end of the hall. "Shit," Tom mutters.

"Daddy," Jack chides, his tongue a pink protrusion between the gap in his front teeth.

"I know, buddy," Tom says, glancing up at me with more than a little naked frustration. It reminds me of the look he started giving me in college when I got pregnant, a look that says, *Couldn't you have done better?* I give him a little shrug, and that seems to make things worse. "How about you go upstairs and check on your sister, okay?" Tom says, nudging a reluctant Jack toward the stairs.

"Fine," Jack says, his footfalls landing on the steps with a little more force than necessary. I take a breath once he's out of sight. It never used to be difficult to breathe around my children, but this new body is proving more difficult to navigate than the old one was.

Tom watches me openly as I take in the house. It's as if he still thinks I can't see him when he's doing it, after all those years when he watched me from just beyond the periphery of my vision. I walk from room to room, biding my time before I go upstairs to the one room I want to see. I have to pretend that I care about it all, the kitchen and the bathroom and the dining room and the den, instead of just wanting to see my little room at the top of the stairs. I take the steps slowly, remembering just how they creak under my weight.

I hold my breath as I open the door, expecting to see my bed with its armchair drawn close, the TV on the dresser across from it. Instead, it's an office. I don't want to let out my held breath, as if this room is a mirage that may still shimmer away and transform itself into what I remember. But no, it remains. Bookshelves, a desk with a computer on it. A calendar tacked to the wall. A heavy shade over the window. My memory stirs, shaking forth a familiar image. This room was Tom's office before the accident. Of course he would revert it back to its former use once I was safely moved into a nursing home. Of course, it's only logical. But it seems Tom's logic has served no purpose but to hurt me in these past eight years.

I take a few steps in, standing where I used to lie, listening to the sounds of my house, remembering the melodic tones of Cora's voice, watching clouds and blue sky and birds from the window. This room, which had been my whole world for a while, looks like I've never been here at all.

Tom follows me into our bedroom, a room I haven't entered in eight years, and it's a different color from the one we picked together when we moved in. I wonder if he still sleeps on the same side of the bed, but when I glance at the side tables there's an equal amount of clutter on each. Books, mostly. How long has it been since I read a book?

The curtains on the windows are different, and that strikes me as probably the oddest thing of all, because what the hell does Tom know about curtains? He'd lived alone in an apartment before we moved in together, and when I first saw his place I'd been appalled to see that he'd stapled a sheet over his window to keep the sunlight at bay. But these curtains are mounted on ornate, heavy rods. They're cut perfectly to the size of the window. The fabric looks expensive. I'm baffled, absolutely baffled, at how these curtains came to pass without my orchestration. I wander into the bathroom.

"Honey," he says, as I'm reaching for my closet door. My hand freezes. He looks like he's steeling himself against something, the way he used to look when we'd drive down to his parents' house in Iowa for Christmas. I imagine his father's gray crew cut and his booming voice. Could I possibly be so fearsome?

I open the closet, and then I understand Tom's hesitance. The ironing board rests against one wall of the little walk-in space. Boxes labeled "Christmas Decorations—Upstairs" are stacked in the corner. My clothes are gone. I step inside. All my things are gone. My shoes. Even the tall, thin dresser that held my belts and scarves and underthings, it's gone too.

"Where . . ." is all I can manage. My vocal chords have wound themselves into a tight little knot at the base of my throat. I'm wearing yoga pants and a T-shirt that Tom bought me at the Target on State Street before I left the hospital, and it occurs to me that this is all I have. My clothes are gone.

"We sold some of it. And donated some of it," Tom says. "But honey, this was years ago. You have to understand, we had no idea." He doesn't finish, but I know what he's going to say. There's no way he could possibly have known that I would be cured. It would be illogical to keep my things, especially when the closet could so easily be used to store an ironing board and Christmas decorations. Why keep around reminders of a wife who might as well be dead?

"Who is 'we'?" I ask.

"Me and the kids."

"Oh." My family. My traitorous little family, ganging up against me. The question swings back at me again, the one I asked Dr. Bernard at the first support group meeting.

"We didn't get rid of all of it. Some of your things are up in the attic." He pauses, waiting for something. Gratitude, maybe? When he doesn't get it, he continues. "We'll get you new things, of course. Tomorrow, we can go out and get you a whole closet of new clothes."

"Sure." After all, what is the loss of my belongings when I've already faced the loss of eight years of my life? I imagine this is what it must be like for families whose houses have burned down, leaving them nothing familiar to call their own. I remember stories of refugees who would not give up their deteriorating shoes because they were the only things remaining from their old lives. *That is what I am,* I think. *A refugee.* A woman who has been so cast out of her life that she will forever be a stranger in it.

"I don't want," Tom begins, and then he gets choked up, wipes at his eyes. Tom has always been the one of us who was quickest to cry. It's amusing in a dark way, how some things never change. "I don't want you to think we didn't miss you," he says, his voice an octave higher than usual because of the strain of his tears. I used to find it endearing, his wealth of emotion and his willingness to display it openly. But I've seen him cry one too many times during the past eight years to see it as anything but useless. Pathetic, even. "We missed you every single day. If I had thought there was any chance at all that you could come back, I would have saved every single thing. But baby, they told me there was no chance. Zero. They told me there was no point in believing in miracles."

"Right," I say, nodding, shutting the closet door. Is this a miracle, this thing that has happened to me? I don't know. It feels too clumsy, to fleshy and utilitarian, to be miraculous. But I don't want to argue with him, so instead I stand there and watch him cry.

The TV is huge. It might be the biggest TV I've ever seen, the kind you'd usually find mounted on the walls of sports bars so a person sitting in one of the back tables can still see the game. It takes up half the living room, eclipsing most of the brick fireplace against the back wall. That fireplace was the clincher for us when we were looking at houses; we imagined ourselves wrapped in wool blankets, sitting in front of crackling logs in the middle of winter, and we made an offer on the spot. We'd actually used the fireplace only once or twice, in the years we lived here before my accident. I wonder if it's been used at all since.

"It's a little much, I know," Tom says from the kitchen, when he sees me standing in front of the big black screen of the television. "It was a sort of family Christmas present last year. I might have gone a little overboard."

It strikes me that we didn't even have a TV when we first moved in here. Our old apartment was so small that we'd watch movies on Tom's desktop computer, and we'd eventually bought an ancient TV at the Brown Elephant when we decided that our kids deserved to grow up on Sesame Street the way we did. But I never imagined anything like this, not for us.

I'm delighted by it. Even the remote is gigantic, nearly as long as a paper-towel roll and twice as wide. It feels like a weapon in my hand when I pick it up. I'm endlessly fascinated by how things feel to the touch, now that I'm more able to discern one sensation from another. It's gotten easier to filter through the chaos of sights and sounds and movement, and I'll find myself running my hands over the wood of our kitchen table or the scratchy fibers of a knitted throw or my own skin, and marveling at the texture and temperature inherent in all of these things. My favorite thing is sticking my fingers into the container of uncooked rice Tom keeps on the counter. It's a shivery feeling, like dipping your hand into water that's not quite water, and I do it again and again when Tom is in another room, feeling my stomach clench every time at the sensation.

The TV remote is surprisingly heavy, and I point it at the TV with one hand and press the red button at the top with my other. The screen flickers to life, like the start of some great engine. The volume is so loud that it knocks me back and I drop the remote, which hits the floor with a plasticine pop, sending batteries scattering. I clap my hands over my ears as Tom rushes around the kitchen counter and fiddles with one of the black boxes in the cabinet beneath the TV, and the volume quiets to a tolerable level. Whatever Tom is saying is muffled through my hands, so I gingerly remove them from over my ears.

". . . had his video game plugged in. He cranks the volume up and the whole house sounds like a war zone. I swear, I'm going to get PTSD, but he and Katie are just happy as clams." He retrieves the remote from the floor. "Where'd the batteries go?"

I don't really answer, because I'm still recovering from the sudden onslaught of sound. I feel shaken, like all of my nerves have been thoroughly plucked, and my palms are clammy. My heart is charging forward like I've had a near-miss on the expressway.

Tom kneels down to fish the batteries out from under the sofa, and then hands the remote back to me. "I'd tell you what's on, but I figure you probably know better than I do, right?" he says with a too-big grin, as if he's said something devilishly funny. I nod, but I don't smile back.

As it turns out, the TV is quite the revelation. I turn it on as soon as Tom bustles the kids off to school in the morning and then departs for his job running his outdoor equipment service. It's bright, so bright that I could probably sit with the curtains closed and hardly tell the difference. The picture has a clarity that I can barely believe; the characters are three-feet tall and I can see every line on their faces. It convinces me even more that Connie would make a terrific actress now, because even the sharpest of cameras couldn't pick up a flaw in the skin of her face. It makes me feel proud in a possessive sort of way, as if I'd created Connie myself out of a perfect piece of clay.

More than fascinating, the TV is a comfort. I fall back easily into the pattern of my days at the hospital. First a morning talk show where four D-list celebrities and one unlucky journalist sit around the table and harp on the latest news in pop culture. Then the local news, endless reports of gang shootings and teacher's strikes and football scores. And then the stories start, inversely ordered by quality, beginning with a half-hour show about a town on the East Coast that's infiltrated by vampires, and ending at 3 p.m. with *Stratford Pines*, the crown jewel of the network's daytime lineup. The sheer size of it, on the big screen, is intoxicating. It feels more real, this close up, like if I just sink back into the sofa enough I could let myself drift through the soft membrane of the TV screen into that world. My world, the one I've always imagined, even after the show ends and the afternoon game shows begin.

It's difficult to sleep with Tom next to me, snoring lightly, turning over and adjusting his pillow and occasionally mumbling in his sleep, while I remain perfectly still. Always, perfectly still. I haven't slept in the same bed with someone in eight years. And it occurs to me one night, a few weeks after my homecoming, staring at the ceiling and listening to Tom breathe next to me, that I'm not sure if the same is true for him. The thought is short-lived though, because he turns toward me and puts his hand on my stomach. I jump, jerking so violently that I nearly knock him in the chin with my shoulder.

"Jesus," he mutters, shifting beside me.

"I'm sorry. I didn't mean to—" I stop talking because his hand is back, a bit heavy, brushing its way back and forth over my T-shirt.

"It's all right." I can smell his breath, like warm mouthwash. I don't remember how this works. I shut my eyes and think of the thousands of scenes like this that have played in my head during the last eight years. They always seemed to be lit differently, more like candle-flicker than this darkness, brightened only by the insistent glowing of Tom's alarm clock and the dots of light on the TV and cable box and Blu-ray player across the room. In my head it was always more passion than practicality, the way it had been so many times with so many characters on *Stratford Pines*. It was never about the fact that two people happen to be lying in bed together. It was rainstorms and torrid affairs and long-lost lovers reuniting for the first time. It occurs to me that Tom and I should belong to the latter category, but my body can't seem to conjure the same heat or the electric thrill I remember, even from imagining it. I'm surprisingly cold, lying here in our bed, even as Tom seems to creep nearer with every move of his hand.

"I've been thinking a lot, these last couple of weeks," he says, his voice a murmur, his hand testing the boundary of the bottom of my T-shirt.

"Yes," I reply, because it seems like the correct response. Two blinks.

"Do you remember what we started talking about right before the accident?" His mouth is close to my ear now, his head in the valley between our pillows. I can't imagine it's very comfortable.

"Yes." I say it before I realize that I haven't bothered remembering much of anything from before the accident. It's the way I coped for eight years, by not looking back. By pretending my life had begun the day before, that there was no world outside the walls of my room. No world but what I saw on TV. That was the way you stayed sane, in a situation like mine. You made yourself believe you'd forgotten your whole life.

"I've been thinking, maybe we should try and pick up where we left off. I mean, we don't know how this works, this whole SUB thing. If you're really thirty-five we could only have a few years left to try."

"Right."

"So," he says, his hand sweeping down then, under the waistband of my yoga pants and into my underwear, as he presses the minty heat of his mouth into the side of my neck. I go rigid, my elbows digging into the sides of my ribs. I keep very still, as if I'm being sniffed by a wild animal and maybe I can pass myself off as an inanimate object until it loses interest. As it is, it takes longer than I'd like for Tom to notice that I haven't moved an inch, haven't responded to the workings of his hand.

"Am I alone in this?" he asks.

"I . . ." I'm supposed to want this, I know. But I can't muster it, that want.

He lets out a long breath, extricating his hand from between my legs. I can't tell if he's angry or dejected. "I discussed it with your doctors, you know, if that's what you're worried about. There's no danger, medically. I think they're actually excited about the opportunity to see what happens. The more data the better."

I'm still not terribly clear on what he's talking about, but I bristle at the idea that he's been speaking to my doctors about me. It feels too much like I'm still paralyzed, something to be cleaned and watered and fed and taken care of by others.

"I don't want you talking to my doctors," I say, trying to make out the fine webbing of cracks in our ceiling through the darkness.

Those are familiar, even if the rest of the room is not. Even if my body is not.

"What?"

"I don't want you talking to my doctors without me there. I deserve to know as much as you do about what's happening to me."

He's silent then. I wonder if I've upset him. I don't remember ever speaking to him in such a way, when I was the old me.

"Fine," he says, raising a hand, miming his innocent frustration to an invisible audience. He's not a very good actor though. Connie would be appalled. "But that doesn't change the fact that we wanted more kids. We've always wanted more. And now we have a chance."

Oh dear. The rest of the conversation clicks into place for me. And he's right, when we were first married we talked about having more children, as many as three more, in fact. But I've just come back to myself now. I have just stopped being something that has to be tended to, something hooked up to machines, something that lives and breathes because other people have made sure of it. How can I tell him that this body is something sacred, no matter how clumsy or fleshy or unfamiliar it is. How can I tell him that I want this body to be mine more than I want it to have his children?

"The doctors want to see what happens?" I ask, imagining them discussing me like I'm a lab rat running in its wheel, observed from behind glass by the men who will decide my future.

"They want to include it in the study data. A healthy pregnancy could go a long way to getting FDA approval, apparently. But that's not really what I'm concerned about," he says, peeling the sheet away from me and dragging up my T-shirt until it bunches under my breasts. My stomach is enviably flat, unmarked by my former pregnancies or Jack's C-section. It's funny, this is the body I struggled so hard to get back to after the kids were born and never could. I guess there really is a price for every wish, isn't there?

"God, you're so different now," Tom says, examining my exposed skin in the darkness. At first, his touch is an examination only, drawing his fingertips over my skin, as if testing to see if it is real. He's pleased. I would be gratified, if this body were my doing, if it were not a lucky happenstance of a very unlucky life. Instead, it feels like just another mark against the woman I was, the body that still feels more kindred to me than this one.

He kisses along the bottom edge of my ribcage, his hand sinking back to its former position. It reminds me of a night in the park, less than a week before my accident. The kids, sleeping in their car seats in the back of my minivan. The sharp roughness of the wooden picnic table under my thighs. There is a price, I think. There is always a price.

"There you go," Tom breathes into the skin of my stomach, his hand more insistent now. I wonder if this body is capable of disobeying me, the way the last one would, my legs and hands and hips moving even when my mind told them to stop. I wonder if this body knows any of what it is capable of. But it is a different body now, I remind myself, as Tom pulls down my yoga pants and rolls on top of me. I'm a different person now.

# Hannah

I stare at my closet, trying to find something that will work, anything to replace the baggy sweaters and the one old pair of jeans that I've been wearing since I got out of the hospital. Jeans from high school, the ones I found folded up in the bottom of my dresser. They're the only ones that fit around the sharp, narrow bones of my new hips. I've all but given up on wearing bras; their wires pinch my ribs and the cups gap around the shrunken remains of my breasts. I feel like a little girl, young and unformed, trying on the silk and lace of her mother's clothing, imagining a world she does not yet inhabit.

Everything I own feels large. Even my shoes are a half-size too big. I don't wear rings for fear of losing them off of the narrow, supple joints of my fingers. And my clothes—clothes designed for a woman, dresses cut to reveal cleavage, high-waisted trousers that hugged my hips, fitted sweaters and pencil skirts and over-priced lingerie—they have been made inanimate. They have been made inanimate on my new body. They hang, lifeless. Even the brightest ones seem to lack color when I put them on.

Penny and Connor are having us over for dinner. Nothing fancy, of course, but still. I can't wear my ratty jeans or any of the thick sweaters I curled myself into when I was sick. Everything in my closet seems wrong, made for someone ages older and much more proper than I am, especially in this body. Clothes that I bought as much for Sam as for me, replacing the T-shirts and thrift-store jackets and hippie skirts of my former wardrobe. Things that would suit the world of newspaper offices and cocktail parties and yacht clubs in which he moved. Things I could imagine Lucy wearing. I think of Lucy, and realize that I hate every scrap of clothing I own.

Instead of getting dressed, I pull handfuls of hangers out of my closet and toss them onto the bed. I retrieve a bunch of large black garbage bags from the kitchen and fill them until they're bloated with artifacts of my former life. I stack the garbage bags by the front door and leave them there. Sam can drive them over to Goodwill or throw them away; I don't care. I change into the one dress I've retained, a wrap dress that looks sad and baggy without breasts and hips to fill it out. But at least it's something. I pull it on, cinching it tight around my waist. All of my heels are too big, but I grab a pair of black flats from the discard pile and stuff cotton balls into the toes so they'll fit, at least for one night. By the end I'm feeling worn out and sorry for myself, as if I've been airlifted out of my life and deposited somewhere I don't quite recognize. I hear Sam arrive home from work; the door opens and hits the garbage bags. They slide across the wood floor. But he doesn't mention them when he joins me in the bathroom and brushes his teeth. He doesn't say anything.

We don't talk on our way to Penny and Connor's apartment. We speed down Lake Shore Drive as the sun falls below the metal and glass of Chicago, and everything is a shimmer of color. Homesickness hits me hard, choking me up. It sits somewhere under my breastplate, a barb of muted grief, though I don't understand it. I've always loved this city so much it makes my bones ache, but it feels impossible to be homesick for a place in which I still remain. Yet as I look at the familiar skyline and the wind whips off the lake, hammering against my window, it's there. That sour agony. And I wonder if someone can be homesick for herself, for the person she was just months ago. I rest my head against the car window and shut my eyes, trying to drive the feeling away.

Penny and Connor live in a one-bedroom on a quiet street in Ravenswood, a place that is perpetually falling apart but has enough early 20th-century charm to make it endearing. The walls sport built-in bookcases with pitted glass doors, the ceilings are high and

framed in intricate molding, and there's a giant claw-foot porcelain tub in the bathroom. It has always seemed the perfect blend of
both their sensibilities; it has a certain artistic rhythm mixed with
an air of antiquity, particularly when its bookshelves are stuffed with
Connor's dissertation research on post-Colonial political violence. It
reminds me of my apartment, when Penny and I used to live there
together. As Sam and I let ourselves in, the air is rich with olive oil
and garlic. *Astral Weeks* is playing in the background.

"Hello?" I call out, heading for the kitchen, where Penny is bent
over a steaming copper pot. The kitchen lights cast a buttery glow
over everything, and for a moment I can imagine Penny's Jamaican
grandmother bustling about in front of her hot little cook stove,
occasionally turning to cool her face against the salty air floating in
through the windows. But then Penny turns, and she's the same wry,
effortlessly modern hippie that she's always been. She grins when
she sees me.

"Should I be afraid?" I ask, approaching the stove with exaggerated caution. "I don't know if I can take anything five-alarm quite
yet."

"Don't worry, Sam called ahead, told me all about your recent
dietary proclivities," Penny says.

"Of course he did," I reply, and my tone is more annoyed than
I expected.

"Would you have preferred I made my mother's chili?" she asks.
I feel like shit.

"No, I guess not."

She offers up a spoonful of white-cheddar macaroni and cheese.
"It took everything in me to keep from putting chipotle pepper in it."

I taste it, and the sharp richness nearly makes my eyes roll back
in my head. "Jesus, Pen, that's phenomenal."

"Is anyone else from your group the same way?" she asks as she
taps a bit of smoked paprika into the pot.

"All of them. The shrink in charge thinks it's because children have all these extra taste buds that die off as you get older, and that hasn't happened for us yet."

"So you're going to be stuck on fish sticks and oatmeal and . . . whatever else kids eat for what, like the next decade or so?"

I shrug. "It's not like anyone's tried this before. They honestly don't know."

"That's a lot of years without a glass of wine," Penny says, brandishing her wooden spoon like a nun with a ruler.

"I'm aware. Speaking of which, Sam brought a bottle of Beaujolais."

"Tasty."

"And he's treating me like I still have a catheter in."

Penny wrinkles her nose. "Not so tasty. So that's why you're so prickly. I would have thought he'd be all over you after what you two have been through."

"I guess it takes some time for the hospital smell to wash off."

"Well I'll have Connor mix you up something with training wheels on it, help you forget your troubles. What do you think, rum and coke? Something with grenadine in it?" Penny opens the fridge, peering inside. "Shit, I can't even remember what we used to drink when we were young."

"A shot of raspberry Smirnoff in our dorm room freshman year," I say, remembering the hot feeling in the back of my throat, trailing down into my stomach.

"With those shot glasses of Lucy's that lit up when you hit them on the table." Penny laughs, her hand toying with the red strings of beads around her neck. "We were such babies then."

"You know, she's pregnant again. Lucy."

Penny gives a short laugh. "Funny, isn't it. How our worst-case scenario is another woman's miracle."

"Do you think she's happy with Roger?"

Penny pauses in her culinary ministrations. "Where does that come from?"

"I don't know. When she came to visit at the hospital," I say, playing with one of my un-pierced earlobes. "She lights up like a fucking Christmas tree whenever Sam is around. And he . . ." I think of the way he held her when she cried.

"What?"

"Nothing. Like I said, must be the hospital smell."

Penny picks up her spoon, gives the sauce a decided stir. Sam and Connor appear behind us brandishing glasses of red wine. Connor hands one to Penny.

"I wasn't sure what you'd want," Sam says to me, the hint of apology in his voice spurring a pinch of annoyance in my stomach.

"Con, why don't you get her a vodka-tonic with some grenadine," Penny says, glancing at me. "That sound good?"

I nod. The music is louder now, thrumming in the background. Penny dances as she tends to the macaroni. Sam stands across the kitchen, sipping his wine, examining the line of cookbooks crammed onto the windowsill. He's wearing the navy blue V-neck sweater I got him for Christmas two years ago. I wonder if it's an attempt to be nice. Then the darker, bitter part of me wonders if he even remembers that I was the one who got him that sweater, and I'm angry again for no good reason.

"Just so you know," Connor says, returning with my drink. "I may have been a little heavy-handed." He adjusts his wire-rimmed glasses, looking about twelve years old despite the sparse goatee he's sporting. "So, proceed with caution."

"Thanks." I raise a mock toast to him and take a sip. It's fizzy and sweet, cold in my mouth and scorching on the way down, with the sharp, slightly medicinal tang of liquor. The burn spreads from my throat to my chest, and I cough into my palm.

"That's my girl," Penny says, clapping me gently on the back a couple of times. "Just like last time. We were hacking like a couple of tubercular old maids after that first shot."

Sam's eyes are on me now, with an intensity in his expression that I haven't seen much since I left the hospital. I think of the way his eyes would always drift to the screen next to my bed, watching my pulse ox drop a bit more every day.

"I'm fine," I say, raising my glass for a second time. "Just burns a little."

He nods, shaking off the look, though it occurs to me that this is what it will be like every time I catch a cold, every time I drink a sip of water too quickly, or eat something with too much pepper in it. I think of how it must be for him, like sleeping with a decaying stick of dynamite under his bed, never knowing if it might go off without warning. I take another sip of my drink, relishing in the fact that it's going straight to my head, driving out the heaviness there, wrapping everything in a fine mist, like breath fogging a windowpane. I don't want to have to think anymore.

We sit down to dinner in the mismatched chairs surrounding their dining room table, which is so crowded with candles we almost don't have room for our plates. Above us hangs the chandelier Penny fashioned out of the painted shards of cut-up aluminum cans. It would be worth an absolute fortune if she ever decided to sell it, but instead it hangs over the dining room table Penny picked up in a garage sale and painted a robin's-egg shade of blue. Penny has always had a hard time seeing the value in things; she would happily sell her paintings for five dollars on the street, instead of thousands of dollars in an art gallery, if I had not forbidden her to do so. It's probably the part of her I love the most, the part of her that is chronically confused by the arbitrary nature of worth and value and societal expectation. She is so different from me, in that way.

"Okay, let's do this," Connor says, raising his glass and nearly catching his sleeve on fire when his hand drifts too close to one of the tapers.

"To Hannah being sprung from the hospital," Penny says, her voice a soft humming, like warm honey. We raise our glasses high to escape the fire.

"Here, here," Sam says. And we drink and dig into our dinners, and laugh and drink some more. I can hear someone walking around in the apartment overhead and wonder if that person is lonely. It's hard to imagine loneliness, surrounded as I am by those who love me most.

"So what are the others in your group like?" Connor asks, as he gets up to change the record. Billie Holiday begins, and I feel the moment when all of us sink a bit lower into our seats, lulled into a near stupor by this combination of song and food and partial inebriation. I try a sip of Sam's wine when Connor cracks the second bottle, but I can only think of the smell of mineral spirits when I taste it and resort back to the sugary fizz of the drink I've been nursing all night.

"There's one, she's probably the most beautiful woman I've ever seen up close. And she's sort of funny, a little brash, not what you'd think. Easy to get along with, you know? It was sort of surprising. I always assumed that the really beautiful people didn't need anyone else."

Connor reaches over, tracing his fingers over the back of Penny's neck, and I feel a hot little stone of jealousy settle within my stomach.

"And there's a woman who spent eight years as a quadriplegic, totally paralyzed from the nose down. She's a little strange. But sweet in a sad sort of way. And then there's the asshole."

"The asshole?" Penny asks.

"My pet name for him," I say, running my palm over my forehead, trying to dispel some of the fuzziness that has collected on the other side of the hard bone beneath my skin. Trying to find the scar that isn't there anymore. My vision is blurring a bit. I have to pay attention to keep my eyes in focus. "David 'asshole' Jenkins."

There's a beat of silence. Everyone seems to sit back up in unison, drawn to attention by the common realization that I'm probably not allowed to say that particular name out loud. And yet, there it is.

"The congressman?" Penny asks, her eyes wide. "Like, that David Jenkins?"

"The Randian neoconservative Antichrist?" Sam asks, his lips drawing thin. "You didn't tell me that."

"I'm not supposed to tell anyone," I say, my head a flurry of alcohol and revelation. I clap a palm over my mouth, as if I can retrieve the words from the air and stuff them back into me.

"Shit. You'd think there would be some sort of litmus test for getting your life saved," Sam says. "Like how many times you've voted to cut Medicaid, that sort of thing."

"Sam." He doesn't meet my eyes.

"I'm kidding, you know I'm kidding," he replies.

"Sort of," Connor says, raising his glass.

"Yeah. Sort of," Sam replies, clinking glasses with him.

"So what almost did him in?" Penny asks.

"Baby." Connor's tone is a bit admonishing, though she's unfazed by it. "She isn't supposed to be telling us any of this."

"She already opened the door," Penny says, both hands raised, as if she's in front of a gun, feigning innocence. "What's the harm in taking a couple of steps through?" She looks at me, her expression daring me to spill. And I can never say no to Penny.

"Brain tumor," I reply.

"Nice," Penny says, nodding in mock approval. "That's respectable."

"But Con's right, I probably shouldn't be telling you all this. God, I signed like sixteen confidentiality agreements."

"Relax, Hannah, no one here is going to the papers," Penny says, reaching over and squeezing my wrist, shooting a pointed look at Sam. "All of this is off the record, of course."

"I'm not working, Penny."

"You're always working," she replies.

"Anyway, I would have thought cirrhosis would have gotten to him first," Sam says. "A buddy of mine went to Yale with him. Supposedly he liked to drink his weight in Kentucky bourbon to prove to all the rich kids he was a good ol' boy. Word out of Washington was he never really slowed down after he graduated."

"Maybe they should make drinking off-limits for SUBs too," Penny says. "You know, since we're throwing stones."

I make eye contact with Connor across the table, a silent plea to keep this dinner from becoming nothing but a pissing match between Sam and Penny. He takes my cue.

"So have you been back to your studio?" Connor asks.

"Not yet. But any day now, I think."

"Well, Penny's spending enough time in hers for the both of you. And now with the Daley Center thing . . ." Connor trails off as Penny shakes her head, a tiny movement, her lips pursed. Connor looks from her to me. I try to make my expression impassive, optimistic even, while everything is curdling with sour envy.

"You got it," I say and even manage a smile.

"I did," Penny replies, nodding.

"That's great, Pen. Really," I say, as Sam echoes my sentiment. Penny gives a little shrug, as if winning an emerging artist commission at the Daley Center is nothing significant. Yet everyone at the table knows what it will mean. It will mean a review in the *Tribune*, citywide exposure, and introductions with the heavyweights in Chicago's art scene. I think of my studio, of the canvases laying against one wall, how many times I imagined them hanging in the lobby of the Daley Center. I scull the rest of my drink, hoping to smother my jealousy with it, like water poured onto hot coals. The room seems to shudder a bit around me, as if it's trying to shake itself loose of its foundation.

Later, when the boys are huddled in the corner, fiddling with Connor's stereo system, Penny pulls me into the kitchen.

"Is David Jenkins the one you told me about? From the roof?" she asks, her hand encircling my upper arm, her grip not hard, but firm enough for me to know she means business. I purse my lips, and it's enough of an answer. She releases me, pressing her palm to her forehead, then brushing back the braided strands of hair that have fallen loose on her face.

"Jesus, Hannah."

"You know, I really don't need a lecture right now Pen." I mean the words to be sharp, but they come out so weary I'm shocked at how piteous I must appear. She nods, then turns away.

"I meant to tell you," she says, picking up the wine glasses and rinsing them out in the sink. "I just didn't want . . . I mean, it's no mystery to me what people in the program are probably saying right now. If the committee had the chance to see your work . . ."

"That's not true," I reply, grabbing a dish towel and fishing the dripping glasses out of the dish rack, desperate for something to do with my hands.

"Of course it is," Penny says. And it is, we both know it. Silence descends, and with it, a possibility I hadn't yet considered. The possibility that I might become the sort of person I've always secretly pitied, the office workers and day-to-day errand runners and stay-at-home mothers. People who go to Florida on vacation, people who have children because they don't know what else to do, people who will never have an article written about them. Ever since I was little, I was convinced my destiny belonged to something extraordinary, and I would be one of those privileged, shining few who would escape the commute and the monthly bills and the midlife crisis. My talent had only reinforced that idea. I never considered that I could fail just enough to slip into the most ordinary sort of life. The thought shudders through me, the thought that this moment might be the genesis of my ordinariness.

My hands slip, and the thin stem of one of Penny's wine glasses cracks against my palm.

I'm sensationally drunk by the time we leave, and Sam catches my arm, leading me down the endless stairs and out into the street. Cold air hits me, pelted with the first snow of the season, and I realize it's November, and that most of autumn has passed away without my notice. For some reason I think of an astronomy class I took where the professor described how the ozone layer would fall around us in white flakes if the sun ever went out. I imagine it, that the snow is really frozen molecules of ozone, that we're all going to perish, that it won't be just me who knows what it's like to be dying. I'm scared in an exhilarating way and I catch hold of Sam's coat as we walk. The warm, damp wool is scratchy on my cold hands. I try and catch a few snowflakes in my mouth, breathing them in, and they have a metallic tinge to them as they melt on my tongue.

Sam folds me into the car, gently, as if I'm something very delicate, an origami flower made of gauzy tissue paper, likely to tear and be ruined. I watch the quick, rhythmic clouds of my breath in the car as he gets in next to me. I reach across and brush my fingers over the light curl of the hair above his neck. He doesn't seem to notice, starting the car and turning on the heat. But as I persist, tracing my fingers onto the skin at the back of his neck, he twitches away, less a flinch than the way someone responds to a fly buzzing at his ear. There is annoyance in the movement, and it stings as I pull my hand back.

"Did you mean what you said at dinner?" I ask. "About there being a litmus test for getting your life saved?"

"It was a joke, Hannah."

"It wasn't very funny. Not to me."

He doesn't apologize. He doesn't say anything, he just cranks the wheel and pulls out onto the street.

"After all, what makes me so deserving, huh? My parents are out there bringing clean water to people in the desert, and what do I do?" I ask. "Nothing. Paint pictures. Lucky a computer picked my number, huh? If they thought like you, I might not be sitting here."

"You know that's not what I meant."

"Well it was a fucking shitty thing to say." I'm drunk, and my eloquence is gone.

"Fine, Hannah. If you want to sit there and try to pick a fight, go ahead. You're just angry because . . ."

"Because what?"

He pauses.

"You could at least try and be happy for her."

I know he means Penny. I bristle at the accusation. "I *am* happy for her."

"But not more than you are sad for yourself. You should have seen your face when you found out."

"That's not why I'm angry," I say, feeling wretched and small, a spoiled child who hasn't gotten her way. I think of his arms around Lucy, the way he avoids touching me, waking up to find him gone.

"No one said you couldn't have finished your pieces. I could have brought you your stuff at the hospital."

"That's not why I'm angry, Sam," I repeat, feeling him drag me away from what I want to talk about.

"Of course you are, you're a terrible loser because you've never had any practice at it. You didn't have to stop painting when you got sick. You could have kept going."

"Jesus Christ, you don't get it at all," I say, my voice suddenly too loud for the little interior of our car. "You've never understood how it works."

"So explain it to me," he says. He's angry; all of his consonants are sharp.

"I can't just pick up a brush and paint. I have to be alone and be able to think. Do you have any idea the effort that goes in to it? On a good day, a really good day, it takes everything in me. You think I could do that in the hospital with nurses walking in and out and machines beeping and people around all the time? You're absolutely fucking clueless."

"You always have excuses," he says. "What about now? You're not sick anymore, Hannah. Everything can't be focused on you all the time anymore."

"I'll stop acting like I'm sick when you stop treating me that way," I say, forgetting to temper my desire to hurt him. It doesn't outweigh my desire to have everything go back to the way it was. I know, even drunk, that I can't have both.

He pulls the car to the side of the street, under the L tracks, a fast move that makes me jerk so much my seat belt locks up. He kills the engine. I think he's going to yell at me, but when he speaks his voice is so controlled it's almost shocking.

"I used to have nightmares about you," he says, shutting his eyes, letting his head fall back onto the headrest. His neck is exposed, like prey, offering itself. "Nightmares about finding you dead when I woke up in the morning, or when I got home from work. I would stay up at night to make sure you were still breathing. You cannot possibly expect it not to have an impact. It didn't just happen to you, Hannah. It's not fair."

"None of this is fair," I say. I want to tell him that I was the one in that hospital bed. I was the one being invaded by tubes and torn by pain, suffocating on dry land. I was the one who knew what it felt like to be dying, slowly. But these seem like horrible victories to claim over someone I have loved for so long.

"You can never forgive weakness in anyone, can you?" he says. "If I faltered, even just for a moment . . ." He trails off. My heart picks up speed. *Say it,* I think. *Just say it, once, tell me the truth. Don't make me ask.* But he shakes his head, running a hand over his face, his exhaustion showing. "But you never forgive anything, do you?"

I think of Lucy. Of watching Lucy cry into his shirt, of the depth of their secrecy, which I am only beginning to understand. I have loved Sam so long for his goodness, and he has loved me just as long despite my lack of it. He should know my answer already.

"No," I say, leaning back into my seat, the only light in the car emanating from the dashboard clock. The windshield and windows are thickening with snow. It creates an eerie quiet inside the car, as if we've driven into a giant snowbank or been buried under an avalanche, irreparably cut off from the rest of the world. There's a certain hum in the air, the kind of low static a record makes when its last song ends, and I almost regret it when Sam starts the car, turns the heat up. He flicks on the windshield wipers and the world reappears beyond the glass, and I'm almost surprised it's still there.

Even amid the hum of the car's engine and the rhythmic motion of the wipers scratching across the windshield, the silence has reawakened between us. I can't say anything to him. I don't know what I would say if I could. Some form of apology, maybe. If not for getting cancer, then for not cutting him enough slack in its aftermath. For putting him through this again, after he watched his father die of Parkinson's when he was too young to protect himself from it. For being the one who was saved, instead of his father. For not being able to forgive.

But I can't find a way into those words. I don't know how to have empathy for someone else when I barely know who I am. I can hardly navigate the smallest moments in my world, the simplest things, the eating, breathing, sleeping moments that everyone else seems to be able to ignore. Still I get the impulse to wake from a heavy dream, as if I've suddenly remembered that none of this is possible, that it's all wrong, that it can't be happening to me. Still I expect to jerk awake and find the life I remember waiting, unaltered, like the world beyond the windshield.

# Linda

The grocery store is so huge and bright and full of people that I think I might pass out. Aisle upon endless aisle is stocked with thousands of products, all with their own brightly colored packaging, leaving barely enough room for people to snake their shopping carts through. Music clamors over everything. I feel sick. For so long, I've been used to processing only one thing at a time that I'm unable to face this onslaught of stimuli. Things flash in and out of my peripheral vision. Somewhere in the store, there's a child screaming and the sound shreds my nerves. I didn't remember how terrifying the world was, at its full size. I follow Tom and Jack and Katie in our little convoy as Tom pushes the shopping cart and the kids load it with groceries. There's a practiced nature to this mayhem, and I imagine that they've done exactly this, every weekend, for years. I follow behind, watching them, getting in the way of everyone around me. I seem to always be in someone's path, blocking the item he or she is trying to reach. I bump into more than one person and forget that I should apologize when that sort of thing happens. I'm so used to being in one place, and having the pieces of my world orbit me like tiny moons, that sometimes I forget that the people around me can even see me.

Being home, being around people, my children, is an entirely different type of difficulty from being in the hospital. I'm the routine-breaker, the woman who staggers out of bed at odd hours, who is preoccupied by the textures of things, losing the threads of conversations as I run my hands over the objects and surfaces around me. Tom makes them change the channel so I can watch *Stratford*

*Pines* on the flat-screen. I am the intruder, stopping hushed conversations between Katie and Tom when I enter a room. I thought Katie would be the easy one when I returned home, the one who would remember me from the years before the accident. But instead it's Jack, my baby, who brightens when he sees me, who wants to show me his collection of Ninja Turtles figures, who needs me with an insistence that borders on the absurd, stranger that I am. While Katie has stopped bursting into tears in front of me, she remains remote, considering me like some foreign cousin who has come to visit, someone she understands little and likes even less.

We're stopped in the cereal aisle. There's a log jam of carts right in the middle, and Tom is waiting patiently for his turn to weave through while the kids are scooting around him, trying to decide if they want the cereal with the pirate on the box, or the one with the leprechaun. They get to pick one box of cereal a week, Tom told me, as if he were relaying vital, top-secret parenting information. Once it's gone, they're back to corn flakes for breakfast. I nodded, thinking about the books I used to read on nutrition and child development, the way I had homemade granola and almond milk for them in the mornings, instead of sugary bits of puffed rice, dyed bright colors. My former self could have been such a good mother, I think, if she were only given the chance. Now I am lost in a sea of fluorescent lighting and flashing machines that distribute coupons hanging from shelves. I shut my eyes, willing it all away.

When I open them again, they catch on a display of chocolate bars wrapped in colored foil. Labels promise all manner of deliciousness—caramel and crispy rice and peanut butter. It's the sort of thing I never would have allowed myself in my previous life, back when I counted calories and ran five miles a day and bought organic produce. But I imagine it now, the rich sweetness of chocolate and caramel, and saliva collects under my tongue. I want it, insistently. I want to cram the whole bar of candy into my mouth and chew it until my jaw aches. I want it with a vigor that's almost sexual, a riotous feeling, something I don't want to ignore for fear it will disappear. I take a quick glance, left and right. Shoppers compare prices and peer at the nutrition labels on boxes of cereal. Tom has disappeared toward the other end of the aisle with the kids in tow. No one is looking at me. My fingertips spark with blood and excitement as I reach toward the display, plucking one of the bars from its place and jamming it into the pocket of my jacket. Someone turns toward me, so I pick up another bar and pretend to read the nutrition label on the back. I scowl, and put it back in its place, as if it has profoundly disappointed me. Connie would be so proud if she saw my performance.

It's only when I move down the aisle, fingering the prize in my pocket, being careful not to crinkle the foil wrapping for fear of giving myself away, that I realize I'm grinning. Excitement pours through me, a rush that makes me want to skip out of the store, run as fast as my new legs will carry me, like a dog running for the horizon and never stopping. I'm nearly effervescent with the thrill of my crime. But I remember the importance of the act, and I shake the smile from my face before Tom catches sight of me again.

"I thought we'd lost you there," he says.

"Nearly did," I reply, trying my best to look mystified and adrift in the cacophony of my surroundings. Jack runs up, jumping on the end of the cart and tossing a box of cereal in, holding on as Tom wheels him forward toward the end of the aisle.

"I decided on Lucky Charms this week," Jack says to me, and it's clearly a decision that has taken some real effort.

"Oh, I see," I say, nodding, wondering at how to respond to something as simple and inconsequential as a box of cereal. I wonder if this is why other parents constantly reprimand their children for the smallest of infractions, for running or speaking too loudly or demanding too much attention, because they don't know any other way of speaking to them. Katie comes up and drops her box of cereal into the cart, Wheaties, of course. Katie is on the basketball team at school and everything in her world seems to revolve around the sport. I try and recall how I was at that age and can't quite remember back that far, now that everything has been clouded by the accident.

"She doesn't care about your cereal," Katie says to Jack, turning her accusatory eyes in my direction.

"Katie, give it a rest," Tom says, handing her the list. "Go see if you can pick out some eggs, okay?" Katie snatches the list from him and walks off, Jack following close behind her. Tom sighs, but says nothing. After all, this is well-worn territory for us at this point, in these months since I've been home.

I eat the candy later, in Tom's upstairs office, while he's helping the kids with their homework. I smuggle it out of my coat pocket and tuck it into the back of my jeans before I scurry upstairs. It's half-melted when I pull it out, but I don't care. I watch the setting sun from my window, the window in Tom's office, and peel back the foil wrapper with the carefulness of an archaeologist uncovering an ancient treasure. I don't eat it all in one bite, no, now the craving has transformed into a need to savor, to draw out the deliciousness of my crime for as long as possible. I take small bites, rabbit bites, letting the chocolate melt in my mouth and the caramel stick to my teeth. My body sings with it, the taste of it, I can almost feel the shiver of chemical pleasure run up and down my spine. *This is mine*, I think. A secret. I've made this mine.

I stole a pair of panties from the sale bin at the Gap once when I was a teenager. It was the only other time I've ever stolen anything. They were black and lacy, with a little fake gemstone in the front, and I yanked the tags off and stuffed them into my coat pocket while I was pretending to try on a pair of jeans. My friends were with me, and we walked out of the store in a little giggling pack. Out in the parking lot we compared our haul—a camisole, a pair of earrings, a tube of lip balm, my thong—and congratulated ourselves on being subversive and rebellious and young. I never told them how painful it was for me, walking out of that store with my sweaty hand balled around that knot of black lace in my pocket. There was no thrill for me; instead my fear was colossal, even after we were out of the store and into the fresh air. I was certain the very moment I thought I was safe would be the moment in which a security guard would clap me on the shoulder and demand that I turn out my pockets. It wasn't until I was home, stuffing the contraband into the top drawer of my dresser and shutting it hard, that I began to feel normal again. I never wore those panties. They seemed to forever be a symbol of my own frailty, up until the point when Tom threw them away with the rest of my underwear.

I knew shoplifting was supposed to be exciting. My friends did it a lot, pilfering makeup and jewelry and even the occasional T-shirt from a thrift shop or a department store. Any time I received a birthday gift from one of them, I was pretty confident it had been brought to me by way of someone's pocket or the inside of someone's bra. I even knew a girl in college who, during the course of our freshman year, stole twelve cookbooks from the Barnes & Noble near campus. When I asked her why she only stole cookbooks, she shrugged.

"Why does anyone do anything?" she asked in return.

But now I understand it. Now, in the office at the top of the stairs, licking melted chocolate off the tips of my fingers, I finally know what it is to steal something and like it. It's not about what you steal. It's not even about escaping the prospect of getting caught. It's about cracking open a little sliver of freedom for yourself. It's slipping into that other world, the one in my head, where nothing bad ever really happens and there are no rules at all. I sit in that room and feel like I've finally traveled somewhere no one can follow, not my doctors or my family or the people I knew in my former life. And I'm the only one who knows it.

Like all good secrets, the story of my adventure begs to be told. I whisper it to Connie as we sit waiting for our meeting to begin. She grins a little, her eyebrows furrowing, and she looks so radiant I want to kiss her if only to see what it would feel like.

"You stole a candy bar? What is this, Mayberry?"

"It was delicious. Maybe the most delicious thing I've ever eaten," I say, shutting my eyes to remember the sheer sensation of it.

"Careful, John Dillinger, this week it's candy bars. Next week you'll be boosting cars."

I giggle, unfazed by Connie's usual surliness. The meeting begins the way it always does, with Dr. Bernard asking if anyone has anything new to share. Connie shakes her head a little to warn me off sharing my story with the group. But of course that's not my intention. I know the thing about secrets, they're like pie—the more slices you share with other people, the less you have for yourself.

It's David who clears his throat. "I uh . . ." he falters as everyone turns toward him. It seems uncharacteristic, for him to be uncomfortable with the attention. "I'm beginning to think my son isn't as okay as I thought he was," David says, elbows on his knees, his hands folded in front of him.

"What makes you say that?" Dr. Bernard asks.

"A lot of things, I guess," he replies, and then he pauses, dragging the fingers of one hand through his short-cropped hair. "When we told him about my cancer, about the transfer, he took it fine. Better than fine, in fact. The boy didn't shed a tear. I was so proud of him, for taking it standing up like that. My son, tough as nails."

I watch as David's face twitches from an expression of pride to something quite the opposite.

"But then he threw up at school the next day. Out of nowhere, in the middle of English class, I guess. I don't know, it was my wife who went to get him. And he's been getting into fights. I thought it was just kid's stuff, but now he's been picking fights with older boys, bigger boys. I think that maybe he's trying to convince me he's tough."

"Does he know that's important to you?" Hannah asks. David looks at her a long time before he answers. It's curious, to watch David and Hannah interact. They seem to have a language all to themselves, one that I can't understand.

"I used to get the shit kicked out of me as a kid," David says, looking at Hannah. Unflinching. "You should have seen where I come from. Dirt roads. Twenty-year-old cars. The best place to eat was the Arby's in the next town over. And I was small. The worst thing you could be in that town was small. They wouldn't just take your lunch money, they'd take your shoes. There was a time when the toughest part of me were the soles of my feet." He pulls a hand through his hair. "Of course being tough is important to me. I'm afraid my son's childhood won't prepare him for something like that. Or worse," he gestures around the room, at all of us beleaguered souls, "it won't prepare him for something like this."

# Hannah

I've been renting a small studio in Wicker Park since my fourth year as an undergrad at the Art Institute. The rent comes out of an artist's grant I won for my senior thesis, a series of paintings of women being carried off by birds, to which one of the Art Institute's many donors took a liking. The studio is small, in that it allows room for an easel and a stool, a few containers of art supplies, a set of wireless speakers, about thirty canvases, a coffee maker, and a mini fridge, while still allowing just enough space for me to turn around, provided the door is shut. The window opens about four inches, too, which is useful in summer because there's no air conditioning. And sometimes it's useful in winter as well, because the heat tends to go berserk, which leaves me painting in my underwear more than I'd prefer. And I love it, my studio, perhaps more than I've ever imagined loving any place in my whole life.

I have to push hard on the door to get it open at first. It warps in the summers, when the damp heat swells the soft wood in its frame, and it never seems to return to its correct shape come winter. When I put my weight into it the door pops open, and I'm face to face with myself again. The painting is still there. Of course it is.

I look scared, my large eyes a mixture of yellow ochre and burnt sienna, overlaid with shimmers of titanium white and warm gray and hooker's green to show their fullness, wet with tears. My hair is dark—Payne's gray, Mars black, and burnt umber—falling in silky waves around my shoulders. I think of the hours I used to spend at the salon under the dryers, breathing that harsh ammonia smell as the chemicals soaking my hair did their work, how straight and glossy it was before the transfer, not the halo of tight curls it is now. My skin is pink blush and Naples yellow, flesh tint, a touch of pistachio, with raw umber and a hint of sap green blended in the shadows under my eyes. There's softness at my jaw, my cheekbones don't jut as much from the smooth surface of my skin, my face more rounded than it is now. My lips are cadmium scarlet and silk purple, dried and cracked with silver and process magenta. There's a little ultramarine there, too, in my mouth. To show sickness. To show a lack of oxygen. There I am. That's the face I remember. That's the scared little thing still living inside of me.

It was a kind of therapy, at the time. Sam's idea, of course. A self-portrait, a way of preserving what I was, in case the transfer eclipsed something or ruined something. Sam never said those things out loud, of course, he would never have vocalized the fears we shared. But when he suggested it, I knew what he was getting at.

And it helped, a bit, there at the end, in my last days before the pain became too great and I went into the hospital for good, to wait out the weeks until the transfer. It felt like I was capturing something of myself in a bottle, corking it tight, waiting to open it and breathe it in when I was on the other side of the cancer and the transfer and all the fear. Now, looking at the girl in the painting, I want to tell her that the fear isn't gone. It's still here but different, more diffuse, maybe. More systemic, not just sitting in the pit of my stomach as it always had. Now it sinks into my skin cells and the enamel of my teeth, my toes and the space between my hip bones.

I take the painting from the easel and put it with a group of others, facing the wall. I can't look at her now. I sit on my stool, in front of my easel, the position that used to leave my back stiff and impossibly sore, full of knots that Sam would work on with his thumbs while we watched TV. I remember that feeling, that sweet, necessary pain, though I've never felt it, not in this body. I've never woken with a stiff neck. Never cracked my knuckles or my back. I can bend over from standing and place my palms flat on the ground. I'm no longer in the habit of crossing my legs, or slouching, or tucking my hair behind my ear. My mannerisms have been scrubbed away, replaced with a profoundly sterling body, capable of things I haven't yet thought to ask of it.

I find a large canvas and set it on the easel, adjusting the mirror clipped above it until I can see my reflection in the small, round pane of glass. I flick on the light next to it and pick up a pencil.

Dread drives its way through me. Where do I even begin? How can I take it all in, when my own face still looks so foreign to me, even after all these months? How do I draw myself when I still see disjointed features, a Picassoian sort of creature, every time I look in the mirror? Then the answer comes, as it always does, as simple as a breath, as plain as a handful of earth. You start with the eyes. Always, start with the eyes.

And then it's easier, knowing that I don't have to do it all at once. Knowing that the fear comes and goes in waves and all I must do is wait for it to recede before I charge on. I rough in the outlines of my eyes in four contoured strokes, two for the upper edges, two for the lower. The width of an invisible third eye is between them, showing me how far apart they should be spaced. Then the bridge of the nose, its rounded underside, the nostrils. The edges of the mouth align perfectly with the center of the irises, and I rough in the outline of its downturned fullness. Then the eyebrows, the ears, and how strangely it all comes into proportion, as if every human being were created using the same map, the same architectural schematics. When I finish with the faint pencil lines I begin mixing colors.

I pick up a brush, wetting the tip and dipping it into the paint, then applying it to the canvas, just the way I have a thousand times before. The brush feels clumsy in my hand. I watch the inky wet tones seep into the canvas, the taut fibers inhale them. I paint the undersides of my eyes, the sunken patches below my cheekbones, the shadows around my nose and below my bottom lip and under my chin. Stepping back, the image looks skeletal with only the darks colored in. I mix middle tones, layering them over the foundation of darkness I've laid down. I rough some taupe into my hair, the basis of my rich brunette, a frizz of curls that now falls to my shoulders. It occurs to me for the first time that I haven't cut it since the transfer, which means it has never been cut at all.

As I work I remember the art room in my high school, watching my teacher's impossibly weathered hands, the paint that clung to the hair on his arms, the gray fullness of his beard. I always imagined in another life he would have been a fisherman, sketching in his bunk while being tossed by rough waves, instead of an art teacher in a suburban private school. He had the kind of face that made you imagine the wind.

I make tea while the paint sets by running hot water through my coffee maker, and it's so bitter without cream and sugar that I can't drink it. I return to the canvas and give myself skin, give myself burnt umber eyes, and rose-hued lips, and dark eyebrows that dominate the jagged moonstone of my face. She still looks skeletal, I find, even with eyes and lips and pink cheeks. Even with dark hair. She looks flawless and tired. A Victorian girl shut up in a tower. A waif. Primed for destruction.

And she's not right. Not even close. There's no life in it. There is nothing close to inspired, nothing close to what I used to be able to pull from a paintbrush. Nothing close to what it takes to get in to the School of the Art Institute of Chicago, or earn a prestigious artist's grant while a student there. I want to burn it, but the painting isn't the problem.

I call Penny. I need her eyes, her honesty, the way I did in the hospital. She must hear the chord of panic in my voice, because she leaves a full grocery cart in the middle of Whole Foods to drive over. I chew all of my perfect fingernails off waiting for her to arrive.

"Oh, Hannah," she says from the doorway, as soon as she sees it. That soulless painting.

"Yeah," I say from my seat, feeling my bottom lip tighten over my upper, the tension in my jaw keeping everything else inside me at bay for the moment. "It's gone."

She shakes her head. "It'll come back, this is your first try."

"I don't feel it anymore. It's one of the many things I don't feel now. I know what a dry spell feels like. This . . ." I swallow hard, trying to clear a path for the words. "It's gone. My muse is hitchhiking down the fucking Jersey turnpike. Gone."

"Honey, it's just your first try."

"Maybe it's because it's not even my goddamn face." I pull the first painting away from the wall, shoving it onto the easel beside the second. The contrast is staggering, both in the quality of the work and the subject of the portraits. It's painful to see them this way, my two selves. It's painful to see that, even though the first is a brilliant painting, the second is clearly the more beautiful subject. Penny sees it too. It's a bereft look. This seems like the end to a horrible fairy tale, the girl who traded all of her talent for a pretty face.

Penny offers to drive me home, but I need to be alone. To think, to wonder who I am, what I should be, if not a painter. The question has never really occurred to me until now; even in high school it was always apparent that I would be an artist, that my life would never be fit for anything else. Through everything, through the screaming matches I had with my parents about my disinterest in an Ivy League education, through Lucy's quiet, placating disapproval, I never felt a single moment of doubt. Now that certainty feels so foolish it sours my stomach. I think of the practical things that I can do with a bachelor's in 2D Art and Design, and most of an MFA from the Art Institute. I assume I could probably get a job at Starbucks. I blink back tears as I climb the stairs to the Blue line.

Maybe I should start over entirely, I think, as the train rattles up and the doors squeak open, releasing a gush of stale, slightly rancid air from inside. Become something that doesn't take much skill, or education. An office assistant, or one of those hippie massage therapists, or a court reporter. I try to imagine myself in a pantsuit, showing up to some fluorescent office that smells like burned coffee and air freshener.

But then another image overtakes me, like a veil of fog eclipsing my vision. Me in an expensive dress, with perfectly manicured nails and Chanel earrings framing my face. Me in pumps, pulling an oversized SUV up to a school's pickup line. Wearing a sweater that strains over my swollen belly, making a cake for Sam's birthday. Going into real estate, or interior decorating, or starting a blog about parenthood. It's a life I've been drifting toward for the past four years; after I took out my nose ring and quit dying my hair, after I let Lucy take me shopping, after I convinced myself that only kids marked time with tattoos and wore clothing with paint stains and holes in them. It's a life I could enter as easily as one drifts off to sleep. I could marry Sam, I could have his children. I could become the perfect housewife and do charity work and paint mediocre paintings that Sam would insist on hanging in our home. It would require nothing of me but to remain on the course my life has already taken. It would require nothing, save to forget the questions that I've been afraid to ask Sam, to repress the memories of waking up in the hospital and finding him gone, of seeing the effortless way he and Lucy smile at each other. It would be easy, to forget who I was before. The artist, the girl with all the talent, the one with the sharp edges.

Sam is making dinner when I get home. I'm exhausted; all I want is to fill our bathtub with piping hot water and submerge myself up to my ears, but he must have heard me come in because he appears in the kitchen doorway.

"Hey. Where have you been?"

I drag myself toward the kitchen, and its stainless-steel appliances, its huge basin sink, its chrome-and-glass splendor. I realize I'm hungry, and it only adds to my exhaustion.

"I stopped by my studio," I say. Sam brightens immediately.

"Yeah? How did it go?"

"Fine."

"Did you get some work done?" he asks, lifting a lid off a pot and stirring its contents. Curry, by the smell of it. It's hugely pungent, a hot aroma, both familiar and shockingly foreign to me.

"A little," I reply, fishing in the cabinet for a bag of pretzels and popping a few into my mouth.

"Dinner will be ready soon," Sam says, not really looking at me. I take another handful of pretzels.

"You really think curry was a great choice?"

"You love curry."

"Loved, Sam." I rustle the plastic bag in my hands pointedly.

"You can at least try it, Hannah. I'm getting a little sick of pasta and peanut butter sandwiches."

"I never said you had to eat what I do."

Sam sighs, rubbing at the back of his neck with tense fingers. "Did you do any painting while you were there?"

"A little," I repeat. I don't want to talk about this, not yet, not while it's still fresh. Not in a kitchen with so many sharp objects around.

"And how did that go?"

"Really well, actually," I say, yanking open the fridge and grabbing a container of cold pasta from earlier in the week. I pop the lid off and dig in with a fork, leaning against the counter. "Another couple weeks and I'll be able to steal that Daley Center show away from Penny."

Sam is calm as he opens the cabinet above him, handing me a plate. "You knew this was going to take time." I hate the way he says it, telling me all of the things I'm supposed to know. You know I had the flu. You know the doctors wouldn't let me see you. You know. You know. I set the plate down too hard on the counter and it breaks with a bright, sharp sound. A couple of pieces skitter along the counter.

"Goddamn it, Hannah," he says, dropping the spoon he'd been using to stir the curry and clattering a lid onto the pan.

"I've got it," I say, trying to preclude his interference by grabbing up the pieces myself. But a sharp edge presses into my palm with such light precision that my skin opens, and suddenly my hand is cupping a map of blood as it spreads through the lines of my palm. The pain is sort of staggering, catching me off guard. I'd forgotten physical pain, in these days since the hospital. It strikes me how delicate this body is, with its new skin and its clumsiness and all of its nerve endings turned up to full volume. Like a child. Something vulnerable, something that must be protected.

Then Sam's got me by the wrist, pulling me over to the sink, turning on the tap full-blast and sticking my hand underneath it. The map of blood is blown away by that gust of water. The pain reaches its way up my arm. He turns off the tap and crushes a dish towel into my hand.

"I know," he says, and then pauses, as if collecting his thoughts. "I know this hasn't been easy. Fuck, it's been an absolute nightmare. But I want things back the way they were, and I know you want that too. We just have to find a way to get there."

I think of the lines in my palm. It's a different map now. And I think of all the territory we would have to retrace to get to where we were. I think of David, and Connie, and Linda. I think of waking in the hospital and finding Sam gone. *I'm a pioneer,* I want to say. My eyes will always be on the horizon, charging forward and making a home wherever I land. Pioneers don't go back.

# David

"Burt," I say into the webcam on my laptop. "How the hell are you?" The blurry, hangdog face of Burt Leeland moves closer to his own camera, filling up more of the window on my screen. I hate seeing the little image of myself nested in the bottom corner, looking even less like me than all of the mirrors. Of all the conference calls I've done since the transfer, S&J's CEO is the first person to warrant a camera on my end.

"Worse than you, looks like. You look like they shaved ten years off your life."

"It's all this clean living," I reply. "Beth won't even let me have a celebratory cigar."

"I'm glad to hear this . . . treatment has done you such good," Burt replies. I've always liked him, this humble billionaire. Both because he is so unlike the insufferable power-players that permeate the private sector and because he's savvy enough to use his affability to his full advantage. He's a snake, like the rest of us. But he's the snake you want to play a round of golf with, and he tips his caddies better than anyone I know.

"It's miraculous." I clear my throat. "Listen, Burt. When everything was happening so quickly, when I first got diagnosed, I'm not sure if I ever properly thanked you."

"Your wife sent us a basket of things. Caviar. Good wine. Tickets to the opera. My wife appreciated it a great deal."

"I'm glad. Beth has always been better than me at those sorts of things. I would be sitting around, wondering what to get for the billionaire who has everything."

Burt sits back in his chair, his hands folding over the round bulb of his paunch. "That's the thing. There is something I can't get for myself. And it certainly isn't opera tickets."

My foot begins tapping, as if of its own accord. Maybe I don't have full control over this body yet; I'd banished all outward signs of nervousness from my old body years ago. "I expected there might be something," I reply.

"Listen, David. I'm tremendously glad that everything worked out for you, and that I was able to play some small part in your recovery, I really am." He taps his fingers on his stomach, but I know it's not nervousness. This man doesn't fear anyone, certainly not me. It's a show, a physical tick to make him appear weaker than he is. To soften the blow.

"I appreciate that." I keep an eye on my reflection in the little window at the bottom of my screen. The trick to these sorts of exchanges is to appear as unfazed by them as you'd like to be. It's the sort of thing that takes practice, but luckily the one thing that the transfer hasn't stripped from me is my poker face.

"The thing is, I'm going to need the FDA to vote against it. The whole program. It can't be approved, not this time."

"SUBlife?" Sweat seeps into my shirt, one of my best shirts.

"S&J's pharmaceutical branch is three months away from developing our own drug for, whatever it is you call it, when they move the memories over. The drug they gave you so the memories would implant in the new body. If ours gets approved, it'll be worth more than the rest of S&J combined. But if the FDA approves the procedure as it stands now, well, there won't be any use for our drug, now will there?"

"Sir, what you're asking is completely beyond my reach," I say, but he waves a dismissive hand.

"I know you have a guy at the FDA. Richard something-or-other. You two went to college together, pledged the same fraternity. You got him his job."

"Rick Preston." My voice sounds hollow. I try to remember

what I told Jackson about not selling the farm, about not giving everything over to this man. I never considered it would be something like this.

"Right. So what I need you to do is to put a call in to this guy and assure him, in that way you do so well, that your committee will eviscerate the FDA's budget if SUBlife passes. Blame your religion if you need to. I don't care. Just kill it."

"If I do what you're asking . . . It will be years before SUBlife can go back up for approval. All of it, the whole pilot program, all of it will have to be done again, at huge expense. This could irreparably damage the program, sir." I think of Hannah. Of Linda and Connie. None of them could have waited years. Neither could I.

Burt Leeland leans forward in his chair, his hands flat on the desk in front of him.

"Son, as I understand it, you're only sitting there breathing because of me. But if that's not enough to motivate you to return a hell of a favor, well, I'm sure your chief of staff has informed you that human cloning wouldn't poll very well in your district. Seems you have a bunch of religious fanatics voting for you, who are apt to vote for someone else if they catch wind of your . . . status."

And in that moment, there is nothing to be done. I think of my career, of the impossible prospect of going up against a man as powerful as this. And I know that if there is any of the redeemed man left in me, the good man, the one who could have changed, my next words will kill him stone dead.

"Of course," I say into the camera, with the most sincere look of admiration I can muster. "It's not a problem, sir." I can see myself in the little nested window on the bottom of my screen, and for a moment I look exactly like my son.

# March

# Hannah

Even though I'm late to Thursday's meeting, I shouldn't be surprised to find David out front, smoking a cigarette. At first I'm appalled that he would flout the rules so openly, that he would risk cancer in his new body after it had already taken root in his old one. But then I remember, it's David. And David does what he wants.

"You could get kicked out of the program for that, you know," I say. He glances up and smiles. It makes me glad, foolishly glad, that he's so happy to see me.

"I have some friends in very high places," he replies. "I'm not worried." I consider for a moment if I should hurry inside to where Connie and Linda are surely waiting, but too much of me wants to remain with David, who doesn't care if he's late. As if I'm inoculated against any blame if I'm with him.

"You're one of those guys, aren't you?" I ask, leaning against the brick wall beside him, enjoying its rough familiarity on the skin of my arms, as I always enjoy sensations that have not changed for me since the transfer.

"What guys?"

"The ones who could get away with anything," I reply. "And took it for granted. Like they didn't know that the world wasn't engineered to revolve around them."

"I'd wager a girl who looks like you could get away with quite a bit of trouble."

I shrug, feeling the first pulse of a blush swarm up my neck. I motion for the cigarette, all the while wondering what it is about this man that brings out everything foolish in me. This man, who believes in all the things I abhor, whom I don't even particularly like. He shakes his head, holding the cigarette a little farther away from me.

"Absolutely not," he says. "Do I really have to give you, of all people, an antismoking lecture?"

"I can't paint," I say. "Reckless things, remember?"

"Since the transfer?" he asks, and I nod.

"It doesn't make any sense. It's not my hands, I can hold a paintbrush. It's something else. Something didn't transfer over."

"Fuck," he says, handing over the cigarette. I take it and inhale, and the sizzling heat of it floats into my limbs. I feel a little dizzy, though I'm not sure if it's the sudden onslaught of nicotine, or if it's the fact that I haven't slept since I visited my studio, or if it's David. I hand it back to him.

"Good as you remember?" he asks.

"Nothing is as good as I remember," I reply. He nods, but he looks away. I wonder if I've admitted something I shouldn't have, a truth that all of us have been trying to avoid.

"You know, my handwriting is different since I had to relearn it," David says, finally. "Maybe it's like that with your painting, maybe it was some mixture of muscle memory and years of practice that made you paint the way you used to."

I hold out both of my hands, palms up, considering the lines on them. The cut from the broken plate is a thin pink seam along my pale skin. I wonder if it will leave a scar. My first scar.

"I've been thinking a lot about those articles you read where people get lung or heart transplants and take on personality traits of their donors. You know, how they might crave a food they never liked before, or suddenly get the urge to listen to a specific type of music? It makes me wonder if it isn't just about the parts of our brain that store memory. I wonder how much of what made me a painter lived in that body, and not just in my head."

"Like maybe if someone got your heart, they would be able to paint the way you used to?" he asks. He reaches forward, brushing a curl of hair off my face. It feels like crossing a line, when he touches me. He's still holding the cigarette between his fingers. Flecks of white ash fall into my hair. I think of Sam, then, how difficult it is for us to look at each other now.

"I think maybe they would be able to do a lot of things that I can't anymore."

His apartment is dark when we arrive, even though it's not quite evening. All of the shades are drawn. It's like we're underground, and the sun is somewhere far away. It only adds to my feeling of disorientation, this inability to judge time or direction. Even in the dimness I can see the money in this place, the same way you can spot an expensive suit. My eyes are drawn to the walls, where huge black and white photos hang in heavy frames.

"Who's your decorator?" I ask. I recognize a photo, one of a series by Carla Abramson that came through the Museum of Contemporary Photography a few months back. It was a study of decay, the corners of the city where the relics of the Industrial Age have been allowed to deteriorate. This particular photo shows the peeling metal of rusted L tracks.

"My wife," he replies, remaining in the entryway as I cross to the frame. "You like it?"

I shrug. "I know the photographer a little. I was never really impressed with her work, but these aren't bad, for what they are." I glance around. "Your wife isn't a fan of paintings?"

"That's my preference, actually," he says. "I'm a fan of the real world. I never had much patience for someone else's interpretation of it." The reflection of movement in the glass catches my eye, and I realize he's crossed the room to stand behind me. "This is normally the point where I would offer you a drink, but . . ." he trails off.

"Right," I say. I don't turn to him. I watch him, the dark silhouette in the glass, as he steps toward me, closing the gap between us until we are one muddled shape against the dim half-light of the window. I shut my eyes before he reaches me. I shut my eyes, and wish they had picked someone else to be saved. Someone good, someone like Sam. Not me, not David. It is a terrible mistake, to play god and save the wrong people.

It has been so long since I've been touched that my body is already alight with energy, every hair standing on end, in the moment before his chest presses into my back, in the moment before his hands slip under the hem of my shirt. It has been so long that it feels like I've never been touched at all. And then the realization comes in that fleeting moment: I have never been touched. Not this version of me.

I have only vague memories of my first time, the first time that came before this one, the feeling of lying on my back in a dorm room with a football game playing in the background, turned up loud so his roommates wouldn't hear us. How comical it seemed even at the time, that it should be so willfully unromantic, as if engineered to be a story my friends and I would cringe at in the years to come. Everything about it, the boy, the room, even the pain, eventually blended into nothing but a vague sense of disappointment within my memory. The shocking insignificance of it proved to be the one memorable aspect of that night.

This time, this second time, is quite different. The strangeness of it is not gone, not when this body still feels so foreign to me, so remote. At times it feels like I'm observing some kind of animal, watching its behaviors and marveling at its reactions, its twitches and whimpers and slow unfurling, as if it were a being wholly separate from me. Its desires surprise me, catch me off guard, because they are not what I remember. I react to the smallest things, his hand hooking behind my knee, or that first icy breath of air when he divests me of my underwear. His mouth between my shoulder blades is enough to make me bite into the pillow. My fingernails make crescent-moon dents in the skin of his arms, and the sight of them on his perfect skin excites me. Sensations become too much for me very quickly, and there are several times when I must reconcile the need to push him away and draw him closer simultaneously.

And the pain, it is both sharper and more insignificant than I remember. It is familiar now, in a way it should not be. David knows to move quickly, after the slow-build of the beginning, or perhaps he simply has no choice once he's inside me. Perhaps he is as much a slave to the whims of his new body as I am to mine. I wonder what we must look like, with our flawless skin and uncoiled muscle, like two marble statues trying to make love. It only occurs to me after he comes that neither of us has thought to use a condom. I try not to dwell on what that bit of mutual forgetting might signify, as we lie next to each other on his bed. I can feel his pillow move when he looks over at me.

"Better than you remember?" he asks, and I can't look at him. All I can do is go feverish with blushing and hide my face in my hands and nod.

# Connie

"Would you get new eyes if you had the chance?" I ask Dr. Grath as we huddle at his tiny mid-century kitchen table, with its vinyl surface and dented metal legs. He's going through his photo albums. It's an ongoing project; I've been helping him scan them into his computer for posterity's sake, even though he can't see them anymore. He has a son, somewhere out east, a teacher at some snooty private high school who calls every couple of months to check in. Dr. Grath thinks that his son might want the photographs someday, so I describe them to him and he tells me how to label the files. It's sort of amazing, actually, how much he remembers. The most cursory description seems to suffice, though sometimes he asks me to describe a photo in more detail so he can augment his mental picture of it. I wonder if I'd be able to remember every photo in the albums of baby pictures my mother used to keep, the ones we'd pour over on my birthday when I was a child. I wonder if those sorts of memories might have grown soft with the transfer, if everything is one degree removed from what it was, a scan of a scan.

"What a question," Dr. Grath replies, waving a liver-spotted hand and blinking hard with his vacant eyes. "Of course I would."

"Even though it would change everything about you?" I ask. "It would change the person you've become in these past few years. It would change who you are."

"Certainly," Dr. Grath says. "But I was a seeing person for much longer than I've been a blind one."

I consider this. Five years seems like such a long time, thinking back on it. It almost seems like I can't remember a time when I wasn't sick; I can't remember how I spent my healthy days. But the time preceding my diagnosis was much longer. Maybe that woman—the beautiful one, the one who had no reason to even consider death as a concept, much less a possibility—maybe she has not been so fully blotted out by my diagnosis as I once believed. Maybe she is alive and somewhere hidden, hibernating, readying herself to spring forth in triumphant return. Maybe I am already her.

"You know, your breathing changes when you're thinking too hard," Dr. Grath says, getting up and going to his side table, which acts as a makeshift bar. He pours us two tiny, crystal glasses of port without spilling a drop, even as he crosses the room and sets mine in front of me. It's only three in the afternoon, but I figure it couldn't hurt. In the faded light that bleeds through the thick layer of grime on his windows, the port shines ruby red in its glass. I take a sip, and it's terrible, like swilling nail polish remover. I choke on it a bit. Dr. Grath smiles at me, amused.

"All right?" he asks. I nod, grimacing, but he can't see me.

"I'm fine," I finally manage.

"What's next?"

"This one is of your wife," I say, clearing my throat, glancing down at the photo for only a moment. It's easy to recognize her. I feel like I know Maureen's face better than I know my own mother's, we've been doing this for so long. "She's young; her hair is long, in sort of a shag cut. She's wearing a rose-colored T-shirt, and the background is dark."

"Is she smiling?" he asks, though I'm sure he knows the answer.

"Yes," I reply. She always smiled for photos, Maureen did. It's amazing the things you learn, watching people in the tiny, split-second moments captured in photographs. I know Maureen always wore sunscreen when they went to the beach, and Dr. Grath seemed ever-interested in documenting her spreading thick stripes of zinc oxide cream onto her gleaming arms and shoulders. I know her favorite earrings, little silver teardrops with turquoise in the center that she wore in almost every photograph for the first year of their marriage. A wedding present, Dr. Grath said, when I asked him about them. I know she drank imported beer and dirty martinis when they went out. I know she read to her swollen belly before her son was born. The things I know about a woman who died back before Dr. Grath went blind. Too much, it seems sometimes. It's too much for any one person to know, any person who never met her or lived with her or loved her. Though I think maybe I love her a little now, the way people like Linda love characters on *Stratford Pines*. There's something about watching someone's life unfold that makes you feel as if you share something deep and warm, even if the affection is only one-sided.

"What if I'm different?" I ask. Dr. Grath considers me, his gray-tipped eyebrows furrowing, as if he's studying me with his blank eyes.

"Different? From whom?"

"The person I was before I went into the hospital. The person who left."

"New vocal chords?" he says, as if it's our private joke. I wonder if he can tell that I don't smile.

"New everything."

He leans forward in his chair, reaching for and finding my hand where it rests on the table. His fingers brush over my knuckles, the perfect bones of my fingers, the soft, impeccable skin. I wonder what it feels like to him, like butter or fine silk or anything that is too perfect to be part of a person's body. He shuts his eyes.

"Is it what they were talking about on the radio?" he asks, releasing my hand and sitting back in his chair. "A few years ago all anyone could talk about was the UN passing an exception to the ban on human cloning. They were saying it was probably for medical research."

"It was," I reply, though I shouldn't be surprised that Dr. Grath would put the pieces together. "There are four of us, in Chicago at least. I'm not sure how many across the country."

"How does it work?" He's very calm, for someone who's just

realized he's sitting across the table from a clone of his best friend. It makes me want to hug him, though I don't.

"They cut into your brain. The process kills you, but they're able to extract pieces of the memory center of your brain and transfer it into a new body, into a clone of yourself. It's sort of like injecting stem cells. The brain matter takes root in the clones and grows there. You become a new person," I say. "Well, the same person, but a new body."

"So, how old are you?" he asks. He looks a little pale. I wonder if it was a good idea to tell him, if he's too old and too fragile for these sorts of revelations.

"I guess, maybe a few months old? But they use hormones to rapidly age the clones so they match up with the age you are at the time of the transfer. I guess they figured it would be a bit unnerving for adults to wake up in the bodies of infants. They're all about the psychological effects, let me tell you. I have to go to a support group every week for a year."

"Who knows about this?"

"Not really anyone," I say. "We had to sign all sorts of paperwork saying we'd keep it confidential. So, you know, don't go shouting it from the rooftops."

"As if anyone would believe me," he says, though it doesn't sound like a joke. He sounds astonished. "What do you look like now?" he asks.

I glance down at the photos of Maureen. I've watched her age, going through these albums. Maureen was always a beautiful woman, with bright eyes and a perfect symmetry to her smile. Catalogue pretty. Girl-next-door pretty. But even she faded slowly, as their son grew. I've watched as lines appeared around her eyes and extra pounds collected around her midsection. Gray threaded through her hair, a lovely enough shade that she didn't bother dyeing it, but gray just the same. And then the speed of her aging accelerated almost exponentially, in those last few years. Suddenly her skin grew puffy and sagged off her face. Her frame seemed perennially bloated, with flat, sagging breasts and pitted flesh at the backs of her arms. Lines deepened. Age spots appeared. And by the end, no amount of brightness in her eyes could have salvaged her beauty. It had been drained away from her by time, the perfect thief. I wonder what Dr. Grath thought of her then, Dr. Grath who is still a relentless student of female beauty, even without his eyes. I wonder what Maureen would think of me now, were she still alive.

"I look like I could be on the cover of *Vogue,* if I play my cards right," I reply. Frankness has always been *de rigueur* with us.

"Give me a comparison. Dietrich? Harlow? Hepburn? Bergman?" he says, rapid-fire. "The other Hepburn?"

"Blonde," I reply.

"Novak? Bardot?" He pauses, as if to give the next name its due deference. "Monroe?"

"Better," I reply, feeling myself begin to smile, as he sucks in a little breath. This is serious business, with Dr. Grath.

"Tell me."

"Kelly," I say, letting my tongue tick against my teeth as I say it. He shuts his eyes, no doubt conjuring the image of her, that slow-motion moment where she leans in and kisses Jimmy Stewart in the beginning of *Rear Window.* Her perfect blonde curls. Her red lips. The string of pearls around her neck. I could hear his intake of breath when I first watched it with him, even though he couldn't see her. The memory alone was enough to make him gasp.

"Well," he says, with his eyes still closed. "If you're not going to drink that glass of port, I certainly will." I smile and slide it across the table.

# Linda

I don't know if it's because everything already feels so strange in my new body, as if I'm being constantly bombarded by a deluge of vivid sensation, but I know immediately that I'm pregnant. It's a strange feeling, to wake up one morning and know that my new body has become a fertile patch of earth in which something tiny has taken root. I imagine I can feel it already, whatever it is, a tiny goldfish swimming inside me, the flutter of a moth trapped under a drinking glass. I know it even before the symptoms come, days later, when the smell of Tom's aftershave has me heaving into our toilet. When I resurface he's grinning so wide, and I feel so heartily terrible that I want to smack him as he leans his face, with its cloying aftershave fumes, close to kiss me. I'm back at the toilet before we have the chance to celebrate.

I was never this sick when I had Jack or Katie. Tom and I didn't realize I was pregnant with Katie until almost the end of my first trimester. We were in college, and it wasn't unusual for my periods to come and go when I trained too hard for the cross-country team or in the months leading up to finals. To this day I'm still dumbfounded at how healthy Katie is, considering the diet of protein bars and sports drinks and domestic beer I thrived on back then. But this time I'm nearly crippled by it, the sickness, spending hours chewing dusty saltines as I sit on the edge of our bathtub, staring at the toilet like a well-known adversary.

I'm not sure whom to tell. Tom is fretting about telling the kids, and has been for days now. He's probably right to worry; he can see exactly what is going on in his house, how Jack careens between elation that I'm home and naked fear that I will be taken from him.

Tom sees that I have nothing to offer the little boy, that I am still unsure how to speak to him or show affection for him or do all of the things that should come naturally to mothers. And Katie is ever-wary of me, keeping her distance, talking around me as if I am not here. As if it were my choice to abandon her at the age of four, when she desperately needed a mother.

But I fear that telling the kids will be nothing compared to what I'm facing. The doctors. The others, Hannah and David and Connie. I feel like I'm betraying them, a little. Leaving them behind, when we were supposed to be in it all together. I've never wanted to be the first at anything; I've never relished the feeling of being special the way others seem to. I would rather follow a well-trodden path, be part of a crowd. I've never been good at blazing trails.

I gaze up at the panel built into the hallway ceiling and then grip the cord that hangs from it and pull. The stairs unfurl to the floor in front of me, and the space exhales a smell of dust and wood, the smell of the innards of a house, of the space between walls. I climb up into the attic, and the light filtering through its cloudy little window is all I have to see by. I wait for my eyes to adjust to the darkness, watching the dust spin through the strands of light around me. I never liked the attic. I only came up here when there was a clothing drive going on, to sift through Katie's old baby things and donate what she didn't fit anymore. I wonder if Jack's box of baby clothes is still up here, since I never had the chance to sort through it.

I find that I like the attic much more now, now that I've become accustomed to stillness and quiet and solitude. The rest of the house seems overrun with the artifacts of daily life; there is always a toy or half-finished art project or article of clothing to smudge or sit on or trip over. The noise of my children is jarring, so different from the babbling and screams of babies, but an ever-shifting din of voices and video games and singing cartoons. This space, by contrast, feels forgotten. I can take a full breath here.

There are many more boxes crowding the floor than I remember, and I hunch to avoid low-hanging rafters as I wind my way through them. None of them are labeled. Tom was never much for organizing, after all. He was much more likely to shove something out of his field of vision and then forget about it. The thought stings a bit.

I choose boxes at random and pry them open. There's a box of Tom's grandmother's china, the pattern that's so flowery it reminds me of a frosted supermarket cake; the china that Tom hates, though he still can't bring himself to get rid of it. Tom has always been like that, sentimental. I'd begged him to throw the damn dishes away when we first moved in together, because his grandmother had terrible taste and besides that she'd been dead for ten years already—Christ, almost twenty now—and they would never be put to any use ever again. But no, Tom held on to them, physically even, the battered box tight against his chest to keep me from taking it to the Dumpster. Now I pull away wadded newspaper, glancing at the headline crumpled within, which is something about the end of the Cold War, and discover that the china isn't nearly as dreadful as I remember. I might even like it, a little, up here among the forgotten things. But it is not what I'm looking for, so I fold the soft cardboard of the lid back into place and move on.

It takes me three more tries—boxes containing a plastic badminton set with a net so tangled it resembles a bird's nest, musty sheets, and an inflatable mattress that's so old its rubber is beginning to flake—before I hit on the box that must be mine. On top is a raggedy old shawl I knitted while I was in college, the one I'd sling over my bed frame to wrap around me when my apartment was particularly drafty. It doesn't strike me as something that holds much significance. But I try to imagine it through Tom's eyes. I wonder how many times I'd wrapped myself in it to venture out of the warm cocoon of our bed, springing to the bathroom and back, wearing nothing but socks.

And it hits me: these are not things he kept in anticipation of my return. These are things he kept to remember me by. There's the journal I kept during our honeymoon in Hawaii, which quickly became nothing more than an inventory of what we ate each day instead of an actual travel log. My little carved wood jewelry box, which I open to find is still a jumble of chains and beads and bent bobby pins. I hunt through the mess with a fingertip and discover the piece of sea glass Tom found during a camping trip on Lake Superior one summer, a hazy shade of emerald green, probably a piece of a discarded wine bottle worn smooth and edgeless by the press of water and sand. It's still there, still green and like silk to the touch, and it makes me think of those chilly mornings, the mist rising up off the lake, before the summer sun climbed high enough to burn away the moisture from the air. There's my hospital bracelet from when I had Katie, which I was able to pry off of my wrist intact when the swelling in my hands finally went down a few days later.

And still, even when I should be weeping at the life I have lost, or the life that has at least been broken through interruption, all I can think is that these things are of no use to me now. These are not the objects I would choose to keep, had I been given a choice. I would want the collection of music I'd so religiously cultivated throughout so many years, music that Tom hated and I loved, albums that he would never have thought to keep. I would want my overstuffed binder of recipes, the dishes I'd made for myself and others countless times, now lost in the ether of my memory. I would want the box full of sewing patterns I never got the chance to make. I would want my bookshelves full of books. A hospital bracelet, a piece of sea glass . . . these things do me no good. I don't need to remember what Lake Superior smells like. I need to remember my life, the day-to-day of it, not the highlights.

I close the box, knowing that there's nothing here to help me, knowing that it's futile to think that some object could drag me back across those lost years, back into the person I was. There is only what I have now, who I am now. I hurry to search for baby clothes because, while my hopes might be dashed, *Stratford Pines* begins in a half hour.

# Connie

I call my mother on her birthday. I can't say it's something I've always done. There were plenty of years when the day slipped past like any other, and then I'd be sending flowers in apology instead of celebration. We're pretty even, though, because I can't remember the last time she called me on my birthday either. Still, this year is different.

"Yeah?" her voice comes over the phone, and it's a little thicker than I remember. I think of what Dr. Grath said about hearing the cigarettes in my voice.

"It's me," I say and wait the obligatory moment it takes her to connect the dots.

"Con," she says. It's her hostess voice, the one she uses to greet customers in the restaurant where she's worked since I can remember. It's a bit overly friendly, trying to cover for the real distance that exists between us. "How are you?"

"I'm good. I'm really good."

"Good, good." I can hear voices in the background.

"I'm not interrupting something, am I?"

"Nah, I've just got the girls over for martinis. Celebrating." My mother's friends are all paunchy and deeply wrinkled, and none of them have my mother's immaculate bone structure to begin with. She's better than all of them, I think. Even now, pushing sixty.

"Of course. Happy birthday."

"Thanks, hun."

"I was going to send flowers. But then I figured I'd call."

"Mmm. You going to church?"

I consider for a long moment whether or not it's acceptable to lie to my mother on her birthday. I decide in favor of dishonesty. "Once in a while."

"Now you know nothing in your life will come correct until you make right with the Lord. That illness you've got, that's the sin you lived for so long. That's why the doctors can't help you. You're not looking to the right doctor, honey."

"I know, Maureen," I say, because using her real name drives her crazy. All of her friends call her Betts, though I've never figured out why. I suppose it's one of the many mysterious things about the woman who raised me, all of those little rituals and bits of wisdom held over from her model days in New York. Drinking ice water will force your body to burn more calories. Coconut oil should be used on the face and hands every night before bed. Vodka is acceptable in large doses, but never a single sip of beer. And Betts, always Betts, not Mom, and certainly not Maureen. It was a veneer of beauty and glamour that had been my mother's religion, and mine, before she found God in the more traditional sense.

She was saved right around the time I got sick. I'm not sure if there was any connection there, if the news of my diagnosis drove my mother further into her own mess of born-again bullshit. All I know is that she seemed to forget all of the laws of her old life just as I was reaping the awful results of living by them. Her ethic of beauty had served only to punish me. And yet, even now, especially now, when I am in possession of the rarest of faces, her laws are still the due north of my compass. I am both too young and too old to trade my religion for a new one, as she has.

"You should come out to my church some Sunday," she says. "It's not too long of a drive. And the ladies would love to see you. It might be good for you, you know? A change of scenery. Some time away from that city."

*That city* is how she always refers to Chicago. At first, because it wasn't New York, and certainly wasn't L.A. And now because of its crime rate and gay bars and liquor stores and its heretic population. I wonder if I'd even recognize my mother anymore, with her dark hair and long neck, now circled with a chain that holds her golden cross. She'd always been a denizen of cities, before I left her with too many lines on her face and too many extra pounds, in a double-wide trailer near the Wisconsin border. Now she's just as wary of my home as she would have been traveling to the Sudan. How easy it is to reinvent yourself, I think. To become someone you would have once hated.

"Something's different, Mom," I say. There's silence on the other end of the line. "Betts, you there?"

"Have you been praying about it?" She sounds stricken, yet resolute. It occurs to me that she must be thinking the worst, that I would call her on her birthday to tell her that I've come to the end of my rope.

"No, Christ, I'm not dying, okay?"

"Please don't." Her voice sounds strangely weak.

"What?"

"Don't say things like that."

"It's the truth. I'm not dying. Not anymore." Silence again. "Betts."

Her voice comes through a bit stronger this time. "Don't say his name in vain. At least, not when you're on the phone with me, all right? I can't control what you do when I'm not around, but I won't stand for it in my presence."

I pull at the tension in my forehead with my fingertips. A few more conversations like this and all of my lines will come right back. "Did you happen to hear anything else I just said?"

"I don't know what you want me to say," she replies. "But the ladies are here. Making martinis."

"You told me."

"They're waiting for me. I should go. After all, I'm the belle of the ball today, aren't I?"

"Unlike every other day?" I ask, and I hear her chuckle.

"Are you getting out at all?"

"Yeah, I'm getting out." I think of Thursday group, and the

short walk to the L from my apartment. It's been sunny these past few weeks. I walk over to my window and pull back the curtains, spilling fresh brightness onto the spare trappings of my apartment.

"Good. Fresh air. It's good for you."

"Thanks, Betts. Happy birthday." I hear the line click and let my hand hover for a second before setting my phone down on my windowsill. What had I wanted to say? I don't even know. Would it change my mother back, if she knew I'd been saved too? That I had been saved in a more physical sense than her, and by the blasphemy of science? Perhaps she would merely think that all of her prayers had been answered, like one final endorsement of her newfound faith. Perhaps nothing can spin her backward, the way I have been reborn in an earlier, more perfect version of myself.

It's ironic, too, because all of my life, my past has been my only liability. No one wants to hear that you were trash, that you'd turned up like a shiny penny in the middle of a rat's nest. I'd glossed over it for years, pretended to be from Chicago instead of the rural armpit of one of its suburbs. But now my history is gone. I released it like the string of a helium balloon, watching it spin upward into the sky, barely bidding it farewell when the wind spirited it away. I don't need a history anymore. I don't need to lie. It's the first time in my life that the truth is much more smooth and solid, diamond hard. I only wish that I could scrub away all those years and all that history for my mother as well. To finally give her the life I robbed from her, all those years ago. But even now, even amid the time of the miracle cure, there are some things that are still out of reach.

I'm not sure where to go at night anymore. I went out for a while when I first moved back to Chicago, before the exhaustion and the general emaciation took over in earnest, but I can't really remember the exact names or locations of those dark, neon-lit enclaves where I would spend my nights. I don't have much to wear either, I discover, when I step out of the shower, the cool air of my little apartment making me shiver as I paw through my closet. The majority of my clothes were chosen for comfort and because they were cheap. But among the oversize sweatshirts and threadbare fleece pajama pants I find a slate-colored tank top with some beading around the neckline and a pair of black leggings. It'll do, I think, as I admire myself in the mirror. I'm deliciously thin; even in such skin-tight clothing, nothing moves much as I twist and turn in front of the mirror. I pull my hair back and slather on thick eyeliner, and suddenly I wish Dr. Grath could see me, because I am Edie Sedgwick at the Chelsea Hotel. I am fit to be someone's muse. But that's the trouble when you're beautiful and your best friend is blind: it doesn't do either one of you much good.

I decide on Smart Bar and hail a cab, brimming with anticipation. It's raining a bit, and as the cab rushes through the damp streets I imagine we're under water, moving through a sunken city whose lights have not yet gone out. I tip the driver way too much when he pulls up in front of the lit sign for the Metro, and he grins at me with Cheshire teeth as I step out onto the damp curb and hurry inside. The beat of the music is there, even before I've been swallowed up by the darkness and the heat and the teeming movement of bodies. It's that hard, thrumming beat that thumps within my chest like a surrogate heart. It's a young crowd here, college students probably, but I'm pulled into the dance floor all the same, and I wonder how old I look to these bourgeoning adults.

I swim my way to the bar and I'm carded, which makes me grin, which makes the bartender prop his elbows on the bar and lean very close to me to take my order. He's pretty enough, tan with dark hair, but I'm more interested in thrusting myself back into the mob of dancers than I am in making small talk with a man who is paid to be here. I order Malibu rum with pineapple juice, and it's so sweet it nearly makes my teeth hurt, but the alcohol doesn't burn as much going down. It's what I drank as a kid, when my friend Tanya's older sister would give us the leftovers from her parties. We'd jump the fence from the trailer park into the apartment complex next door and sit in its empty pool among the dead leaves and condom wrappers and drink until we could barely climb our way out again. I think about it now, nearly twenty years later, what it was like to be fourteen and newly minted and so full of promise. It feels a little bit like how I feel tonight, though the drink doesn't taste familiar at all when I sip it. That's the one bit of disappointment, but it's fleeting, and soon I'm worming my way back in between the clatter of bodies and bobbing to the music and the flash of colored lights.

I haven't been dancing long when I spot him. Or rather, when I see him spot me. He's young, fuck he's young, maybe twenty-five, with stringy blond hair and arms that show veins and thin fibers of muscle beneath his skin. A sort of a punk kid, I think, catching the glint of a silver ring in his nose. I take a gulp of my drink and pause in my dancing as he makes his way toward me. He's very pretty, almost feminine, the kind of pouty youth who is born to stare shirtless from Levi's ads or lounge on rumpled beds for Calvin Klein. It's a sort of comfort, his beauty. We're of the same breed, he and I. He wears combat boots and a stocking cap. I lick my lips, making the red stain of my lipstick shine in the overhead lights.

"You all right?" he says, loudly, into my ear. He smells thickly of sweat. I smile, clearing my throat, which still burns hot and raw from the alcohol. The heat is starting to spread downward, though, curling its way out of my stomach, sinking heavily into my limbs, and settling low beneath my pelvis.

"Fine," I say, baring my teeth at him. He's matched his movements to mine, and while it's not quite dancing as much as it is pulsing with the rhythm of the backbeat, it feels good to be in motion. When he smiles, his two front teeth angle slightly toward each other, and I think maybe this boy and I have more in common than even I imagine. I picture him growing up in the rural southern reaches of Illinois, a beautiful young redneck working in the sun. Maybe he picked me because he recognizes the girl I was, once, like a smell of motor oil and cheap wine that will never entirely wash off.

"What's your name?"

"Edie."

"I'm Colin." He offers a hand and I take it, clasping it between us. "You roll?"

"Not lately."

"Want to?"

I cock an eyebrow at him. I'd done my share of Ecstasy in my former life, though I cut out pretty much everything since I got sick. But it was fun, and I'm in the mood for some fun. I nod, and he leads me by the hand into the darkness that clings to the club's walls, away from the brightness of the dance floor. He pulls something out of his pocket, and I catch a glimpse of clear plastic before it's spirited back into the tight denim of his jeans.

"How much?" I ask, leaning in close, smelling the pungent tang of his skin. He shakes his head.

"For you? First one's free." He brushes his hand to his mouth and then leans toward me, closing his lips over mine, his tongue pressing something small and round into my mouth. I swallow the pill easily and then stand on my tiptoes to press my mouth back into his.

"How old are you?" I ask. He looks at me a little suspiciously then, so I smile, widening my eyes, trying to look a bit more like an ingénue.

"Twenty-four." His mouth slides under my ear. One of his hands has attached itself to the crease between my ass and the back of my right thigh. "Why?"

"Just curious." Christ he's young. He was in kindergarten while I was drinking in that empty swimming pool. But he's practically glowing with that golden youthful swagger, and kissing him is like drinking in my old life, waking up that side of myself that has been sick and dormant for the past five years, or has never been awake at all. Not in this body.

"You've got about a half hour before you'll start to feel it," he says, the hand on my leg hitching me up a bit onto his thigh, pulling me closer. "Want to go somewhere?"

I nod, and soon we're out into the damp streets, and he's leading me by the hand, hailing a cab. The drugs kick in just as he's tipping me back onto the musty futon in his tiny studio, with its dirty windows and scuffed wood floors. And just like that, everything is shining, shimmering like a mirage of water on a hot desert road. Everything seems to fit into place, with the satisfying soft click of puzzle pieces sliding together. I can see that every moment in my life has conspired to bring me here, and all of my selves—the gangly little brat of a girl, the blonde teenager in cutoffs and flip-flops drinking in the fallen leaves, the actress shooting up in the bathroom of a five-star restaurant, the invalid with the papery skin and the foam of yeast clotting in the corners of her mouth—all of them have folded themselves into me, like matryoshka dolls, each self hiding a smaller, former self. And I, at this moment, can feel them all held within me, all of those lost, beautiful girls, and everything we've ever wanted. I shut my eyes, reach out, but my hand collides with the skin of the boy's chest before I can even realize what I was trying to grasp out of the empty air.

He's pawing at me with one hand, undoing his jeans with the other, but I'm too awash in my own euphoria, I can't differentiate one sensation from any other. I seem to slip easily out of the present moment and into some void within myself, where all of my history is held, and when I look up to the dirty windows I can see that something is painted there, some scene of lovers or animals, something difficult to discern when it changes shape in the darkness. It's a long moment before I realize it's a reflection, that I don't recognize myself, with my hair splayed out on the pillow beneath me and my eyes heavy-lidded, and this boy shoving down his jeans. He's tan down to his waistband, but his ass looks thin and soft and very white in the reflection, and it makes the whole image suddenly ugly and I have to close my eyes. He's sliding my underwear down and flipping me onto my stomach when I decide I've had enough of this.

"Stop," I say, as I shove his hands away.

"What's wrong?" he mumbles, grabbing my bare hips and trying to pull me to him as I squirm away.

"I'm going," I say shoving him back again and pulling my underwear back into place.

"Come on, baby," the boy says, his hands encircling my forearms. His grip is strong; I can see the muscles tense in his biceps and shoulders, and I know his leanness is hiding the tensile strength of iron rebar. "You can't just leave."

*This is the moment,* I think. The delineation. Things can go badly now, very badly for me, on the whims of this boy alone. I can feel my control slipping; I can feel danger pressing in, alarm bells going off too late. But I think he sees the sudden fear in me because he releases my arms then. He looks surprised, that I could be afraid of him. But I know more about the world than he does.

"All right," he says, showing me his palms. "Whatever."

I don't intend to let this sort of luck run out, so I pull my clothes on and stumble out into the hallway, pausing at the top of the stairs to pull on my shoes as his door slams behind me. When I'm out on the street the night air seems to hum, full of the glistening dots of city lights and the smell of rain. And I want to reach into myself, into that place beneath my sternum and pluck out that pretty teenager with her Malibu and pineapple juice and tell her see, see, look at me, and how much I have seen, and I still am no wiser than you, little girl.

# Hannah

Sam has to fly to San Diego on a business trip, following down a lead for an important story. *Of course,* I think. The stories are always important, always a crusade. His leaving is a relief, after weeks of shuddering silences, of nights spent tossing and sleepless, avoiding even brushing an elbow against each other, avoiding all of the subjects we can't talk about—my painting, our theoretical engagement, anything to do with Lucy, and, of course, his absence at the hospital—and finding we have nothing much left to say to each other. He leaves me alone, a stranger in my own body, without anyone to ground me in the subtle routines of my old life.

Sam's absence make the presence of David in my life seem that much more potent. Memories of that day in his apartment swarm up like bees when I'm the least prepared for them, when I'm rinsing my hair in the shower or chopping cucumber in the kitchen—which nearly cost me the tip of my brand-new finger—or lying awake in bed, trying not to think of David. How marked this body must be by the one man who has possessed it, if David is right about storing memories beneath our skin. My body is as traitorous as my mind now, reacting as it does with toe-curling insistence every time I think of him.

I look out my kitchen window on to Printer's Row, newly coated with a sheet of ice that makes everything glitter in the cold sunlight, and try to clear my mind of David. Watching the movement of the city in winter is always a comfort, the way Chicago seems relentlessly disinterested in its inhabitants. It makes my own difficulties feel like part of a greater pattern, a whole city of people who are walking against the blinding cut of the icy wind swept in from Lake Michigan. As if we are all struggling to make it through in a place where, not so long ago, people fought simply to outlive this cold. The people who were foolish enough to make their homes on the edge of a fallen glacier. Pioneers, I think. People who are made to endure.

My doorbell rattles me from my wistfulness, and it's Lucy calling from the street outside, begging entry. I buzz her up and pull on a sweater and jeans over the tank top I slept in. I glance at myself in the mirror on the way out of my bedroom and am met with the reflection of my own wan scowl. Lucy, on the other hand, appears at my door flushed and positively incandescent. Her coat hangs open around the tight fabric of her sweater, her stomach swollen and melon-ripe beneath it.

"God, Lucy, didn't you notice it's still winter out there?" I ask, ushering her inside.

"Please, I have my own internal heater these days," she says, kissing me on the cheek and heading for my bedroom. She's carrying shopping bags.

"What exactly . . ."

"Look, honey, Sam told me that you're having some . . . wardrobe issues," she says.

"Sam called you?"

"I called the other day. You weren't up yet." She stops in the doorway, surveying the rumpled bed and last night's clothes still on the floor. I slink by her, picking up the few discarded garments and pulling the comforter over the twisted sheets. I'm pretty sure her three-year-old is already learning how to make his bed.

"Anyway," she says. "I decided to pick you up a few things." She presses the shopping bags into my hands. "Go and try some of them on. I had to guess your size, so I just took mine and subtracted ten."

"It's not your size if it only lasts nine months," I say, setting the bags down on the bed and sifting through them. It's a mess of linen pants and oxford shirts and cardigan sweaters, all bright colors and designer labels. The sort of thing I used to buy because it's the sort of thing Sam likes. "What is this, the entire J. Crew catalog?"

"Until I have a little girl to shop for, you're it," she says, pulling a lavender blouse out of one of the bags and holding it up to my shoulders. "Just try something on, okay? Humor me."

I take it from her as she selects a pair of tweed pants to match. I drop them on my bed and strip off my sweater and jeans right there. I can feel the heat of her jealousy as I stand momentarily in my underwear. I know what she sees, the body she once had, unaltered by stretch marks and breast-feeding and pregnancy weight gained and lost. A body that has only ever seen cold winter sunlight, a tightly wound bud yet to bloom.

"You don't have a mark on you, do you?" Lucy asks from behind me.

"Not yet. But I'm expecting the first freckle to show up any day now." I pull on the blouse, buttoning it halfway up and then step into the pants.

Lucy sighs, buttoning the blouse the rest of the way up and then pulling me in front of the full-length mirror. "You look lovely," she says, gathering my hair back in one of her fists.

"Come on," I say, to cover how much my reflection bothers me. Standing before me is the sort of bland-looking, endlessly mediocre creature I endured ink and needles and piercings and countless bottles of hair dye to blot out in my formative years.

"Sam would love you in this," Lucy says.

"You're probably right," I say, stripping back to my underwear. I think of Penny when she turned to Sam in the hospital, when she looked at my unmarked arms. *Better for the country club,* she'd said. Smoothing out those rough edges. "But it's too much, Luce. I can't accept all this."

"Of course you can. It's the least I can do for you right now. I know it hasn't been easy, coming home." She pauses. "You've been back to your studio?"

"Did Sam tell you that, too?" I ask.

"He mentioned something. He said you had a fight."

Of course, he can still talk to Lucy when he can't talk to me. I laugh a little, a dark sound, handing the clothes back to her. "I'd say we had a disagreement."

"It'll get easier," she says. It's the sort of thing that people say like a mantra, without any conviction. Because, of course, she doesn't know that some silences have a core, a root, and, like a weed, the silence cannot be killed until the root is torn out. Or, perhaps, she knows more about the root of Sam's silence than she is letting on.

"Where did Sam go the weekend before the transfer?" I ask, before I can stop myself. It looks like I've startled her, because she steps back a bit, a slight flinch in her otherwise calm demeanor. Her hand goes to her stomach, and I know it then, that she sees this particular question as an attack.

"What do you mean?" she asks, going back to the bags of clothes and refolding them, even the ones that are still untouched and perfect.

"I woke up and Sam was gone," I say, as if explaining to a child. "He was gone for days. I want to know where he was." He wouldn't have stayed away unless it was something terrible, unless the guilt was so huge that he couldn't face me after. Deception isn't something that comes easily to Sam. Lucy, however, is a woman accustomed to getting what she wants.

"He had the flu. You know that," she says. *You know that.* He said it the same way, after I woke up from the transfer. You know I only stayed away because the doctors told me to. You know. I imagine how it might have happened. She cried into his shirt and he held her while I was there in the room. How might they have comforted each other when they were alone? "He was run down, Hannah. Exhausted. It was only a matter of time before it caught up to him. The same thing happened in high school, when his dad was at his worst." She talks fast. Lucy is itching to leave, to not have to answer any more questions, and she makes a big production of checking her watch, feigning surprise.

"Shit, I've gotta run if I'm going to make my prenatal yoga class.

But are you sure you don't want to hold on to these?" Lucy asks, holding up the shopping bags. How easily I could accept them. Become the woman I imagined, Sam's perfect wife, vacant and bland as a sheen of dust. A girl with smooth edges, almost as perfect as Lucy, but for all the dark history and desperate impulses that have followed me into this new body. It's a life I might have chosen, once. But I can't surrender to it, not now that I'm beginning to understand the nature of Sam's silence, of Lucy's evasion. Now that I know what David Jenkins tastes like. There are too many things I would have to choke down, breathe around, to become a perfect wife for Sam.

"No," I reply, trying to keep the bite out of my tone. "I'm having a hard enough time recognizing myself as it is."

# Linda

I don't tell them about the baby. It is too colossal of a secret, too tectonic. Instead, I tell them about the accident. I want to share something, some secret with them. Because I'm awake, now.

"It was all I could think about," I say, staring into my cup of hot cocoa, the fluorescent light of the hospital conference room turning it an olive green shade of brown. "After I woke up. Because it felt like it happened a second ago, even though it had actually been weeks by the time I came to. I don't know if any of you have ever had something like that happen, something you wish you could take back so badly it makes your stomach ache."

I remember that sick feeling, that swarming acidic bile that was present even though I could no longer feel my arms or my legs or my lungs. The feeling was there, even though there was nothing in my body that could feel it anymore. "I went over and over it in my head. Wishing it away. I was never really religious. I mean, I went to my mother's church when I was younger, but I never really believed any of it. But I spent weeks asking God to give me that couple of seconds back so I could do it differently."

David nods, looking solemn, his politician look. "I think people are right when they say he works in mysterious ways." Connie snorts at this, but David ignores her. "He didn't abandon you, Linda. The fact that you're sitting here with us is proof of that."

"Come on, David," Hannah says. "Let her talk."

How few words we have in our language. For instance, there is no word for the looks that Hannah and David share, the knowing antagonism, the intensity, the admonishment, the sort of shared expectation that sparks in the air between them. It's the sort of thing that must be observed, the sort of thing I'm good at seeing, from those years when words were of no use to me. One for no. Two for yes.

I spent endless hours in that hospital bed, trying to conjure the prayers I remembered from my childhood. My mother's church held services in Mandarin, and I could hear strings of phrases in my head, though their meanings were no longer attached. Was I praying to God? To Jesus? To the Blessed Virgin? I didn't know. I would have prayed to anyone who could have lifted me from that bed. I would have prayed to the devil himself if I'd known the words. But I don't tell David this.

"I had some letters in my car that I was going to mail, just bills and things, but I decided to stop at the post office on my way home. I kept thinking that I should have stopped there before I got on the highway. But I was so anxious to get on the road, I didn't want to take the time."

"Where were you going?" Hannah asks.

That, of course, is the question. The one Tom has forgotten to ask, eight years later. He asked me right after the accident, clutching the rail on the side of my bed, imploring me for an answer I could not give. But by now, the importance of my destination has been diminished by so much time. I try to remember it all. My cell phone ringing. Checking the clock in my kitchen, 3:34 p.m., plenty of time to get to Highland Park and back before Tom got home from work. Dropping the kids at Sarah's down the street, claiming last-minute errands, a couple of hours tops. Getting on the highway. Changing lanes. Once. Twice. Checking the clock on the dashboard, 3:56 p.m. Looking up to see brake lights. Close. Too close.

"I was going to see a man," I say, raising my eyes to the room. "Scott. A friend of a friend who played saxophone in a jazz quartet. The man I was going to move in with, once I left Tom." Something in David's face twitches. I wonder if its disgust. Or maybe empathy. Hannah looks at her hands. Connie is the only one who meets my eyes. It's impossible to shock Connie. Maybe it's even impossible to surprise her. But maybe she looks a little impressed, like she didn't think I had it in me. Not the way I am now. "I was a good person. All my life, I did everything a woman like me was supposed to do. Track scholarship. Two kids. On my way to a Ph.D. And the one time . . ." I can't finish, the anger of it closes my throat. I swallow, hard. "I guess for a long time, I was certain God was punishing me."

"For committing adultery?" Dr. Bernard asks, and only then do I remember. He's writing all of this down.

"Maybe," I reply. "Maybe for once, just once, doing the wrong thing because it was what I wanted."

"What happened to Scott?" Connie asks.

"After the accident? I don't know. He never visited me in the hospital. I never saw him again."

"Bastard," Connie says, and she seems genuinely angry. I'm flattered she feels so strongly toward someone who would hurt me. "Fucking bastard."

"Can you blame him?" I ask. "I was as good as dead. It was easier for the people in my life to act as if that's what happened."

"Not Tom," David says. "He didn't forget you."

I think of Scott, our stolen hours in the backs of movie theaters and on picnic tables in the middle of the night, the scratch of the wood against the back of my thighs, the wanting so furious it made me forget who I was, made me someone new. And Tom, who came by the nursing home every weekend with flowers for my room. Who kept me as his wife long after our marriage had been ground down to powder and ash. And I wonder how anyone is supposed to understand love when it is always changing forms, each with its own name, in a language that cannot be spoken. One for no. Two for yes. How useless these words are.

I toy with the idea of telling Connie, just Connie, about the baby. Connie, who cannot be shocked. We're walking south on Michigan

Avenue, and it feels good to be out in the open air after the claustro-
phobia of the meeting. It's the time of year when everyone assures
each other that this will be the last week of winter, though it never
is. The wind is cold, and we've both got scarves tied under our chins,
our hands thrust into our pockets. We look like mismatched twins,
with our straight spines and our even gaits. I think maybe a person
could pick a SUB out of a crowd, if he knew what he was looking
for. Bodies that show no evidence of the burden of time or effort.
How different I will be soon, with stretched skin and backaches and
hips pushed wide. How altered, how lived-in this body will be.

"Think they're fucking?" Connie asks.

"Who?" I say, a particularly strong gust of wind and her question nearly knocking me sideways.

"Hannah and David. All they do is make eyes at each other.
They don't argue anymore," she says, pulling her scarf a bit tighter.
"Maybe they've found a new way to direct all of that energy."

"Oh. I don't know," I reply. This sort of gossip has always made
me nervous, even back when it was the other mothers on the playground.

In the distance I hear a saxophone playing a stilted rhythm, the
sound of it warping in the wind. The winter air tastes crisp and the
bridge over the Chicago River shudders a bit under our feet as traffic
speeds past. It's my favorite place in Chicago, that bridge, the place
where on a bright, perfect day you can see the glass of the buildings
and the water shimmering in a perfect harmony of light and lack of
color. It feels like heartache now, looking at it, like driving by your
childhood home and finding another family living there.

"Want to stop for some cocoa?" Connie asks, motioning to Café
Descartes on the corner, its windows fogging a bit from the heat of
cramped bodies and the steam of espresso machines. Yes, I think.
Cocoa would be nice.

"What if I had a baby?" I say. It sounds more like a question
than I mean it to. Connie halts so suddenly at my words that a man
in a wool coat nearly runs into her. I have to pull her forward by her

sleeve as we weave our way through the throngs of shoppers. She looks at me like I've said something complimentary about Hitler. All right, I've found Connie's threshold for surprise.

"Why would you want to do that?" she asks, and even the smoky puffs of air escaping her mouth are lovely and delicate. But her words open up a well inside me, like pulling at a loose thread until things begin to unravel.

"We've always wanted more kids. We talked about it, way back before the accident," I reply, but she shakes her head.

"You know, the more you try to convince your husband that you're the same person as you were before, the worse things are going to be for you." Her nose is pink and running a little, and she bats at it with the sleeve of her coat. "Christ, Linda, you just said you were going to leave him. You're not just trying to go back to your old life, you're trying to go back to a life you didn't even want in the first place."

I realize, too late, that she doesn't understand that I'm already pregnant. She thinks I'm asking her whether or not I should try. I start back down the street, making her follow. Connie catches up to me halfway down the block.

"Why would you even ask me?" she asks.

"What do you mean?" I pull the collar of my coat up around my throat. The temperature is dropping and I feel a bit feverish. I think back to when I was pregnant with Katie, how my temperature ran high for a month before I figured out that I wasn't fighting off a virus.

"You have your mind made up already, don't you? Why would you want my opinion?" Connie asks.

"I wanted your opinion because I thought we were friends," I reply, though I know it's petty and unfair of me. She grabs my arm then, pulling me toward a bench out of the streaming path of people walking down Michigan Avenue. People are ice skating at Millennium Park, making the most of the lingering cold, winding in lazy circles around the rink as a cheesy song from the eighties plays in the background. A song that seems familiar, though I can't place it. I can't remember how I know it. This is how music is, now. Even when I can remember a song's lyrics, its melody, it never takes me back. I never feel anything when I hear it.

"We *are* friends," she says, looking up at me, and it's the first time I realize that I'm taller than she is. Her face is intent on mine. "We are friends," she repeats, her cold hand clasping mine. I get an odd sort of sexual thrill out of it, a feeling so potent I have to take a deep breath to crush it back down. "Which is why I think you asked me so I would talk you out of this.

"You just got control back," she continues. "For the first time in eight years, this body is yours. Do you really want to give that up so soon?" Her hand is still in mine, and I'm so dumbfounded by this, by the weight of my uncertainty, that all I can do is get angry. I wrench my hand away from her.

"Maybe I thought you'd be happy for me, that I'm getting on with my life," I say, wanting to tell her that it's too late. That it's too late, and now I wish I could take it back. So all I can do is defend it. "But you don't want any of us to move on, do you? Because you don't have anything else."

Connie doesn't say anything to this. She just turns and begins to walk again, but I don't follow. I watch her back as she moves, the perfect delicacy of her limbs, the slope of her shoulders underneath her wool coat, and it feels like a part of my secret world, the beautiful place, has cracked off and pulled away from me, an iceberg splintering under the heat of the sun. And once again, the horizons of my life seem to constrict around me.

When I get home I head straight to the attic. On the days when I'm alone, when Tom is locked up in his office and the kids are at school, I scale those dusty steps and kneel down on the floor and retrieve my artifacts from their dark little home. I do this now, because my conversation with Connie has left me shaken, left me feeling feverish and disconnected from the world inside me.

I lay them out in front of me, my treasures. There's the wrapper from the candy bar. I flattened it out, the perfect silver foil of it, between two books from the shelves downstairs, like pressing a flower to preserve its beauty. There's the little metal-and-glass salt-shaker from the pizza place where we ate a few weeks ago, which left a dusting of gritty white crystals in the seam at the bottom of my purse. Next to it is a pair of earrings from the trashy little jewelry store in the mall where Tom bought Katie a basketball pendant for Christmas. They're little ladybugs, red with black spots, and they looked like a pair of forbidden apples tempting me from their rotating metal rack. I was surprised how easy that one was, considering the mirrored ceiling and the hawk-eyed salesgirls. Though, of course, they were keeping a much closer eye on the teenagers bopping around the store than on me. There are other things too, a pen, a votive holder, some 9-volt batteries, a tester bottle of perfume from the cosmetics stand at a department store.

I spread them out on the floor and run my fingers over them, reveling in the sweet tingle that erupts within me like the baking soda and vinegar volcano Jack made for science class. Connie's words grow dim, eclipsed by the remembered thrills of all these pilfered items. Just looking at them lights up something inside me, as keen and sharp as a memory.

# Connie

I use the last of my final disability check to book an airline ticket to Los Angeles. The fact that it was my final two hundred dollars made the decision, which I had been ignoring ever since the transfer, suddenly unavoidable. I'd spent the past few years living on the paltry sum I received from the government for being too sick to hold down any substantial sort of employment, subsisting on ramen noodles and peanut butter bought with food stamps, wearing my clothes until they were threadbare in my tiny, dirty apartment. But even I can't live on nothing, and I'm not about to endure my landlord's greasy stare, his innuendos and loaded suggestions, if I have to beg for an extension on my rent.

At 5 a.m. I take the Blue Line to O'Hare, dressed in the only outfit I have left fit for such an errand, a white shift dress and ancient Christian Louboutins that I could never bear to get rid of, with their four-inch heels and snakebite-red soles. It's a classic sort of look, sexual in its simplicity. Hollywood glamor. It's the outfit I was planning on being buried in.

I'm not staying over in L.A., so I carry only a purse containing lipstick, my ID, and the one credit card I have left that isn't maxed out. That's the thing about assuming you're going to die, you don't make smart financial decisions when it comes to planning for the future. Which is another reason for my trip; ever since my disability checks stopped, the creditors have begun calling. I glance at my reflection in the glass of the train window as we dip underground. I look jagged and fierce, a version of myself that is a little sharper-jawed and sunken-cheeked, something like the way I looked when I was sick. The image is ghastly and too familiar, all of that beauty spoiled by poor lighting and murky glass.

When we reach O'Hare, I check in at my terminal and begin snaking my way through the security line, pulling off my sunglasses as a blue-gloved TSA agent scrutinizes my ID photo, glancing back and forth between the card and my face. I know what she sees, a woman who is undeniably the same, yet nearly completely different from the photograph. Any sign of my age has disappeared, all the worldliness is gone from my face. I am blank, and pure, and alight with possibility. She seems perplexed by what she sees, but she shines a flashlight on my ID and then hands it back to me. For a moment I think she's going to ask me the name of my plastic surgeon, but then she waves me through without a word.

My earrings set off the metal detectors, of course. And I get that familiar panicked prickle in my skin when I'm waved over to a secured area to be searched. A female TSA agent pats me down, but all of the men in the vicinity watch with wet mouths and fixed eyes. I don't look at any of them. I show my defiance in the absolute boredom on my face. They are insects, a trifle. I show them that I submit to them only because I can't bring myself to care enough to resist. Another familiar feeling.

I'm flying coach, which I detest, wedged into a sticky foam seat, staring out the window while the businessman next to me tries to make conversation. I ignore him, mostly. He's not bad looking, but after all, he can't be too impressive if his company flies him coach. Instead I play over the whole scene in my head. What I will say. How I will look, in my simple dress and my sex-kitten heels, with a fresh lick of red lipstick across my mouth. It will be all right, all of it, the greedy press of my landlord and my ringing phone and my empty mailbox. If I can look half as good as I imagine, it will be just fine.

I was probably twelve when men began to notice me. They noticed my mother first, of course, because who wouldn't notice Betts? At least, back before she found God and let herself go. I remember sitting on the front steps of our trailer while my mother smoked a slow succession of cigarettes, the midsummer sun shimmering off the sweat that collected in the base of her throat and in the crease between her breasts. I was enthralled by her even then, the beauty of her, and my own importance in being her daughter.

"Don't slouch," she'd say, glancing at me out of the corner of her eye before going back to observing the rows of trailers that surrounded us, like a monarch surveying her kingdom. "You remember those ballerinas on TV? Those are the rarest sort of women in the world. Rich people pay obscene sums of money to sit there and watch them move. Imagine two thousand pairs of eyes on you, and you never have to say a word. Imagine being that powerful. Do you think they slouch when they sit down?"

I'd shake my head, straightening my spine until my back ached with the effort. What would two thousand pairs of eyes feel like? Even one pair often felt like too much, especially when it was Larry, who lived across the way with his small pack of Dobermans. I could feel him looking at me, the nicotine-stained fingers of his hand scratching across the round sack of his belly as he watched me leave for school in the mornings. It was a hot feeling, being watched by him. Like breaking out in hives. Two thousand pairs of eyes felt like an impossible number. I imagined splintering apart under the press of all that attention. But even then, there was a part of me that grew excited at the thought. There was already a part of me that reveled in the idea of being wanted that badly.

After a while it wasn't just Larry. There was Hank, whom my mother hired whenever the plumbing in the trailer wasn't working, which was nearly all the time. Later in my teens I'd point out to my mother that Hank probably didn't know what the fuck he was doing, considering the pipes seemed to always be broken, no matter how many times he fixed them. And later still, it would occur to me that Hank probably had a stake in keeping those pipes in poor shape. But at twelve, doing my homework at the card table in our kitchen or lounging on the couch watching TV, I wasn't sure why I'd suddenly been caught within the focus of Hank's gaze. He'd whistle under his breath as he clanked around under the sink, and he'd call from the kitchen to ask me for a glass of water from the tap in the bathroom. He'd look up at me when I obliged him, from his place on the floor, and I'd feel ten feet tall hovering over him and handing him the glass. He had a blond goatee that was flecked with gray, and he wore square glasses with silver frames. I'm sure I'd find him very attractive now, but back then I never did know what to think.

"Does your mother let you out of the house wearing that?" he'd say, motioning to my shorts, cut off so high on my legs that white triangles of pocket hung below the frayed edges of the denim. I'd shrug, snap my gum. I wasn't much for talking back then, trying to have no use for words. "What kind of music do you listen to? You like Johnny Cash?"

He started bringing me mix tapes when he came over, labeled in black marker, and I'd play them in my mother's boom box while he worked. It was a lot of country, which I didn't much care for, but there would be the odd song by the Rolling Stones or Led Zeppelin that I'd recognize.

"Dance, Chicklet," he'd say, using the pet name he'd chosen for me. I didn't know if it was because he called all the women in the trailer park "chicks," and I was a miniature version of them, or if it had something to do with the gum I always chewed. I never did ask. I never danced for him either, but I did bring him water, and I'd stand there as he drank it, feeling him watch me as he swallowed it down, feeling like I was a tacit participant in an exchange I didn't fully understand.

The women in the trailer park, the ones who didn't have husbands, or who had husbands who weren't worth a damn, used to talk about Hank like he belonged to them. I'd leave my window open at night and listen to my mother and her friends tease him in the dark as he walked home from the bar down the road, their voices making the night wind feel even slower, even hotter, as it drifted in through my screen. I used to imagine myself talking to men that way, with those long, heavy tones. I'd listen to him tease them back, his voice a bit too loud, and listen to their laughter. I wondered if I belonged to him the way he belonged to them, if there was a pecking order and I was at the end of it. He fixed the sink when my mother asked, and when he asked I brought him water and stood there as he looked at me. I wondered if desiring something made it yours already, just a little, simply through the act of wanting it.

Then there were the boys at school. Older boys, teenagers already out of junior high. My friends and I would pass by the high school's football field on the way home, and the boys at practice would shout at us, calling me "blondie," trying to get us to stop. We didn't stop because that was where our power came from, to be wanted and to have the ability to deny ourselves to others. Instead we'd walk to the 7-Eleven and buy pops and smoke cigarettes in the parking lot until the sky darkened above us and we were no longer afraid of being recognized walking in the direction of the trailer park. It was easier that way, better to be from nowhere than to be from there. Better to be anonymous, to be wanted from afar and always called a name that wasn't my own. Up close was when things got difficult; it was harder to be perfect when you were spread out beneath some boy in a truck or in his grandma's basement, hearing the blare of Telemundo on the TV upstairs, the mildew of the carpet permeating everything and making your skin itch. Up close I'd have to close my eyes and imagine Hank and the way he looked at me to get myself to come. And I never felt powerful afterward.

I learned my mother's lessons well, in those years. What she meant when she talked about the ballerinas, women so beautiful they could command silence and stillness and admiration from crowds of onlookers simply by the way they moved. I understood that beauty was a currency, so highly valued that it burned ancient cities and ruined the most powerful of men, so potent that it could pluck me from my meager upbringing and wipe out all of my history like a tide washing away footprints in sand. If you had enough, it didn't matter who you were. You could be anyone.

I can feel it as I walk east on Wilshire Boulevard. Even in the corners of L.A. where wealth and culture and beauty are at their most concentrated, I can feel people notice me. Some pause for a moment, trying to place me, wondering if I'm some young starlet they saw in a movie once. Some pretend like their eyes aren't tracking me as I pass, women mostly, looking at me with expressions that range from admiration to unadulterated envy. And then there are men, who seem not to care if they're caught staring, men with eyes like two dark challenges, who want me to look back at them. Men who look me up and down as I walk, men who honk from taxis or cat-call from construction sites. I've forgotten how intrusive it is, to be the object of such universal male attention. Sort of like being naked and on display. Sort of like having no skin at all.

My old agent, Harry Kramer, has an office in one of the high rises that are ubiquitous along Wilshire. I don't realize how cold I am until I'm in the lobby, where the light from the antique chandeliers overhead seems to bathe everything in warmth. I bypass the front desk and head straight into an elevator, my ears popping as it lifts me to the twentieth floor. Harry's office is the same as I remember it, all polished wood and frosted glass, though the girl at the desk looks so young I nearly turn back around as soon as the elevator doors open. But she looks a little startled when she sees me, and there, the powerful feeling is back. I take off my sunglasses, the large Audrey Hepburn frames, and smile at the poor thing.

"Is Harry in?"

"He is but . . . do you have an appointment?" she asks, faltering a bit, her eyes flitting between me and the blue glow of her computer screen.

"No, but he'll want to see me. Tell him Connie Kavanagh is here." I give her my stage name, because telling her that he'll want to see Connie Duffy would probably ruin the effect. She's too young to recognize my name so she just nods, pressing a button and speaking into her headset, her eyes on me as I stand there tapping a fingernail on the glass countertop. I should have a manicure, I realize, though I've been enjoying the clear smoothness of my bare nails, now that they aren't thickened and discolored with the fungus that overtook them in the past few years. It's all in the details though, this business, so it's a mistake I'll have to correct by the next time I see Harry. The girl presses another button and looks up at me with wide eyes, like a teenage babysitter who's been caught smoking a joint after the kids are asleep.

"He's on an important call at the moment, ma'am. But I can set up an appointment for you if you'd like to come back. Maybe sometime next week?" I know how this goes, I've partnered in this particular dance before. Harry became an expert at dodging me after I got sick, back before I realized that my career was already gone. He'd cancel appointments and reschedule me and have business trips or personal crises pop up at the last minute. Once he even stood me up for lunch in Chicago, leaving me sitting alone drinking glass after glass of chardonnay at the Park Grill until I finally staggered into a cab and cried all the way back to my apartment. I heard later from a mutual friend that he'd had a minor breakdown over my diagnosis and spent the next six months bingeing on OxyContin and having panic attacks until his own HIV tests came back negative. It didn't make much sense; we'd had a brief string of sexual encounters years before I started doing heroin, but he apparently didn't take my word for it. *Serves him right,* I thought at the time. That's what he gets for his aversion to condoms.

It occurs to me again that I should find a different agent, that Harry's behavior—and our history—should disqualify him from benefitting from my newfound advantages, but the only thing more dangerous than having Harry on my side is having him find out I've started working again with someone else. Hollywood has a fifteen-minute memory for people like me—actresses with all the potential in the world who never really make it past that first starring role—but agents like Harry never forget a face they've represented, no matter how altered it's become by time or cosmetic surgery or genetic rebirth. No, I need him working with me to keep the transfer a secret, so I smile at the girl at the desk until she practically wilts in front of me, a flower burned by too much sun.

"Listen, sweetie, a word to the wise—I know you're about fifteen years old—but women like me are always 'miss,' never 'ma'am,' understand? Very important." I tap my finger on the desk to emphasize my point. She turns the color of an under-ripe tomato, her blush competing with an almost green tinge of nauseated embarrassment.

"Of course, miss," she says.

"Well, if you don't mind, I'm just going to pop in and say a quick hello." I move toward the frosted glass of the door to Harry's office and the girl half-rises out of her chair, unsure how to halt me in my progress, or maybe debating whether or not to try to warn Harry of my impending intrusion.

"But, miss—" she says, though I'm already through the door. Harry is at his desk, a paper napkin stuffed in the collar of his shirt and what looks like a ham sandwich spread before him on his desk. He nearly jumps from his seat when I enter, forgetting to remove the napkin, and I watch his face transform from shock to outrage and back again with almost comic rapidity. He's a short man with round glasses, and, though he still has most of his hair, the years of sunning himself in the Bahamas have caught up to him in the soft mesh of lines on his face. He gapes at me like a well-dressed trout.

"Afternoon, Harry," I say, wishing I'd worn white gloves that I could pull off and tuck in the crook of my arm. But, despite my lack of props, I make a good show of dropping into one of his chairs and crossing my legs. The dress rides up a bit. "Please, have a seat," I say, motioning to his chair. He drops back into it like he's been knocked over by a gust of wind. See, I think, this is the man whose attention I begged for five years ago. This is the man who swept me off his desk like so much old paper. But now he's sitting down, in his own office, in one of Los Angeles's most fantastically expensive high rises, because I told him to. This is the power my mother worshipped so enduringly.

"Connie," he says, bringing his hand to his mouth and brushing the napkin as he moves. He glances down then yanks it from his collar and balls it up in his fist.

"It's been a while," I say.

"Yes, and you look, hell, you look . . ."

"Better than the last time you saw me, I'm sure," I reply, unwilling to let him say anything until I've finished. "I'm ready to start working again, Harry. Despite how we left things, I decided I owed you the professional courtesy of coming to you first with the opportunity of representing me."

He looks at me like I've propositioned him using the most pornographic language imaginable; it's a mixture of carnal awe and blind disbelief. "Representing you?"

"I've decided to return to acting. I assume you're still an actual agent and this isn't all just for show?" I motion around the office. I feel like I've turned up a winning hand in high-stakes poker and I'm watching the man across from me debate whether or not to call. It's a moment of pure, vengeful jubilation.

"Of course, but . . . my god, Connie. What on earth has happened to you?"

"Modern medicine, my friend. Now, would you be a dear and get me a glass of water?"

I detect a bit of a tremble in Harry's hand as he reaches for the button on his intercom.

# Hannah

I bring the awful second painting home, propping it up on our kitchen table, and wait for Sam. His flight got in this afternoon, but I know that he'll stop at his office before coming home, getting some last moments of work in. Since I've recovered from my illness, he's recommitted to his job with the fervor of a kid diving into summer vacation. As if his work is the reprieve from everything outside of it.

I don't know what I expect when he arrives, but he lights up when he sees me with a canvas. He barely kisses me hello, a chaste peck on my forehead, before his eyes alight on it.

"God that's incredible," he says, picking it up and holding it at arm's length. "It's really, really great, Hannah."

"No, it's not," I say, already weary at his ignorance. He warned me about this, I remind myself. That night in the gallery, he told me he knew nothing about art. And I have grown to resent him for it, his disinterest regarding the hinge on which my whole life moves.

"Of course it is. It's the best painting I've seen in a long time," he says, setting it down on our coffee table. "It's just great that you're painting again. Reentering that part of your life."

"All this does is prove the fact that we've been avoiding this whole time. I can't try and force everything back to being the way it was," I say, willing him to understand, to stop avoiding all the ways in which we are ruined. In which I am ruined.

"But you did it," he says. "It's right here. And it's great."

"It's not *great*." I say the word like it's something sour and raw I need to expel from my mouth. "It's not even close to great. It's a failure. That's what it looks like to fail at the only thing I've ever been able to do."

"You just need to keep working at it," Sam says, though now his voice is threaded with tension. His veneer of calm is wearing thin.

"It's not going to make a difference."

"Fine," he says, throwing up his arms. "So paint for yourself then. Forget what anyone else thinks. It didn't matter to me what prizes you won. It never mattered to me."

"Of course it mattered," I say, because this is what I want. This argument. It's why I brought the painting home in the first place, for this reason alone. Because losing my ability to paint is perhaps the most profound tragedy of my life. And for Sam, it doesn't even register. The thought of it makes me so angry, I have no compunction about going for the throat. "It mattered. That's the thing about being a hotshot journalist, isn't it? It looks damn cheap if your girl-friend's only marketable skill is taking her clothes off for worthless art students."

"I don't care what it looks like." I can feel him disengaging.

"Of course you do. This is what you want. This is just the right turn for you, isn't it?" I think of the expensive clothes I threw out, the perfect apartment I helped create. How hard I tried to become the sort of woman he could love. Someone wholly unlike the girl I was. "There was always too much about me that wasn't what you wanted. And that was fine in the beginning, because you were twenty-seven, right at the point in your life when everything you liked started to seem boring. That's what made it interesting at first, that there was a lot about me you didn't like."

"I never asked you to change anything," he says.

"No, you didn't ask. But you've always wanted it," I reply, step-ping toward him. "Don't you like me like this? All perfect for you now?" He is grinding his back teeth together, everything in him straining away from his own anger. But I want it, I want his rage, I want something from him that will match my sadness, my guilt. "Maybe I can be what you want now, hmm? Maybe I can be what you've always wanted, the perfect replacement for Lucy, staying home and keeping your house and having babies for you?"

There are tears in his eyes when he looks at me. And I hate him, in that moment. Hate him because he can't be as strong or as cruel as I am. He is no match for me, for the things of which I am capable. Hate him because he is a good man, and so all of his cruelty is born of weakness. "What the fuck is wrong with you?" he asks. "What makes you think I deserve this?"

"You know," I say, everything in me hardening with resolve. "You know. Don't make me ask."

He shakes his head, unfastening his tie and throwing it on the table. Doing anything he can to keep from answering. Finally he looks up at me.

"I don't know what you mean."

A laugh tears its way out of me. It's all become so absurd, absurd to the point of comedy, that we could keep this farce going even a minute longer. I want to tell him that this body isn't his. My old body might have belonged to him, but not this one, not anymore.

"Do you really think saying it out loud will make any difference?" I ask. "How about this? I'll go first," I say, because I've forgotten not to hurt him. I can feel all of the sadness and regret wash out of me, my anger like a purifying fire. "I slept with David Jenkins. Your turn."

Both his hands come down on the table, fast, and I jump at the noise. It silences me, both of us. We stand there. He doesn't look at me. And his expression changes then because he finally understands what this is. He knows that this is how it ends.

"Goddamn you," he says, his hands tightening into fists as he straightens to face me. "Fine. I didn't have the flu. All right? Is that what you want to hear?"

"Maybe," I reply. I think of Lucy crying into his shirt, the way he held her, the intimacy there. Yes, I want to hear all of it, every detail. If for no other reason but that it will wipe away my guilt over David. "Tell me about what happened with Lucy."

"She covered for me. She lied, even though she didn't want to. She did it because I begged her to."

"What happened, Sam?"

"I couldn't stay," he says. "The doctors, they told me that you wouldn't survive the week, your numbers were too low, you weren't going to make it to the transfer. And I couldn't stay there and watch."

"What?" I have never heard this. No doctor has ever told me this. But the pain of that week was so intense, so wrenching, I know it must be true. I know that I was dying.

"I couldn't watch that, not with you. So I got in my car and . . . drove. For days. Just drove, to Montana, Wyoming, I think. Waiting for Lucy to call and tell me . . ." He's crying. I'm not sure I've ever seen him cry, in all the years I've known him.

"Oh god." I grip the back of a chair. My palms are wet. There's a taste of metal on my tongue. I sit down carefully, my mouth pressed into my hand.

"I was out of my mind. I can't even . . ."

"You need to go," I say, but there's no air behind it, it's the barest of whispers. This is too much, too much for this new body, maybe. I'm cold, a deep cold. As if this truth, the one I had not prepared for, has set off some terrible chain reaction within me. I'm worried it's more than this body can take. "Please. I don't want you to come back here."

"Hannah." He drops to his knees in front of me, clasping my hands in his. He is so warm that I want to curl into him, let him gather me up. But I can't. I can't stop remembering what it was like to wake up day after day and ask for Sam, because Sam was who I asked for when I was scared. And he was gone.

"Please. You have to go." I can ask this of him, and I know he will give it to me. His body shudders a bit, and then he straightens.

"I'm sorry. Please, know that," he says. I can only shake my head. He should have chosen someone good, someone like him. He knows that I am not one for forgiveness. So he takes his keys out of his pocket and works the silver one off the ring, setting it on the table between us. Then he picks up his suitcase and leaves.

# David

Hannah calls me in the middle of the night, but I'm awake. I haven't been sleeping well since Beth left to go back to Wisconsin to be with David Jr.; since the call with Burt Leeland. The apartment feels foreign, cold, and hard around me like everything in it has been carved from stone.

"I need to talk," she says, a strange crackle in her voice that I mistake for the static of her cell phone.

"It's a little late," I say, and then wait for a response. "Hannah?" Nothing comes. I let out a long breath. "All right, come over. You remember the address?"

"Yeah," she says.

She shows up at my door and she looks bad, like she has an awful head cold. But when she steps closer, steps inside, I can see that I'm wrong. She's not sick. She's upset. She glances around the darkness in my apartment, the flicker of the television strobing against the living room wall, the college basketball game I've been dozing in and out of for the past hour or so. Her eyes look hollow in the dark, her hair lank around her shoulders.

"What's wrong?" I ask, but she shakes her head. It's a cold feeling, when she kisses me, so different from the scorch of that kiss on the rooftop, or Beth's tepid embraces. Even her skin under my hands feels chilled by the winter air, and she tastes of salt, and I think of water, huge expanses of dark water. And I know that I've been lying this whole time, when I've been shouting to myself and anyone else who will listen that I'm a different person. A better man. That I've changed, that last time was a one-off, a misstep that can be corrected. Because this girl, this damn girl, knows me too well already. She knows that I can't say no. Not here, alone in the middle of the night in the darkness of my apartment, with this cold girl in my arms, where the possibility of daylight feels very remote. Here there is only going under. Here, there is only giving in.

It strikes me anew, when we're upstairs in the muddy street-light flooding my bedroom, how different her body is from the other women I've known. She feels like bone beneath my hands, and her skin is distractingly flawless, so different from Beth's marks and moles and the dark seam of the C-section scar that traverses her belly. Hannah is thin and supple and pliant beneath me, and I want her with such force I'm afraid of hurting her. There is something so tender and vulnerable about her, like the skin of a nectarine, as if I could bruise her with simply the press of a fingertip. And it's all a little sickening, the strength of my desire and the ferocity with which she answers it. This is how people are ruined, I think. This is how kingdoms are toppled. Wanting, like this.

It's only after, when she's lying facing away from me on the bed with the sheet curled around the jab of her hipbone, that I think of Beth and the second chance I've already begun to squander. The thought makes me angry.

"Where's Sam tonight?" I ask, because I want to be a little mean to this girl, as she has been to me by showing up at my door tonight.

"Gone," she says, her voice flat. She doesn't cry, or even breathe any differently after she says it. It's as if all the emotion has been drained from her, left her still and empty, and I think that I've been the tool of this transformation.

"His choice or yours?"

"His," she says, but I think she's lying. My lower lip is bleeding from her teeth. Tonight was a palate-cleansing sort of fuck, like she's trying to blot out the memory of someone else. And she doesn't seem like the sort of woman that men leave.

"Too bad."

"Where's your wife?" she asks, and there's more than a little cruelty in her voice.

"Wisconsin. With my son."

"Must get lonely for you here."

"Sometimes."

She turns to face me then. "Does she know?"

"Does she . . ."

"About your extracurricular activities." The way she says it makes me want to kiss her, or throttle her, to wipe the smugness out of her expression.

"What makes you think I've done this before?" I ask.

"I would think you'd look a whole lot guiltier now if you've never done this before."

I sit up, finding my boxers in the mess of blankets and pulling them on. I don't want to look at her because she's right, I should feel guiltier. But she's wrong, too, in a way. This body that was supposed to be my clean slate. This body that was supposed to make me better.

"Do you want me to leave?" she asks, and the easiness in her voice is sort of astonishing, considering the state she was in when she arrived. It strikes me for the first time that she might be dangerous, this girl. She might be made of tougher mettle than I ever imagined. But now it's me who doesn't want to be alone.

"You can stay if you want," I reply, getting up and walking to the bathroom, taking a piss with the door open.

"I realized something the other day," she says, her voice floating in from the bedroom. I splash some water on my face and chest from the sink.

"What's that?"

"I don't think I've dreamed at all since the transfer."

"Dreamed?" I reenter the bedroom, and she's lying half covered with the sheet. She doesn't look real, lying there in the streetlight. I want to sink my teeth into her, like stepping into new snow. I want the satisfaction of it, to mar something that is too, too perfect.

"At night. I used to dream a lot. I used to wake up tired in the mornings from it, these really long, realistic dreams. But now I wake up and I can't remember a single thing. I can't remember if I've been dreaming at all."

It's a bit unsettling, because when I think about it there hasn't been a single night since the transfer that I haven't slept in complete oblivion. "I don't think I have either."

"Doesn't that make you sad?" she asks, as I settle back on the bed beside her. "The idea that maybe we can't? It's like being told that you'll never see the stars again. You don't think much about them until they're not there anymore."

It's too much to think about all we've lost. To tally all the bits of ourselves we've had to shed to stay alive.

"Sometimes I think I could spend the rest of my life waiting for the things I've lost since the transfer to come back," she says, and I know we're thinking the same thing. "But then what good would the rest of my life be?"

I don't answer her. I don't have an answer. Instead I pin her wrists at her sides and go to work on the skin at the inside of her right hip bone until an angry wheel of color shows under my mouth.

Jackson arrives early the next morning, before I'm even out of bed. It used to be disconcerting when I was first running for Congress, the sort of access that my staff required, how people seemed to be constantly letting themselves in and out of our hotel suites or our home in Wisconsin. Now it just feels typical, as Jackson raps twice on my bedroom door and pauses for permission to be admitted. I sit up in bed, rubbing a crust of dried saliva from the corner of my mouth.

Hannah is already gone. I never expected her to stay the night, but still it feels a little unfinished with her absent. There are probably still things for us to say to each other. But it's better this way, now that Jackson's here.

"Yeah," I call toward the door. Jackson enters in one brisk, economical movement, though his eyes are on his cell phone.

"Good morning, sir."

"What's the word, Jackson?"

"I've got your call sheet for the morning," he says, dropping a folder stuffed with papers on the bed in front of me.

"And let me guess, is Rick Preston's name on it?"

"For the fifth week in a row, yes," he replies. "And I'm not sure the best course of action is waiting for another call from Leeland before you get this done."

I open the file. Rick Preston's name is indeed at the top of the list.

"The FDA vote isn't until August. And I don't intend to jump the minute Burt Leeland snaps his fingers. If he's going to have a Labrador in Congress, he's going to understand that it's a reluctant one."

"I understand, sir. But, while Leeland might seem like a sweet old man, he has an itchy trigger finger when he feels like he's being tested."

I shut the file and toss it toward my feet. "So, theoretically speaking—"

"Because you know how much I love it when we get theoretical." Jackson's tone has an insolence in it that he tempered better before I got sick. And I'm in no mood this morning.

"Jackson, I know I'm sitting here in my boxers, but let's not forget that I'm a U.S. Congressman, all right?"

He blanches, straightening his glasses. "Of course, sir."

"To absolutely flog a metaphor here, what happens if we take the ammo out of Leeland's gun?"

"If we?" Jackson makes a motion like he's about to sit on the corner of the bed, then immediately thinks better of it and pulls up a chair.

"We make a statement about my involvement in SUBlife. 'It's a lifesaving procedure with far-reaching benefits to humanity,' that sort of thing."

Jackson looks like he's bracing to be slapped. "Theoretically speaking?"

"Humor me."

"Well, you can kiss S&J's campaign contribution good-bye, for starters," he says. "Though, that point would probably be moot." He stops then.

"Why?" I ask.

"With seventy-eight percent of your district identifying as Christian, devoutly Christian, all the money in the world couldn't buy back the votes you'd lose right there. And that gets even worse if Leeland leaks how you got your way into that study in the first place. Then you're a man who took a seat in a lifeboat from some-one else. It's not out of the realm of possibility that someone would attempt to bring criminal charges against you."

"Jesus." For the first time, I can feel how little sleep I've had. My eyes feel raw. My limbs ache.

"I'd say your chances for reelection would fall somewhere around the likelihood that the Cubs will sweep the Series this year." Jackson looks as if he's regretting the words, even as he says them. He paws a hand through his hair, everything about him scrawny and tired. But I know there are limitless reserves of energy there, under the surface. This is a man who doesn't know how to stop fighting his particular war. "Sir, you knew there were going to be times like this. Where it's not about right and wrong . . . where right and wrong has nothing to do with being smart."

I nod. "Sure, except it never seemed to matter as much before."

"I know."

"It matters now," I say, though it's impossible to resolve my desire to be good, to do the right thing, while I'm sitting wrapped in the musty sheets recently vacated by my new mistress. And despite the fact that it's barely ten in the morning, I want a drink so badly my jaw aches.

"Of course, sir," he says and hands me the phone.

# Hannah

In the morning I end up on Penny's doorstep. I don't want to go back to my empty apartment, not now, not yet. I use my spare key to get into Penny's building and wait on the steps below the third floor landing for her to get home. I could let myself in, curl up on her couch in one of her beautiful old quilts and sleep a little. I could sit in her kitchen with a drink. But I don't do any of those things. I wait on the steps, all lank hair and overused muscles, smelling of David's sweat, because anything else doesn't feel penitent enough.

I can hear Penny on the phone when the door bangs behind her. Her voice floats up the staircase before she does, and at first the exactness of her diction sounds strange and jumbled, until I realize she's speaking French. She's talking to her father. She pauses on the steps when she sees me there and then sits down next to me. She's carrying a bag from Chicago Bagel Authority. It's the first time I realize I'm hungry. When she hangs up she squeezes my shoulder.

"Rough night?" she asks.

"Sam and I . . ." but she's already nodding.

"He called. I went by your place but you were gone. I was worried."

"Please tell me you didn't know," I say.

"Of course not," Penny replies, and my trust in her word is absolute, as always. "I'm not in the business of keeping Sam's secrets for him."

"Right, because that's my sister's job."

"At least you know they weren't having an affair." Penny opens her paper bag and offers me a bagel. I shake my head. The idea

203

of eating, of anything that will serve this traitorous body of mine, which will lie down so easily for a man like David Jenkins just hours after the love of my life walks out the door, feels sacrilegious. And vindictiveness is my new religion.

"This is worse."

She shuts the bag, setting it on the step next to her. "Yes, it is."

"Anyway," I say, rising from the stairs, feeling my legs protest under me. "You busy?"

"Not particularly. Want to get some coffee?"

"I don't think I can face the world right now," I reply. She doesn't rise. It seems uncharacteristic for Penny, who is always the one charging forward, always the leader. "You want to talk about this out in your hallway?"

"See, Hannah, the thing is," Penny begins, but it hits me before she even has a chance to say it. That stinging realization, that wire of truth uncoiling inside me.

"Sam's here," I say, and then carefully press a hand to my mouth so I don't scream something awful at her. Impulse control does not seem to be this body's forte.

"He needed a place to stay," Penny says, on her feet now, speaking fast. "I figured better he stay here, give you some space for now."

"You hate Sam," I say, taking my hand from my mouth, feeling tears creep up. "You've hated him ever since you've known him. And now? Now is when you choose to take his side?"

"I'm not taking his side, Hannah," Penny says.

"He can afford a hotel. He doesn't have to stay here."

"I was worried about him, all right?" she says, standing now to face me, everything in her animated with her usual righteousness. Penny, who has never questioned a step she's ever taken. "The way he sounded last night . . ."

"What about me?" I ask, a child pulling at her mother's skirts. Perhaps selfishness is my new religion. I don't care. "You're supposed to be the one who is there for me. When I need you."

"And if you'd shown up here, I would have been," Penny replies.

"But I'm not the one you went to last night. And I have a pretty good idea who that was."

"Fuck you," I say, shaking my head, trying to take a full breath as I begin to descend the stairs.

"You're making the wrong choice, Hannah," Penny says. I pause, though I don't turn. "You're not capable of loving someone like him. You know that."

"That's pretty much the whole point, Penny," I say, continuing down the stairs without looking back.

# Connie

I stay a week in L.A. instead of a day. Harry puts me up in a very expensive hotel in Beverly Hills, like he used to when I was very young and very pliant and the idea of dating an older man seemed chic, even if the older man was my slightly slimy agent. I can't quite tell if he's trying to get back into my good graces or under my skirt, but it doesn't really matter to me when the spoils are the same. I spend my days working on my body's inaugural tan by the pool, and in the evenings Harry takes me out to what is always the newest, the next big restaurant.

It feels a little garish to be so ornamental for this man. Harry has an excellent reputation as an agent and as a womanizer, and I get the impression that people think I'm serving his latter persona more than his former. It's bad enough that I'm letting him buy me dinner, but he's also buying the dresses I wear, and the combination makes me feel a little like a call girl, a kept woman.

If only he knew, I think, on my last night in Los Angeles, my skin pink and raw with sun, sticking to the leather interior of his town car in a way that is just this side of painful. I watch the street-lights tick by outside and think of all the things I haven't done in this new body. It's not that I want to be celibate. It just seems to have turned out that way, in the months since the transfer. It's turned into a bit of a game, in fact, a test for me, like those women who create contests around who can go the longest without eating carbs or chocolate. As if denying yourself pleasure could hone you into something more perfect, something more essential.

Harry, of course, doesn't want to take the hint when he drops me at my hotel that night. His hand snakes down to my ass when I kiss him on the cheek, and my body responds without waiting for the approval of my head. I'm not attracted to this man, not at all. I'm a bit repulsed, in fact, but it's been so long since I've been touched. I have to take a breath before taking his wrist and drawing it away from my skirt.

"I'm reinventing myself, Harry," I chide. "It's about breaking my old habits."

"It's hard to argue with something that makes you look like this," Harry says, adjusting his belt buckle in a way that seems obscene. "But I'm willing to give it the old college try."

"Maybe some other time," I reply, and adjust his tie as I escape back into my hotel room. I wonder how long I'll be able to hold Harry off. That's the thing about men with power, they're not accustomed to being denied the things they want. They don't worry at all about being sharp, about being essential.

I fly back to Chicago in the morning with a suitcase full of new dresses, courtesy of Harry's American Express card. Dr. Grath's apartment door is partway open when I get home. I'm simultaneously worried and annoyed. Worried, because what if the old man is lying dead on the floor and a robber is tossing his place as I stand here in the hallway? And annoyed, because I know there's no burglar, but Dr. Grath knows I'll still have to check to make sure. I put my own keys away and cross the hall, making sure he can hear the animosity in the click of my heels.

I push the door open and stalk in. Dr. Grath is waiting for me, a book open on his knee, his hand moving across it as his eyes track limply in middle space.

"Your door was open," I say, even though it's obvious, because I want him to know what a stupid thing it is to do to get my attention.

"Funny," he says, and goes back to his reading. I stand there tapping my foot, unwilling to break the silence myself, and unable to go now that I'm here, in his damp little apartment, with him sitting there by himself in one of his threadbare sweaters.

"You need something?" I say, finally, because my feet feel like shit in the heels I'm wearing. They're new, of course, and not particularly ideal for walking home from the L. They're made for women who can afford cab fare.

"You've been making yourself scarce," Dr. Grath replies. "You missed *To Kill a Mockingbird* last week."

"I've seen it."

"Of course you have," he says. "But it's the sort of film that can't just be seen once, you know."

"Sure," I reply, still standing in the doorway.

"Sit down," he says, motioning to the other chair in his living room.

"I just got in. And I'm tired."

"You want to stay, honey," Dr. Grath says. "It's *Casablanca* tonight."

I sigh. The man is good, I'll give him that. It's the perfect trap, and I've stepped right into it, and now I can feel its cold jaws snapping shut around my leg. He knows, too well, that there is a part of me that can't refuse this. *Casablanca* was the first movie I ever watched in this tiny apartment, only a handful of weeks after I moved back to Chicago. I'd followed the pot smell down the hall and found Dr. Grath watching the flickering black and white of the screen. The movie had left me in tears that night, even though I'd seen it before and never thought much of it. Somehow things felt much more potent in this apartment than they ever have in the rest of the world. Now I stalk in, shutting the door behind me with a little too much force, dropping into the chair with bratty resignation.

"I'll stay for a few minutes," I say.

"I'm glad you can work me into your schedule," Dr. Grath replies. "You've been quite busy lately. I thought you disappeared off the face of the earth again."

"I was in L.A.," I reply. "Seeing my agent."

"Seeing him?" Dr. Grath asks, eyebrows rising.

"Not like that. Well, at least not for me. He's going to get me some work. Modeling. Maybe a movie."

"Picking up where you left off, eh?"

"Just, you know, taking the new body for a little spin," I say. "He's going to fly me back out in a month or two. When he's got meetings set up with producers and such."

"Of course," Dr. Grath says, with a hint of mockery in his tone. "Just as long as that new body of yours doesn't catch anything you can't get rid of with a strong course of antibiotics."

I laugh, throwing my head back, and it feels like something I've forgotten. How to laugh, when it's genuine. This week I've found myself giggling, like a reflex, even when the person across from me isn't the slightest bit amusing. It's an unnerving habit, like smiling at strangers, or flipping your hair. Something that's done purely for another person's benefit, something completely artificial. It makes me wonder what I'm teaching this new body, what habits I'm creating that have nothing to do with what I'm thinking or feeling, that only involve being seen in a certain way.

"I appreciate the concern, old man. But I caught the virus through the needle, remember?" I say. "Now how about you turn on the goddam TV?"

I end up falling asleep on Dr. Grath's couch halfway through the movie, waking only to hear Bogey send Ingrid Bergman on her way with the uptight Nazi-fighter and drag myself back to my apartment in a stupor. I didn't realize how badly I needed sleep.

My apartment is reassuringly spartan, after the clutter of Dr. Grath's. After those first few nights it wasn't enough to get rid of the mess that had built up in my five years as a hermit. I had to get rid of everything save for my bed, my better clothes, an old lamp, and the mugs and plates that weren't overly chipped. The rest had to go. Everything that belonged to that sick girl, everything that could be linked back to my former life.

I wonder, sometimes, why I came back here from L.A. when I got sick. It's a puzzling sort of question because it would have been much easier to wither away in the warm sunshine of the West Coast than here, where the winters can just about kill a person without trying very hard. All I can think is, on some level, I must be like my mother. She was in New York when she got pregnant with me, and she dragged herself back here, to the city where she grew up, to have her baby and live out her years in a suburban trailer park and lament her lost dance career. Some part of us must still be wild, I think, like a wounded animal that drags itself back to its home to die.

# Linda

The only recipe I can remember is my mother's recipe for chocolate chip cookies. I used to make them when Jack and Katie were little, on rainy days or when February grew particularly cold and dreary, when I needed something to fascinate and occupy the little girl who sat with me on the kitchen counter, dipping her fingers into the bag of flour and delighting in the silky grit of its texture. Cookies are necessary now, I think. I need to make something sweet and simple and full of fleeting happiness. It's the sort of task I've always associated with being a mother.

I haul my big stand mixer out of the attic, where it sat collecting dust for the past eight years in a box labeled "Garage sale??" I wonder why Tom didn't sell it, when it would have fetched an easy hundred or two from some neighbor on our street. I imagine all of my things, my only things, spread out on the blacktop of our driveway for neighbors to paw through. I wonder if Tom and the kids have made cookies since I've been gone. Somehow, I doubt it.

In the kitchen, I whip coconut oil and sugar together with vanilla inside the stainless-steel bowl of the mixer, and the sound of it draws Katie down from her room. She glances at the frothy liquid spinning around the sides of the bowl, and then looks up at me. She's nervous, I think. I recognize it, because it mirrors the clench I get in my stomach whenever my children are around. I think of this next child, the one I'm carrying with me, and wonder if she will feel so foreign to me as well once she's born, or if she will be connected to this body in a way that Katie is not.

"What are you making?" Katie asks. Her dark hair is pulled into a high knot, so slick and tight that I can see the shape of her skull underneath.

"Cookies. Chocolate chip," I answer, measuring out flour and baking powder and rolled oats into a separate bowl. I think of my daughter like a skittish cat, one who will dash off if I acknowledge her too directly. My reticence pays off after a moment, when she perches on a stool on the other side of the counter.

"When we make cookies with Daddy they come out of a tube. But Jenny's mom makes them herself. Only it doesn't look like that," she says with an artful expression of disdain and suspicion, motioning to the oil that has settled in a shining, sugary pool at the bottom of the stainless-steel bowl.

"That's because I use coconut oil instead of butter," I reply.

"Why?"

I shrug. "My mother didn't eat butter. This is her recipe." Katie looks suspicious as I add eggs and beat them in with the oil and sugar.

"Can I help?"

I hand her a cup measure, and we're off to the races. By the time I'm mixing in the chocolate chips with a wooden spoon, I'm pretty confident that only half the dough will make it onto the cookie sheet. And I'm nearly effervescent with my success, of luring my daughter into a solid half-hour of interaction.

"You're practicing for the basketball team?" I ask, rifling through what little trivia I know about my own daughter. I'm sick with it, the paltry knowledge I have of who this child is now, after knowing every bit of her for her first four years. Now I know more about the lives of the characters on *Stratford Pines* than those of my own children.

"Junior league," she replies, with such a swell of confidence I can barely imagine she's only twelve years old, and not some capable young woman in full possession of her own abilities. "But Coach says when I'm in high school he can see me going straight to varsity. He says I've got speed."

I grin at this. "I used to have some speed myself. I ran track and cross country when I was younger, all the way through college."

"I know," she replies, pulling a couple of chocolate chips out of the bag and popping them into her mouth. "Daddy says I've got your feet. Pegasus feet. With wings on them."

She plants one of her sneakers on the slat of her kitchen stool so I can see the little cartoon wing she's drawn onto the heel. I think of my own collection of battered running shoes, the ones Tom threw away after my accident, with their identical little wings inked onto them. *This girl is mine,* I think.

"What's your favorite subject in school?" I ask.

"Art," she says, her face twitching from contemplation to dissatisfaction. "And Mandarin. Both of them are cool."

"You're taking Mandarin?"

Katie nods. "Daddy said I should. That it's important."

"It is," I reply, as if it were my idea in the first place. It was something we talked about, Tom and me, when the kids were little, how I regretted my youthful rebellion against my mother. I'd taken French in high school, despite the fact that I'd picked up enough Mandarin at my mother's church and from listening to her talk to my grandparents on the phone that I was nearly conversational. *I'm an American,* I told her. I pretended it was endearing when kids at school called me a Twinkie. I never had friends over to my house because there was nothing worse than having a mother who was not only sad, but who also couldn't order pizza without having to repeat herself.

"Why didn't your mother eat butter?" she asks, picking up another gob of dough and licking it from between her sticky fingers.

"Being healthy was very important to her," I reply.

"But isn't she dead?" Katie doesn't see me flinch, but she looks up at me when I don't answer right away. "I mean, I remember going to her funeral. Me and Daddy and Jack."

"Yes, she is," I reply, trying to focus on my work instead of dwelling on the past. The trick I learned in the hospital. Pretend you're born the day before. You have no history. No history. It occurs to me then, that maybe I learned that trick well before the hospital.

"So I guess she wasn't that healthy then, huh?" Katie asks. "If she died so young?"

"She didn't die from being sick," I reply. "She died from being sad."

"Daddy said she got sick," Katie says, and I can tell she's looking at me even though my head is down, my eyes are on the batter clinging to my spoon. My mother's recipe.

My mother was always fragile, the kind of person who could be tipped over by a careless word. She'd met my father in Wuhan while he was teaching English and she was working in a restaurant near the university. He was an American boy through and through, though his parents were both Chinese, and there must have been something exciting in that for her because he'd badgered her into coming back to the States with him when his visa expired. I sometimes imagined my mother as a young woman, back when she could still fool herself into believing she had the fortitude to uproot herself from ancient, familial soil and travel somewhere new. By the time she realized the truth, by the time she must have finally admitted to herself that she should not have come to the other side of the world, she was already a wife and mother to an American child.

I'd spent most of my childhood protecting her, trying to fend off the world, warding off all of its unkindnesses, like keeping a lion at bay with a whip and a chair. She seemed to carry the distance with her, as if she were far away from everything because she was far away from home. I remember thinking what a good mother I'd be one day because I had learned so well how to care for someone. Because I would never be the sullen sort, the kind who escaped into her head, the kind of mother whose children couldn't reach her. The reality that I've become like her, just like her, makes my hands shake to the point where I must put down the spoon so Katie won't notice.

But no, I'm not just like my mother. I have more resilience than she did. She was so easily bruised, so easily discouraged, the sort of woman who would dump a half-cooked omelette into the trash if it began sticking to the pan, or burn the drapes in the fireplace when she noticed her hems weren't straight.

It was not such a great shock to me that my accident was a tragedy she could not handle. It was not so great a shock when Tom came to me in the hospital and told me that she'd taken pills and walked off the end of the dock near our family's house on Lake Michigan, her pockets filled with stones. I'd hated him for telling me. He could have lied, could have made up an entire life for my mother and I would have never known. He could have created a different death for her even, cancer or blood clots or pneumonia after a fall. His honesty felt cruel, more for him than for me. That was when I began to be born yesterday. To have no history at all.

"I guess she did, in a way," I reply. My nose is running a little. I go to the sink and dab at it with a paper towel. "I guess she did get sick."

"Too bad she couldn't get a SUB like you," Katie says. "If she was still alive maybe you could have gone to live with her."

I turn back toward her then. "Why would I go live with her?" I ask. "You and Daddy and Jack are here."

"I just mean, maybe you'd be happier with someone you know, that's all."

"What makes you think I'm not happy?"

She avoids my eyes. "But you're not, are you?" she says. At first, I don't know what to say. I can't answer her, and she nods, as if I've only confirmed her suspicions. As if she's somehow let me down, as if my sadness is her doing.

"Katie, don't you want me to be here?" I ask.

"I don't know," she says, the pitch of her voice rising, as if I'm accusing her of something. She gets up fast from her stool. "What if I don't?"

"That's all right," I say, but it doesn't stop her. She's off, running up the back stairs to her room. I hear her door slam. I want to tell her that she's not required to be happy that I've come back, and come back altered. I can't begrudge her hating me a little, just like I always hated my mother a little, no matter how much I loved her. But I can't tell her that, because of the little bit of something, the little pea of tissue that's combusting with life in my stomach. It scares me too much to think that I'm the same as my mother. To think that I could hurt these kids the way she hurt me, through her own weakness. And still, still, I find myself dumping the cookie dough out in the trash instead of baking it because it has been ruined, this afternoon, and more, perhaps much more along with it.

# David

Hannah shows up at the worst possible moment. I'm on the phone with Beth because David Jr. broke his arm jumping the fence into the neighbor's yard this afternoon, and she seems to think that the bone will heal faster if I hop in my Audi and drive up there immediately. Ignoring the fact that the kid will have been asleep for hours before I've even crossed the state line. Ignoring the fact that I technically shouldn't be driving. And I'm right at the point of really needing a drink, at the point where Beth's words bounce off me like hot little pellets of asphalt, where everything in me is dying to call her a spoiled cunt and throw the phone across our well-furnished living room—that's the moment Hannah arrives.

She shows up this time with a bottle, something with pink frosted glass. Fuck.

"Hey," she says, before I can cover the mic on my phone, and then Beth is in my ear asking who the hell is coming over at this time of night. Hannah takes a sip as she slips off her coat, leaving it in a soft puddle on the entryway floor, her mouth on the neck of the bottle doing something vaguely pleasant to my spine, setting off a little thrill there.

"Beth, I've gotta go," I say, and I don't even wait for an answer before I end the call, dropping the phone into my pocket. My anger evaporates at the sight of Hannah. She doesn't have much on under her coat, it looks like silk in the darkness, a little pearlescent slip that shows off her breasts wonderfully, insubstantial as they are. The lace at the hem of it slides up and down her thighs like a tide as she leans back to sip from the bottle. This was the sort of girl I've always known would be my undoing. Not as elegant as Beth, or as staggeringly, pristinely beautiful as Connie. A girl who didn't instill the kind of hesitance that those other women would, the subtle, almost unintelligible fear of marring them in some way, as if the blunt instrument of my body could strip them of some of their perfection. As if I could be made to want them less, by having them.

My sexual fascination with Hannah runs no such risks. This is a girl with sharp teeth, hard as bone, standing there with my other favorite devil clutched in her hand, wafting off her breath.

"What's the matter?" she asks.

"You brought your own refreshments."

She giggles a little. "It felt like that sort of night. Maybe it's a full moon. Who knows?"

"Wine coolers were never my favorite," I say, stepping toward her. She steps back a little, teasing in the dark, silhouetted by the orange glow of the streetlights on the window shade.

"What was?"

"Scotch, mainly."

"And you haven't had a drink since the transfer?" she asks. I shake my head. "Well, then I'm not sharing with you." She takes another sip. She's unsteady on her legs, I can tell, because she stumbles a little, raising that scrap of silk even farther. My self-control is in tatters.

"Yes you are." I take a few steps toward her, and she retreats again.

"Nope."

I chase her around the room, taking advantage of the moment when she bangs her shin on the glass coffee table to divest her of the bottle. She doesn't seem pleased as she reaches down to rub her leg, which is already starting to bruise. "Asshole," she says, in a voice that tells me she's not even close to kidding, but I'm not listening. I'm holding the bottle, looking down its neck as if it were a wading pool positioned beneath the towering ladder of a high-dive. I take a sip and it's sugary and sort of floral-tasting, with a harsh bite underneath. Not what I remember, not even close. I wait for that report of pleasure within my body, that familiar click of a switch flipping, opening all of my channels at once. But still, there's nothing.

"Well?" Hannah asks, straightening up, her hands on her hips. I shrug.

"It's not very good."

"It cost seven dollars. It's not exactly Chateau Margaux."

I take another swig. The burn of it is sort of pleasant, like easing into a hot tub. "Why do you keep coming back here?"

"Do you not want me to keep coming back?"

"My chief of staff certainly wouldn't."

"And what's his name?" she asks, closing the distance between us and popping the buttons on my shirt, one by one.

"Jackson."

"Jackson."

"Is it because you can't paint?"

Her hands drop, finding their way back to her hips.

"Chatty tonight, aren't we?"

"Explain it to me. There are a million ways to make it rich in this country, take it from me. You don't have to be able to paint."

"Getting rich wasn't the point," she says, dropping back onto the couch and crossing her legs in front of her. "It was about being extraordinary at something."

"And being ordinary . . ."

"Is just about the worst thing I can imagine," she replies, making slow circles with her ankle. She's wearing heels. It seems absurd to me now, because I'm pretty sure it's pouring outside tonight. Everything about her is suddenly a mix of sadness and absurdity. "But you can understand that, can't you?"

Of course I can. We are so much the same, this girl and me. I take another drink. The trill of my phone's ringtone goes off in my pocket. I glance at the screen, and it's Beth. I silence the call, and then shut my phone off.

"Who was that?" Hannah asks.

"Concerned citizen," I reply, unwilling to get off-topic, like the politician that I am. "So what are you going to do now?"

She shrugs one shoulder, making her collarbone appear and disappear beneath the smoothness of her skin and the strap of her slip. "Maybe I'll marry a congressman. A Democrat."

Clever, this girl, I think, even as I'm striding toward her and hauling her up by her wrists. I forget the bottle on the glass of the coffee table. I forget everything for a little while.

# Hannah

David calls me on a Tuesday morning. Early. I ignore the call at first, afraid that it's Sam, again, leaving a voicemail that I will again delete, unheard. I try to get back to sleep. But when I realize the effort is completely futile, I check my phone and realize it's David who called. He picks up on the second ring.

"What if I'd been on a ledge when I called you?" he says, without even a greeting. "What if I was calling so you'd talk me down? You really think you could live with yourself if you left me hanging?"

"Are you on a ledge?" I ask, yawning.

"No, I'm in the middle of a conference call with the CEO of a fertilizer company. If that isn't enough to make you want to off yourself, I don't know what is."

"I don't know, isn't dealing with excrement something that you're used to as a member of the Republican Party?"

David laughs on the other end of the line. "Ouch, Reed. You really know how to hurt a guy."

"How exactly are you talking to me if you're on a conference call?"

"I have the linkup muted. You'd be surprised how much this guy has to say about fertilizer."

"I'm sure I would," I say, turning back over.

"Are you in bed?" he asks.

"Yeah," I reply. "It's a little early here in the world of the unemployed."

"Can I come over?"

"No."

"Come on," he chides. "I want to see your place."

"Why?" I ask.

"I want to see what you're really like. See what books you have. Go snooping through your medicine cabinet. That sort of thing." I think of bringing Sam to my old apartment, the one that held so much of me. David would learn nothing from this moneyed, sanitized version of my life.

"Sorry to disappoint you, but you're not going to find out much about me here," I reply. Then a thought occurs to me. "Hey, you want to see what I'm really like?"

The painting hangs in the Museum of Contemporary Art, where it has ever since Trevor won a commission for the lobby of the Wrigley Building two years ago and became the most in-demand young artist in Chicago. Penny was apoplectic about the whole thing, of course. It was all I could do to keep her from crashing her car when I told her.

"That pretentious weasel doesn't have half of your talent," she'd yelled, her voice careening around the interior of the little vehicle. "Why aren't you more pissed about this?"

I hadn't been, not at the time. Perhaps because I knew, in the back of my mind, that it was only a matter of time before it would be my work hanging in the galleries and the historic lobbies. Perhaps because I knew that Penny was right, that his talent couldn't touch mine. That my time would come.

I'd come to visit the painting every once in a while before the transfer, as if it were an abandoned child, left in the city its maker had outgrown. Trevor was in New York, last I heard, dating a chef from the Food Network and failing to follow up on his early success. Now, standing in front of the painting again sends a low thrill through me, like running into an ex-lover on the street and smiling at each other a little too long. But there's pain there, too. Because I can understand what Trevor must be feeling now, to have all the potential in the world and worry it will never be realized.

I'm quiet as David's eyes move over it, taking in the lines, the warm color of my skin in the lamplight, the lavender tendrils of my hair, the tattoos on my arm and wrists and hip. I have an odd sense of déjà vu, of standing in front of this painting with a man and testing his reaction.

"This is you?" he asks.

"About five years ago, yeah."

"You were a bit of a punk, huh?"

"Yes, grandpa. A bit."

He adjusts the Cubs cap he's wearing, no doubt an attempt to disguise himself out in the world. I wonder what he thinks of me now, now that he's seen who I am, who I was. I wonder if he knows what he's gotten himself into.

"It's not how I imagined you," he says.

"How exactly did you imagine me?" I'm a little afraid of the answer. He shifts again, and it's then that I realize he's uncomfortable. The great David Jenkins is uncomfortable here, standing in front of a nude painting with the girl it portrays standing next to him. Except this time, unlike last time with Sam, I doubt anyone would make the connection between me and her. How I miss her, I think, looking up at those dark lines.

"I don't know. Not so rough, I guess."

"Rough?" I can see his expression hardening in front of me, like he's making the conscious decision to be a bastard. I've seen this look before.

"I never understood why perfectly attractive young women would want to mark themselves up like that."

"You know, you have a real gift for paying someone a compliment while you insult them. Is that something that comes with the office?"

"All I'm saying is, it's not my cup of tea. I've never been a fan of that sort of thing."

"Well," I say, injecting as much acid into my voice as I can muster, "Lucky I didn't do it for men like you."

"Did Sam like it? The tattoos and the piercings, and having a girlfriend who doesn't mind stripping down for some schmuck with a paintbrush who couldn't get into a decent college?" he asks. His expression is so smug, so painfully superior, that the desire to spit in his face is barely within my control.

"Even if he didn't, he liked everything else." It's absurd, to be defending Sam, after everything. To be defending our relationship to the man I've used to break it apart.

"Not anymore, apparently."

I walk away from him then, because staying for even one moment more would break the last thread of my control. It's not that I'm afraid of the ferocity of my anger, or the ramifications of screaming at him in public. It's that I'm afraid I might cry, the pressure of my anger is so intense it closes my throat, and crying is the last thing I want to do in front of David. It would ruin it, to cry in front of him, to put him in the position of having to apologize or, god forbid, comfort me. This, this interaction I have with him, it only works if I can hate him. Hating him makes it better. And even as I leave him there, winding my way through the exhibits until I reach the lobby, banging through the doors into the bracing air of the street outside, even then, even though he's a bastard, and I certainly know better, I'm already anticipating the next time we'll meet.

# Linda

I go to see Dr. Shah. I've always liked Dr. Shah the best of all my doctors. I was surprised by her age when I first encountered her in the hospital, when she leaned over my still, supine anchor of a body. She comes into the examination room smelling like bubblegum, her hair held up haphazardly in a tortoise clip, her white coat loose over a precariously short pink dress. She is a half-decade younger than I am, though she possesses a list of accomplishments that would have been impressive for a doctor twice her age. Now she's as fresh and enthusiastic as ever, almost comically so considering the program she's charged with overseeing.

"So how's it going, Linda?" she asks, perching on the stool across from where I sit, her eyes wide under thick, long eyelashes.

"Well, I'm still on my feet," I say with a meager smile.

"Phenomenal, isn't it?"

"Most days," I reply.

She nods, sagely. There's a small imprint on her nose that I'm sure once held a piercing.

"Having a hard time? Let me say first, it's very normal for survivors to have a difficult time reentering their lives in the beginning. You've been through a very intense physical and psychological trauma, even if it wasn't in this particular body." She speaks in the way I imagine a sorority girl might when explaining the house rules to new pledges. But I listen with rapt attention because I know her manner belies an almost savant-like understanding of medicine.

"I'm pregnant," I say, all at once, the way I couldn't with Connie on the street. And then I think I've said absolutely the wrong thing,

225

because Dr. Shah's brow creases so severely I wonder if it makes her forehead ache.

"Pregnant," she says, and then everything in her forehead smooths out and she smiles, a little less exuberantly than before, but no less genuinely. "That's wonderful Linda. Congratulations."

"The problem is, I think," I say, stumbling a bit in the middle. "I think maybe I don't want to go through with it."

"With the pregnancy?" she asks, as if I could be talking about anything else.

"I think it's too soon after the transfer," I say, trying to remember all the things that Connie said that made her argument seem so bulletproof. "I've only just gotten my life back. I don't think I can handle any more complications."

Dr. Shah taps her forefinger to her lips. I look down at her from my perch and wonder if I've ever seen the bubbly light in her so dimmed.

"The thing is, Linda," she says, looking up at me with her huge, earnest eyes. "I don't have authorization to allow you to terminate a pregnancy."

"What?" The examination room seems to be growing colder by the minute, the harsh bite of alcohol in the air chilling the insides of my lungs.

"I would have to get authorization from the SUBlife committee to even prescribe the most basic of medications to you. I don't have authorization to perform a surgical procedure, much less terminate a pregnancy." It's as if she's explaining the rules of bridge. It's all I can do not to pull on my clothes and run from the room.

"Can you get authorization?" I ask, my voice a little more pinched than a moment ago.

"Linda, the sort of data this pregnancy provides the study is literally unprecedented. I can't see them approving anything that would limit the sort of knowledge they could gain from this."

"It's my body," I whisper. She nods, looking a little sick.

"Of course it is, of course it is. But in the paperwork you signed before the transfer, you specifically consented to allow the SUBlife committee discretion in your medical treatment for the next five years."

"My husband."

"What?" she asks.

"My husband signed that paperwork. Not me." I must be pale. I must be shaking. Something. Because she rises quickly from her seat, placing a steadying hand on each of my shoulders.

"Think of this as an opportunity, Linda. To begin again with your family. This could be the beginning of something . . ." she searches for the word, and breaks into her cheerleader grin again. "Something great."

I consider how wonderful it must be, to be a brilliant young doctor, now that we live in the time of a miracle cure. When there are fewer lost causes, when nothing is incurable. I think of the future, a future in which people will only fear the most acute sort of deaths. Car accidents. Gunshot wounds. Unexpected, irreversible conditions. How lucky she is to be able to administer the cure without needing it herself.

I nod, giving her my well-practiced smile. Make her think it will be all right, that it could even be great, though none of it is true. It's the story I've told myself every day since the transfer, but none of it is true.

# Hannah

The story breaks on a Thursday morning and it takes me a moment to realize it's Sam's name in the byline. I'm too caught up in the fact that it's happened, so soon, and so completely. The *Chicago Tribune* has published a piece about the Northwestern SUBlife trials. And worse, it names Congressman David Jenkins as one of the study's participants.

I'm actually a few paragraphs into the article, skimming through a brief description of the transfer procedure and details about David's illness, before I recognize the writing. I've read so much of Sam's work—everything, really, that he's published since we've been together—that the voice is immediately familiar. I barely have to glance at the byline to know that it's him.

And, of course, it's all there. Everything I've mentioned to Sam in the months since the transfer, all of those little details I'd foolishly assumed I could trust him to keep secret or, at the very least, not write about for the papers. Mercifully, the rest of us are only mentioned in passing, as the "three other members of Jenkins's support group, each with their own terminal or degenerative condition." But David is drawn in pitiless detail, everything from the number of times he's voted to cut Medicaid, to allegations that he used his political influence to buy his way into the pilot program.

And there's more. Things I didn't know, paragraphs I have to re-read standing up at my table after I've kicked over the nearest chair. Confirmed phone calls from David to an official at the FDA. Threatening calls. Mounting evidence that David has been trying to keep SUBlife from being approved.

I stuff the paper into my purse and bang my way out of the apartment. There is only one place in the world I can be right now. And even though group doesn't begin for another three hours, I have the sneaking suspicion that I won't be the only one arriving early today.

There are already protesters outside the hospital. It's almost impressive that they can congregate so quickly, considering the story just broke this morning. As if they're all part of some sort of Evangelical call-tree, like mothers who phone each other when school is cancelled because of snow. Maybe all it takes is a phone call to mobilize twenty people who don't mind screaming at strangers in the name of Jesus.

They have signs. Some of them hold the newspaper in front of them, David's campaign-smile showing in the muddy black and white of its photo. Others have hurriedly painted posters in the same shade of bright red. Abomination. Sin. Satan. I can only see single words, something in my brain has clicked off, something that has made it difficult to comprehend anything beyond single words and the mass of angry voices being hurled at anyone who dares enter the hospital. Adrenaline, I think, feeling my heart still pounding as I get through the doors and escape into an elevator. Fight or flight. It's not important to be able to read when you're running for your life.

I'm the last to arrive, in fact. Even Dr. Bernard sits with his hands cupping his jaw, waiting for me to appear. I feel like I might be late, forgetting for a moment that none of us are supposed to be here yet, not for hours, but I am too cracked open to think clearly. David is on his feet, though, and my vision tunnels around him. I fish the paper out of my purse.

"What have you been doing?" I ask, my voice so much calmer than I would have expected.

"I could ask you the same thing," he replies, not calm, not even a little. Almost shouting, stepping toward me. I throw the paper at him, halting him as he bats it away.

"Okay," Dr. Bernard says, on his feet as well now, stepping between us. "I think we all need to take a minute here."

"Yeah, sure, doc," Connie says. She's sitting with her arms folded, unreadable. I'd think she was bored, if I didn't know her so well. Linda's face is half covered, her nose and mouth eclipsed by both of her hands.

"You think I don't know who Sam Foster is?" David yells, flushed down to his collar, the veins standing cable-rigid in his arms as he gestures at me. I realize, for the first time despite the nights that we've spent unclothed together, that David has become physically formidable in these months since the transfer. "Your self-righteous journalist boyfriend? You think I don't know where he got his information? Where he got my name?"

This is not my fault. He cannot possibly make this my fault. I'm worried, suddenly, that I might cry. It was a lifelong annoyance, the tendency of my old body to dissolve into stupid, useless tears when I was angry. That particular weakness seems to have trailed me into this new form, and it makes me doubly furious, as I swallow against the raw ache in my throat, that this body has retained all of the wrong things.

"Well I certainly didn't tell him that you've been trying to keep SUBlife from getting FDA approval." Good, my voice has some volume now. I think Linda may be crying, but I can't stop. "What is it, David? Is it okay with God that you saved yourself as long as you make sure no one else can?"

"You rotten bitch."

I can't recognize any of the man I've known in David. I have known his wants, the way every bit of him feels. But I've never before known his anger, the venomous rage in him. He's probably more alive than I've ever seen him.

"All right, that's enough," Dr. Bernard snaps. Then one quiet voice comes through, clearer than all of the rest.

"What are we going to do?" Linda asks, raising her face from her hands. She's not crying, after all. I wonder what it would take to make this woman cry, this woman who has withstood more horror than the rest of us can imagine. "Did you see the people outside? How are we going to be able to meet here, with them out there?"

David laughs, a bitter sound. He reaches down and picks up the newspaper at his feet. "This? This means that everyone knows what's happening here. You honestly think we're going to be able to keep meeting after this? Come on, Linda. That's naive even for you."

"Get out, David." It's Connie who speaks. She's calm. Her face is a study in well-controlled wrath, and it's a fearsome thing to behold. "Get out of here. This is over for you now." We are all still, waiting to see what comes next.

"Fine. Fuck it," David says, pulling a cigarette out of the pack in his jacket pocket and lighting it up right there, his pose careless, flouting the rules. There he is, the boy who would joyride in stolen cars as a teenager. No wonder I was drawn to him. "It's not like this was doing any goddamn good anyway," he says. Then he drops the barely smoked cigarette on the floor, stomps it out with the toe of his shoe, and heads for the door. Dr. Bernard sits back down, smoothing out the fabric of his dress pants as if he's been in a scuffle. I, too, drop into one of the open seats.

"What do we do now?" Linda repeats, looking from Dr. Bernard to Connie to me.

"I'll confer with the other doctors involved in the study," Dr. Bernard says. "This is a serious breach of confidentiality. And if the lottery was compromised, it might put the whole study at risk. The FDA votes in only a few months . . ." He chews on the inside of his cheek as his eyes land in middle space, vacant with the furious calculations that must be going on in his head.

"No one else recognized him?" I ask, but no one answers. I am left to wonder what it means, that I'm the only one who knew exactly who he was, all along.

# June

# Hannah

I run into Linda at Trader Joe's. At first, I can't place her. She's out of context, away from the hospital and the rest of the group, dressed in ill-fitting jeans and a baggy T-shirt. She has her kids with her, a skinny, sullen-looking girl in a Chicago Sky T-shirt and a boy whose smile reveals half-grown-in front teeth. We spot each other at the same time, at opposite ends of the aisle. At first we both hesitate, unsure of the rules, if we're allowed to acknowledge each other after everything that has happened. But then Linda starts toward me and so I maneuver around other families with carts until we meet in front of the shelves of dried fruit.

"You look tired," she says by way of greeting. It's forever our function, it seems, to evaluate and comment on each other's physical appearances. She glances down at her kids. "This is Katie and Jack. Kids, this is Hannah. She's a friend of mine. From the hospital."

I give them a little wave, trying my best to portray normality as best as I can, as if I'm the person who must confirm for them that their mother wasn't abducted by aliens or grown out of a pod. It makes me wish I'd showered today, rinsed some of the thick grease out of my hair. They look at me blankly, unimpressed in the way only children can be.

"Why don't you two go get those ice cream bars that you like, hmm?" Linda says, shooing them toward the freezer cases. She sighs when they're out of earshot. "I hope it's ice cream bars they like. It's so hard to keep up with all of it. Jack's cutting me slack, but it's still eight years' worth of stuff I don't know."

"It'll get easier," I reply.

"Sometimes I get the distinct sense that Katie is angry with me. And I can't tell if it's because I was paralyzed in a bed all their lives, or if it's because I decided to wake up and change everything without asking them first."

"They probably just need more time to adjust," I say, because I have little else but platitudes to offer Linda. I am as lost as she is, knocking around my empty apartment, watching daytime TV in my pajamas, sleeping in taxing, fitful shifts. This is the first time I've ventured outside in days, and it's only to replenish my stores of peanut butter and potato chips. I have yet to find this body's upper limits when it comes to the consumption of junk food, but I'm not one to back down from a challenge. "I've been watching *Stratford Pines*," I say, offering a consolation for my lackluster advice.

"Oh, isn't it great?"

"It is," I say, because while it is indeed a terrible show, there's something satisfying in its simplistic melodrama. It's easier to think of the world as a place where love and hate and betrayal are threads that do not cross, instead of existing in a constant jumble, a knot I cannot even touch, much less try to untangle. "I'm trying to figure out who the stalker is."

"If you've been watching as long as I have, it gets pretty easy to figure out," Linda replies. "But I won't spoil it for you." I'm struck by how different she is now, how present and capable compared to the woman who would barely speak after the transfer.

"Have you heard from any of the others?" I ask. I imagine Linda and Connie meeting in a coffee shop, or in the bright sunlight of a park somewhere. They're not at the hospital, at least, not on Thursday afternoons. I know because I've been going there, staking it out, just in case I spot one of them. But no one comes. Week after week, I stand there alone.

Linda shakes her head, looking pensive, wistful even. "No. I haven't heard from either of them. Not since the last time. You?"

I shake my head. "Though, I keep waiting for a call from David's lawyer, for violating the confidentiality agreement. Ruining his career."

Linda smiles a little. "I think you underestimate his feelings for you," she replies, and I wonder how much she knows, how much she has suspected.

"It's harder, isn't it? Doing this on our own? I never would have expected it could get harder."

"It won't always be like this," she says. "Give it time."

I'm not sure if she's even aware that she's handing my same useless platitude back to me. But I can see something in her now, a patience, something that makes her seem older than I remember. It's motherly, that way about her.

There's not much else to say, but we both linger a little longer. It feels good, running into Linda in the long drudgery of my daily life, like finding money in the street. Something unexpected and a little bit thrilling, a change of luck. Linda must feel the same way because neither of us seems to want to leave.

"Maybe you and I can meet and talk, once in a while," I say, desperate to keep some connection to the three people who know me better than anyone, even when they don't particularly know much about me at all. "Watch some *Stratford Pines*?"

"I don't know, Hannah," Linda says, drawing a hand across her stomach. "I've haven't had as much time to keep up with it as before. You know, with the kids."

"Of course," I say. "Of course, I understand." She gives me a squeeze on my arm and wheels her cart away from me. I blink hard, waving again at her kids as I pass them. They eye me with unguarded suspicion.

I glance back at Linda just in time to see her slip a package of trail mix into her purse. She tucks it under her arm and goes back to consulting her shopping list like any other mother on a grocery run. But she's not. She's not like everyone else. She's a woman who lived in a white-walled room, unmoving, for eight years. I think that Sam was right, that it has to have an impact, everything the members of our groups have had to endure. So, while I myself don't steal anything from the store, I can understand the impulse.

# David

I work my way back up to Scotch. It takes time and a lot of dedication because my taste buds have reverted back to the days when I'd drink sugary sodas and dump a long succession of creamers into my coffee. But as the months pass I move from faux wine to Jack-and-gingers to Old Fashioneds and then there I am, finally, sipping Scotch and hating it in some hipster bar on Lincoln Avenue. The lady bartender has an intricate tattoo of a mermaid running from her shoulder to her elbow. It makes me think of that painting of Hannah and, though the bartender is nowhere near as pretty as Hannah, I find myself chatting with her for a little too long. She has a silver ring in her nose and bleached-blonde hair, and she laughs heartily at my jokes, which are subpar at best. I wonder if she'll go home with me if I ask. And then I do ask, more to quell my own curiosity than anything else. She smiles.

I buy another drink, running down the clock until this tattooed little college dropout is off work, and I catch my reflection in the mirror above the bar. I've been avoiding mirrors since the transfer, since the self that I imagine when I close my eyes and the self I see in the mornings are two very different men. But now it looks like all the working out has paid off, because I can see muscle definition through the sleeves of my shirt. I've let my beard grow back. It's easier, now that my new face has been splashed all over blogs and newspapers and magazines, because people don't recognize me as easily with facial hair. It's too unexpected. They don't make the connection; politicians never have facial hair. I don't look like me, not really, but I don't look that bad either. It's no wonder this little bartender is interested.

There are three missed calls from Jackson on my phone. He is in such a constant, furious state of damage control that I've begun ignoring him so I can get drunk in peace. The people of my district are furious with me for taking part in a treatment that involves human cloning. The rest of the country is furious that I bought my way into a clinical trial from which I should have been disqualified. The guys in my caucus and the Republican leadership are incensed that I'd get caught trying to tamper with an FDA study. People are talking about recall elections. People are talking about hearings in front of the disciplinary committee. I've been accused of everything from corruption to blasphemy to murder, ostensibly of the person whose life should have been saved in place of mine during the pilot program. I've done my best to ignore most of it. Beth is holding up like any good political wife would, keeping a stiff upper lip and shaking off the media attention with her trademark WASP-y coolness. It's Jackson who can't seem to let our presidential dreams go.

Jackson has been insisting lately that we sue Hannah for breach of confidentiality. She's from a wealthy family, it seems, and my impending political fights look like they might be costly. But thinking of attacking Hannah brings with it an exhaustion I can't understand, much less handle. How can I explain it to Jackson, how badly I want to hurt this girl and how sick it makes me when I think of it—simultaneously. I justify it to myself by considering the fallout that could happen if she reveals our affair to the public on top of everything else. I could lose my family, all that I have left, if she takes that sort of revenge. Going after Hannah would be breaking the cease-fire. Mutually assured destruction. So I ignore Jackson's calls. And I get drunk in peace.

It bothers me, a little, that I'm attracted to the bartender because she looks like Hannah. It's not unexpected, by any means. I've been hate-fucking girls who look like Hannah from one end of Chicago to the other for months now, since the article came out. What bothers me is that the hate has begun to soften, while the attraction remains. I find myself scrolling through the handful of text messages we exchanged while we were together, mostly arrangements of times and places where we would meet, but still, it feels good to see something she's written. I've gone back twice to the Museum of Contemporary Art to look at that painting of her, naked and lying in some lousy painter's sheets, and the hate and want and jealousy I feel is like getting hit by a linebacker. It makes me feel weak, to still want her despite everything.

I take the bartender home and fuck her from behind on the living room sofa, watching the birds tattooed on her back dart about as she moves. She and I share a cigarette when we're finished, and that makes me want a drink. It's a disappointment, like everything is a disappointment, every moment another signpost of my failing, my squandered chance for redemption. But it also feels good, like slipping back into my favorite leather jacket for the first time each winter, its fit perfect even after all those months of waiting for me. I've missed this part of myself, I find, the part of me that revels in surrendering to my vices. The boy who yelled into the wind at ninety miles an hour in a borrowed car. The part that Hannah dug up from where I'd buried it. The part of me that was never meant to stay dormant for very long.

# Hannah

When I can no longer stand the sight of my couch, surrounded as it is by empty glasses and takeout containers, its quilt permanently wrinkled in the shape of a nest for my little body, I decide I need a project. I clear out my studio on a Friday morning, the kind of day where the city seems painfully bright, all sun-bleached asphalt and piping-hot glass. I box up my supplies, unplugging the fridge and throwing away the abandoned water bottles and the single beer that I had left there. I wrap the canvases in heavy paper and twine. Everything else goes into boxes that I tape shut and label, trying not to focus too much on one object or another because it will be too hard that way. If I allow memories to start slipping in, I'm sure I'll be lost.

I do pause, however, on the antique Minolta I find behind a stack of canvases. It's a film camera from the 60s, an old SLR with a heavy metal body and a short, wide lens. It was my grandfather's, I think, though I can't really remember why I have it here. I'd used it for a while in junior high while I took an introductory darkroom class at a community college one summer, but I don't know why I'd have brought it to my studio. Yet, here it is, and when I check there's still film inside.

I get the photos back a week later in a thin paper sleeve, with the negatives tucked in back.

There's a photo of my old room in my house in Lake Forest, with its large vanity mirror and the huge classic rock posters on the walls. There's Lucy, so young it nearly takes my breath, all fresh-faced teenage beauty, with her dark hair falling around her like billows of smoke. There's a photo of Candice, my best friend in junior high, playing her cello in a nondescript schoolroom. There's one really excellent photo of my art teacher, with his white mop of hair and his kind, deep-set eyes. A couple are of objects, like an arrangement of flowers on our kitchen table or a stack of books on my desk. There's an earnestness to the photographs, as if I was really trying to convey something with them, though I can't remember what it was. Yearning, probably. Yearning for a life more like the one I have now, silly, foolish child that I was.

I stop when I find the photo of Sam. At first it feels insignificant, as if it would be strange not to find a picture of my boyfriend amid a stack of my old photos. It takes me a moment to realize that the photo is out of place, that it shouldn't be there, that he was not mine yet, back then. But still, there he is, at seventeen, shooting me a grin from under a stocking cap, with a plastic cup in his hand. He's in front of a campfire. I vaguely remember the night, a party my sister threw when my parents were out of town, the only time I was allowed to creep out of my room and explore the world of my sister's teenage friends. I stumbled upon a couple kissing in the living room and ventured outside to find Lucy. I must have found Sam instead. And I must have had my camera.

I don't remember taking the picture. But I remember him sitting there in front of the fire pit on our patio. He smiled when he saw me.

"Aren't you cold?" he asked, motioning to my pajama pants and the light jacket I had wound around me. I nodded, unable to speak for fear of saying something childish or stupid.

"Here," he said, taking a flask out of his jacket and unscrewing it, adding a bit more of its contents to his party cup before handing the thin metal container to me. "Take a little sip, just a little. It'll warm you up."

I did as I was told and it burned like battery acid and tasted just as bad, and I coughed into my hand as soon as I swallowed it down. Sam smiled.

"That's my girl," he said, taking the flask back from me and refastening the cap. "Don't tell your sister, okay?"

"I won't," I whispered.

"Don't tell me what?" I heard Lucy approach behind me, ruffling my hair a bit before crawling onto Sam's chair with him.

"Hannah and I are going to run away together," he said, winking at me, and I must have been crimson from head to foot from my blush and the heat of the booze and the campfire.

"Just as long as you call me from wherever you end up," she said, pressing her mouth to the side of his neck. Then everything was hot inside me too, scorching from the fire and whatever I drank and the total futility of being twelve and the shocking intensity of my own jealousy. I went back to my room and watched out my window as the fire flickered on the faces of the people around it, unable to hear what they were saying. Holding that moment with Sam like the bright hardness of a gem inside me, knowing that no matter what passed between Sam and Lucy, he would always be the one who drew me into adulthood for a quick moment on our back patio. He would always be the first to take my hand and lead me forward.

I never told Penny that the shot of raspberry vodka we took together in our freshman dorm wasn't my first drink. I never told her that someone had gotten to me first, already broken down that barrier for me. It felt good, like a warm little secret, a perfect sliver of time I could hold on to that belonged to Sam and me and to no one else. Something a bit wrong and just a little dangerous, and so much better of a secret because of it.

And I realize that in all the years Sam and I were together, we never spoke of that moment. The memory of it had faded by the time we were together, been eclipsed by so much else, and the realization that we've both lost that bit of our shared history hits me harder than the anger that still wells within me when I think of him, think of his article, think of his abandonment. It scares me a little, to consider how much you can lose simply in the process of living on.

I buy film for the camera, black and white film from an online store because so few camera shops carry it anymore. I buy a bulk box of it, stashing it in my fridge and snapping whole rolls of it at a time. I'm hesitant with the camera at first, with its ancient light meter and the confusing shutter speeds and f-stops. The mechanics of it make me pause and consider what I'm trying to capture, if it needs a shallow or deep depth of field, if I want the image to appear grainy or smooth, if I want to capture motion or freeze it in a split-second. The camera, in all of its clumsiness and cumbersome settings, makes me look at the world again. To look at the world in a way these eyes have not yet, not ever, seen it.

# Linda

There's a little figurine of a dancer on one of the shelves, and it glitters under the fluorescent lighting of the store. It looks beautiful and lonely, standing there, frozen in the middle of its most graceful pose. I don't even hesitate as I slip it into the front of my jacket. It's one of mine, it's there for me; I can tell just by looking at it.

The trouble comes when I'm leaving the store. I can hear the commotion begin among the salesgirls, the notes of intensity in their voices, harsh whispers, someone hitting all the wrong notes on a piano. At first, I'm truly mystified as to what the trouble is. Then the security guard approaches.

"Forget something, ma'am?" he asks. He's a middle-aged Hispanic man, and he looks like he could be very kind, the sort of man who would shovel his neighbor's driveway, if he wasn't looking at me as if I might bolt at any moment.

"No, just going home to my family," I say, and smile, the way Connie would. The way she does to make people trust her. But it doesn't seem to work because he says something into the little radio clipped to his jacket, and I hear the crackle and buzz of a voice coming over it in reply.

"Can I see what's in your jacket, ma'am." He says it like it's not a question. And I know that I should hang my head and comply, to pretend like I was going to pay for the figurine all along, but the moment seems so hilariously impossible, so out of sync with the normal order of my life, that I think I must be dreaming. Dreaming, or having slipped across some thin membrane into my secret world, where exciting things do happen. Either way, I know the best course of action is to run.

It's David who gets me out of lockup. I can hear the CPD officer at the desk on his phone, his tone apologetic, a child being admonished.

"Right away, sir," he says over the line and then hangs up the phone. He disappears through the door to the outer office of the police station, and I remain where I am, of course, locked in a concrete cell that smells like a port-a-john. I don't really want to touch anything. It's like sitting in one of the more dilapidated L stations, a place you know is contaminated with all sorts of human waste. My fingers are still tinged gray from the fingerprint ink, and I think about what Hannah once said, that our fingerprints are probably different from those of our old bodies. It gives me a strange stirring of freedom within my chest, the thought that I'm anonymous here. No ID. No credit cards. Nothing in my wallet but some cash and a couple of business cards. Just the little bit of something inside me, just me and her. I could be anyone, I think. If I disappeared right now, if I left this station and hopped a train and kept going, no one would ever be able to find us. There wouldn't even be pictures of me to post.

When the officer returns, David is with him. The sight of him is jarring, in this awful place, particularly because it's the first time I've seen him in a suit. He looks like a congressman, though he smiles and gives me a little wave when the cop busies himself with opening my cell.

"Terribly sorry about the misunderstanding, sir," the cop is saying. "I have a grandmother with Alzheimer's myself. I know what it's like to lose track every once in a while."

"And of course, I'd appreciate it if you'd keep this to yourself," David says as the gate to my cell swings open. He hands the cop a few bills. "Come on, sis, let's go home, okay?"

I can't help but rush to him and throw my arms around his neck. It is so, so good to see him, especially here, though I am thoroughly flabbergasted by what has happened. "Am I not arrested any-more?" I ask when I release him.

"No, not anymore. Come on," he says, his voice low. He pretends that he's not as delighted to see me as I am him, but I know better. I follow him out of the building and into a very expensive-looking car.

"How did you know I was here?"

"You had Dr. Bernard's business card on you. They called him, but he's at his vacation home in Michigan. I guess he thought I'd be a good runner-up."

"What did you tell them?" I ask, as he opens the car door for me and I duck inside. It smells like new leather. It has the feeling of the inside of a museum, of still, expensive air.

"That you're my mentally handicapped sister-in-law, and you wandered away from us at the mall."

I can feel my mouth fall open. "That's terrible."

He grins at me. "Want to go back in there and tell them the truth? That you're a cloned coma patient who likes to commit petty larceny in her spare time? Or I can have them call Tom, if you want."

I fold my arms over my chest. "I wasn't in a coma. I was conscious the whole time. There's a difference."

He chuckles as he starts up the car, pulling it out into traffic. "You live in Evanston?"

I nod, though I don't bother to inquire how he knows.

"So what were you doing lifting a six-dollar figurine from Water Tower Place?" he asks. "This is how you spend your time now that you don't have the support group to go to?"

"It's a long story," I reply, feeling the purr of the car's engine through my seat.

"Well, this could be a long drive. I have to go the speed limit. No license," he replies. I give him my best reproachful-mother expression. We cruise through Grant Park, heading toward the Lake.

"I'm pregnant," I say, testing it out, trying to shock him. At first I think he hasn't heard me because nothing shifts in his expression. "Aren't you going to say anything?"

"What does that have to do with you shoplifting a piece of junk from the mall?"

I shrug. "I don't really know. Maybe nothing. It feels good though, to do something secret. Something just for me."

"Most women, I don't know, take up knitting. Read romance novels. That sort of thing."

"Yes, us little women and our simple hobbies," I say, and we both smile a little because I sound like Connie. "Well I can't knit anymore. New body. My hands don't remember it." I hold them up in front of me like a couple of foreign objects, their skin smooth and supple and enduringly perfect. "Don't you ever want to do something wrong? Simply because it's wrong?"

We pull on to Lake Shore Drive, picking up speed, and David lets out a low whistle. "Boy, if there's going to be an epidemic of this sort of behavior for everyone who goes through SUBlife, the program will never get past the FDA."

"Maybe you should have let us crazies sabotage it for you," I retort.

His hands tighten on the wheel. "I didn't get a chance to explain last time. About the FDA. I didn't have a choice."

"Maybe if you tried to explain, we would have understood. But you were too busy yelling at her." We both know who I mean.

He nods. "Want me to explain it now?"

"No," I reply. "It doesn't matter now." The damage has already been done. There is no taking it back, not for him. Certainly not for me. I sniffle and realize that my eyes are full of tears. It's as much a surprise as before, when Cora would wipe my face with tissue and not even pause in what she was saying. But I know it's different now. I know this body feels too much for my tears to ever be involuntary. "I don't know if I want it," I say. "The baby."

He fishes in the center console and pulls out a pack of tissues, which he thrusts at me. "I think I'm the wrong person to talk to about this."

"Because you're a Christian?" I ask, taking the tissues and using one to wipe my nose.

"Because most of the time I'm a lousy parent. Even when I'm actually trying," he says. "And yes, I'm a Christian. So I'm not the one to be discussing your options with."

"I don't have any options," I reply. "Courtesy of all the paperwork we signed. Or in my case, the paperwork my husband signed." I can't keep the tinge of anger out of my voice at the idea of Tom still directing the course of my life without my permission.

"You know, someone once told me that there are two kinds of unplanned pregnancies. There are the babies you don't want. And then there are the spouses you don't want," David says.

"What if it's my whole life that I don't want?" I ask, before I can catch myself. I put a hand to my mouth. "Jesus, I shouldn't say things like that. My kids." He reaches over and grasps my shoulder. It's a reassuring feeling, fatherly. I pull my sleeve up and dab at my eyes with it. "I imagined running away this afternoon. Just going, not looking back, not ever. Disappearing. Again."

"Well, I can take you anywhere you want," David says, tapping the steering wheel with his palm. "Just say the word."

"The worst part is, I don't even know where I'd go," I reply, even though it's a lie. I know exactly where I would go, if I could. If such a place existed.

# Hannah

I think very seriously about selling my apartment. It seems, at first, like the smart thing to do; I've put so much work into it over the years that I'm sure I could make a solid profit on it. It's difficult to wake there every morning, to live alone within its walls for the first time, that I think it might be easier to tear every last scrap of my old life down and build a new one from its rickety foundations. Sometimes I think it might be easier if everything in my life is unrecognizable instead of just my body.

The tiny second bathroom, nestled off the room Sam used as an office, finally convinces me to stay. For no other reason, but that it would make a perfect darkroom. I buy the supplies for a small fortune online—darkroom components are terribly difficult to find now and most of what I order is second-hand and remarkably overpriced—but I'm up and running within a few weeks. The man from Home Depot looks at me like I'm crazy when I ask him to remove the toilet, explaining to me about the condo's resale values as if I were a child, and then finally, begrudgingly doing what I ask. I put an enlarger in its place, set up a shelf of trays over the bathtub. A row of red safelights go over the mirror, which I cover with black acrylic paint so I don't have to look at myself, my new self, in that muddy amber light.

The rhythm of the darkroom is soothing; that I remember from the class I took when I was a kid, how easy it was to slip into the patterns of light and darkness, the timed agitation of trays of chemicals—developer and stop bath and fixer and stabilizer and water wash—the patience required to get it right, just right, before you can dare bring your print out into daylight. I lose time in the darkroom, like I used to in my studio, with my little radio blaring away on a shelf above me, the music keeping stilted time with the click of the darkroom timer.

I spend my days scouring the city for photos, walking through its streets with my camera, snapping shots of children playing at a park with their grandmother, or an overgrown aloe plant pressing its waxy leaves against a shop window, or a group of tight-jeaned teenagers standing under the Melrose Diner's blaring neon sign at three in the morning. I forget to eat, some days, hunting around with film cassettes rattling in my pockets. I bring my spoils back to my darkroom and follow my days of excursions with more days spent in darkness. It's a strange pattern into which I've fallen. I am both explorer and hermit. I study the faces of people and speak to no one. I am invisible, behind that camera. I have become something new.

I sit down with a pencil and paper, trying to sketch out what I have in my head. The thin, spindly feathers, the swirling lines. The feeling of movement. But it doesn't work, everything looks thick and flat and lifeless when I put the graphite to paper. I crumple it up, toss it into the wastebasket, and get my phone. Penny picks up on the third ring.

"Hey." Her voice sounds tight. These last few months are the longest we've ever gone without speaking. I wonder if she's angry at me.

"Hey," I say to her now. "I need you to draw me something."

She pauses, and I can almost feel her bite back a reproach. "Okay," she says, finally. "Okay, I guess."

An hour later we sit, huddled in my spare bedroom until the floor around us is littered with sheets of discarded paper and Penny's drunk the last of my emergency coffee stash. Late afternoon sunlight cuts swirling, dusty paths through the air around us.

"How about this?" Penny says, holding up the drawing she's been working on.

"I think that's probably about as close as we're going to get."

We've both relaxed a bit from when she arrived, when we greeted each other with forced smiles and anxious glances, testing each other out before we dove back into the deep waters of our friendship. But now, even before she speaks, I know what's coming.

"So let me get this straight," she says. "You left Sam for the Antichrist?"

"He's not the Antichrist," I reply, though my attempt to defend David is admittedly feeble. "And I didn't leave Sam for him. I left Sam, and David happened to be around."

"That doesn't sound like a good enough reason to fuck a Republican."

"Well, it doesn't matter now anyway. Sam's article put a stop to it pretty quickly. Which, I assume, was his intention."

"Please," Penny said, flicking her hand dismissively. "You think Sam published that article to punish David because you were sleeping with him?"

"Why else would he single him out? Go after him like he did?"

"Listen, I don't know where he found out about David trying to kill the FDA vote. But can you imagine Sam, the white knight of truth and virtue, sitting on that story for any reason? Come on, Hannah, he wouldn't be the guy you loved if he did."

"Even if you're right, none of it matters, anyway," I reply. "The article has nothing to do with why Sam left. Neither does David, not really."

Penny's head drops back against the wall. "He told me what happened, Hannah. He was wrecked," she replies.

"Yeah, so was I." I think back on that night and imagine how different things could have been if I'd gone to Penny in my grief instead of David. "I can't forgive him, Pen."

"I know. I understand," she says. "That's what we've always loved about each other, isn't it? That we're both merciless, in one way or another. Kindred spirits." She glances at me and I nod, a confirmation. "But then I think about Connor. And if it came down to watching him go through something like that and closing my eyes, I don't think I would have an ounce of strength to keep them open. I don't know if I could have stood it for as long as Sam did."

"Jesus," I say, "would you really want to be with someone who would leave you to die alone?"

She starts to cry then, and it's an appalling thing to watch. Penny, fearless Penny, the one who has always been the fiercer of us, crying there on the floor of my little spare room. She claps her hands over her face. I don't know what to do. I'm helpless before this wash of emotion from someone who is always so controlled. She wipes at her eyes.

"You wouldn't have been alone," she says, her voice so tight it's almost a whisper. "I would have made sure of it. I would have been there."

I take her hands and kiss her knuckles. They're rough. Artist's hands, made for utility, for transmission. Mine are like a child's hands, wrapped around her dark fingers, useless and unformed.

"I love you, you know I love you," I say, and she sniffs, nodding, shaking off the lingering emotion the way someone else might flick away an insect. "But you're not the one I would have needed to be there."

We take the drawing to the little tattoo shop on Irving Park that Trevor used to swear by when he lived in Chicago. I'd never gone there before, since I always went to a shop in the Ukrainian Village for all of my other work. But there's no way to explain to Garry, my former tattoo artist, why all of his previous work has suddenly disappeared from my body, so I had to find an alternative. Inside this shop is a woman with long auburn hair, and she looks at the drawing, then from Penny to me.

"You're really jumping into the deep end for your first tattoo. You sure about this?"

"This isn't my first tattoo," I say, grinning at my own private joke, and she shrugs and leads me to her chair. Two and a half hours later, I walk out of the shop with the beginnings of an ornate phoenix spanning the space from my left shoulder to my elbow, its lines like lacework in Penny's delicate, perfect detail. It's hot and aching when the cool evening air hits it, but it's that good ache, like sore muscles, the kind of pain that's born of living.

It feels good to watch it heal during the next days and weeks. It crusts over, grows dry, as my body tries to rid itself of the ink deposited in the low wound. But the marks remain, too deep for this body to be rid of, and that feels like a triumph. Like I'm reclaiming myself, an inch of skin at a time.

# Connie

I'm spending too much time alone. There is nowhere for me to go without our weekly group meetings, waiting for Harry to summon me back to Los Angeles. He got me a modeling job in Chicago to hold me over, a few days of photo shoots for some Midwestern makeup company, which felt briefly exhilarating until they handed me a check and sent me on my way. Now I spend hours holed up in my little apartment, the way I used to when I was sick. I keep thinking about my mother. I think about the way she was when I was a child, her ferocity and strength of will, her unyielding authority. And I think of her now, imagine her in that trailer, a dried-up shade of what she was, because of me. I want to talk to Linda, to ask her what she thinks of my depression and its source. But there's no way for me to find her. I don't know how to even begin trying to track her down.

I consider confiding in Dr. Grath, but things have grown a bit frosty between the two of us since my trip to L.A. I returned so certain of my future, so sure of my impending departure from this broken-down apartment building. It's probably only natural for us to begin to drift apart, since a more permanent separation is probably imminent. But without the group, without Linda, and now without Dr. Grath, I find myself with nowhere to turn when the familiar depression begins to plague me. All of the things I press back seem to seep forward when I'm alone for too long.

Finally, after the third fitful week, I decide that the only way to resolve my psychic imbalance is to go to the source, so I rent a car and drive north on I-94. Within minutes, Chicago's buildings give way to corporate offices and hotels, then car dealerships and the occasional restaurant. By the time I exit, thick walls of greenery line the highway. It's all fast-food and auto shops and dollar stores, everything dingy with age. Compared to my silver city, it may as well be a different country.

It's cool and rainy when I arrive, pulling my rental car through the overgrown driveway at the trailer park's entrance. The place feels deserted, with all of its inhabitants tucked away and not strewn around their yards and porches, calling to one another over the din of their children. I pull up to my mother's trailer, though it takes me a moment to figure out which one it is because this place feels smaller now and the trailer hasn't held up very well. Its paint is peeling and the screen in the front door is torn, a piece of it dangling like a pennant within its wooden frame. My mother's lawn chairs are still out, though brackish water collects in their seats and their metal joints show a red dusting of rust.

I pull open the screen to knock on the door, and as I do my thumb catches on a sharp splinter of raw wood, which imbeds itself in my skin. I curse and am in the middle of prying the splinter out with my fingernails when my mother opens the door. For the briefest of moments, I think I have the wrong trailer. The woman standing there looks much too old to be my mother. Her mouth is puckered with lines, and her eyes seem to have grown smaller, surrounded as they are by skin that droops down from her eyebrows and pools underneath, hanging in bags above her cheekbones. She looks like a wax figure that's beginning to melt in the sun. Her dark-blonde hair has thickened with gray, becoming wiry and coarse, hanging around her face in an uneven bob. For a moment I think that this can't be her. This can't be the woman who taught me to worship beauty the way ancient tribes worshipped the sun. But then her saggy eyes widen. And I remember that she worships something else now, especially when I see the little gold cross nestled in the rumpled skin of her throat.

"What in the heck," she says, and her voice is the same, that's how I know it's her. "Connie?"

"I couldn't explain over the phone," I say, all of the words I'd practiced during the drive up seeming to slip away from my grasp, like shimmering minnows in shallow water. "I wanted to come here. To show you that I'm better now." That things can go back to the way they were, I think, looking at the cross again.

"Better?" she says, and then she must realize she's still holding the door open, as if I'm a salesman who must be kept at bay, because she steps back and ushers me inside. The inside of the trailer hasn't fared much better than my mother has. It's dingy, with a strong smell of must or wet animal or both. The cloudy sunlight doesn't seem to make it through the windows with any force, and the effect is like walking into the dim dampness of a cave. "You want some lemonade?" my mother asks, and I nod without thinking. I sit down at the card table in our little kitchen, which is covered by a cheap-looking white tablecloth with embroidered edges. My mother sets a glass in front of me, and when I take a sip the lemonade is cloyingly sweet, with a tinge of the foul sulfur taste of well-water. I try not to grimace as my mother sits across from me with her own glass. I decide maybe talking will keep me from having to drink more.

"There's this new treatment," I say. "It's experimental. They're only testing it on a few people. But it works."

"What sort of treatment?" my mother asks, her face awash with something that looks like horror. "Stem cells?"

"Does it matter?" I reply. "I'm better, Maureen. Does it really matter to you what saved my life?"

"Of course it matters," she says in a hiss. I lean back in my seat and take a long breath.

"Do you have anything else to drink around here?" I ask. There were always bottles of vodka in our freezer while I was growing up.

"Drink your lemonade," she says, motioning toward my glass. There's no air conditioning in the trailer, and the glasses are sweating rings into the tablecloth.

"I was thinking of something a little stronger," I say, but she ignores me.

"You can't buy your health through sin, Connie," she says, fishing into the pocket of her sweater and pulling out something. She sets it in front of me, and I realize it's a small prayer book with a gold-embossed cross stamped into the leather of its cover. "You can't buy salvation through unnatural means."

"So, you'd have me what, pray the AIDS away?" She winces when I mention the name of my disease, and it reminds me of the way my grandmother would whisper the word *cancer*, as if saying it out loud would tempt an angry twist of fate. I think of all the words that will lose their power, now that SUBlife has begun.

"Maybe if you'd been right with the Lord you'd never have had that pestilence to begin with," she says. I bang my way up from the table.

"Maybe if you'd been worth a damn as a mother, I wouldn't have been shooting up in a bathroom somewhere to begin with," I say, yelling now. She looks at me, a hard look, and I can almost glimpse the diamond-brightness of the woman who raised me within this simpering exterior. "Maybe if I had valued anything but being beautiful, and what that could buy me, maybe I could have avoided a lot of the shit that's happened to me."

She moves then, toward me, pulling me to her. I'm so surprised by it that I wrap my arms around her on reflex alone. I can probably count on one hand the number of times my mother embraced me when I was a child. It happened so infrequently that I stopped wanting it after a while. So this sudden motherly affection leaves me a little stunned.

"I'm sorry," she whispers into the hair above my ear. "I'm so sorry." She pulls back, cupping my face in her hands, and suddenly I want to cry, to sob into her shirt like a child. But her next words stop me, freezing everything in me that is still soft and tender and in need of a mother. "I'm so sorry I didn't raise you with the Lord."

The rain has stopped, but the temperature outside is dropping when I leave the trailer, or perhaps it just feels that way after the stifling heat of my mother's kitchen. Instead of heading back to the car, I turn and walk to the chain link fence that separates the trailer park from the apartment building next to it. I jump the fence, which is a bit more intimidating a maneuver than I remember, despite the fact that my body is as youthful and supple as it was then. It's my mind that has aged, grown more afraid. But I do it, scraping the heel of my hand on the top of the fence as I drop down, and I wonder absently if a tetanus shot was included with all of those vaccinations I had after the transfer.

But then I'm at the edge of the pool, and my mind clears of everything else. It's full of water, rippling a bit as droplets fall from the surrounding trees. I've never seen this pool full, not in all the years I lived here. The apartment building has a fresh coat of paint on it. The windows look new. *Progress,* I think. They probably charge extortionist rates to live here now. I imagine the children who probably swim here, the mothers in their bulging one-pieces, the lenses of their sunglasses flecked with droplets. Teenage babysitters. Little boys doing cannon balls. None of them could probably guess what happened there. It's been too long since the pool was neglected; no one who lives here could probably imagine the sorts of things that went on inside of it, when it was all moldering leaves and empty bottles. None of them could guess what might have happened to a girl who went there alone one night to escape the sound of her mother and her mother's plumber friend fucking through the thin walls of their trailer. Or what happened when a man followed her in.

It was the dog smell that made me realize it was Larry. And by the time he was close enough for me to smell him, any chance I'd had of escape was already gone. Maybe that was the night I had in mind so many years later, when I sat down among those pale beauties in that bathroom, their works spread out before them on the tile floor, the low light making them look skeletal and fierce when the flame of the lighter clicked on and the liquid within the spoon began to bubble. Maybe it was thinking of that night in the pool that made me ignore what I'd heard, the rumors that there was something going around, a bad strain that had shut down the Valley's porn production for the summer when two of their actors tested positive. Perhaps I was remembering in that moment, as my career was about to take off, how precarious a position it was to be on the verge of being seen and wanted by so many people. Maybe I already knew too well the danger there.

He'd wiped himself off in my hair when he'd finished. And I'd stumbled home and found my mother's kitchen shears, taking them to the bathroom and lopping off chunks of my hair until it hung like strips of soft straw from my scalp. I'd been modeling pretty regularly for a year or so at that point, mostly magazine work, but the money went a long way in our little trailer. The booking agents loved blondes. Mother smacked me in the face when she saw it the next morning, when she first glimpsed the ragged short ends of my hair. It took three months and three expensive trimmings at a salon in the next town over to get me back to the point where I could start booking jobs again, and my mother barely spoke to me in all of that time.

I stand in front of the pool and think of it, the fact that I've finally gotten what I'd wanted so desperately then, a new body. But I am not rid of that night, despite the fact that every bit of me has been made new. It was a difficult lesson to learn at sixteen, that all the power bestowed to me by luck and youth and beauty was not enough to keep me safe. That maybe the power inherent in beauty is false, and to be desired is to receive a dark, illusory exchange where a man pretends to relinquish his power and never really does.

I think of my mother, and the horror with which her old self would look upon the age of her current face. How jealous and proud she'd be, looking at my new face compared to hers. And it occurs to me that maybe things are better now, since I got sick and Betts found God. Maybe it was too painful for her to worship beauty as she did, when hers steadily faded with each year. Maybe she's happier now, despite her fleeting thoughts of her dying daughter. And even though I've lost the mother I remember, the one whose standards I've finally lived up to, maybe her approval will always be out of my reach no matter the circumstances. Maybe it will be easier to think of my mother as content in her new life, when I think of her at all.

# Hannah

Lucy goes into labor on a Thursday morning. At 2:53 a.m., to be exact, because I'm the first person Roger calls when her water breaks all over their bedroom floor. I can hear her in the background of the call, saying something laced with profanity and a couple of angry-sounding grunts. I pull on my jeans, and assure Roger that, yes, Penny and I will meet them at the hospital to wrangle the kids during the delivery.

"We betting on the sex?" Penny asks as we get into the car and pull out onto the empty roads. The orange hue of the streetlights gives the night a strange, otherworldly feeling, as if everyone has disappeared but the two of us. We drive north, past my usual route to Northwestern, heading instead to the Illinois Masonic Birthing Center, where Lucy's midwife works.

"What are the stakes?"

"Dinner at the Pick Me Up."

"I bet it'll be a girl."

"Dammit, I wanted to bet on a girl," Penny says, and for a moment it's as if nothing has transpired between us but the easy progress of friendship. There is no Sam or David, or cancer, no subtext in our words, no strain of jealousy or regret. She grins at me, and I grin back.

When we arrive at the birthing center, Roger looks like he's just been asked to eat something disgusting for money. There's a kind of grim determination in his sweaty pallor, in the inherent uneasiness of his demeanor. It's a look that knows what's coming, and I'm thoroughly relieved that Penny and I have been relegated to babysitting for the duration of the delivery. I'm not good with things like this. Things that involve tubes and pain and fluids. With bodies—my own or anyone else's. And then there's the familiar feeling, the dark creep of something sour in my stomach and the muscles of my arms when I think of Lucy giving birth to another baby. Something very much like jealousy, or regret.

I stop in to see Lucy as Penny begins to wrangle the boys, who are sword-fighting with discarded paper-towel tubes when we arrive. Lucy looks puffy and puce-tinged.

"Hey," I say, approaching her bed and taking her hand. There's an odd sense of déjà vu in it, when I consider that not too long ago, I was the person in the hospital bed. The room is actually lovely, decorated more in the vein of a high-end spa than a hospital. "Nice digs."

"I know. Just a step down from getting a hotel for this right?"

I perch on the edge of the bed. Lucy and I haven't spoken since Sam left, and now I have no idea what to say. I motion to her stomach. "How is it so far?"

"Like the others. I keep forgetting how awful it really is, for some reason the memories never really measure up. I swear, this is it. After this, Roger is getting snipped."

"I don't think you should tell him that just now," I say, taking the cup of ice chips by the bed and feeding Lucy some. "I don't think you want Penny to have to scrape him off the floor. Or me in here during the delivery."

"You'd be able to step up," Lucy replies. "I think we've proven your toughness by now."

"Right." I help myself to a few ice chips from her cup and crunch them with my molars, hoping it will keep me from having to talk about anything that matters. Lucy, however, is not so easily dissuaded.

"I'm so sorry about everything that happened, Hannah."

I nod, though I don't look at her. I showed up because that's what I do when Lucy needs me, but that doesn't mean I'm not still stinging from her secrets.

"Want me to stay for a while? Give Roger a break?" I ask, praying she says no.

"Go on and help Penny. I'm sure she'll need it," she says, and then her face crumples into a red, wet agony, and her hand squeezes my fingers with enough force that I'm afraid of the damage she might do. Even now my fingers are slender and delicate, their muscles under-developed. I worry she'll pull them from their sockets, like a parent who grabs his child's arm too quickly and dislocates it. My fingertips are colorless by the time she lets go. I move them gingerly, testing all the connections.

"You okay?" she asks me, and it's a silly question, considering she's the one in labor. I wonder if I look a little pale, a little panicky, maybe a little like her shell-shocked husband.

"Yeah," I reply, getting up from the bed. "Aren't I always?"

The baby is born at 2:15 p.m. I'd spent the morning silently hoping that she'd be born quickly, like her older brother, out in three hours or so from the time we all arrived. But no, not the third child. The girl, who comes into the world dark-haired, like a wet, worn beanbag. Emma Christine. We all huddle around Lucy, a chorus of cooing faces, and I try not to watch as Roger kisses Lucy's hair, the way he looks at his daughter. Lucy is drained and wrung out, but still glorious with the triumph of motherhood, and the envy I hold for her is finally whole, complete; a perfect sphere I can barely choke back as it rises inside me.

I stick around when Penny heads home, and Roger takes the boys to the cafeteria for snacks. I know it is the wrong time for this, for any of it. I'm exhausted, so Lucy must be half-dead. But I'm worried, in a way that I've never been before, that this might be the last chance for honesty between my sister and me. She must know it too, because all I have to do is sit on her bed before she starts to cry.

"I'm sorry," she whispers, wiping at her eyes, making them even puffier. "I didn't want to lie to you."

"I know," I reply. "Sam was always the one person you never could say no to."

"It wasn't that," she replies. "I was there, Hannah. Both times. I watched him lose his dad, and then nearly lose you. And I kept his secret, I lied to you, because he deserves to be forgiven after everything he's been through. And I knew you wouldn't be able to." We're both silent for a moment. Is this what they think of me, the people who love me? Am I this vicious? I must be, because while it hurts to think of Sam, sometimes I relish in the pain because it allows me to hate him. It lets me ignore the damage I've done.

"I wish I could," I reply. I think of our parents, half a world away from both of us, saving other people when their daughters need so badly to be saved. "Anyway, he's probably better off." The knowledge lingers, how David and I never even considered using condoms in all of our time together. How I will never be a perfect wife, a wife like Lucy. Maybe that is why I let Sam go, in the end.

Lucy brushes a hand down the side of my face. "What is it, Hannah?" she asks.

"I don't think any of us can have children," I reply.

"What?" She sits up a little straighter in bed, propping herself up with her arms. "What are you talking about?"

"The SUBs, all of us in the pilot program. And I think we all know it, too."

"What makes you say that? Have the doctors said something?"

"No," I reply. "I don't think they know. It's this feeling . . ." I trail off, try to find a way to explain. "You know I got pregnant once, right?"

Lucy nods. "Freshman year."

"Yeah. It was like walking into a house and forgetting to lock the front door. You know? You're walking around, hours later, doing something else and you just realize. The front door is unlocked. That's how being pregnant was for me. All of a sudden, I knew, it

was a fact. I didn't even take a test before I made the appointment."
I glance over at the little bassinet next to the bed, at the gurgling,
soft little girl inside. "That's sort of how this feels. I know it, without
having to be told."

"Jesus," Lucy says. "That's awful." I laugh a little.

"It's karma," I reply, reveling in the dark irony of it. "I think it's
Mother Nature being a rotten, vindictive bitch because we finally
beat her at her own game."

# Linda

There's a puddle of hot blood in my underwear. I can feel that something is wrong right away, there's a tight burn right between my hips, and the rest of me feels sweaty and tense. I find the blood in the bathroom, with my jeans bunched around my knees. I blink. No. One blink. Again and again, because I can't even form the word, can't even whisper it. No, no, no.

It happens fast, all in a gush of pain, a river of it, doubling me over. I grip the edge of the sink, my hand clammy and sliding against the smooth marble. I can hear the small sound of something falling into the water beneath me. At first I think it can be saved, like a bird's egg fallen from a nest, that if it is kept warm and safe it might still become the thing that it's meant to be. I rummage around under the sink and there's nothing to catch it with, nothing I can use to rescue it. Instead I peer into the rusty water in the toilet bowl and it's there, that little clot of tissue. It's a mass of pulp, an alien thing produced from an alien body, a body that was never meant to create anything because it itself was not created by any natural means. It's a feeling like falling down; everything in me has fallen, every bit of me.

Tom knocks on the door. I've been in here for a while. I wonder what someone does with a thing like this, a thing that is something and nothing at once. All potential, unrealized. I could tell Tom. I could go to the hospital. I could lie on the floor and pretend to be paralyzed. All of it seems futile. There's nothing left to do but to get rid of it, like a dead goldfish, to staunch the bleeding with a maxi pad and open the door to face Tom. I tell him it's the flu. A stomach

266

bug. Something vague that will keep him at a distance, lest he catch it from me.

I drift, in those next few days. I find an old bottle of sleeping pills in Tom's cabinet and take two at a time, until he has to shake me awake in the evenings when he gets home from work. It frightens the kids, to see their father frightened. Even Jack keeps his distance now. Tom is worried, always worried, wants me to see Dr. Shah, or my ob-gyn. I know what he thinks, that I'm defective, that there's something wrong with my SUB. I can't bear to tell him that he's right.

When I don't want to sleep anymore, I curl up on the couch and watch *Stratford Pines*, or go into the yard and lie on my back in the grass and listen to the trees. I want to cry, but I'm not sure this body knows how. It's difficult to conjure that pressure, that physical insistence. I think of the phantom tears I used to cry, the ones Cora would dab from my face with those embroidered handkerchiefs of hers. My body, always a betrayer, always giving me the opposite of what I need.

The next few days are worse, because once the shock of it wears off, once my new body bounces right back into humming and click-ing in its normal, well-oiled efficiency, I begin to feel it. Somewhere deep inside me, there is the tiniest kernel of relief. And I hate it, and love it, that feeling. Hate it because it is selfish and cruel, it puts me in league with all the women who wish their children away, who leave their infants locked in cars on hot summer days, or feed them too much cough syrup to quiet them, or abandon them in front of fire stations. And I love it too, that feeling, because it's proof I'm still alive. That there is still something for me to want in this world, even if it's to want all the wrong things.

I climb the stairs to the attic, pulling out my artifacts and press-ing each between the skin of my palms. There is no thrill of elec-tricity, as if something has waved a magic wand and rendered them inert. It feels like loss, surely, as if the little embryo took the keys to my secret world when it left my body, as if it pulled all the dreams out of me as it left. But another thought occurs to me, as I sit there. Perhaps the dream world has receded because this world has begun to unlock itself. I think of all sorts of possibilities that could exist for a woman risen from the dead, all of the ideas that occurred to me in that jail cell, when I realized I could disappear. I think of open water and mountain tops. Things I've never allowed myself to dream, after that night in college when the stick turned pink, when the choices weren't mine alone anymore. All of this, the accident, the transfer, even my miscarriage, have all conspired to give me the chance to do what I've wanted to do since I can remember. How could anyone fault me now, after I have been so torn from my life and it has healed itself with me on the outside? I have been given the world now. How could anyone fault me for leaving?

# David

David Jr.'s arm is in a navy blue cast that reaches from his palm to his elbow. It's a completely helpless feeling, for my son to be injured every time I see him. To be so far away, avoiding my district and all of those unanswerable questions and probably subpoenas, unable to protect him because I can't even protect myself.

"I'll be home in a month, buddy. Mom says you'll have your cast off by then," I say, imagining the time we can spend before I return to Washington to face the Ethics Committee. Everything hinges on the FDA vote. If SUBlife passes, I might avoid charges for tampering with the study.

Maybe I'll take David Jr. fishing. Maybe I'll start him out hunting, even. I started younger than him, and maybe handling a gun will give him the sense of patient confidence that it instilled in me when I first went out with a rifle over my shoulder. But David Jr. looks confused by the sentiment.

"I thought Mom said you weren't coming home," he says, brow furrowed.

"Of course I'm coming home, buddy," I say.

But again, he shakes his head, adamant.

"What exactly did your mother tell you?" I ask, apprehension squaring my shoulders.

"She said you were going to stay in Chicago with your girlfriend."

"My girlfriend." There it is, I think. Beth, showing her cards through our son. A winning play, if I ever saw one. "David, go get your mother and put her on the phone," I say, trying to keep my tone even.

"She said she doesn't want to talk to you," he says.

"Tell her she should call me in the next five minutes or I'm driving out there right now so we can talk in person, okay?" I say. David Jr. nods. "Okay, you keep your chin up son, you hear?" He nods again, and then my screen goes dark.

Four minutes later, my phone goes off. It's Beth. "At least I know now what it takes to get you to drive up here," she says as soon as I answer.

"What have you been saying to our son? You told him I'm not coming home?"

"I figured it might be better for you to stay in Chicago for a while," she replies, her tone controlled, dispassionate even.

"With my girlfriend?" I ask, trying to sound both weary and condescending. "I don't have a girlfriend, Beth. I don't know what the hell you've dreamed up there."

"Well, then, whoever it was I heard at your place, the night David Jr. broke his arm. Connie, is it? She's certainly pretty enough. Though, no matter how tough you think you were once, you never really had the stomach for the junkies, now did you?"

The mention of Connie feels like a punch below the belt, like going after someone's sister. Veins of anger open up in me. I feel like there is something hot and dark and molten at my core, and every wall I have built to keep it hidden, keep it contained, is cracking apart. I'm angrier than I should be, if I intend to continue this conversation without imploding our marriage. But maybe ending our marriage is exactly the intended purpose of this conversation for Beth.

"Or maybe it's Sam's girlfriend," Beth continues. "What's her name again?" I jerk to attention.

"Sam?"

"Sam Foster, the journalist," she says, and I begin to see, faintly, the outline of something treacherous here.

"How exactly do you know Sam Foster?" I ask, feeling like I'm about to be sucker punched and there's no way to get out of its way.

"I found him through those files of yours," Beth replies. "Ironic, isn't it, that one of them had a journalist for a boyfriend? It never occurred to him to write about SUBlife until I called and told him all about you. He seemed pretty adamant that his girlfriend be left out of it, but you he was more than willing to write about."

I lean forward, resting my forehead in my palm. I've known Beth to be a lot of things. But this cruel, this calculating, I never knew she was capable of this. I'm almost impressed, which sickens me a bit, because I have indeed married the perfect political wife, someone who is just as capable of terrible, deceitful things as I am.

"I've helped you out a lot over the years, baby," she says. "I've been whatever you needed. But not this time. You lied to me, when you told me things would be different. You lied to my son, too, and you should've known that there would be a price for that."

"Our son," I say. She doesn't reply. "Our son, Elizabeth."

"Well, I guess we'll see what the courts have to say about that," she replies. I end the call by throwing my phone across the room. It ricochets off the wall, leaving a dent in the paint and raining pieces of plastic onto the wood floor.

# Hannah

When I get home, my camera slung over one shoulder and a bag of takeout from Tamarind in my other arm, David is sitting outside my apartment door. My first impulse is to simply walk past him, to pretend he is so irrelevant to me that I don't even recognize him, but the slump of his shoulders makes me pause. He has a beard now. It makes him look older, a bit more grizzled than I remember. I wonder, in these few months since we've seen each other, if I have changed as well. And, despite everything, seeing him is the most potent relief I've felt in weeks.

"How do you know where I live?" I ask by way of a greeting. He looks relieved that I've acknowledged him at all.

"Your records," he replies. "I had my chief of staff get them for me."

"Jesus, I should have guessed," I say, still hurt and angry despite the fact that everything in me wants to throw my arms around him. "Opposition research, right? Or does Jackson do that sort of thing with all the girls you sleep with?"

"Can I come in?" he asks, motioning to my apartment door. Part of me wonders if he's crazy enough to think we could pick up where we left off.

"No," I reply. "Not until you tell me what you want."

"I want to apologize," he says, running his hands through his hair. It's longer now; he probably hasn't had it cut since the last time I saw him. I get it. He's less recognizable this way. "For everything I said about you, about the article. I know now that it wasn't your fault."

"What are you talking about?" I ask. He stands, and the size of him surprises me. He's muscled now, more imposing.

"Hannah, can I please come in?"

We sit at my kitchen table, though I don't offer him anything to drink. Politeness is still a bit beyond my capabilities when it comes to David. As he looks around my place, I wonder at how little of me is reflected in this home, how much of it is the person I was when I was with Sam, the girl who didn't mind her parents' money, the girl who was more than willing to smooth out her rough edges for him.

"What do you mean about the article?"

"Is that one of yours?" he asks, motioning to a huge painting hanging above my sofa. It's one of my favorites, one that I could never sell, the first of the series that won me my artist's grant. It's so detailed it's nearly photo-realistic, a woman being dragged away by her hair, a flock of ravens doing the dragging. The background is 1920s dustbowl farmland, and all of it is bleak and desperate except for the woman's expression. There is something there, something like surrender, a bit like peace, as if the woman knows there isn't anywhere those birds could take her that could be worse than where she's leaving.

"Yeah," I reply, glancing at him, recalling what he said about paintings when I first visited his apartment. "My version of reality, I guess."

"I like it," he replies.

"What are you doing here, David?" I ask again.

He pauses and then nods. "I know you weren't Sam's source for the article. I'm sorry I accused you of that."

"So where did he get it?"

"My darling wife," David replied, shaking his head. "Lady Macbeth. I promised her everything would be different when I bought my way into the program. That's how I justified it to her, and to myself, I guess. It would be worth it, to take someone else's spot, because I would be a better man. I would use my influence for good."

"And then?"

"And then she realized that I wasn't going to change. Realized it before I did, actually. She was always the smart one."

"How did she know to contact Sam?" I ask, but then the dots connect in my head before he has a chance to answer. "Your opposition research, of course."

"She's good at this sort of thing," David replies. "She's lived with me for long enough, she's picked up on my talent for exacting the most damage possible with the littlest possible effort. I would be impressed if she didn't ruin my whole life in the process. And if she wasn't threatening to take my son away from me."

"I'm sorry," I say, and for the first time in a long time, I mean it. I realize what a colossal mess of things we've made, how we've been given our lives back only to take them apart ourselves, of our own accord. And I wonder if our SUBs have, in fact, made us more human than we were, less able to tamp down our fears and our desires, made us feel too much all at once. Maybe people aren't meant to feel things so powerfully, as we have, and to act on them.

"Why did you do it, David?" I ask. "Why try to keep it from passing the FDA?"

David lets out a long breath, sits back in his chair. "Turns out, that was the price of getting me into the program. One of my corporate donors wants their drug in the next trial, so this one can't go through."

"Jesus, that's disgusting."

He nods. "I wish you were right. I wish it had something to do with God. At least I'd have some . . . conviction to cling to. But it was just blind self-preservation, in the end."

"And the crazy thing is, I understand," I reply, remembering sitting on that bathroom floor with Sam's arms tight around me. How riotous the fear was. How I would have offered up anything I had to the person who could spare me everything that came after. "But unfortunately for you, it's just another of those things that I can understand, and no one else will."

He walks to the window, peering out over my view of Printer's

Row. "You know I always hated this city? The Democratic machine, the corruption. God, the winters. But it's really sort of beautiful now, isn't it? I can see why you love it the way you do." He turns back to me. "I've missed you. Even when I was busy hating you, I missed you."

I look away, because I can't return the sentiment. I have missed David, but in the way I've missed Connie and Linda and even Dr. Bernard. When I wake up at night and instinctually reach across my bed, I'm not reaching for David. I try to divert the subject from my own lengthy hesitation.

"You know, I ran into Linda at the grocery store a few months back."

"Yeah, I ran in to her a while back too," David replies, a bit of a smile breaking across his face. "I think it's safe to say that none of us really knew each other at all, no matter how many meetings we went to."

"Sure, but we still knew each other better than anyone else."

"You're probably right." He looks wistful, and then he clears his throat. "So what are you going to do now? Seems like you have a pretty clean slate to work with here."

"I don't really know." I don't tell him the truth, about how, for the past few months, I've been seeing everything in shades of light and darkness and texture, everything as a potential photograph. The way I can feel myself changing, when I hold my camera, when I peer through the lens. That secret bit of hope is mine for now. Something for me to cherish alone.

"If you still want to be reckless, you could come with me to Washington. I have an apartment there."

"Be your mistress?" I ask.

"Or a friend. I don't have many friends there. Gets lonely," he replies, though his expression hasn't changed. He doesn't appear as vulnerable as he sounds. He could just as easily be making small talk.

"I'm not your friend, David," I reply. "We were never friends, were we?"

"No," he replies, shrugging. "I guess we weren't." He brushes my hair off my shoulder, a familiar, intimate sort of gesture.

"I'm going back there in a few weeks. I finally have to face all of this shit. And for the first time in my life, I have no idea what to say."

I lean forward and kiss him. A last kiss, to match all of the firsts we've enjoyed together. And I realize how good it feels, to be kind to David, despite all of his failings. To forgive him, a little, because of everyone in our lives, we're probably most like each other. And it feels a little like forgiving myself.

"You tell them what you told me," I say. "You tell them that God put a gun to your head, and you did what you had to do to stay alive. And that not one of them would have done any different."

"You think that will be enough?" he asks, his face so open, his exhaustion so evident that I wish I could draw him. Instead, I rise and get my camera.

# Connie

Harry arranges a business lunch at Cointreau, one of the new Los Angeles restaurants that keep cropping up, lasting for a few glittering months, and then dying off when everyone realizes you always leave hungry. It's me and Jay Cunningham, whom I knew when he was John Carrion, the up-and-coming producer. It seems he's arrived, as I spot him and Harry at a table across the room. I stride in past the well-manicured clientele, catching stares as I pass in my red skirt and white blouse, clothes that on anyone else would look simple, bland even. I may as well have walked in wearing a bikini, the way these businessmen are looking at me. I hated the looks I got when I was withered and sickly, the stares that were so much worse than the people who would not look at me at all. This is an entirely different feeling, but just as invasive.

My model friends and I used to joke that Jay was so greasy he must have bathed in Vaseline, and the sentiment holds true even now as he takes my hand before I drop into a seat across from him. He's tan, very tan, L.A. tan, almost orange. Like he's been hitting the salon to compliment his day-to-day sojourns out in the merciless California sun. His hair is slicked back and the green of his eyes, which would be pleasant on someone else, clashes with his fake skin tone and gives him the look of a viper sizing up his dinner.

There's already a dirty martini in front of my plate. I raise an eyebrow at him.

"You think I've forgotten what you drink?" he asks, lifting his own drink in a mock toast. I smile and pretend to sip, though even bringing the glass to my face, even breathing the fumes of it as I wet my lips, feels like huffing wood varnish.

"Jay is trying to find someone for the indie flick he's filming here next summer," Harry says, motioning lazily back and forth between the two of us with a thick hand.

"Straight to business, hmm?" Jay says, folding his hands in front of him. "He's right. Our talent got pregnant and dropped out. Can't shoot her pole dancing when she's the size of Texas, now can we?"

"Pole dancing?" I ask, though we're interrupted by the waiter, who takes our orders and bustles off with admirable efficiency.

"It's a dark comedy about a single mother," Jay replies. "Late twenties, early thirties. Struggling, with an over-bright but difficult little kid. Takes up a job at a gentlemen's club where she meets a down-on-his-luck doctor with a gambling problem, and what do you know? Sparks fly. Now, the studio is fighting us on this, but we're looking for an R rating so there might be some nudity. Nothing gratuitous, of course."

I smile. Of course, there's nothing gratuitous about playing a woman who takes her clothes off for money. Or being a woman who takes her clothes off for money.

"That's not a problem," Harry chimes in. "Right, sweets?"

I bare my teeth at his pet name, the name he calls all the girls, and I want to call him out for being the overpriced pimp that he is, but instead I nod. "Of course, it's not a problem," I reply. "I've got no reason to be bashful."

Jay grins. Harry grins. I pretend to drink my martini. The food arrives and it's fancy shit, stacked up like tiny sculptures on huge white plates. All of it tastes strange, too strong, its spices and sauces and textures sharp and overpowering. Jay and Harry dig in. I wonder if the waiter would bring me some macaroni and cheese if I asked really nicely. If I smiled at him, flashed my eyes in that way men like. I know all of the things that men like by now, and how they relate to me. Men like the way I sway my hips when I walk. Men like it when I bite my bottom lip, particularly when I'm wearing red lipstick. Men like it when I pretend I'm not interested. I shrug at Jay.

"You think this is the sort of movie to break back into the business with? It all sounds a little overdone."

"I think this movie will show that you're willing to take risks," Jay replies. "Get your face in the theaters. Maybe some international exposure. I think you try to relaunch your career any other way, and you're just wasting your time."

"Makes sense to me," Harry says.

Jay glances at my plate, which is nearly untouched. "You don't like the fish?"

"I'm picky," I reply. A sly smile spreads across his face. His teeth are peroxide-white, so white my own teeth begin to ache just looking at them.

"Of course you are," he replies.

We end up in his hotel room. Of course, we end up in his hotel room. This is how these things work. This is how I remember it. Harry left us at the restaurant, claiming he had some emergency appointment with another one of his actresses, the way he always played us against each other, keeping us on edge, constantly currying for his favor. I'm too old to play those games now. But then Jay has a town car waiting downstairs, and I'm pretty sure my mother had a rule against refusing rides from powerful men when they're offered. So we end up in his hotel room.

I remember this. I'm pretty sure I've slept with Jay already for a part, back in the day, back when his name had something to do with rotting flesh. It's kind of hard to keep track. He pours us each a drink.

"I can't believe you go out in public wearing that," he says, handing me a crystal glass. The hotel room is expensive, with towering views of the city around us. He really has arrived, our little John.

I glance down at myself. I'm covered from knees to shoulders, but I know what he means, though I pretend I don't. "Wearing what?"

"Anything but a burka," he replies, downing his drink. "It should be illegal. You could cause car accidents. Plane crashes. Mass hysteria."

"You always did have a talent for exaggeration," I reply, touching my lips to the glass, leaving a bloody mark on the crystal rim. This is going to be a lot more difficult without the benefit of inebriation.

"Stay here in L.A.," he says. "What are you doing, hiding out in Chicago?"

"I like it," I reply. "There's no artifice there. Chicago suits me."

"Chicago is small potatoes. Christ, you might as well be living in Shitsburg, for all the exposure you'll get there."

"Not if you have anything to do with it," I say, and he smiles, stepping closer to me.

"You know, there were a lot of rumors about why you dropped off the planet for a while."

"What sort of rumors?" I ask, playing coy, though I know where this conversation is heading. It is, I suspect, the same reason Harry has backed off so easily at my rebuffs for the past few months. No one is sure what my status is anymore.

"Some of the girls from the *Pines* said you were sick."

I look him square in the eye, because there can be no question of this, not if I ever want my career back. "Do I look sick to you?" I ask, and smile with each and every one of my teeth.

Apparently it's all the answer he needs, because he leans in then, his mouth closing over mine. He tastes sour. I set the glass down on the side table, leaning into him as he loops a hand around my waist. I can feel the damp heat of his palm through my blouse, and I imagine oily handprints on my clothes.

I think of how I was back then, that little girl, wide-eyed and straight off the plane in Los Angeles, shedding her trailer park clothes for men who promised her fame and fortune, her face up on billboards above Hollywood Boulevard, every camera turned in her direction. How easy it had been, in that body, the one that already felt tarnished at nineteen. The one that didn't feel quite like it belonged to me. It was easy to loan it out, to give it away. This body, however, has not yet become a mere tool for someone else's satisfaction. I have not yet wrought a value from it, weighed and measured its worth in trade. I have not yet put it to work.

I have no desire for Jay, in his expensive suit, with his slicked-back hair and fake tan. I can't even rummage around inside myself and find a shadow of interest, something to pull me through to the other side, the shape of his hands or the scrape of his stubble or any of the other things that would set me shivering, were Jay another man. But no. I've learned long ago that the most difficult battle is trying to make yourself want something. It's easy to learn to love, or to hate, or envy, or even forgive. You can teach those things, you can learn them. But desire is that most elusive of birds, perched in the high branches of the tallest tree, ready to take flight with the smallest provocation. There is no snaring it, no coaxing it down. And I'm no longer sure if I can make love to a man without it.

Jay tries to hold on to me as I twist away, as if one moment more will shred my resolve and have me tumbling into him.

"What?" Jay says, his eyes still heavy-lidded and unfocused.

"I'm going to go." I remove his hands from my waist. And then, because I have nothing to lose, "I guess you can contact Harry about sending that script." He smiles, and I know that the dream of that indie film has evaporated as well.

"I'll send him the script if you stay."

It's my turn to smile now, and I'm not sure if it completely hides my disdain for him. "My price is much higher than that, Jack."

"All right," he says, "I'll give you the part if you stay. I'll give you whatever you want." He steps toward me, brushes the backs of his fingers down the column of my throat. And just like that, it appears. That little seed of wanting. It is the wanting of anonymous sex in public bathrooms, of faceless bodies on a dance floor, of disembodied voices on the other end of a telephone. It is a human wanting, so human it is too shameful to be acknowledged. A desire that can only exist alongside revulsion.

He screws me up against the wall. Facing the wall, my cheek

pressed against the beige hotel paint. It hurts just a bit more than I imagine it would if I'd already taken this body out for a spin. All of the blood drops from my head when he comes, and my knees go weak. I don't fall, he has me pinned, but he slips an arm around my waist and it reminds me of how my mother would hold me when I was a child, getting sick over the rim of the toilet. How I hate that arm, hate needing it to steady me.

The whole messy affair is so much like what I remember of sex. I thought it might be different in a different body, in this more perfect body. But there is that same sense of relief when he finishes, a curtain falling on a great performance. Though I don't care about this man, don't care about what he has to offer me, I care that I have been perfect for him. It is the greatest bit of sadness for me, the realization that still, even now, no one cares less about my own pleasure than me. I only care about how I appear to him, ever-beautiful, ever-willing. The stuff of fantasy. I wonder, as he holds me there, if I am real at all.

# Hannah

The Daley Center is all lit up in golden light, a shining meteor of chrome and glass in the hazy Chicago darkness. The space is crowded, and I catch Penny's eye from across the room, winking, a silent sign of solidarity borrowed from years of going to loud, crowded bars together. Nights when pushy men would con us into dancing, when a wink across the room would signal the need for an escape route. Or other nights, like the night I met Sam, when a wink meant that I'd find my own way home. Tonight, she smiles at me, knowing that my signal means she's done well, that I'm here, and that she'll be all right. It was the same wink she gave me when I turned, glancing back at Sam and Penny and Connor before I was wheeled into the operating room.

Her work is phenomenal. It hangs, suspended on wires from the ceiling, huge, wall-sized collages of gauzy paper, sheets layered by the hundreds until they have form and depth and shape. Like terrain, or long expanses of skin. Painted pale watercolor shades and cracked through with light and shadow. I stand in front of one that is all sun-bleached peaches and creamy grays, the one that's called *And Again*, a battleground of long tears and smooth, polished expanses of color. It feels alive, as I stand in front of it. It looks as if it could breathe.

Penny breaks away from the couple she was talking to as I move toward her. "So what do you think?"

"It's pretty decent, actually," I say, pulling her close. She's her usual jangle of bracelets and earrings and necklaces, all sterling silver and shining against the black silk of her dress.

"Connor is somewhere around here. Jesus, I've already lost track of my own boyfriend. I'm already a prima donna in the making."

"Those are some lovely paintings."

"Want to know which is you?" Penny asks, and I choke a little on my drink.

"Me?"

"Of course. They're all people. Connor is right over there." She motions with her wine glass at a canvas that is all shades of turquoise and sand. The longer I look, the more I can see the calm and subtle quirk that could easily be Connor.

As I look around at the rest I can see it now, the cadmium red and burnt umber of her grandmother in her hot little kitchen, flecked with a blue so clear it could only be the scent of salt water coming in gusts through the windows. Her parents are side by side, the violet and silver of her mother next to the sea green of her father's eyes, the smooth exactness of his temperament. I look back at the one that drew me in initially, the one that seemed sad and beautiful and alive. And I understand why she titled it *And Again,* because it is not me as I was before. It is now, it is my living, breathing present. And somehow, in a way I don't wholly understand, I can see myself in it. A clearer vision than any mirror has yet been able to provide me. And I think, if nothing else, this will sustain me. This will draw me forward, at least for a little while.

"Thank you," I say, and I know Penny sees it in my face, that I understand.

"I started it the day you told me you were sick. The bottom layers are black. I would just coat whole sheets in India ink. I burned some of it, until it was tarry and charred and just desolate. You can't see it anymore, there's too much covering it now. Even where I cut into it, I couldn't go down that far." Penny looks so sad as she speaks that I nearly have to glance away. I wonder about the sum total of pain I've caused the people I love. I wonder if it hangs over my head, a butcher's bill, waiting to be called up. Or perhaps I'm already paying my price.

"It's a shame I had to stop," Penny continues. "Imagine if I'd been able to work on it for another year. Imagine where you'd be then."

Sam stands in front of my painting. The sight of him makes me seize up, sends a jitter of nervous energy through me. I thought he might be here. I've spent most of the night trying not to look for him. But I approach him, end up standing next to him, because I'm nothing if not a glutton for punishment.

"See, I recognized you this time too," he says, motioning up at the canvas, before he even looks at me.

"You got it out of Penny."

He shakes his head. "I'd know you anywhere. In all your forms," he says, meaning it to be a joke, but there's a stab of poignancy to it as well. "I like your tattoo."

I glance at the lacy phoenix threading its way up my arm. It's the deep black of a new tattoo, not yet muted by time and sunlight. It's like me, in a way. All of our wear is yet to come.

"No you don't," I say. "You don't like tattoos, remember?"

"I liked yours." He must see my skepticism, because he continues. "You never understood, I liked what it meant, that you had them. That I could walk into the office's Christmas party with you on my arm, and everyone could see that I wasn't like them. Because I was with you, and you didn't play by their rules. I loved that about you."

"I thought that was what you loved least about me," I say. It's hard not to be wistful in front of something so beautiful. "You know, I was thinking the other day about my first drink." I take a sip of my current drink, which is ginger ale with a splash of gin.

"Which one?" he asks.

"The first one," I reply. He turns toward me, his eyes on mine.

"You mean the time I gave a twelve-year-old a shot of Jack Daniels in her backyard?" he asks. "I thought we'd agreed never to speak of that again."

I grin then. "I didn't agree to anything. I forgot about it. I assumed you had too."

"I didn't forget," Sam says. "I wouldn't. That night was the first time I really saw you. Not just as Lucy's sister."

"What did you see?" I ask, thinking of myself now. What am I but a being made from memory, my flesh and blood a copy of the body that came before it, my mind a knot of history that cannot be untangled, cannot be relived? There is nothing for me to do but move forward and hope that whatever bits of me that housed my soul have been re-created here.

"I saw what I always see." He doesn't say more, he doesn't explain. He doesn't have to.

"You know, I've spent a lot of time trying to forget every single thing about you. Nothing else worked. Everything else hurt too much."

"I'm sorry," he says. I reach forward, brushing my thumb over the crease between his eyebrows, the price of loving me. No matter how badly Sam has always tried to do the right thing, it was always his weaknesses, his failings, that I loved the most. It seems terribly unfair now, that I can't forgive them as well. I let my hand drop.

"We made such a mess of it, didn't we?" I say, thinking of cities razed to rubble. High towers fallen. A perfect love story, gone to ruin.

Sam nods sagely. "We should keep that in mind for next time."

I glance up at him. "Next time?"

"I got it from my source in the FDA," he says, stepping forward and drawing his thumb over my cheek. "Looks like SUBlife's going to be approved at the vote tomorrow. And I figure, if we're all going to live past a hundred, you and I have time to make a mess of things at least once or twice more."

I can't tell if he's kidding as he kisses me, a patient kiss, one that calls back all of the memories I've tried to hide away, and walks off into the crowd.

# Linda

Tom is eating cereal in the kitchen when I return to the attic. I know he is, because that's what he does every morning. He sits at the kitchen table with his *New York Times* and he eats a bowl of Cheerios. Even before my accident. I remember hating the exactness of his routines even then.

I'm not in the attic for long. And I have plenty of time, because Tom likes to linger over his paper, slurping the excess milk from his bowl in slow, dripping spoonfuls. I saw the suitcase when I was up here before, and it takes only a few minutes before I find it again, wedged between an old lamp and the box to an inflatable kiddie pool. It's dusty, but I recognize it immediately, the suitcase I dragged with me on our disastrous honeymoon to Hawaii, where it did nothing but rain and I was laid-up with Braxton Hicks for three days straight.

I carry it down the attic stairs and stash it in my closet for later, when Tom picks the kids up from school. Until then I consider what I will take, what I even have to take. I think of my artifacts, my stash of pilfered items, which have so wholly lost their magic that I don't even feel the need to look at them anymore. None of them will do me any good out in the world. None of them has any real value. They're like Tom's box of keepsakes in the attic now, the shawl and a piece of glass.

I fold my clothes, the pairs of jeans and T-shirts and cardigan sweaters and socks I bought to replace the things Tom threw out. I stack them up, ready to be dropped into the hollow stomach of the suitcase. I go into Tom's sock drawer and find his roll of emergency cash, and I take all of it. I collect a hair brush, a toothbrush, a photo of the kids from before the accident. It's a paltry little life I have here, ready to be packed away. It feels fitting, because my life has been small, so small, for so long. The difference now is that the world is big. It's huge, and frightening, and all I want is to see as much of it as I can.

The difficulty of this life, I have found, is how little magic there is in it. How little possibility. Here, imagination is foolish. Impractical. *Stratford Pines* is treacle and melodramatic, unrealistic dreck. It is hard to resolve the realization that I dreamed more—in waking and in sleep—lying in that hospital bed than I have since my own personal miracle occurred. It seems like the greatest crime of luck or fate that I have left a hopeless situation only to find myself unable, now, to even dream of hope. There will be no baby. There will be no other men. There will be no blind corners to turn, no unexpected delights or rushes of excitement. There will be no other path for me but as a mother, as a wife, if I do not leave this place. And there is nothing like eight years of solitude to teach you selfishness.

I thought about leaving Tom a note. Telling him about the affair, about the years he wasted waiting for a wife who was already gone, even before she was still and silent and confined to her bed. But it seems doubly cruel now, to tell him all of that, and to leave as well. It was so much easier when all of our conversations were distilled down to two words. One for no. Two for yes.

I think about leaving something for the kids, for Jack and Katie. There's a gnawing ache within my chest when I think of them, like hunger, as if my heart is starving at the thought of them. But I still think of them as babies, as the children I had before the accident. I feel like a wicked stepmother now, the usurper of their idea of a mother, of the perfect image they'd grown up envisioning when they looked at old photographs of me. I am a woman who does not know them now.

I will leave tomorrow. I will leave this house in the morning and board the Purple Line and head into the city. I will have my suitcase.

I'll buy a ticket for the bus. And I will be gone. No fingerprints. No ID. No pictures of me; no way to track me down. The possibility of it is so massive I feel as if I could drown in it like an avalanche of cold snow.

Maybe I'll get off the bus in a small town somewhere. Maybe there will be a diner, somewhere I can ask if they're looking for help waiting tables. And maybe it will be the sort of place where people fall in love easily. Maybe it will be the sort of place where long-lost people congregate, where twins impersonate each other and babies are born to the wrong people and families are built and shatter and reform again and again. Maybe they'll be waiting for a woman who spent eight years paralyzed before getting a new body, a woman with a world full of secrets inside her. Maybe that'll be the sort of place I'll go.

# Connie

Dr. Grath's door is closed when I get back from L.A. I'm a bit disappointed, but not altogether surprised. I wonder if he assumed I wouldn't be coming back this time. It's not exactly out of the realm of possibility; after all, it was only yesterday that I learned Harry was not prepared to pay for my flight back to Chicago. I had to pawn one of the necklaces he bought me, all while he left pleading voicemails on my phone, imploring me to reconsider Jay Cunningham's offer of the lead in *Almost Ruins* in the strongest terms imaginable. But I don't want it. I don't want to be paid for.

I knock on Dr. Grath's door, already smelling the skunky whisper of smoke drifting out into the hallway. I hear him mumble something from inside, so I let myself in. His eyes are half-lidded and bloodshot, and he sits slouched in his chair.

"Who is it?" he asks.

"It's me," I reply, sitting on the couch next to him. The TV is off, and something in that bothers me. I wonder when he's eaten last, or last ventured out of his apartment. "It looks like you started without me, old man."

He chuckles a bit, raising the joint in his right hand. "Well, you've been a bit tricky to track down lately. Not like the alley cat you once were, always showing up for supper. One can't wait forever, can one?"

"I guess not," I reply, taking the joint from him and inhaling.

"I thought you'd be off somewhere warm, making love to the camera by now," he says. "Every time you leave, it gets harder and harder to imagine you coming back."

I hold the smoke in, letting its itch turn into a burn within my lungs before I let it out in a long stream. I contemplate my options.

"What if I lied to you?" I ask, passing him the joint.

"Lied? About what?" Dr. Grath's blind eyes widen just a bit.

"About what I look like now. You know, Grace Kelly. All that."

"About the cloning?" He's confused. His wiry eyebrows try to touch like trapeze artists attempting a midair catch.

"No, that was the truth. I just . . . exaggerated the rest a bit. A lot, maybe."

"Oh," Dr. Grath says, and I can't tell if he's at all surprised. Maybe he's disappointed.

"I went to L.A. To see my agent. Hoping that he could get me an acting gig, maybe some modeling." I sigh, trying to sound dejected. "He said he didn't have anything for me. He said he couldn't market a look like mine anymore. Too classic."

"I like classic," he says. I laugh a little.

"I know you do, old man. You don't have a choice."

"So what are you going to do?" he asks. I shrug, though I know he can't see it. It's habit. A habit that was born long before I entered this body; impossible to break.

"I guess I just stay here. My agent said he might be able to get me some more work here in Chicago."

"Surely you can do better than that," he says, and I shrug again. "I know what's going on here. You're waiting for me to qualify for this SUBlife thing, so I can look like Monty Clift again, and we can run off together, is that it?" I smile and there are tears in my eyes, though he can see neither. I suspect he knows what I do, that Dr. Grath is one generation too old for immortality, that he will grow old and die the way people were always intended to, a death that is the sort the rest of us have always hoped for.

And if he did get his sight back, everything would be ruined. He would see my lie, see that I am every inch what I described myself to be after the transfer, and that I gave up all the possibilities that my beauty afforded me and stayed with him, in this dingy apartment building. Because I don't want to be bought by men like Jack Cunningham. And because even now I'm afraid of what might happen to Dr. Grath in my absence, that without me he'd drift into some final oblivion, stop eating or watching his Turner Classic Movies or going through his photo albums. That he would grow lost in this little apartment. I want to be here to keep him from drifting away. And he would never forgive me for that.

"Exactly," I say, turning my hand over so I hold the roughness of his palm in mine. "Exactly."

He doesn't think he will ever be selected for SUBlife. He's lying, and I know it, and I let him. I wonder if he knows I'm lying too, and is letting me just the same. Either of our truths would mean I have to leave here, to leave him behind, to go out into the world and live through all the danger and possibility afforded to a woman born with my face. I don't want to leave. He doesn't want me to go. So there is nothing left for us but to love each other, and lie.

# Linda

I wake early on the morning I'm going to leave. Tom is still asleep next to me, breathing in heavy, open-mouthed snores. One of the kids is up, I'm not sure which one, but I hear the TV on downstairs. I try not to think about them. They will be better without me, without a mother like mine, silent and remote, a mother who will leave them eventually anyway, and will make the leaving their fault. I lay in a bed for years pretending I had no history, that I was no one, because my mother chose to see my tragedy and raise it with her own.

Still, memories wash up. I indulge today, only today, because what I am about to do is such a high crime that any little indulgences along the way will be surely, fully eclipsed later. I play the game, the one I never allowed myself to play in the hospital, tracing my way back, trying to pinpoint the moment that would have prevented my accident and spared me all of this. Don't change lanes. Don't get in the car. Don't answer your phone. Don't sleep with Scott, again and again, no matter how much you want to. Don't wish you hadn't married Tom. Don't marry Tom. Don't get pregnant three months before graduation.

That is where I must stop. Because I cannot, no matter what I do, wish away my daughter. I can remember, so clearly, that morning. Fainting after speed work at cross-country practice, how panicked Tom looked when he met me at the health center, wrapping me up with both of his arms and taking a deep breath of my hair. Anemia, they said. Could I be pregnant?

I told them I wasn't. There was no way, we were always so careful. But as Tom drove me home we talked about the nights when we weren't so careful. Admitting to each other the things we couldn't admit to anyone else, as we always did. We stopped at Walgreens on the way home, and I waited in the car while Tom bought me a pregnancy test and the biggest bottle of water they had. I chugged while he drove.

I made him wait outside the bathroom of our little apartment, because no matter how long we'd been dating, I still couldn't pee when he was in the same room. Then I made him plug his ears and sing Tom Petty outside the door so he couldn't hear, and he did so with such gusto that I was laughing so hard I nearly missed the stick.

"I'll buy you dinner if it's positive," Tom said when I finally let him back in the bathroom, as we sat on the counter and waited for the timer to run down.

"And if it's negative?" I asked.

"No way."

"Cheapskate," I said, just as the pink lines appeared in the window of the test. It was a feeling of my entire world clicking out of joint, a train derailing at high speed, running along without tracks for a few perilous moments while everyone inside held their breath, waiting for its inevitable tumble. Tom's face fell in a small way, and I saw my first glimpse of the look I would come to know so well, the *couldn't you have done better* look in his eyes that seemed to make all of it my fault. But then he took a breath and smiled, and there was resignation in his expression.

"Well," Tom said, "where do you want to go to dinner? And will you marry me?"

I check again to make sure I have everything I need, ruffling gently through my stacks of clothes, the money I've pilfered from Tom, the hair brush and toothbrush and box of tampons. These are the things a person needs for life, I think. Not a trunk of keepsakes or a collection of stolen artifacts. These things, the practical things, should belong to a person without history.

I leave the suitcase in its place for now. It's too early to drag it down, to catch a train into the city, to buy a bus ticket at Union Station. It's still dark outside. Tom is still asleep. So I descend the stairs, with my mind's eye still firmly on the suitcase, on my escape. I've had good practice at this, being a woman who resides in two worlds at the same time.

The TV is flashing a bright Looney Tunes pallet of color across the carpet, but no one is watching it. I can hear a commotion from the kitchen, and I walk in just in time to see Jack on his knees on the counter, reaching into a high cabinet and pulling something down, bringing down a glass measuring cup with it. The cup shatters on the countertop beneath him. I can see a shard of glass open up the skin of his leg, and he's so startled by it that he teeters on the edge of the counter.

Something kicks me forward, an impulse so ingrained that I don't have to think before I'm moving, grabbing Jack by the waist. He lets out a little wail of surprise, then bursts into tears. I haul him over to the sink and sit him on the edge of the counter, wetting a paper towel and pressing it to the bleeding cut on his leg.

"Mommy," he says, between hiccupping sobs. His face is crumpled and wet.

"You're okay," I say, remembering how I would say it to Katie when she first started walking, when she would plop down onto the cushion of her diaper, looking up at me with huge eyes, trying to gauge by my reaction whether it was a fall worthy of tears. I react the way I used to with her, wiping the fat little teardrops from his cheeks and kissing him on the forehead. The smell of his hair is different from what I remember, the powder and milk smell of babies. My boy. "My poor boy," I whisper.

"I was trying to make pancakes. For you and Daddy," he blubbers. "I couldn't reach the mixing bowl. I broke one of the good measuring cups."

"That's all right," I reply, checking his cut. "Don't you worry about that." It's not deep, just a glancing touch of sharp glass. The bleeding is starting to ebb even now. "Oh, this isn't too bad," I say. "Where does Daddy keep the Band-Aids?"

He motions to a cabinet over the sink. There are two boxes, one Cinderella, one Batman. Tom is good at this, this parenting thing. I pull out a huge Batman bandage and apply it to Jack's leg. He seems pleased. His tears are beginning to ebb as well.

"Why were you making pancakes, Jack?" I ask, as my phone begins to vibrate. I ignore it.

"It's July eighteenth," he replies, and then he looks at me expectantly.

"What's July eighteenth?" I ask. He looks puzzled, then must assume I'm playing a game with him, because he breaks into a smile. My phone buzzes again, cutting into our conversation. Who on earth would be calling at this hour?

"Your anniversary with Daddy," he replies, clearly proud that he passed my test. "We celebrated it every year you were gone." I nod, because suddenly I can't speak anymore. Instead, I pull my phone from the pocket of my sweatpants, clearing my throat before I answer.

"Hello?"

"I didn't wake you, did I?" comes the voice over the line, a familiar voice. A male voice, his tone so wry I can picture the self-satisfied grin that must be playing over his face.

"No," I say, and feel myself smile, as if I were an observer of this body's impulses.

"So, tell me Linda, are you staying out of trouble?"

I set Jack up with some cereal at the kitchen table and go upstairs, returning to our bedroom. I sit on the foot of our bed. Tom glances up at me when he feels the mattress shift.

"Hey," he says, propping himself up on his elbows. There's a red crease in the side of his face from the pillow. "What's up?"

"I'm not pregnant," I reply.

"What?" he sits up, fast, as if there was a task he's forgotten to handle and the result has been the loss of our child. "What are you talking about?"

"I'm not pregnant anymore." I say it slowly, trying to keep my tone even. Trying to keep from repeating it again and again until he finally figures out what the words mean, that it's too late for anything to be done, that all of his questions are useless.

He's silent for a moment, staring at me aghast. "When?" he finally asks.

"A few weeks ago. I didn't want to tell you."

"Oh God," he says, and reaches toward me, his arms outstretched. I put up both of my hands to ward him off.

"No," I say. I can see it when he changes gears, when anger pours into his expression.

"Well, why the hell wouldn't you tell me when it happened, Linda?" he asks, his voice a bit too loud for the quiet, lingering night.

"Because I wasn't sure how I felt about it. I needed time," I reply, still calm, trying to stay calm.

"Jesus, what about what I need?" he asks, nearly shouting, his voice high, an almost comical pitch. "All of these years, all of it. I can't even remember what it feels like to need something and to get it."

"What did you need, Tom?" I ask.

"I needed," he begins, but catches himself. He slumps a bit, his bare shoulders sagging. He's a very pale shade of white, as if he hasn't seen the sun in a while. Small, wayward hairs curl at odd intervals on his shoulders, the first true sign of age. He is so sad, and so decent, that he will not answer. So I do it for him.

"You needed me to die. In the hospital, in those eight years. That's what you needed."

His knobby fingers cover his face. "Yes," he whispers. "Because I loved you. And it was awful. I just lost you, and lost you, and there was no end to it."

"You know, it's funny," I say, wishing I could cry too, to prove to him that I'm still human. But it's impossible to conjure the emotion. For me, it's a simple truth, one from which I did not need to hide. "I wished for the same thing."

"God, I wish it could have been different for us," he says, his voice strangled. I want to love this man, love him enough at least to comfort him. But I don't have it in me.

"I know." Thinking back, this is not so different from how we've always been, even before the accident. I've always been the strong one, the one who sets the course for us. It must have been so difficult for him, with me gone.

"I know about Scott," he says then. *Scott*. I think of the park bench, my children asleep in the back of our van. "He came to the house a few weeks after your accident. I had no idea who he was, until he broke down sobbing in our living room. He said he needed to see me. That I was the only one who would understand what he was going through. We ended up talking, for, I don't know. Hours probably."

He pauses, and I can't imagine anything that might come next. It is as if my entire estimation of Tom, and everything he is capable of, has evaporated into the air.

"It was, in a strange way, just what I needed," he says. "To talk to someone who knew you the way I did."

My body is rigid with astonishment. I almost want to take my pulse, to make sure everything has not shut down from the surge of shame and confusion roiling within me. When I speak, my voice is breathless, a child's voice.

"Why didn't you leave me there? Divorce me? If you knew?" I think of all the different ways his life might have proceeded without me, all of the mothers my children could have had. Mothers who were more capable and more selfless than me. Tom reaches forward and takes one of my hands. His is so warm, I feel only half-alive by comparison.

"Because you would have had no one," he says.

I pull my hand from his. There is nothing else to be done, because I will never be able to love this man in the way he deserves.

I think of my suitcase in the closet. I think of the world, the whole world, that exists outside this house and the people in it.

"We can try again," he says. "For a baby."

"It's not going to make a difference," I reply.

"Are you going to leave?" he asks, and he looks so much like his son, our son, with his red, blotchy face, that I can almost love him for the resemblance alone. Almost.

"Did you want to have a baby to keep me from leaving?"

He doesn't reply. We are at an impasse, we look at each other for a long time. Finally, I blink. Once.

"Jack tried to make us pancakes and broke a measuring cup. Can you clean it up?" I leave before he can say anything, shutting myself in the bathroom and listening as he plods down the stairs to the kitchen, where my children are eating their breakfast and trying to avoid the shards of glass.

I put on the terrible sneakers I found in the attic, the ones with the wings inked into the heels, and creep down the back stairs and out into the lingering pre-dawn darkness. It was always easiest to run just before dawn, when the shadows of night are only beginning to recede, before the sun rises and heats the brick and concrete of the city until the air is thick with humidity. There's an hour, when the sky begins to lighten in the east, before the city stirs, when everything is soft and cool and brimming with life. It is the hour in which I could always forget the things that weighed on me.

I run down Hinman to Main and then east to the lakefront. The water looks swollen and choppy, like it might rise up and chase me as I skirt its tide, and by then all of my muscles are warm and loose, and I find another gear. I wait to grow tired, for my limbs to take on that familiar lactic-acid heaviness, for my chest to tighten and protest the exertion, but this body does nothing but obey. It does not protest. Every breath becomes the first breath after being underwater, kicking hard for the surface and splashing up, gulping hard to get enough air. Every breath feels that sweet.

I pass other people on the path, couples with strollers and people walking dogs, other runners. I can feel my body charging forward, my heart drumming the pulse of blood through my limbs, synapses firing like roman candles, my breath, the patter of my feet on the pavement. Everything is rhythmic. A machine, churning away, breaking through the air around me, my gears and pistons and joints well oiled and endorphin-soaked. The world around me shimmers, resplendent with morning light and the gleaming magic of moving fast, effortlessly.

I fly along as the lake begins to glitter with the first bits of sunlight breaking over the horizon, and my body feels so good, so crazy good, that I can almost convince myself that it was all worth it, just for this. Just for a moment like this. I know the feeling will end as soon as I turn back and head for home, rejoin my family, unpack my hidden suitcase. But for a little while, the ability to forget is not a curse. Sometimes forgetting is a gift, too.

# Hannah

I wake the morning of our last group meeting startled and breathless. Unsure, for a moment, of where I am. And then I cross the thin veil of sleep, when the whole world and all of its truths wash inward in that one potent moment. I remember it all, in an instant, rushing back like forgotten memories. But that doesn't blunt the feeling held over from moments ago, and a kind of muted joy sits in my chest. I walk with it, through my morning and out into the world, all the way to group. With that feeling of being held.

We meet in the conference room, as we always have. We take our normal seats. It's David's doing, that we're all here. David, with his opposition research. He was the only one who could bring the rest of us together in the end, for our final meeting, one year since we opened our new, light-blind eyes for the first time. We all look a bit worse for the months we spent apart, and I think of all the things I have not told these people, about Sam, about Lucy, about what has happened between David and me. About how I can still see the world in that old, beautiful way even though I cannot paint it. I wonder what secrets the rest of them must be keeping as well. I wonder how much has gone unsaid between us, all along.

"So, here we are," Connie says, clasping her hands together. "I don't know about you, but I think it feels good to have the band back together for this little reunion tour."

"Well I haven't missed you that much," David replies. "I see you almost every time I take the Red Line. Those goddamn ads are inescapable." I smile at this too, because I've been just as startled as David when I board the L and see Connie's face lining the cars, staring out from her ads for some new anti-aging cream. It's Connie winking at the camera, her face pale and pristine, her lips bright red, her hair all slick golden-blonde. The text reads, *Ask my age, I dare you.*

"You don't think it's false advertising? I mean, me hawking a fucking wrinkle cream?" Connie glances at Linda, who shrugs.

"I think if that's the most morally ambiguous thing you've done since the transfer, you're lucky," Linda replies, and we all exchange unsteady, knowing glances. "Maybe they shouldn't have left it to chance. The lottery. Maybe they should have picked someone stronger than me, someone who would have been better at everything that comes after."

"People who deserve it more," Connie adds, the straight line of her front teeth capturing her bottom lip. I'm sure we've all thought the same thing, more than once. I know I have, especially now, after all the damage I've caused.

"I think we were foolish, in the beginning," I say, unable to keep myself from looking at David, or thinking of all my towering mistakes. "To think that going through what we did wouldn't have an impact. To think we could just keep going in spite of it."

"Whatever the case," Dr. Bernard says, "I think you all need to appreciate what a singular experience you're having. This might be the next frontier of human evolution. I think you need to reflect on your place in history."

*Pioneers,* I think. *Blazing the trails.* And then Connie snorts.

"I'd love to reflect and all, doc," she says, smirking from under a messy knot of blonde hair. "But all I really want is a nice strong cup of coffee." We toast to this, raising our cups of cocoa.

"I had a dream last night." I can feel the pulse of disbelief around me as soon as I say it, followed by a thrill of elation.

"What?" Connie asks, leaning forward, her hands tight around the sides of her chair. "Are you sure?"

"I know what it's like to dream," I reply, before thinking that our last meeting might be a good time to temper the snippy edge in my tone. "I'm sure."

Connie breaks out into a smile; Linda clasps her hands together in front of her mouth. Even Dr. Bernard gives a small, sharp chuckle.

"You know what this means?" Connie says, her eyes wide. Linda speaks before I do.

"Maybe it will all come back," she breathes. "Maybe if enough time passes, the rest of it will come back too."

Dr. Bernard adjusts his glasses, uncomfortable with the direction of this conversation. I can tell he wants to warn us not to grow too hopeful, that dreaming is one thing, while being able to drink coffee or paint or have children is another thing entirely. But he remains silent, perhaps because it's our last meeting, or perhaps because he realizes how much we all need to hope irrationally for a little while. For now, it'll be enough.

We're all talking at once, our voices crisscrossing our little circle, notes of laughter bouncing from person to person. And then Connie shouts over everyone, silencing the room until it's all one muted note of expectation.

"Hey, Hannah. So what did you dream about?"

I take a moment to remember, pull it all forward, to drape myself in the feeling of it. Standing at the water's edge. Feeling the cool wind on my face. Feeling him approach behind me, warm and solid, the way you can in dreams when you can feel the whole world because the whole world is inside your body. Waiting an extra moment, savoring the weightlessness of it, feeling myself drifting out of my skin, pulled by the wind until I'm sure I could let go of my body and fly out over Lake Michigan if I wanted to. But instead I hold on. I remain. And then I take a breath, and turn.

# Acknowledgments

I would like to thank Rebecca Johns Trissler for being such a wonderful mentor. Thank you for so much, but especially for never letting me second-guess my work. Many thanks to my agent, Melissa Kahn, for her skill in championing this book and her patience in guiding me through this process. I am so grateful to my editor, Sally Kim, for her enthusiasm, her kindness, and for providing such insightful answers to all of my questions. Thank you also to the fantastic team at Touchstone for making this process such a joy.

Thanks to Jeremy Barr for his lawyering skills and for being generous enough to let me put my writing first. Thank you to Mandy Graber for being such a wonderful source of support and advice along the way. Many thanks to Valerie Paulson, Janet Hickey, Daniel Stolar, and everyone who made DePaul University feel like a second home. To my support group, the incredibly talented class of writers who lived through the first draft of this novel with me, thank you for the early advice and for always keeping my feet on the ground.

Love and thanks to Vanessa Bordo and Ashley Grebe for keeping me sane for over a decade. Thank you to my brother, Christopher, for being my 3 a.m. phone call. And, finally, thank you to my Mom and Dad for giving me a childhood filled with stories. This one is for you.

# About the Author

Jessica Chiarella grew up in the Chicago area and has a Master's in Writing and Publishing from DePaul University. She is currently a student in the University of California, Riverside's MFA in Creative Writing program, where she received the Chancellor's Distinguished Fellowship Award.

# And Again

Four terminally ill patients receive the chance to enroll in the SUBlife program, a scientific advancement that gifts them with brand new bodies free from their old illnesses and the ravages of time. They're exact replicas of their former selves . . . or so it seems.

The four patients are Hannah, an artist who cannot seem to recapture her prior inspiration; David, a politician whose meddling with FDA approval for the SUBlife program is a secret he's hoping to keep; Linda, who spent eight years in a "conscious coma" and is trying to reconnect with the family from whom she became estranged; and Connie, a soap-opera actress trying to revamp her career. *And Again* raises the question: is getting a second chance at life as miraculous as it seems?

# For Discussion

1. When David wakes up with his new body, he vows to be a different man who won't drink, won't smoke, won't indulge in extramarital affairs. How much of our habits are tied into our psyche and our genetics? Do you think old habits die hard? Or can we really re-train ourselves?

2. Speak to the ways in which each of the four characters sees their body as a tool, an object separate from them, something not their own, after the SUBlife program. Hannah cannot summon her old passion for painting. Linda feels helpless after her husband signed consent papers while she was in her coma. Have you ever felt separated from your physical body? How much of your personhood do you think lies within your physical body?

3. Despite their external differences, what bonds do you see between Hannah and David that might lead them to be attracted to each other? If they had never met inside the SUBlife program, do you think they would begin an affair in real life? Have you ever been drawn to someone who seemed completely wrong for you? Why?

4. Connie's life with Dr. Grath, a blind man with a love for old black-and-white movies, contrasts sharply with her life in Hollywood meeting sleazy agents and managers. Why does Connie find sanctuary with Dr. Grath? How much does his blindness factor into her sense of comfort around him?

5. Hannah is drawn to personalities like Penny and Connie, women who are unafraid to speak their minds. Think about Hannah's voicelessness compared to Linda's literal voicelessness. How would Hannah's life be different if she spoke her mind more?

6. Though our society does not currently have something resembling a SUBlife program, author Jessica Chiarella's alternative present does not seem far off. What similarities and topical themes did you notice throughout the book, from stem cell controversy to Linda's lack of choice in having her child? How probable does SUBlife seem to you in our current society?

7. Linda feels a close bond to Connie due to years of watching her on *Stratford Pines*; this bond sometimes verges even on the sexual. What do you think spurs this false kinship, and why is it especially keen for Linda?

8. When Hannah learns the truth of why Sam was not at the hospital when she was at her illest—not that he had an affair with Lucy, but that he fled the state—she throws him out in a rage. In what ways is this worse than an affair for Hannah? Which would be a worse betrayal in your opinion, and why?

9. Is there a part of your anatomy worn by time that you'd like to reverse? If you had a SUBlife body, what parts of your old body would you miss?

10. After blinking YES or NO as her only form of communication for nearly a decade, Linda finds it difficult to relearn how to communicate the breadth of her feelings with her partner Tom, and with the therapy group at the hospital. Imagine yourself in her situation—how do you think it would cause you to rethink

how you communicate and what you choose to share? In what ways would you feel frustrated, and how might it be a relief?

11. Hannah makes the decision to re-ink her new body with a tattoo of a phoenix designed by Penny. If you had to choose a defining tattoo for yourself in this moment of your life, what would it be?

12. When the four SUBlife participants encounter one another in real life, outside the realm of their weekly therapy sessions, they share with one another an intimate secret, a special bond. If these four had not gone through the SUBlife program, do you think they would still share a bond? Do you detect a similar thread of experience that still binds them together?

# A Conversation with Jessica Chiarella

**How did your training at DePaul University prepare you for writing your first novel?**

Being a student in DePaul's writing and publishing program really made all the difference for me in writing this novel. I wrote the first draft in a two-part novel-writing class run by Rebecca Johns Trissler, who has become a wonderful mentor to me throughout this process. The class was essentially a novel-writing boot camp, where each of us wrote sixty thousand words in ten weeks, took a week off for spring break, and then came back and revised those drafts over another ten weeks. There were about fifteen students in the class, and we were absolutely exhausted by the end, but I walked away with the raw material that eventually became *And Again*. It turned out to be an extremely rewarding way to write a first novel, because I was sharing the experience with such a talented group of students, and we all sort of leaned on one another for advice and moral support during the process. I don't think it's a coincidence that the novel included a support group that met every week, because that's exactly what class felt like by the end!

**Why did you choose these four characters to explore and investigate in their SUBlife journey? Were there others you discarded in your drafting process?**

There were absolutely other characters that I had to lose as I revised the novel. The first draft was written from only Hannah's point of view, and as soon as I finished I realized that I was spending most of my time thinking about the other characters in the support group, wondering what their lives and futures would look like. There were originally six or seven members of the support group, so when I finally decided to write from the other points of view, I knew I had to create composites of some of the characters to keep the novel from becoming too crowded with perspectives. I still think about the characters I cut though, because there are so many different ways I wanted to tackle SUBlife's effects, such as through issues of gender identity, disordered eating, and mental illness.

**Which character do you find yourself relating to or empathizing with the most?**

Each of the characters has traits or attitudes that are drawn from my life, and each has some that are diametrically opposite to me as well, so that answer has shifted a lot depending on where I was in the writing and revision of the book. But in the end, Hannah is very close to my heart. I think her duality is something with which I strongly identify—her perfectionism contrasted with her rebellion against societal standards, the ways in which she grapples with her own privilege and yet still gives in to her selfish impulses—those are the things that made her come to life for me. She makes some very poor choices out of a very human desperation for connection. Sometimes she held up a very challenging mirror for me. But I knew that the more uncomfortable she made me as I was writing her, the better a character she would be.

**How do you envision these characters' lives ten years after getting their new bodies? Do you think the SUBlife program could happen in real life?**

I think they would certainly be more at home in their new selves. The initial shock of it would probably have worn off, though I think they would still be contending with the aftermath of some of the choices they made in that first year. They'll probably all have some serious regrets regarding how they reacted to the transfer initially. But I think, ten years out, they'll have stopped thinking of themselves as patients, stopped thinking like people who have dodged a bullet, so their problems will be more practical and less existential than they were in that first year. I've always been amazed at how adaptable people are in the face of profound change, so I wouldn't be surprised if they spend whole weeks without thinking about the transfer at all, after a decade.

I'm not sure that something like SUBlife could happen in real life, but I think the idea behind it—that the miracle cure will not be a pill, will not be something we're anticipating, but something much more holistic—is possible. I spent a lot of time thinking about human flight while I was writing the book, that it was less than a century between the Wright Brothers and landing on the moon. I think the next big medical advance will happen that way; there will be very little time between the first breakthrough and its logical conclusion.

**What inspired you to write this story? How do you think you would cope if you were a member of the SUBlife pilot program?**
The book started out as a love story, as an examination of how a relationship would be altered if a person went through a transformative physical experience. But very quickly I realized that something like SUBlife would have such an impact on the patient herself that everything in her life would be transformed, not just her relationship.

I'm not sure I would fare any better than the characters in the book if I had to go through SUBlife; I'm not great with change as it is, so the idea of such a profound physical alteration would be incredibly difficult. I've spent a lot of time thinking about losing my tattoos, and it's always an upsetting idea. Then again, the idea of a fresh start is very appealing. I would probably spend a few months falling apart, and then thank my lucky stars I'm still alive and march myself straight to a yoga class.

# Enhance Your Book Club

1. Re-tell a chapter of this story from the point of view of the main characters' partners: Sam for Hannah, Beth for David, Tom or Katie for Linda, and Dr. Grath for Connie. Share your chapter with the group and see how the narrative changes.

2. Create a piece of art that you feel conveys your physical body as it is today, affected and informed by a lifetime of experience. Then have a friend in your group do the same, objectively drawing your body as a physical entity. How is it different? What surprises you?

3. Research articles in the news today about stem cell research and the advancement of cloning underway. Then look back on archived stories about Dolly the Sheep dating back to the mid-nineties. How have our society's views on cloning and even stem-cell research changed? How do you think they will continue to change?